Fatespinner

S.K. AETHERPHOXX

Copyright

Fatespinner

First Printing: 2016

Thoughtweft Publishing
281 Moubray Rd.
Kelowna, British Columbia, V1V 1V2
www.thoughtweft.com

Cover Art by Daniel Kamarudin

ISBN
Paperback: 978-0-9952112-0-9
Hardcover: 978-0-9952112-1-6
E-Book: 978-0-9952112-2-3
AZW: 978-0-9952112-3-0

To Noboru and Nobuko Ikesaka
I'd be a lesser man without your love and support.
This one's for you.

MY INSTRUMENTS

You believed, and I became

Darlene Bournival
Christopher Ikesaka
A-Jay
Chiisairan
Joelle Fuller
Sundee B.
BergEdelweiSS
Viktoriya Prudnikova
Koby Kaminski

MY FATES

You inspired, and I flourished

Nina Bournival
Matt "Ruffus" Fuller
Colleen Glendinning

PREFACE

Like most great stories, this one begins with a girl.

I wish I could say this was my lifelong dream finally come to fruition, or that some life changing event brought to light the words that were locked up inside of me, but no. At the time, I was just a guy trying to impress a girl. She was a screenwriter with huge ambitions and I got the bright idea that writing a nice short story might catch her eye.

The base of my ideas for Fatespinner sprung from my closest friends. Once a week, every week, for about thirteen years we would play Dungeons and Dragons, Mutants and Masterminds, Exalted, Scion, and a copious number of other RPG style games. It was from those fond memories that I began to weave this new tale, and what began as a short story grew into a novella – then a novel. Finally, I decided only a trilogy could truly let me tell the story of these characters in the depth and detail I wanted. The joy of creating came easily, but the words did not.

It was hard. Really hard. Fortunately, what began as me trying to catch someone's attention had somehow flourished into something I simply enjoyed doing. More importantly, I enjoyed doing it for myself. I got the girl for a while, but it was only after we parted ways that I realized I wanted to finish this journey. For me and no one else.

Writing this book brought me more identity. I've learned so much more about myself as I inadvertently reflected different aspects of my psyche across my spectrum of characters. *Turns out I have a lot of different personalities, so I've included a character reference at the back of the book in case you forget who is who.*

Whether you are an experienced writer, a new writer, or someone who has never written at all, I hope you find your words as well – because words change perspective, and perspective changes everything.

PROLOGUE

The world of Elanta is a Pangaea. A vast stretch of land greeted by ocean on all sides. Mountains, swamps, deserts, forests, and jungles each create a distinct realm to feature their own politics, race, and traditions rich with heritage and culture; knowledge and lore; love and war. Yet, no matter how vast their differences may be, there lies one common bond to connect the threads of their existence – the potential of their souls. The majority of Elanta lives simple lives, but there are those in each culture that learn to harness the energy within themselves and channel it into something greater. The path of unlocking the potential of their soul is a journey that takes years, often times decades to accomplish, but makes them capable of great works. Some use their power to heal grievous injuries or disease in the course of an evening, while others put silver in their words to bend the minds of their peers. Many forge their soul into weapons, to conquer any who oppose, or protect those they adore most. These empowered mortals are referred to as 'enlightened' and are often in high regard by their rulers.

It is because of this potentially volatile power, hinged on the convictions of those who wield it, that four powerful beings conspired to create a means of watching and manipulating the multitude of potential destinies electing the best future for the sake of all of Elanta. These four became known as the Fates, and their omnipresent realm of fate-spinning spiders was the Weave. Few people knew the Fates used an unfathomably massive cluster of webs to foresee the potential future and even fewer knew that each fate spinning spider within that cluster was connected to a living soul in the mortal realm – weaving a timeline that both connects and disrupts those it interacts with.

The sky of Elanta has never once held the sun, never embraced the moon, and never shone a single star. Since the beginning of time, Elanta has been surrounded by a perpetual and eternal mist that engulfs it like a cage – aglow during the day and pitch in the night. No one knows what lies in or beyond the mist, but anyone or anything brave enough to sail or fly into the disorienting and mysterious haze is never seen again.

Some speculate there is a promised land beyond, where the souls of the dead reside and mortal flesh may never tread. Others say it is the edge of the world, where the chaos energies of the universe begin to unravel from the stability of reality. The cultists, however, believe it is a barrier meant to shroud their homeland from that which lurks hungrily on the other side. Several rumors and theories hang heavy in the air and whisper in the ears of Elanta's denizens, but it is the world they both know and accept. It had always been and always would be unless something substantial were to happen.

1

MISTBORN

The night was a vexing stillness of dark whispers that trickled across the cobblestones. The scent of fresh rain lingered beneath a minty overtone of herbal patchouli, as lantern light glistened across the small puddles that littered the streets. This was the great city of Whitewater, capital of the realm of the same name.

A figure hurried amidst the shadows of closed shops and homes of the common folk long since retired. The dark fabric of his cloak hung heavy and damp in the trail of his footsteps. He soon approached a small wooden hovel, boarded up and seemingly vacant, just before the massive stone wall that encircled the outskirts of the city. He placed his hand to the door, where an eerie green light shone beneath his palm and highlighted a sigil that stretched across the surface. With a nearly inaudible click, the sigil faded and the door slowly crept open. With a subtle flourish of shadowed robes he vanished into the darkness within. The door slowly closed behind him and the sigil flared and faded as it sealed shut.

He was immersed in a thick fog of sandalwood and musk that led him beyond the abandoned rooms and down a flight of rickety stairs to the cellar below. Guiding him were clusters of candles that nested in sconces, thick with wax that oozed in globs.

As he stood at the base of the stairwell he gazed upon a circle of five magi, each clad in dark robes similar to his own. A low chant vibrated the air as their voices, in unison, seemed to resonate amongst the small white pillars of crystal that stood before them. They each knelt before a crystal and held out an open palm while unsheathing a *kris* from beneath their lapels – the wavy edges of the short blades flickered maliciously in the candle light. The steel cut deep as they severed the soft flesh of their hands, allowing the blood to drip and splatter across the pristine white surface.

He knew better than to disrupt them. They were performing a ritual they had meticulously prepared for months. However, the urgency of his news was surging across his heart like lightning. He would hold back as long as he could, but an imminent danger would soon befall them and his silence could be their undoing.

The metallic tinge of their blood trickled down his throat as he watched the crystals slowly turn pink. An effect he had never seen before, though through study he knew to expect it as the crystal drank their life force. The resonance in the air grew deeper and he could feel his organs vibrate as the ritual began to reach its climax. The stones were reacting to their dark energies much faster than initially predicted, which was good news in their dire situation.

The hum slowly began to fade as the crystals, now completely rose, became docile. The cloaked figures labored as they dizzily clambered to their feet and staunched the bleeding with clean cloth. "What is it?" asked one between shallow breaths. His voice was both deep and scratchy, who everyone in the room easily recognized as that of their leader, the powerful bloodmage, Kalen.

"Master Kalen, I have come to inform you the guard captain has discovered this location. He is en route with a unit as we speak."

The inquisitor pulled back the hood of his cloak. Thin white hair hung drenched in sweat across wrinkled features and clouded eyes. "Don't worry," he said calmly as he wrapped the cloth across his wound. "All that's left is to place the stones and activate the circle. When they arrive, we will kill them and proceed with our plans."

"Master, Whisper is among them." Urgency filled his words, enough so that it caused Kalen and the others to stop and look to each other for answers.

"The King hired the mistborn girl?" Tension wrought into the cloud of incense that softly stung their eyes. His wrinkled eyelids squinted over a ponderous gaze as he stared at the floor.

Whisper was a problem he hadn't expected. Most people wouldn't know she was a mistborn, as she was very diligent in shrouding her traits of mis-creation from the common folk. However, her name was renowned throughout the higher governmental powers and infamous amidst the underworld criminals she was often hired to hunt. Very few lived long enough to determine the origin of her mutations, but it was widely assumed she was a human, kissed with dark, demonic influences that resided beyond the mist. Her unique hybrid form had enlightened her soul and allowed her to channel essence into feats of incredible strength and reflex – some say more. It was a common affliction amongst infants born too close to the mist, though it was rare for one to survive the fatal persecutions.

"All of you will delay her for as long as you can while I attempt to summon something to defend us." His eyes grew dark as he gestured for the others to make haste. "Be alert. They bear no shackles for us, only coffins."

***

The soft clinking of half plate resounded through the streets as a dozen royal guards positioned themselves outside of the hovel. With swords at their side and spears in hand they proudly bore the Whitewater colors of silvers and blues and studied the building intently as their commander issued their orders.

The commander was a noble man of broad stature and experienced armor. Rough, bristled skin adorned with a grievous scar across his cheek held their respect as someone who had earned his rank through vicious combat and difficult decisions. As he spoke, his voice drew their full attention.

"Commander." A scout appeared from the darkness and approached him.

"Agent Dask, where have you been?"

Dask bowed his head in apology, then brushed his oily brown hair from his eyes. "I've swept the perimeter," he began, "It seems the Orbweaver sect have set lethal enchantments all across the property. I recommend an approach of absolute caution."

This was not news to him, as he was well aware of the Orbweavers renown. They have been wanted for treason and the practice of dark arts since their emergence several months ago and he knew to handle them with extreme prejudice.

"We are not here to approach any further, we are simply containing *her*." The commander gestured behind him with a tilt of his head.

Dask's eyes nervously looked beyond. The silhouette of a young woman with a heavy white robe on her shoulders leaned casually against the building across the street. Fireflies danced around her eerily. The robe hung open, with a cord that connected the lapels. Beneath, she wore simple cloth wrappings across her chest, while the broad and flowing legs of her hakama pants flared down from her waist.

The left sleeve of the robe had no arm and was folded up and fastened to the shoulder – her right hand hung in the other sleeve with the weight of a heavy clay jug at her fingertips. With a subtle turn of her head she swayed the hair from her eyes and lifted the jug to her lips, taking a small sip of the liquid inside – presumably wine.

She was very petite. Feathery black hair, cut and styled short in the back and sides gradually tapered longer in front to sweep across and conceal her left eye. Hardly a day over twenty years of age, with skin of pale porcelain and a very slight frame.

"Why have we hired the mistborn to do our job for us?" Dask pondered aloud. "They are unnatural, demon-tainted creatures." His hand fell to the hilt of his short sword, nervously scratching at the metal with nails blackened in filth.

The commander reached beneath his breastplate and revealed a decree with a broken royal blue and white wax seal of the Judiciar. "The Orbweavers have been sentenced to death and Whisper is better equipped to confront them." It was no secret he would have preferred to capture the sect himself, but he understood that the decision was made to minimize casualties. He then turned to the woman and signaled for her to approach. "Whisper, we're ready."

The one armed woman carefully placed her wine jug on the cobblestone and sealed it. The sound of fired clay scraped the stone as the cork squeaked. She gave her robe a gentle brush and walked through the flickering fireflies that faded in and out of the darkness.

"I have been informed the premises is heavily trapped with enchantments. Will that be a problem?" the commander asked.

As Whisper approached, the lantern light washed across her face. It was then that they could see the icy blue, demon-kissed eyes that hid beneath her hair – slitted pupils wrapped in a brilliant cobalt blue iris. Though nearly impossible to see beneath her sweep of dark hair, fine opalescent scales adorned the skin surrounding her left eye. Likely the reason she fashioned her hair the way she did. It was impossible to hide both her eyes, but covering the more conspicuous of the two would, at the very least, minimized the negative attention she received from the bigoted. Mistborn were extremely rare, and therefore highly vilified.

"It won't be a problem." Her voice was sharp and unimpressed.

"Is everything alright?" asked Dask. He could tell her mood seemed pointed, though he wasn't certain if this was out of character. "You seem uninterested."

"I fight warriors. Not old men in nightgowns." She sneered and turned her nose as she proceeded towards the hovel. "The only thing interesting is how you couldn't do it yourselves."

***

"Master Kalen." One of the shrouded magi approached him from behind. "The guards are outside now. Whisper will be here in minutes."

The scent of blood slowly overpowered the incense as Kalen put the final touches on a large glyph he drew on the wall with his open wound. His breaths were severely labored and he staggered slightly as he drank the remnants of his waterskin so much blood had been used and he needed to replace the fluids in his body as quickly as possible. He stepped back to examine the cultic mark and wondered to himself if he would have the strength to make it work. The only time he had ever completed a summoning of this degree was when he was at his peak, a mere half decade ago, but he knew anything less would pose no threat to the mistborn girl. He referred quickly to a leather ledger that lay open at his side and confirmed his glyph with the one in his notes.

"I can help you summon," the mage offered.

Kalen shook his head. "This ritual is too advanced for you, I will have to do it alone."

"But it will kill you."

His cloudy eyes glanced at the rose crystals that sat in the center of the room. "We have fulfilled our purpose as Orbweavers by completing the crystals. If I am going to die, I will do so instilling terror into the hearts of those who oppose us."

The mage bowed. "We will give you as much time as we can." He turned and disappeared up the stairs.

With deep breaths and heavy hands, Kalen forced his pale palms against the wall and began to chant beneath his breath. Tiny red sparks flashed through the smoke as the glyph ignited in heatless orange flame and the room began to fill with the unmistakable stench of carrion.

★★★

Whisper slowly ambled up the pathway towards the hovel. The soldiers behind her dared not make a sound, beckoning in a silence that was as cold and unsettling as the night itself. Just as she had been warned, her approach seemed to activate a glyph that was carved into the base of the steps. A sickly green flash illuminated the darkness as the sigil ignited and bursting forth came a half dozen iron spines.

Whisper snatched them from the air, the slender spikes laced between her fingers. More hints of green flame began to emerge from various locations around her, but as quickly as she had caught the spines, she released them, flicking them with a snap of her wrist.

She was relatively uneducated on the use of glyphs, but in her limited experience she learned that the passage of energy throughout the symbol was key to its ignition, and if she could disrupt the path before it released then the destructive essence of the glyph would destabilize and implode. Fortunately, hitting something with enough force it would burst was her specialty.

Her demonic eyes were renowned for being acute and she could spot and react to each glyph as it began to flare, piercing the solid markings with the spines she had caught from the first failed attempt on her life. Surely enough, the remaining traps that had begun to trigger were quickly broken and burst into dazzling flares of green flame that immediately folded in on themselves.

She was terribly bored. A challenge of reflex and sight was no challenge at all and she spared every bit of temperance yawning on the doorstep. She was certain it had been sealed, but was certain it wasn't strong enough to keep her out. With a swift kick, the surface of the door shimmered briefly and shattered like glass as the wood and paneling exploded inwards.

The smoky concoction of incense and blood assaulted her senses, nearly distracting her enough to miss the faint glimmer of a blade that sought her heart. She immediately parried and countered with a strike to the mage's throat. The disturbing crackle of cartilage echoed as the guards watched the mysterious body plummet from the shadows and tumble down the steps. Whisper then slipped into the veiled darkness and disappeared.

Though the home seemed sparsely furnished and vacant, the abusive fog made the simple rooms disorienting. With light, careful steps she followed the dim glow of orange fire that flickered from the cellar stairwell. A faint creak of floorboards gave away the positions of the three magi flanking her and she quickly spun to defend herself.

They each wielded a vicious kris and dashed towards her in hopes of exploiting what they thought was a small window of opportunity. Though they were cloaked quite heavily she could sense they were all nerves as they hesitated in their assault.

As the first mage thrust his dagger, she struck his wrist and quickly drove her fingertips into his windpipe, crushing both. Before the body had time to fall, she turned to the second and dislocated his shoulder before he could complete his swing. As he buckled to cradle his arm, she clutched him by the face and took a wide step through the open archway into the adjacent room, whipping his body and plunging him through the heavy wooden wall that separated the two spaces.

The third froze momentarily as he watched the split second massacre and dropped his blade. He turned to flee, but felt weightless as his feet were swept from underneath him, dropping him hard to the floorboards. He felt her wrap her hand around his ankle and before he could plead for his life the world was a spinning mess of dark shapes. Throbbing pain surged across his body as he struck something hard and traveled through it. The last light to flash across his eyes was the fire of Kalen's ritual as he crashed through the floorboards into the cellar below.

Kalen paid no mind to the disruption behind him, but could distinctly hear the soft, malicious footsteps of Whisper as she descended the stairwell. He mustered the energy, though it would consume him in the end, to complete the summoning, but he needed just a little more time. Though he tried not to break his focus as he poured his life into the glyph, he nervously anticipated her killing blow. However, it didn't come. Instead, her sharp voice sung behind him, laced with curiosity.

"What is that?" she asked.

He couldn't afford to look at her and break his concentration, but he could manage a sentence or two. "A summoning circle."

"What are you summoning?" Intrigue filled his ears as she watched him work. The fire from the glyph had spread across the whole wall to create a flaming portal that shifted and rippled with unstable energy.

"A species of demon, called a havnus." He struggled, still flushed with confusion over her lack of intervention.

"Is it powerful?"

He chuckled as blood began to trickle from his nose, ears, and eyes. "Not the strongest, of course, but the strongest I can call."

There was a pause that lingered between them and stretched so long he grew suspicious. Then her voice, rich with sinister thrill, caught his ears. "I'll wait."

★★★

The royal guards stood uneasily as the scene grew quiet. It had only been a few minutes since Whisper had entered, but after the initial sounds of violent altercation everything had gone still. The faint orange glow that eerily shone through the smoke within the hovel had slowly grown brighter, and they nervously adjusted their stances and grips.

A faint rumbling began to tremor beneath their feet, which drew their attention from the hovel. Through the confusion and high tension the commander ordered they hold their positions and prepare themselves. He had seen the aftermath of Whisper's work in the past and had expected collateral damage as a worst-case scenario, though the trembling earth was tragically unforeseen.

The tremors grew deeper and louder as the unit neared their breaking point. Large beads of sweat trickled down their brow and stung their eyes. Jaws clenched and ached as they forced their valor to hold them steady. The orange glow then burst into a flash of light and quickly receded back into the darkness as the tremors immediately subsided.

The commander stood ready, listening and watching with the utmost intent, trying to decipher the situation, but nothing happened. The half plate armor of the platoon shifted in the silence and the tension slowly began to unwind.

Without warning, the hovel exploded in a cacophonous roar of splintered shrapnel that shook the stone beneath their feet as a massive creature burst from the wreckage and hurled a body across the street and through another building. The havnus had a thick reptilian body that glistened black and red against the ambient light and pried itself from the debris with a dozen spindly arachnid legs.

The guards immediately stepped back and trembled in awe as the creature's jaw unhinged from its sockets in a hollow chord of grotesque cracking and popping to form an abyss of jagged teeth and wrath. The monster turned its attention to the nearest group of shaken guards and charged them, savaging the slowest to flee with its razor fangs.

Across the street, from the building through which the havnus had hurled the body, a soft glow of white light began to pour from the scraps of shattered wood and broken thatch. Wind began to whistle through the streets, bearing a fervent animus that felt like razors against their skin. Emerging from the wreckage, bathed in a shimmering corona that flicked roiling tendrils of searing white flame, was Whisper. The coils of fire lazily licked deep, grievous scars across everything they touched, wood and stone alike.

Her head hung low as her cobalt blue eyes locked onto the havnus and brimmed with calamity. However, it was her smile that made the commander question which demon was more terrifying. It was a smile that stretched sharply from ear to ear, projecting both unfettered amusement and incalculable ruination.

She shrugged off the folded left shoulder of her robe and allowed it to hang behind her from the tether attaching her lapels. The commander began to approach, but stopped in his tracks as he caught the opalescent shimmer that gleamed across the left arm he didn't even know she had. It was widely assumed she had lost the arm, but instead, she was hiding it. For good reason as well.

It was entirely demonic in nature, bearing jagged opal scales that armored from her shoulder down to the three claws of her hand. Though the arm was proportionate to her size, it was remarkably toned with lithe lines of muscle definition that traced throughout.

Beyond the commander's initial astonishment, he realized her white corona had created a wind funnel that completely engulfed her while the tendrils of flame slashed through everything they touched. He knew better than to approach, as he would be shredded. Instead, he did what he was there to do in the first place, contain the situation as best he could and let Whisper work.

He quickly turned to the remainder of his unit, who were futilely attempting to drive their spearheads through the creature's thick skin. "Disengage!" he yelled. "Clear the district! Get the civilians to safe distance!"

The guards immediately aborted their efforts and obeyed the orders, dashing down the streets and banging on doors.

What had started with a walk slowly turned into a run as Whisper charged the havnus. The monstrous creature caught clear sight of her roiling aura and diverted its attention from pursuing the guards to devouring her. It lowered its unhinged maw and lunged at her in attempt to swallow her whole, when its forward momentum abruptly stopped. Whisper managed to clasp onto its upper and lower jaws and push back with equal force. The havnus twisted and flailed as it attempted to free itself to no avail. Her heels dragged through the stone as she used all of her strength to ensure he couldn't overpower her.

The vortex of wind and flaming corona that encircled her began to lash at the monsters thick flesh, and it writhed in pain as she slowly felt its strength wane from the overwhelming onslaught of splitting skin. With a feat of sheer force she drove its head into the ground, crushing the rock and sending an explosion of fissures that wove beneath her feet. She forced the havnus backwards and dredged its head across the stone as its spindly legs flailed.

The advantage was clearly hers and the commander held his breath as he watched her force it to the perimeter wall. The creature forced a gurgled shriek as it tried to twist its mouth from her grasp, but as the hurricane of energy continued to flay, the focus needed to overpower her was fading rapidly. The corona seared across its leathery skin, shattered rows of sharp teeth and violently ripped the soft tissue within its open mouth.

Once the havnus had become so weak that its many legs could barely hold its weight she began to repeatedly crash its head into the perimeter wall. The ground shook with every shockwave of fissured stone and shattered bone, and even after the massive body fell lifeless, Whisper wouldn't stop. There was a terrifying delight in her eyes as each strike turned into an unpleasantly soft gushing of flesh and blood.

The commander approached, being sure to keep enough distance that her aura couldn't devour him. "Whisper! Stop!"

She pummeled its lifeless body into the wall once more raining rubble from a massive network of fragmented masonry. Her head hung low and her shoulders slumped as she reluctantly let the havnus' head fall to the ground with a slimy, boneless splatter.

Though her demeanor had grown calm, her aura was still thrashing wildly. "You're going to bring the whole wall down if you don't stop this witchcraft!" he warned.

There was a pause that hung heavily between them, but eventually the wind began to recede and the white glow dissipated. Her hair hung down and shielded her face from his judgement as she stared at the bloody corpse with unfamiliar eyes, seemingly dazed by her overreactions. "Disappointing," she sighed as she feebly attempted to regain her composure.

The commander was at a loss for words and simply watched, her head hung low, as she turned and retrieved her clay jug from the street. The cork was quickly removed as she drowned herself in a mournful drink and pulled the robe back over her left shoulder to conceal her mutation. Without another word, she slipped into an alley and vanished.

Blood had overcome the musk and minty patchouli now, trickling its metallic distaste across their tongues as they assessed the damage around them. The hovel lay in ruins, tattered limbs of the valiant strewn through smears of cooling blood, and the perimeter wall was on the verge of collapse.

The commander looked upon it with a heavy heart. It was even worse than he imagined.

2

WHITE HAIRED WITCH

The outskirts of Freestone were an ocean of pink, red, and white blossoms that waved and danced in the breeze. Sweet aroma filled the morning air and pacified the city at its heart. The soil, both rich and bountiful, had made Freestone renown across every realm in Elanta for its incredible peach trees.

A wise and elegant woman stood before a row of oak casks – vibrant green eyes and ghostly white hair, with words renown for being softly sung from seductive red lips. Exquisite silk cascaded down her shoulders, delicately accenting her adornment of intricate jewelry. An older man stood behind her with a quill and ledger bound in leather. With an outstretched hand, a worker amidst the casks bowed and carefully placed a round glass of amber liquid in her palm. She observed it carefully as it swirled and presented its aromatic bouquet, and after a small sip she fell into deep contemplation. Her distillery, the Scarlet Ribbon Estate, had been crafting the realms most coveted peach brandy for years and she held incredibly high standards for the product that would carry the name.

"Perfect," she said sweetly. "Bottle it."

The worker smiled and bowed once more as she handed the glass back to him. "You honor us, Lady Rhoswan."

She turned her head just enough to gesture to the man behind her that she was addressing him, though not enough to make eye contact. "Mister Breon," she started, "Please check the inventory and see the current orders are filled. The remaining bottles are to be stored in the cellar for private sale."

Breon readied his ledger and proceeded to walk down the row. "As you wish."

"One more thing..." He had stopped and turned to meet her eyes. "Where is Grove? I have enchantments that still need to be made." Her attention was drawn to a stack of freshly crafted casks she had been waiting to have blessed and purified.

The practice of occult wasn't uncommon in the realm, as you didn't have to be enlightened to learn and use the basic principles of the art. However, gifted practitioners were few and far apart and Grove was well worth his weight in coin. As mortals went, he was a master of his trade.

"I haven't seen Grove as of late, Lady Rhoswan," Breon said shaking his head. "I have sent him your commission, but not yet have I received a reply."

She pursed her lips slightly. "I will visit him personally. We may need to hire a new enchanter, please look into it and provide me a list by tonight."

He bowed his head and returned to his work.

She turned her attention back to the worker as she readied to leave. "You have done excellent work." She gently placed her fingertips under his chin. "Please, take a bottle for yourself and provide the others with one as well."

"If I may, Lady Rhoswan, could I forgo my bottle to see my daughter?"

She gently slid her hand through his hair and met the yearning within him. "How old would she be now?"

"Six, milady. It's been two years since her passing."

Rhoswan gently nodded, and with an ivory blaze that drew glyphs across her pupils, she gazed into him. A smile stretched across his face as he began to cry, awash with the sight of his lost daughter. The laughter, the grass, the feeling of her little hand in his as they walked the peach groves. Even the tone of her voice as she regaled him with her rich and beautiful experiences in the afterlife. What was a matter of seconds as the glyphs began to recede, was a reunion of hours to him.

"Thank you so much, Lady Rhoswan. You are so good to us." He bowed, wiping the tears from his cheeks.

She merely smiled and glided wordlessly to the doorway, leaving her worker's adoration in her wake.

3

WHITEWATER LEVIATHAN

The King's court was vast, and simple words could not do it justice. Lengths of violet silk hung from the ceilings of white marble while light shone in through great windows that towered in pointed arches of stained glass. The halls were filled with an ancient wisdom, having stood strong for centuries as a home and symbol of hope for the many townships over which King Whitewater ruled. Upon the spire of the castle itself was a coiling dragon of pure platinum and gold that wrapped around the building to the tip, holding in its jaws a massive ruby only slightly smaller than the throne upon which the King sat. The massive ruby was a landmark, a symbol of boundless importance and stature that was recognized across the world. Whitewater was a city nearly as amazing and intricately planned as the very marble mosaic that lined the great hall's northern wall, portraying a woman of exquisite beauty holding a feather in her palms – an artist's rendition of the fabled Shiori Etrielle, said to be the creator of all things.

"This way please," a soldier of Whitewater spoke. He then turned foot and proceeded down the hall. Whisper was always surprised at how agile they were, considering the heavy silver plate in which they were clad.

She peered down the hall at her escort and followed. A feeling of vexation churned within her stomach. She had taken this walk a few times before. Once for a slight misunderstanding of the word 'subdue', and another for using a carriage to beat someone to death. She was certain she could have avoided the brunt of her scolding had the horse not still been attached. She assumed the King was upset about the collateral damage. Regardless, she prepared herself for the worst.

They arrived in a room with an over-sized mahogany desk with a proportionate chair behind it. Vast bookcases of dust and knowledge filled all four corners, while papers and diagrams lay strewn about in a barely ordered manner.

"Please, have a seat. The King and his Voice will be with you shortly." The guard gave a shallow bow and left the room, closing the door behind him.

The King and *his Voice.* Whisper focused herself and took a seat at one of the regular sized chairs. The thought of meeting with the King was unnerving at best, but to have the presence of his Voice as well was an overwhelming idea. If the King was the most important figure in the realm, his Voice would easily be the second. Whisper was, however, renown as a cold and relentless lawgiver and wasn't about to let her nerves show over a chat with the King. Again.

Moments later, the door creaked open and a giant of a man entered the room, adorned in relatively casual noble attire. He stood well over seven feet tall and was proportionately broad and muscular. Long, beautiful white hair flowed down his back, while powerful blue eyes met hers with a glimmering compassion and grace. True to his name, he was the prime lineage of tribal giants known as leviathans, long since lost. It had been nearly a half century since the leviathans were erased from existence – a cleansing that swept three realms into a war that stretched for years. Tens of thousands of lives were lost driving the rebel tribes from the mountains, and when the dust of victory settled on humankind the last leviathan had fallen to the blade of the former King, Leomund Whitewater. It was amidst the rotting corpses and blood soaked gravel that the young Liam had been found, and though the King had been adamant on the destruction of every last one, something changed his mind about this last little survivor. It was widely rumored that Leomund was approached by a messenger of the Fates, who convinced him that raising the leviathan as his own would somehow play an important role in the strength of the realm. Surely enough, as Liam matured, his strength became a cornerstone to his father's empire. Through decades of loyal contribution he eventually inherited the throne in full when Leomund died at the dawn of the Dragon War, nearly two and a half decades ago. With his new crown brought new rules and the people quickly accepted him as the Whitewater Leviathan.

Whisper stood and bowed her head, catching glimpses of another behind him. He was slightly taller than herself, just under thirty, clean cut, and remarkably handsome. His emerald eyes greeted her beneath black hair that was thrown back, voluminous, and beautifully messy – a highlight of dark violet subtly kissed the ambient light. He was dressed in a high collared military coat, tailored to fit, with a simple white shirt and scarf of indigo. A small smile crooked in the corner of his mouth that somehow softened her. The King sat, but the young man chose to stand.

"Your majesty," she bowed "It's an honor."

The King waved a hand and she took her seat. He casually leaned to the side of his chair. For being such a powerful man he seemed incredibly laid back. Since inheriting the throne from Leomund he had decided to rule as close in stature with his subordinates as he could, to create an air of fairness and the illusion of equality, something he was well known for. He owned no servants, no cooks, and no squires. He tended to his own meals, cleaned his own messes, and dealt with his own affairs. It was known as Whitewater Equalitarian Rule, implemented the moment he bore the crown. He always preached that noble wealth made mice of men, and decided to use the portion of the taxpayers money intended for the Kings comfortable lifestyle to instead promote culture within his cities and fortify their borders with elites in the finest gear one could buy. More recently, the scholarly city of Lyre to the north was being heavily funded to research advanced technology and chemistry.

He was an immaculate amongst the common folk and a blight to the lords, though he never yet forced his opinion into law. His empowerment of the people gave them the leverage of a coupe should they be treated poorly. This fear kept the lords and dukes in check without the King ever having to lift a finger. Since his rule, the realm had become a beacon of hope for the common man and a land where swords bowed to kings over coins.

"Whisper, this is Salem Eventide, from the city of Freestone."

She had heard of him before. A man rewarded with a powerful position in the King's court for his contribution to the thriving economics of Whitewater. Though the realm of Whitewater encompassed several large cities, only three were of true note. The capital city, named for the founding family of Whitewater, was home to several generations of kings. The second, and oldest, was the city of Lyre, a bastion in the cold northern border-marches where Leomund Whitewater constructed the Great Library, which held the world's largest collection of literature and ancient texts known to man. Lastly, and most recent, was the city of Freestone. It was a small town of little significance until the arrival of a mysterious woman from the south, who called herself Rhoswan Gray. She and a business partner invested in a distillery they called the Scarlet Ribbon Estate, from which they began to create some of the finest and rarest vintages fit for any royal dignitary. It wasn't long before the humble town of Freestone transformed into a hub of trade and tourism.

It was no secret to anyone that behind the success of each of the three major cities, Salem played a significant role. The funding to Lyre's research and development, the silent partner of the fabled Scarlet Ribbon Estate, Voice of the King himself – all Salem Eventide. She'd even heard that his capacity for diplomacy and negotiation had somehow convinced their elusive neighbors to the east, the Setsuhan tribe from the Realm of the Snow Leaf, to open their borders to trade after a millennia of isolation.

"I employed you to confront and execute the Orbweavers yesterday," the Leviathan spoke.

"Indeed your majesty."

"I have been informed that you were successful. However, I have concerns over the practical application of your skill."

"Your majesty, they summoned a demon," she iterated.

The Leviathan nodded as he glanced over a report on his desk. "According to this, you detained the creature prior to damaging the perimeter wall."

Whisper knew he was right and didn't feel comfortable trying to convince him otherwise. She was fairly new to the city, as she spent her whole life in the confines of a remote monastery, deep in the mountains to the northwest. Though she was displaced from the rest of the world in her youth, she was highly educated by the monks and recognized that, when all was said and done, you truly only had three things – your name, your integrity, and your word. "Yes, I guess I got carried away."

He appeared to appreciate her honesty, though she knew it wouldn't change his ruling. "You will repay my people by assisting the stone masons as they repair the excessive damage you've caused."

Whisper swallowed hard, but maintained her focus on his eyes, showing no fear. "Your majesty, I have no skill in masonry."

"Then it will be a good learning experience. To understand the damage of your recklessness, you must understand the meticulous scrutiny and fickle temperament of the art repairing it."

There was an awkward silence and the King gave a heavy sigh. He relaxed his arms on the rests and tilted his head to one side, as though pondering her fate.

"I like you, Whisper," he started, "You're the first person I've met who is stronger than me, though arguably your lack of discipline comes with great expense. As mistborn go you have shown great prospect in the short time I have known you, but with every silver talent spoiled on your path of ruin I must consider the economic impact for your militaristic contributions."

She shifted uneasily, anticipating the rejection to follow. He had every right to terminate her contract or even ban her from the city should he wish.

"Your power is too chaotic and your growth is far too sequestered to safely reside within my walls any longer. I wish to propose a more ambitious use of your talents." He allowed his words to settle in, but she wasn't oblivious to the idea that this was a passive exile.

"Your personal contribution to the wellbeing of this kingdom and the unwavering loyalty to the protection of myself and my peers makes me honored to have your skill in my realm. It is with this great admiration that I offer you a privileged position." He turned back to Salem and extended a hand to present him. "Salem is my chief adviser, ambassador of the city of Whitewater, and Voice of the King. His words are the only of this realm I declare equal to my own and his presence is crucial when mine is not possible. He will be conducting an investigation into the disappearances of several of my realms most recognized enchanters, which have shown strong connection to the rise in Orbweaver activity. Should they be linked I will need him well guarded, and he has specifically requested you."

Whisper bordered between curious and uncomfortable, finally breaking a short silence. "Requested me?"

Salem smiled politely. "I hear you have beaten a man to death with a horse."

Whisper recalled the incident that last landed her a similar scolding from the King. "A carriage, actually." She knew it didn't matter, but felt the need to correct him anyways. "The horse just happened to be attached."

Salem seemed very pleased. "Imagine the tombstone."

Though he was soft spoken there was something about him that projected undeniable authority, making her unsure whether or not to laugh.

"Dear Whisper." He lowered his head and looked at her with enticement as his words flowed with milk and honey. "I am investigating conspirators against the realm, a task that involves a significant amount of danger. Truth be told, you possess a strength, mobility, and discretion I cannot receive from a unit of elites."

A smile swept across her face as she fought an uncontrollable peace within her – compliments were few and far apart in the life of a mistborn. However, there was something more, something... unnaturally alluring. His smile, his eyes, his words, all wrapped around her in a way she wasn't used to. A truly odd sensation for her, whose natural state involved more agitation than attraction.

"Let's not mix words, Whisper," The Leviathan said. "With a single decree I will name you 'Ward of the Voice'. Now tell me, can I trust you to protect the second most important figure in the realm?"

"I accept," she replied without thinking, hearing the words flow from her mouth as though they slipped on instinct. It was an immense title, one often only given to highly ranked and trusted veterans of the King's army. How she was worthy of it was flattering and to turn it down would be foolish.

The Leviathan took a quill and parchment from his desk and began to write. "It's settled then. I will arrange your official papers and have them ready within the week." He stopped and smiled at her. "Until then, you are an honorary stone mason's apprentice."

She looked out the window for a bird's eye view of the disaster she had caused. "Fickle temperance," she sighed, "Certainly not my virtue."

4

GROVE'S ESTATE AND THE BLADE BEYOND THE SHEEN

It was a relatively long walk to Grove's stead, but Lady Rhoswan enjoyed the quiet time through the trees in the spring. Birds flitted from branch to branch as they welcomed her presence. A short four years ago, Freestone's orchards hadn't extended this far out. Before she established the Scarlet Ribbon, the city would export their product to the neighboring cities and realms for mediocre market values. As her distillery prospered she purchased vast acreage, provided ample jobs, and kept the majority of the peach industry localized. Before long, Freestone was brimming with commerce and tourism, earning its rite as Whitewater's secondary capital.

When she first moved from the southern plum country village of Blackthorne, the people did not accept her gently. Though she was charismatic and graceful, her unusually white hair had people spreading rumors that she was a witch. It wasn't until the persuasive young Salem Eventide, now her business partner, had brought to light her economic contribution and had everyone eventually referring to her as 'their' witch.

In truth, she liked the nickname. It made her feel mysterious and powerful, as though she were revered for her unique traits and skills, instead of feared. She liked to largely take credit for the prosperity of her business and the fruits it bore for everyone else to reap, but she had help. Whenever she needed that extra push, the fresh new idea, or foresight in the market, Salem would slip in unnoticed and whisper in her ear. Inspiring things. Grand things. She was the machine that made the system turn and he was the oil that kept it running as smooth as silk. Though she had no idea where Salem Eventide had come from, she thought it best to keep a close eye on him. After all, no mere mortal could have such consistent insights.

Lost in thought, it had taken only moments for her to travel the several miles of orchard back into the city. The people bowed and greeted her pleasantly as they gave her ample berth to pass. They loved that she was *their* witch and gave healthy respect to her personal space. A smile spread across her face. The townsfolk perceived her as enlightened, as well they should, having watched her peer into one's eyes and allow them to *see*. For each person it was different. A loved one, a lost one. For as much as people revered her ability to breathe life into their memories and dreams, the fear of her scorn ever animating their nightmares was looming possibility that kept them willing to please. A power so great would have taken a significant amount of training, but her power ran far deeper and greater than they could ever know, because she was keeping a great secret - she was blessed with her enlightenment. Spoiled with a flush of power she did not have to earn, where not a single day passed with training or meditation. It was an extremely rare occurrence in human history, and they were known as 'Champions', 'God Touched', or 'Instruments of Fate'. The rumor was that the power is attained by being chosen by one of the Fates, who were unseen gods of destiny and worldly balance. Whether or not this was fact was never truly known to mortal men, for if it were the very knowledge thereof could imbalance the line of time.

The Grove estate was a touch more elegant compared to the other buildings in the area. It stood two stories tall with a sweeping steepled roof of orange clay shingles that contrasted against its white and grey cobblestone walls. Rippled glass windows in frames and shutters of rich dark wood allowed for plenty of natural light. While most of the homes in this part of Freestone were built close together, the Grove estate was on a small gated plot of lush green land that gave his work much needed privacy. Grove was a very talented enchanter and had made a comfortable living from it. She unlatched the heavy iron gate and walked up the front steps. No one appeared to be home, but she knocked anyways, allowing some time to pass with no answer. She thought it peculiar. Grove always had terrible time management skills, but was consistent with excuses for his absence. A sigh, laced with irritation, brushed her lips as she turned to the street and crossed her arms. She wasn't fond of hassles.

Moments later, a hefty man clad in fine vestments politely intercepted her as she passed through the gate. He bowed respectfully and tipped a formal hat. "Lady Rhoswan," he said, a mischievous sheen flashed across his eyes, "What does a wren weigh?"

There was brief silence that muffled the ambient sound of people walking by until Rhoswan smiled coyly and pulled a folded fan from her sleeve – the noble white lace opened across her lips. "A pound, of course." She then turned and walked away, feigning ignorance to the man's mysterious words in case anyone else had seen or heard their brief interaction.

The man bowed once more and smiled, nervously looking around to ensure no one else was around. "Aye," he muttered under his breath. "A pound."

***

"My lord Eywin!" A soldier loudly knocked on a cold, reinforced wooden door. "It's very important!"

After a few moments delay it opened, where stood an elderly man shaken from his sleep. Soft, velvet robes adorned him from shoulder to toe. "What is the problem?" he asked, being sure as not to mask his agitation.

The soldier bowed deeply. "In the mines, sire. Something has been discovered that requires your immediate attention."

Derin Eywin, the Duke of Lyre, waved his hand and followed the soldier briskly through the stone halls and into the courtyard. The late evening air was both cool and still, as it often was this far to the north. The city of Lyre was an ancient place. It had long withstood thousands of years of war and weather until it came to peace under the reign of the former Leomund Whitewater, allowing them to annex the city into the realm. In Leomund's later years, the Great Library had been constructed to house the realms' most ancient codexes, manuals, and historical texts. Scholars from all over the world flocked to its ancient stone streets to become the best in the fields of medicine, history, philosophy, and thaumaturgy. Aside from the monasteries haphazardly scattered across the world, the Great Library was possibly the largest and safest place for one to attempt the arduous journey of self-enlightenment. With access to a multitude of educations, one had all the tools necessary to discover the power within themselves and how it intertwined with the energies of the world around them. It was the last remaining bastion city from the Dragon War, with walls several meters thick and more soldiers than the capital and Freestone combined.

High aloft one of the Library's spires, dedicated to alchemy and medicine, a young woman's attention was drawn to the window as a row of cloaked horsemen hurried across town towards the city walls. The escort of lantern-lit geldings seemed to come from the duke's keep, which could only mean something was awry.

"Do you think father is down there?" she asked, gently rubbing a leaf of lamb's ear before placing the fuzzy plant into a mortar.

The man to whom she spoke, a few years older than her, strode across the room and peered over the ledge, his freezing breath drifted slowly into the night. The sigil of a tree with the trunk of a sword played with the ambient candlelight that flickered across his vestments. It was the symbol of house Waylander, one of the most recognized houses in Lyre. For six generations the Waylanders had dedicated their name to the dukes of Lyre, enlightening themselves and serving as protectors, practitioners, and healers. He was the eldest child and only son, Casamir, with one sister, Katya. It was his destiny to one day complete his training and enlighten to join the ranks alongside his father, and since he had lost his mother to illness when he was young there was an unspoken weight that made him feel he would dishonor her if he didn't.

Once she was old enough to understand that illness took her mother, Katya Waylander devoted herself to the art of medicine. Now at sixteen years of age she was finishing her third year of official academic study. Already, she had begun to feel the connection between herself and the nature with which she worked, which was a good sign she was on the right path to breaking down the wall within herself and being able to utilize the energy within her in conjunction with poultices and elixirs. Excellent news for her, but stressful for Casamir, whom after nearly six years of extensive education had yet to feel his soul connect to anything at all.

"It's possible," he replied. "There are enough horses for it to be Lyre's Elite."

The Lyre's Elite were a group of soldiers known as Moths, all enlightened and specially trained under the careful watch of their father, who was referred to as Elder Waylander. They were peacekeepers, counter-intelligence operatives, highly specialized tacticians, and assassins – whatever the duke needed, whenever he needed them.

***

The duke was hurried across town to a mine outside the city walls. Though they rode at a rushed pace, the city was so large it still took them nearly twenty minutes to reach the portcullis and beyond. The duke dismounted and proceeded into the mine, which was teeming with an overabundance of workers and scholars. A sage, who was essentially a highly ranked scholar and was identified by the royal blue and white robes in which he was adorned, approached him excitedly.

"My apologies, my lord." He bowed briskly, recognizing the six Moths on horseback behind him. Dark cloaks and leathers, concealing all but their eyes. Each wore a heavy, golden trimmed scarf around their face and shoulders, which proudly displayed a large brushed steel brooch of a moth, identifying them as the Lyre's Elite – dark sapphires glinted in the eyes of the wings.

"What is the meaning of this?" the duke asked.

"Please, this way."

They dismounted and maneuvered down a long series of shafts as the foreman nervously spoke, shifting his eyes between the path ahead of him and the six Moths behind. "As you recall, my lord, not long ago we struck a vein of quartz."

"I read something about it somewhere, get on with it."

"Well, we had begun to remove it when we noticed that the deeper we dug, the harder it became to break."

The duke rolled his hand, as if to gesture for him to get to the point.

"Ah... yes, my lord." The foreman quickly bowed his head, embarrassed. "We did not want to trouble you with such petty complications. Instead, we began to dig around the vein, and well..." His voice trailed off as they entered a larger chamber filled with workers, all standing before a narrow wall of hewn crystal.

Suspended within the crystal was a curved sword of incredible and exquisite craftsmanship. It appeared to be made of pure platinum, with an edge of solid gold that traveled from hilt to tip. The guard was also golden, with three curved blades that chased each other within a solid ring that fused to their tips. The hilt was wrapped tightly in black and silver cloth, but what was most unique was what hung from it. An ornate chain with a little charm on the end. It looked like a little piece of white cloth, wrapped and tied around something spherical to make it appear as a tiny fabric ghost, hanging by the top of his head. There were even two little black lines for eyes, making it look as though it were sleeping. The sage raised his hand to direct attention to the artifact.

The duke leaned in and examined it more carefully. As he approached, he realized it was not actually a solid piece of crystal, but a hollow, transparent box made of thousands of tiny crystal hexagons. Veins of the hexagonal crystal stretched from the top and bottom of the cage to hold the hilt and tip of the sword in place, creating the illusion of suspension. "It's incredible!" he said in awe. "This crystal certainly isn't natural, and the sword is unlike anything I have ever seen before. Do we know anything about it?"

The sage opened a codex so old that the bindings cracked and crumbled beneath the weight of the paper and referred the duke to a page within. In the text was a unique crest, an elegant rune of lost language and unknown origin set before a blazing phoenix. "This is the mark of Shiori Etrielle," he said excitedly, "The Immaculate Artisan from our oldest texts of thousands of years. This was her signature, her mark of supernatural excellence. A being from beyond our space and time, believed to have created our whole world from the chaos of the mist itself."

The duke listened intently. He was certainly familiar with the theory that the world of Elanta had been created by an incredibly powerful being from another plane of existence, and with the feats of the enlightened growing more impressive with each passing day who was to say it wasn't plausible. There was hardly any worship or occult following in her name though, as the only proof of her existence were a few codices, badly damaged or destroyed over time. This particular text was the only fully intact copy of her work, and even it was written in a language far too archaic to completely decode. If she truly was the Immaculate Creator of the world, someone had gone to great lengths to make sure no one knew for certain. So far as he knew, only the Fates were powerful enough for such a conspiracy.

"My lord," he directed Eywin's attention to a golden symbol embossed into the base of the platinum blade. It was definitely the same. "This is the seal of Shiori Etrielle. Not only an incredible piece of history that is likely powerfully magical, but a long lost artifact created by the same hands many believe crafted the very world itself!"

Eywin stood before the sword and slowly allowed the awe to trickle in. Even if this *Etrielle* person hadn't actually created the world, she was clearly powerful enough to hold the reputation for several millennia despite the abysmal lack of proof.

The sage smiled. "It's invaluable, my lord. The incredible things it could be capable of... I can't even imagine the possibilities!"

One of the Moths looked upon it with suspicion and scoured the room. "This tunnel is far from the projected mining schematics."

The workers whispered amongst each other, confused yet fearful.

"What makes you say that?" replied the foreman.

The Moth turned to confront him. "I've seen the projection, counted my steps, and kept careful note of each change in direction as we walked. Where we stand is roughly one hundred and fifty paces north, and two hundred and twelve paces east off of the main line."

The foreman's nervousness piqued once more. "Um, yes sir. You are correct. A tiny, albeit forgivable slight, considering the find."

The Moth's dark brown eyes struck him from beneath his leather cowl, eyes meant to tear one apart from the inside out. "Why?"

"What do you mean?"

The menacing figure began to cross the stone, stalking silently forward as though affixed on prey. "Why had you veered off course in the first place?"

The foreman laughed awkwardly and looked to the duke for help. "A simple miscalculation, my lord. I deeply apologize."

The Moth never once shifted his gaze, nor did he seem to blink. However, his head began to tilt slightly, as though he were smelling something faint. "I don't believe you." He grabbed him by the lapel and held his face close, crushing him with intent.

Confronted, the man began to stutter. "I... well..." With a splash of warm blood, the foreman's lifeless body was ripped violently from the Moth's grasp as a heavy pick embedded itself in the side of his head from across the room. As quickly as the Moth looked to see who had thrown it, the assailant, a worker hidden amidst his colleagues, was riddled with knives from another of Lyre's Elite. The soft orange glow of the lanterns shimmered over the half dozen silver hilts that littered his body and clanged against the stone as he fell to the ground.

"What, by fate!?" duke Eywin scolded.

The largest of the Moths stepped forward and approached the second body, crouching to collect his knives from the corpse. "My apologies," his deep voice resonated, "I was not quick enough."

The first Moth knelt alongside the foreman's corpse and closed the open eyes with the palm of his hand. Moments later, he arose and revealed to the duke a narrow kris from a harness hidden along the man's calf.

"These men are Orbweavers, my lord," he exclaimed as he examined the wavy blade, smelling the faint blood and patchouli that lingered from prior use. A scent he had caught upon entering the mine. "We should notify the King and consider destroying the sword."

"You can't do that!" cried the sage. "This is a precious piece of history! We need to lock it up and study it!"

"Absolutely not," the Moth retorted. "The Orbweavers clearly have divine access to information. If they found it buried beneath a mountain of granite they'll definitely find it in the King's vault, and can we afford to attract that much attention? For all we know, the Fates buried it here themselves."

"And as the Fates mold our destiny, the mere fact we have found it means they wanted us to." The sage directed his attention to the duke. "My lord, please consider. If the cultists seek it, then it must be powerful. Let us not destroy it as a weapon to be feared, but wield it as a symbol of rule."

"Ignore his petty cries," replied the Moth. "His words are that of selfishness. We must consider that the Orbweavers decided to bring your attention to its existence because they needed you to make their scheme work in some way, otherwise they could have excavated it and vanished before anyone knew it existed. Your desire to keep it is calculated into their plan, so we should do exactly the opposite."

"Nonsense!" Eywin retorted, his harrowed eyes grew ever darker as his desires overtook him. "You killed the two spies. And a weapon like this could win me the throne... perhaps more."

"Sir," the Moth implored, leaning in closely to whisper his words. "Perhaps discretion would be best, as what you speak of could be deemed as conspiracy against the King."

The duke wrapped his fingers around the scarf of the Moth and pulled him closer. "You will not counsel me on wisdom," he said sharply. "I'll say as I please, as I'm pleased to say. And you, Elder Waylander, will mind your tongue, or lose it."

Waylander closed his eyes and bowed his head in apology. "Yes, my lord. I misspoke." He turned as the duke released, glimpsing one last time at the sword encased beyond the sheen. Though he could not say, his instincts continued to warn him. If this sword was truly that of Shiori Etrielle's, it stood to reason that powerful, other-worldly things would be drawn to powerful, other-worldly things.

"Break it loose," the duke ordered the workers. "Now."

The sage approached. "My lord, though it appears to be a crystal of sort, it's completely impregnable. We believe it to be honeycomb stone, created by the dragons before their untimely demise." He gestured for them to stand back as one of the miners readied a heavy iron pick in his hands. With a hard swing from high above his head, the iron collided with the surface and shattered into several heavy pieces that crashed to the ground. The crystal bore neither chip nor scratch as the pick lay broken at their feet. Sheer bewilderment engulfed them all. Save for Elder Waylander.

"I want it freed as a whole, then. Dig over, under, around. I don't care. Find a way to get the whole thing into my keep." Eywin arduously pulled himself away and addressed the Moths that stood at the ready, specifically the outspoken in the midst. "Oversee the extraction and assist with your enchantments. No one comes close to this without proper authority and all miners are screened going in and out."

Waylander met his gaze with disapproval, imploring him with unspoken words to reconsider while Eywin remained unwaveringly resistant. "Escort it to me personally once it's freed, Waylander. I'll have you watch as I take my first step to the throne."

5

KOAN AND THE KITTEN IN THE WOODS

The smell of mortar sat heavy in the air as Whisper stood back and watched the King's masons examine her work. It had been a long week, hauling slabs of cut stone and repairing the wall with her bare hands and feeble knowledge. Fortunately, the masons were kind to her and she learned very quickly the basics of the art. She felt confident as the mason turned to her and smiled in approval, and couldn't help but breathe a sigh of relief. A hand gently rested on her shoulder and she turned to see Salem, praising her by smiling simply with the corners of his eyes. In the short time she had gotten to know him, she began to realize that regardless of what he was actually saying, his words were in his gaze. It was a progressively powerful realization as she learned to feel instead of hear. Often times she would feel the full emotional and inspirational effect of his intent, but have little to no recollection of the words that got her there. In his other hand he was sipping from a small ceramic cup filled with plum wine.

"Wonderful job, dear Whisper," he said softly.

She blushed and feigned nonchalance.

He removed his hand from her shoulder and looked to the east. "As soon as you are ready to depart, we will head to Freestone."

Whisper was quickly confused. "Freestone?" she asked. "I thought we were investigating the Orbweavers in Whitewater?"

Salem reached into his lapel and revealed a small note, sealed with an exquisite red wax. "A letter from the esteemed Rhoswan Gray. It would seem a good friend of mine has gone missing. A master enchanter, I am afraid. I hazard to think the disappearance is connected." He paused a moment to feel the breeze across his face. "If anything, it is fortune in disguise. Though I spend much of my time here in Whitewater, my home is in Freestone. I have investments to check up on also, of course." He nursed the violet liquid and held it to his nose, breathing it in. He had not yet revealed any emotion beyond relaxed, though in the week's time she hadn't seen anyone be anything less than congenial in his presence. Men and women alike approached him with the utmost benevolence, partaking in his ever grand symphony of modest tone and enlightening words. A man like that, she imagined, would have used his silver tongue to pull the hearts of all the beautiful women that flocked to him. However, though the masses were both radiant and svelte, he seemed to pay them as much attention as he did everyone else. No man was that humble. She knew something was unspoken.

He interrupted her thoughts. "I will give you some time to gather your belongings." Salem put the cup to his lips and sipped the wine carefully, as though he were not drinking but simply splashing it on his palate to savor the flavor of every drop. "Meet me at the east gate in one hour." With a bow of his head he walked away, leaving the scent of plum wine to linger in the air.

She had never been to Freestone before. As a child of the northern ice fields who now lived in the central realm of Whitewater, she hadn't actually seen much of the world at all. It had only been a few short years ago, on her eighteenth birthday, that she set out on a pilgrimage from the Monastery of the Eternity Ring, hidden deep in the mountains of the western fire realm of Emberwilde. She spent her whole life there, being forcibly separated from her parents as an infant.

Her short journey led her to Whitewater and she had settled in since. The King treated her with respect and offered her work from time to time. She didn't have much to her name and needed the resources, so she obliged. Over time, she was permitted to purchase a small home near the castle gates. Having been raised in the monastery, everything she had ever owned she had to learn to make for herself, so buying her new home in Whitewater was a bittersweet balance of both pride and shame.

She ascended the stone steps leading to her front door. At her request, a local enchanter had etched a rune of silver into the center of the entrance before he mysteriously vanished with the rise of the Orbweavers. He told her, at the time, that it wasn't always the symbol that was important in enchanting, but the power and intent placed behind it. Taking that into consideration, she customized the design after a charm her father left her in their last moments together, and the enchanter filled the rune with fortune and prosperity. It was a simple charm, a vortex of four opposing lines swirling in on each other, with a brilliant ruby in the center. To this day, no scholar had been able to identify its purpose, meaning, or origin. The general consensus was that it was the crest of a family line long since lost, though crafted by exquisite hands.

The interior of her home was sparse, cool, and clean. A breeze gently blew through light drapes and crossed the small, empty space. The kitchen and living area were attached to each other and stairs led to a loft bedroom that overlooked the bottom floor. She walked up to her room and began sifting through her dresser. Her wardrobe was tragically drab and monotonous. Eighteen years in a monastery wearing the same color and style every day can have that effect. And the weight and fit were the only she had found, so far, that would conceal her left arm from public scrutiny as effectively as it did.

With her single free hand she gathered together a few changes of clothing, some traveling essentials, and then pressed her fingertips to the center of her chest. She could feel the silver charm beneath her wrappings and took a deep breath as the wind kissed her cheeks. It was a fragment from her past she wanted to keep close to her at all times.

The sight of her baggage saddened her. Three years in the free world and she was still the same person, with the same clothes and habits. A victim to her comfort, a prisoner to orthodox.

She proceeded down the stairs and stopped in the kitchen. From a cupboard she withdrew a maroon bottle and unfastened the clay jug from her shoulder. A smile of relief crept across her lips as she listened to the wine slosh into it – one new habit she had developed, at the very least.

She waited patiently at the east gate, the distinct smell of horses and hay drifted from the nearby stables. After what she would have sworn was exactly an hour, Salem approached. He had no bags nor satchels in hand, save for a fancy sling carrying a bottle of wine hung over his shoulder. His smile paralyzed her. "Right on time!" he spoke with his eyes. "Freestone is a few days ride from here, we should depart immediately."

She bowed her head slightly to acknowledge his request.

"Might I ask you, dear Whisper," he started, "Would you prefer to ride or walk?"

She tried to hide her confusion, as she couldn't bring herself to see a man of noble attire walking for any length of time when he could commission a horse. Aside from that, transportation was a new and convenient luxury in her life. "I'd like to ride there." Her attention drew to a beautiful white horse tethered to a stall.

"Interesting," he replied, "But we will be walking."

Her eyes grew unimpressed. "Why would you ask me? Just to suggest the opposite?"

He shook his head and placed a hand on her shoulder. "Dear Whisper, the question was not to determine the opposite response. We were walking regardless. The question was to see what you would say."

She waited for sweet irritation to sweep her, as it normally did, his words were so well laced in tact she couldn't help but feel accepting of his baited response. Barely.

He released her shoulder and began to walk through the gates. "Your time away from the monastery has weakened you," he said without turning to look her in the eyes. "You bring dishonor to the lessons of your elders with your impatience and poor self-control."

She was astonished by his forthright accusation, and without the softness of his eyes to buffer the words, they bore deep into her character and infuriated her.

"These words stir you?" he asked firmly.

She ground her teeth silently as her eyes grew dark.

"They are meant to. Shame can be a tool from which we learn." He turned and pierced her with his gaze. One that roughly wrapped around her throat. "Now, will you crumble beneath its weight or use it to remind you of the convictions your elders taught, and walk?"

Angry as she was, she knew he was right. Patience was strongly enforced in the monastery and since leaving she was allowing herself to slide on all the codes and ethics she felt were too hard to uphold. She choked back her pride and caught up to him. A small part, beneath the shame, was grateful and relieved. She had finally seen a second emotion from Salem, and it pleased her that it was one that would scold and command her fickle respect, even though he was a bit of an ass. This walk was one she should have taken a long time ago.

★★★

They walked in silence for nearly half a day. She admired the scenery and allowed its beauty to ease her inner storm as best it could, but it still churned beneath her skin. She couldn't help it. Forgiving and forgetting weren't mistborn traits to say the least, regardless of fault.

She was pleased to see the hills and plains were beginning to turn into tall trees and brush as they exited the massive influence of the capital city. Despite the rough start it felt like she was beginning an adventure, and the thought of finding someone or something powerful enough to test her made her heart race.

Salem caught a brief glimpse of the cruel excitement in her eyes as she stared ahead, lost in her thoughts. Though he was plenty skilled at deduction, it didn't take much to read her love for aggression. An elevated heart rate flushed her porcelain features, the muscles in her jaw tightened as she clenched her teeth. Even her pupils dilated to indicate pleasure, while her head dropped to watch the road from just under her brow.

They finally reached the dense forest that was to be their path for the next few days. The road was clean and well traveled by merchants and scholars, but these forests were home to many eyes. It was unsafe to travel at night or without protection. Fierce animals were rare in these parts, often being frightened or dissuaded by large groups or loud sounds – it was the bandits one had to watch for. The bandits here weren't the most cut-throat of the realm at least. They discovered they could, oftentimes, bully the wealthy for a donation or toll over multiple encounters throughout each season. Keeping them alive was viewed as a long term investment. The soft rustling of the trees was all the reassurance Salem would get knowing he was far more likely to have to negotiate his release than have his throat slit as they slept.

"Tell me about yourself, dear Whisper," Salem said as he pulled the cork from his wine.

"There's nothing to tell." She peered off into the trees to distract herself from the conversation.

"I understand you grew up in the Monastery of the Eternity Ring."

"It's none of your business."

"I suppose not," he looked to the sky, "but if I am to trust you as my guardian, I must fully understand the depth of your thirst for revenge."

Whisper's heart began to race and she took a quiet moment to calm herself. "Who says I want revenge?"

He took a deep breath and gathered his thoughts. "If I may," he began, "I believe that, before your very eyes, you experienced the passing of your mother and father."

She slowed her pace and continued to give him a cold shoulder, though deep down inside she wasn't sure she wanted him to stop. "Tread softly, Eventide."

"Firstly, the charm you keep beneath your wrappings. I notice you touch it from time to time. Keeping it so close to your heart leads me to believe it is something of significance. As a monk of the Eternity Ring, I can only imagine it would be a trinket from your prior life, short as it may have been."

Whisper challenged his theory sharply. "It could be anything, you don't know it's a charm."

"I do know it is a charm, because the significance has been projected through the sigil you enchanted on your doorway in Whitewater. Certainly not one of any occult significance and therefore one of personal origin. Clearly that of a charm and nothing less. Most people would touch the charm to ease themselves, however, when you do, your heart rate increases, amidst other physical reactions such as sweating and nausea. You use it to remind you of the events of that day, traumatic as they may be, never allowing yourself to let go.

"Secondly, your loss of control with the Havnus. That, coupled with the discoloration beneath your eyes tell me you have trouble sleeping. Nightmares or mental anxiety I presume."

Out of reflex, she gently pressed beneath her eyes before realizing she couldn't determine the color of her skin.

"These signs are clearly symptoms of post-traumatic stress, connected to your parents with the other information I had earlier deduced. You exhibit no despair in these reactions, discarding abandonment as a root. This simply leaves your anger, which directly ties to, what I feel is, the dramatic passing of your lineage."

With a touch of the charm beneath her wrappings, she experienced everything he just spoke of. It was astonishing he was able to see so much within her from such minor mannerisms.

"Nearly every night, I remember," the labored words shuttered from her lungs. "Even though I was only an infant."

Salem sipped the wine and listened carefully, brushing his free hand along the leaves of a low hanging branch while they walked.

"My mother was upset, arguing with my father. She was going to leave, he begged her to stay. Pleaded, actually. But she was brimming with... something. Conviction, I think is the word you would use?" She looked to Salem and then back to the road. "There was a fear for her life, but also an acceptance of death. It felt like she was leaving to meet someone she knew would kill her." She tried to recall the specifics of her memories, but it was so long ago and she was cursedly fortunate to remember what she had. "She left, and that was the first and last memory I have of her."

"Your father?" he asked.

She shook her head softly and raised her eyes to the leafy canopy above them. "For some reason I can remember so much more about him. His face. His features. Even his voice." Her demeanor grew cold as she recalled the last mournful look he gave her before their parting.

"It must have only been hours, maybe even a day since my mother had left, that someone approached my father and told him she was dead. I couldn't see the man's face, but my father was nervous. The most unusual sensation emanated from the stranger, one I could never forget." She rubbed her fingertips together as she recalled the feeling. "There was a heavy static in the air, thick with power. It weighed on me like soft lightning that stretched across my body and forced me into shallow breaths. My vision even began to tremor as the pressure built in my head. It was so intense that I lost consciousness. My last memory before waking up in the monastery."

"Static? It must have been a very powerful aura. The root of your drive to pit your strength against the strong."

Whisper nodded. "The enlightened I have killed so far didn't have nearly as much energy as what I felt that day. Though occasionally I feel the exact sensation, without ever finding the source."

Salem thought deeply. "Peculiar. Do you think he is watching you at times?"

"I do," she replied. "He mocks me. Letting me know he's near, but never shows himself."

"Dear Whisper, perhaps you could consider the *aura* you feel may simply be a form of psychological manifestation of the trauma you have endured."

She stopped abruptly, fighting the anger within her. "He's real!" Her voice grew wicked as she pierced him with her slitted eyes. "I'm not crazy. He's out there and I'll find him."

Due to the advantage of her mistborn traits, energy was as good as a fingerprint. Its frequency, taste, scent, visualization, radiation all subject to her acute senses, enough so that it held as much recognition as physical appearance. She was hunting for the owner of that aura. Hunting for the man that killed her family, and struggling with the feeling of being hunted herself.

"This man took my family from me. He is very real and his blood will prove it." The wind began to rise slightly as the leaves danced, beckoning her next question for the self-informed 'know it all' of Whitewater. "What else can you tell me?"

Salem shook his head. "Only that I believe your father was an enlightened enchanter from the southern fields of Whitewater. Perhaps the city of Blackthorne or even Freestone."

"How can you be so sure?" Of course, she had her doubts, but if he had proven anything so far, it was that he had the eyes to see beyond what she was capable of.

"The charm. I notice you gesture to it moreso when speaking of your father, which leads me to believe he was the one who gave it to you."

"Fine, you've uncovered that much, but how..."

"You may not have noticed," he interrupted, "but when you touch it, the wind brings the faintest smell of lavender."

She hadn't noticed, to be honest, as the charm would occupy her mind in other ways. Not to mention she was far better known for her eyesight.

"Though rare in the border realms, the scent of lavender is a common secondary trait of the pacifying enchantments often placed on warding talismans made in Whitewater's floral fields. A superstitious signature, in truth. They feel it irritates creatures of darkness. Hence, beneath your wrappings is a talisman of Whitewater origin, given to you by your father, an enchanter of the realm."

"An enchanter?" She paused. "Could his death be connected to the Orbweavers?"

Salem sighed. "Certainly possible I suppose, though enchanters only began disappearing a few months ago. It seems a stretch to claim your father's disappearance twenty years prior was at the hand of a sect only just breaking the surface at present."

She slowly reached into her robe and pulled the charm from the bindings. It dangled delicately from a thin chain. Now that she was made aware of it, the smell of lavender was much more prominent, and it helped bring her temper down slightly. The ruby glinted in the ambient light and she lost herself in it. "You seem to think you have it all figured out." She locked eyes and challenged him. What little peace the lavender had brought was quickly lost in conviction. "What does it mean?"

Salem smiled coyly. "I cannot tell you that."

"I can't get you to shut up about anything else and now that you have information I need, you're an avatar of peace." She couldn't contain herself anymore and roughly grabbed the front collar of his silver trimmed peacoat. The charm's chain wove between her fingers to keep from falling alongside the button she had abruptly torn from the wool. "Tell me."

"Or else? Will I rue with toothless words?" He leaned forward and pressed his collarbone further into her grip to assert his iron will. "It is a koan, dear Whisper. A deep riddle. The answer, to which, is a journey only you can take."

"But I have no idea what it means or where to start!" Her eyes seemed angry, but he could tell they were filled with a desperation she had no experience in channeling.

"To rob me for answers, is to rob yourself of revelations." His eyes were solid, piercing emeralds – hard, beautiful, and sharp. "You are so clouded with remorse, intemperance, and shame that you lash like a child, kicking and screaming."

"How dare you act like you know me, and call me a child, no less!" She gruffly pulled him to her face. "We'll see who kicks and screams in a moment."

Salem didn't waver, and instead slowly pushed his face closer to hers. He felt her weight shift to her back leg as she pulled away slightly, indicating either intimidation or confusion. "Do not assume bravery is the same as confidence. You may don the fangs to stake your claim, but you are still a wyrmling."

"I'm entirely confident, Salem. I'm undefeated," she growled.

Salem let a pause settle. "I would wager you packed your bags with one hand," he said. "Too ashamed to free your other arm, even in the privacy of your own home." Her gaze began to shift back and forth between his eyes. "You have already defeated yourself. Defeating others is simply a way to ease your pain and lick your wounds. Fill your abysmal lack of self acceptance with small victories."

She wasn't sure what to say. Her rage was all encompassing, but deep down inside she felt he might be right. Why would she never reveal her arm and shadow her eyes? Why did she associate praise for her victories with importance? Why was she the only one cursed with such physical mutation? Why call it a curse at all?

"Yours is a journey of finding identity, not this static in the wind. Revenge does not define you, you define yourself. You have incredible power, even with such an unstable soul, but you have no idea what the true meaning of that power is, yet." Salem cupped the charm as it hung from her grip and presented it in the palm of his hand, the many facets sparkled in the light of the shifting canopy above. "The journey to learn the answer is as important as the answer itself," he said. "That is why it is a koan."

She thought heavily and slowly began to ease her grip when a faint rustling drew their eyes. Emerging from the bushes were a dozen men, donned loosely in hides and leather but armed to the teeth with decent steel. The leader of the group was a very broad and unkempt man, standing over six feet tall at least ⊠ a giant compared to Whisper's short and delicate frame. Though his thick, shaggy beard hardened his features, Salem and Whisper could both tell in his eyes he was young and green.

"Afternoon, kittens." The man smiled confidently as he tossed an empty satchel to their feet and tipped his head, gesturing for them to fill it. "The woods be gettin' dark soon and you'll be needin' to pay some protection."

Salem met him with bemusement and turned his head as much as Whisper's grasp would allow. "You mean to rob us?" He then pointed to Whisper. "Did you know she once beat a man to death with his own horse?"

"It was a carriage," she defended sharply.

"What does it matter? A horse sounds better. If I say carriage then people wonder *'Was it small or large? Did it have cargo? Was the horse still attached?'*"

She twisted her grip a little tighter. "I don't want people thinking I hate horses!"

The burly man loudly cleared his throat to regain their attention and pointed to the empty satchel once more. "I hate to interrupt the lover's quarrel…"

"Oh, I was just getting her riled up for you," he smiled mischievously, "Best of luck, sir."

The man chuckled with his band and winked at Whisper. "I'm sure I'll need it. I gotta warn though, these woods make slaves of kittens." The eyes of his men flared with a dark sickness and calculated voracity – like sinister dogs waiting anxiously for something innocent to wander within range of their chains. "In fact, the pretty ones get it worst."

Whisper's eyes began to dilate again, wrenching her grip on Salem's collar. The fabric tightly wrung into his neck and his face flushed red with blood. His eyes began to water as he gently tapped at her arm in submission, but she wasn't paying attention – or didn't care. Salem flared with labored confusion as he struggled to make eye contact with the gruff man before them, "Kitten?"

6

HONEYCOMB STONE AND THE WEIGHT OF A WREN

The Lady Rhoswan awoke abruptly from the surface of her escritoire, strands of her white hair hung from her lips as she caught her breath. Heartbeats pounded against her chest as her vision refocused. It was another dream, another memory, from a life that wasn't hers. Ever since her power had awoken she would receive vivid memories from the few Instruments of Fate before her. Some pleasant, most not.

It was still light outside and she gracefully preened her hair with her fingertips as she proceeded to look over the list of enchanters that was provided to her earlier in the week. Steam still curled from a cup of tea she had steeped before she dozed off – its sweet aroma blossomed in the office in which she worked. Though the Scarlet Ribbon Estate was the prominent feature on her acreage, her office and chambers were in a smaller building hidden deep in the trees behind it. A beautiful pagoda of rich redwood surrounded by stone lanterns, rock gardens, and a pond laden with white lotus blooms. A small wooden bridge arched over the water and led to a pair of red lanterns that illuminated the entrance.

Dazed from her brief nap and unmotivated to work, she arose and changed into a flowing robe and corset, fastening her hair back with a headdress of feathers and jade. She stood vainly before the mirror and admired herself in the dying light. Her concentration broke when she heard the ring of a tiny bell, drawing attention to the window. There she saw a raven on her messenger's perch with a small cylinder attached to its back. Her bare feet silently crossed the room and she carefully removed the message from within. It was a Whitewater raven, sent by Salem with a simple note that informed her he had received her information on Grove and would be returning within the week to investigate. With a deep breath she sighed in relief. The last thing she needed was for her business to be delayed, and the sooner Grove was found, the better.

Though Salem's visit seemed professional in nature as he investigated the missing enchanters for the King of Whitewater, she was certain he was also coming to Freestone to enjoy the celebrations at the Scarlett Ribbon's seasonal auction, the Lantern Garden Gala. It was a tradition they began only two years ago, but the turnout and profit was far more than initially projected. They would make decent coin from premium bottles, cases, and whole casks. However, it was the main event that attracted kings, magistrates, lords, and nobles from all stretches of the world.

A few years ago, Salem managed to acquire a forbidden fruit known as dremaera from the Realm of the Snow Leaf, never revealing how. Each year he would get enough to make five bottles. The wine was so rare and sacred that they decided an auction would best reap the maximum profit for the product. And so the Lantern Garden Gala was created. Each season, a line of valuable products would be sold to the highest bidder, with the main event being a single bottle of dremaera wine. A portion of the profit was used to purchase the land that surrounded the Snow Leaf, hire a permanent regiment to keep the borders secure, and bribe Whitewater officials from ever considering expansion into Snow Leaf. This protected the supply by protecting what the Snow Leaf wanted most – privacy. Perhaps this was the cornerstone of Salem's negotiations that helped him attain the fruit, but who knew.

With the remainder of her share, thus far, she had nearly doubled her acreage and influence in Freestone. Though her investments were clear, Salem's were not. In truth, she had no idea where his cut of the money went. His home was still the same small cottage in the city that used to double as a clinic, before he collapsed his medical practice to become much more politically inclined. It was of no matter to her, though, as curious as she might be at times. His acquisition of dremaera doubled the coin in her treasury and that made him her best friend. For now.

Together, they were a lethal combination of foresight and charisma, and it was exactly the motivation she needed to endure her current issue with Grove. She was more than capable of convincing people to do what she wanted, but he was better at reading between the lines and deducing a person's character. In truth, she was still clinging to the hope that, sooner or later, a hungover Grove would show up in a gutter somewhere from a week of uncharacteristic overindulgence.

From the escritoire where she had awoken, she closed the small, bound ledger she had been working on and placed it into one of the drawers. The ledger was Salem's record for the quarter, outlining the Estate's earnings, expenses, and his portion of the profit. She was meticulous at accounting and every coin was documented. This year had been very successful, a combination of her public relations and his continued outreach to the neighboring realms.

Night was falling and her servants were lighting the stone shrines along the pond's edge. The candlelight shimmered across the still water as the darkness descended. Then, the first of many came. A man, dressed in fancy garments with a small wooden box in his hands. The Lady Rhoswan slid the door to the pagoda open and greeted him outside. She examined the contents of the box, and allowed him entry. One by one, men and women of status would approach her home with an identical box in hand and the process would repeat. As the night continued, nearly a dozen people arrived and disappeared beyond the paper doors.

"Lady Rhoswan," a familiar voice said, "You look stunning, as always."

It was the nobleman she had met as she left Grove's stead. She allowed him to kiss her on the cheek and present his wooden box. Rhoswan smiled as she accepted it, her fingertips traced the intricate detail etched into the surface. A single branch with three blossoms stretched from corner to corner. "It's a pleasure to see you again," she smiled coyly.

He smiled back and looked into the empty space behind her, eagerly searching for something he could not yet see. Though many had come in the passing hours, the room was completely empty. She carefully lifted the lid of the box and gazed upon two half pound bars of silver nestled on the soft red velvet cushion within. A sweet smile gleamed through her eyes as she closed the lid.

"The weight of a wren," she said softly and allowed him to enter.

***

Liam Whitewater strode the marble halls of his castle and pressed his hands to the smooth ridges of two massive wooden doors, each inlaid with abalone and alabaster. The weight of the wood groaned as they slowly swung open to reveal the High Council patiently seated in a circle of elegant chairs, all facing the throne upon the dais – a single seat meant for Salem Eventide remained empty.

"Sit," The Leviathan commanded as he crossed the room and took his seat, placing his hands over the onyx-marble orbs that accented the ends of the throne's arms.

The Great Hall was the oldest part of the castle, being built first, with the rest constructed around it. It was a masterful piece of architecture that had no equal and held the distinct signatures of the dragons that helped his forefathers build it. Tall, open arches flooded the room with natural light, allowing waterfalls of vines and blooms to cascade down the precious stone. It was the first and only hall, to their knowledge, that was constructed without the support of pillars or arches, relying on the draconian science of honeycomb stone to create a calculated and precise support that no other could replicate.

The hexagonal honeycomb stone that was set into the hall's white marble was a rich ocean blue, which shimmered with multiple facets against the light of the room. Though it looked like hexagonal gemstone of crystal or glass, it was actually completely hand made ⊠ a product of alchemy that could be a variety of different colors. It was the result of a chemical formula and resin setting technique that was developed centuries ago by the dragons, and had been perfected to the point where it was the sharpest and hardest substance in all of Elanta. Seemingly indestructible, the dragons did hint once that when they refined the process they gave it one specific weakness, just in case. However, because the formula remained exclusive knowledge to the founding dragons and their Queen, Savrae-Lyth, all hopes of mankind ever learning it and its secrets died when the

Queen was slain at the end of the Dragon War. Alchemists continue to explore its mysteries, but none have been successful.

"What concerns my people most today?" Whitewater asked, gesturing for one of them to take the floor.

A man clad in silver chain mail stood and adjusted his aggressive posture. Though his face bore no scars, he had the eyes and chiseled demeanor of a man who had seen and survived the worst the world had to offer. He was no stranger to any man, woman or child in Whitewater, as he was the highest ranked military official in the realm and the trusted face of every defense protocol. He was Alexander Tybalt, Judiciar of the High Council, responsible for the entirety of Whitewater's military and the royal judicial system. "I have the detailed investigations report from last week's engagement with the Orbweavers." He withdrew a folded document and proceeded to hand it directly to the King.

Whitewater immediately recognized the seal was broken and looked to Tybalt for an immediate explanation.

"Salem Eventide, your Grace. He reviewed it before he left for Freestone with the mistborn girl."

Breaking a seal intended for the presence of the council was a serious offense, nonetheless, the King begrudgingly sighed and continued to read the contents.

"Eventide is given too much lenience, if you ask me!" chimed another seat.

Tybalt recognized the voice as Victor Fairchild, Treasurer of the High Council, and turned to express his disapproval. Though the King was forgiving of opinionated outbursts, Tybalt was a man of much more rigidity.

The bald and heavy set Victor Fairchild leaned back into the luxury of his fine silks and played with one of the large golden rings that decorated his pale hands, meeting Tybalt with challenging petulance. "Please, Alex. You were thinking the same thing."

"It is not your place to say," Tybalt replied sternly.

"Stop!" Whitewater's voice shook the floor beneath them. "The degree of my lenience towards any infraction is my own business, Fairchild, and you will refer to Tybalt by either his family name or title in the presence of the High Council. Is that understood?"

The chubby treasurer averted his eyes and sulked. "Of course, your Grace."

Whitewater carefully folded the letter and handed it back to Tybalt, who then took his seat. "There is nothing in here I have not yet heard."

"Let me see," asked Fairchild, who flicked his fingers in the air at Tybalt to gesture compliance, to which Tybalt obliged. "The damage is so extensive and for only five Orbweaver casualties. As Royal Treasurer I must state the obvious expenses that mistborn girl has incurred."

Tybalt made no effort to hide his impatience with Fairchild's ignorance at any opportunity. "Her presence was necessary, in case you had forgotten the demon they were rushed to summon. Without the pressure, they could have had time to call more and our military would have suffered greatly."

"You're right, Judiciar," Fairchild replied. "If only our military wasn't so helpless."

"The Orbweavers are a force that you..."

"Enough!" Whitewater commanded once more. His attention turned to the last of the seated council, Vaughn Cross, who sat pristine and unbothered – hands folded, eyes closed. Wavy jet-black hair hung down to his shoulders and rested on the white and navy cotton of his official uniform that which Alexander Tybalt was not required to wear with his armor, and was apparently not good enough for Fairchild.

Cross was the youngest of all but Salem, with an intellect and reasoning that quickly made him Chancellor of the High Council, but kept him in contention with the Eventide prodigy. Where Fairchild and Tybalt consistently locked horns, so was the same for himself and Salem. Each always trying to out think the other.

"Why the hovel by the main gate?" Cross asked.

Though Tybalt considered the thought, Fairchild was confused. "What does that matter?"

Cross' voice was as calm, dark, and as sharp as the eyes that peered through his slender features. "There are many empty properties across Whitewater, why would they choose that one?"

"They had to set up somewhere, it means nothing."

"True, it is likely that is holds little, or even no importance," Cross continued, "but assume that, for the sake of argument, it was necessary. We should look into other details of the property."

"Eventide has already issued an investigation into both current and prior title holders, and what other lands they may own,"Tybalt said.

Though most had missed it, the King caught the subtle twitch that hung in Cross' eye at the mention of Salem's forethought. "Good, but we should also examine other aspects."

"Like what?"Tybalt was genuinely interested.

"What is under it, to start. Are there any constructs, or is it simply stone, or even ore. Something they can attune to, or something that assists them in the practice of their dark arts? We must assume the location was important until we have proven it was not."

"There should be no tunnels," Tybalt began. "If there were, it would have been paramount I know for the sake of the cities defense."

"Hire some geomancers to inspect the area,"Whitewater ordered Tybalt.

Fairchild was quick to chime in. "Your Grace, the treasury has taken a large loss as is, perhaps one would suffice."

"I want two. This Orbweaver pestilence will not take root within these walls because of frugality." The Whitewater Leviathan leaned forward and rested his elbows on his knees, looking over the council with both severity and aggression. "This is my realm."

7

THE PUREBLOOD ENCHANTRESS

Loud coughs echoed through the forest as Salem braced himself on his knees. Much to his relief, Whisper finally released him and prepared to do what she did best. Her eyes went feral as she arched her back and glared menacingly at the dozen men before her. All were armed with swords or axes, but only the leader had yet to draw his.

"Now now," the leader said, smiling as he rested his hand on the hilt of his blade. "You should think first."

Whisper held her charm out for them to see and then placed it back in her wrappings. It certainly looked expensive enough to pull their full attention. "Come take it."

The burly leader chuckled and looked to the ground as he ran his dirty fingers through his mottled hair. He turned and shrugged to the men behind him. "As the lady wishes." He waved his hands to gesture for them to engage. "Relieve the young lady, but don't rough her up too much."

Four men sheathed their weapons and advanced, two each. Salem gracefully stepped behind Whisper and gave a light pat on her back. "Make this quick, I have an appointment in Freestone."

"I don't do slow deaths," she growled in sinister undertone.

Three turned their attention to her as Salem took refuge behind, but the fourth strayed wide to try to get him.

The air grew cold and still as Whisper slid a foot back and prepared to receive, raising an open hand. The first bandit lunged in for a wide swing, but before he could engage the muscles and forward momentum, she made her move. The faint sound of her sleeve in the air was all the warning he had before he felt radiating pain and numbness. In a blinding half second, she thrust her fingertips so deep into his throat his spine could be heard breaking amongst the unnerving crunch of cartilage. She scooped her hand behind his head and threw him aside to clear her line of sight.

She immediately crouched and spun beneath a swing from the second, sweeping both of his legs out from under him. As he fell, she finished her low spin with her back towards him and leapt in the air, completing a backflip with tight arc. The sound of the wind leaving his lungs was all they heard as he landed flat, followed by the breaking of bones as Whisper tucked both of her legs back and landed on his chest with pointed knees. Ribs cracked, his sternum buckled and all that remained was the gurgle of blood in his lungs as he drowned in flooded breaths.

Using the continued momentum of her flourished tumble, she quickly rolled back to her feet and shifted her whole upper body towards the third bandit. Both of his feet flew off the ground and his body hurdled back as she crashed her forehead into his face. A horrifying explosion of cracked bone resonated as he sustained so much blunt force his whole face collapsed into his skull and snapped his neck. The body soared several yards back down the road towards his comrades, tumbling through the hard dirt until it lay a bloody, mangled, unrecognizable mass of gore and pulp.

The fourth managed to sneak by and engage Salem, who threw his hands up in non-confrontation. "Wait, wait, wait…" he said quickly, just as the bandit threw a jab that snapped Salem's head back. He bellowed, staggering backwards, holding his hand over his eye. "Why the face!?!"

The bandit stopped and looked at his fist, seemingly confused. As he watched Salem gripe, a hand grabbed the back of his head and he was hurled straight down, face first, into the ground. He died instantly. The earth shook and a few gentle leaves fell from the trees above them, then all grew quiet once more, save for Salem's ranting. Whisper turned to face the leader, thick bandit blood streamed down her face and dripped from her hair, but it was only now that they could see the unnatural fury slitted in her terrifying eyes. She watched them. Pierced them. Stalked them with eyes they had never thought possible.

The remaining eight were motionless as they stared in horror at the gruesome mess before them. Blood pooled into the grass and dirt, tickling their senses with iron. The leader stood enfeebled and the other bandits remained deathly still.

A familiar feeling washed over her. A buzzing electricity in the air that tingled across her skin and made her vision vibrate. It immediately reminded her of her childhood, bundled in blankets and staring into her father's eyes for the last time. It was unmistakable and her heart leapt into her throat as she frantically tried to determine its source. As quickly as it came, it dispersed, and nobody else seemed to notice.

"Stay back!" the leader yelled as he backed away slowly, drawing his sword and waving his other hand to gesture a soft retreat. "I don't know what you are, but we'll be leaving you alone." He continued to fearfully withdraw as his sword trembled in his grasp until he bumped into someone. He turned to see one of his men fall backwards, stiff as a board. The rest were all just... standing still. Paralyzed. Their eyes shifted in their sockets as they struggled to move. He turned back to Whisper just as she struck a nerve in his wrist, forcing him to drop the weapon, then immediately clasped her hand around his throat and began to squeeze. He grabbed at her arm and tried to force his release, but he was no match for her supernatural strength.

"Stop!" Salem called to her, nursing his squinted eye. "Let him go."

Whisper's narrowed gaze pierced him in disbelief.

"He is too weak to matter to you anyways, killing him is no victory." He placed a soft hand on her arm and gestured for her to release the grip.

With great reluctance she threw the bandit leader to the ground and turned her back to him. "You know best," she said with great sarcasm.

Salem approached the leader and crouched. "What is your name?" he asked.

The man panicked and scrambled backwards. "Get away from me! I'm sorry!"

Salem locked eyes with him. In Whisper's experience it was very hypnotizing, and it seemed to calm the bandit's nerves enough to remain still. "What is your name?"

He sat prone with his hands raised and dared not move. "Norven Swordhand."

"Really?" Salem seemed surprised. "What a great name! The Swordhand part, of course, not Norven. Norven is terrible, but Swordhand... wow... Swordhand." He loved how it sounded and even mouthed the word to himself before continuing. "Dear Whisper, please release the other men. I think they are far too traumatized to be harmful now."

She seemed confused and frustrated. "Idiot."

He turned his head back to her and glared in disapproval.

"It brings me joy when you're wrong," she chimed, growing ever alert to the trees around them. Her eyes traced through the shadows and carefully noted every branch, leaf, and blade of grass. "I didn't freeze them. It was *him*. I could feel *him* here."

Salem nervously inspected around him with no success. "Swordhand," he started, "can you explain what has happened to your men?"

Norven shook his head. "I... I don't know. Nothing in these woods do that, I've never seen... never... anything." Too scattered for full sentences.

"I'm going to sweep the perimeter," Whisper said as she disappeared into the darkness. Skilled as she was at combat, she was terrible at moving stealthily – he was aware of her presence at all times as she cleared a large circle around them.

"Listen very carefully, Swordhand." Salem looked him in the eyes again and his voice became harmoniously entrancing. "In exchange for your life, you and your men will ensure our safe passage through the forest."

"Safe passage?" Norven knew there was nothing in this forest that could contend with a demon, so why bother.

"Okay, perhaps 'safe passage' was not right, but unhindered. You know the other bandits out here, all you have to do is convince them we are not worth the trouble."

Norven nodded in compliance, though he knew he had no choice.

"Should you or any of your men give us problems, however, I will not stand in the way of my companion's grim resolve." Salem smiled, winked, and gave him a good slap on the shoulder. "I feel confident, after the demonstrations of today, that you will not do anything stupid." He held out a hand to help him up.

"You can't be serious!" Whisper objected from somewhere in the brush. "The man is a criminal, you can't just let him go!"

Salem hung his head. Clearly she didn't understand that she was blatantly giving away her position, making a sweep near pointless. "Men take up the sword for many reasons, dear Whisper," Salem said as Norven clambered to his feet. "It is better to extend a hand of understanding than one of condemnation."

She had emerged further down the path, frustrated and shaken. The aura had vanished completely, but to have felt it once again flushed her with all of the rage that had wound within her since childhood. Clenching her fist tightly she roared into the trees with agonizing vexation. Uncomfortable silence, thick with volatility, weighed heavily on them all.

She huffed angrily and placed her hand on her hip while standing next to one of the paralyzed men. Salem turned to her and watched as she waved in front of his face.

"Fine. Whatever you want." She gently pushed the bandit and let his rigid body fall to the ground. "They're alive. Conscious even. They just can't seem to move."

Salem approached cautiously and knelt before the one Whisper had knocked over. Through a short series of basic tests, he discerned their paralysis was neurological in nature and neither the work of cantrip nor sorcery. Everything autonomic seemed to function properly. Eyes dilated and contracted in response to the shift in light, they seemed to register pain when he pinched their cheek, they were still capable of blinking and, most importantly, they still had a heartbeat. After a few minutes, most of the men were regaining the ability to move their fingertips.

"I do not know what could cause a phenomenon like this," Salem declared, troubled by his lack of understanding. He was certain that, whomever Whisper felt, was responsible, though it would seem the mysterious energy was of a frequency only she could sense. Whether it was because she had felt it before, or simply because she was enlightened. "It is the effect of sorcery, without actually being sorcerous in nature."

"Will they be alright?" Norven asked, being very careful to give Whisper a wide berth and prevent eye contact.

"I believe so. Some are starting to move again. It seems the effect is wearing off very slowly." He looked to the sky beyond the canopy above them. Fortunately, they had a few hours of daylight left. He sighed deeply in thought of their situation. He was very uncomfortable with the phenomenon that had just occurred and wanted out of the forest sooner than later, just in case it happened again, or whomever did it returned. His mind couldn't shake the obvious question of *why* yet, but it was far too complicated to answer with so many variables.

Salem turned his attention back to Norven. "We will drag the bodies into the brush, while you run ahead to warn the others of our passing through."

Whisper hung her head back and sighed heavily. "Fiiiine," she whined, grabbing the prone bandit by the collar and dragging him to the next. Salem watched, entertained, as she grumbled to herself and effortlessly slung two bodies over her shoulder, dragging a third by his ankle.

"Does your demon only have one arm?" Norven asked as he watched, slack jawed.

Salem shook his head and frowned. "No, she is simply stubborn and will not use the other."

"Your word she won't harm us?"

The corner of Salem's mouth shrugged. "Simply keep to our arrangement and do not do anything to set her off... which I dare say is most things. She is not actually a demon, but she might grow fond of you if you keep calling her that."

"But her eyes..."

"She was born too close to the mist. Not many people realize it because it is so far off the shoreline, but the mist in close proximity has a unique effect on infants in the womb. Its chaotic energy mutates and disfigures the child, oftentimes being stillborn or euthanized at birth for being monstrous. Whisper was fortunate to be so beautiful and owes her life to the love of her parents." Salem refrained from explaining her story any further, as it wasn't his to tell.

"She's enlightened."

"Yes. Eighteen years in a monastery, but she is unique. Most enlightened are... well... more enlightened." Salem held his hand over his heart to emote what his words meant. Norven didn't seem to be well educated and couldn't be trusted to understand context.

"I didn't know power could be raw. I always thought it was like breathin' or blinkin'. Imagine she learns to control it," Norven replied.

Salem sighed and watched her drink from her wine jug, calming her nerves. She was certainly wasteful with her energy, turning into an inferno of uncontrollable and chaotic surges that were as unpredictable as they were dangerous. "She certainly is a tempest." He turned back to Norven and gestured for him proceed down the road. "Clear the way, Swordhand. May next we meet be under different circumstance."

The shaken bandit hastily withdrew and vanished beyond.

"You shouldn't be letting them go," Whisper scolded as she indelicately threw one of the paralyzed into a mess of ferns and underbrush.

"Please, dear Whisper. If he had not been so harmless before, he certainly will not be now that you have instilled the fear of the Fates within him. He is a coward, that is why he is an exiled soldier."

She cocked her head and pondered the consequences of delving deeper. "I have few questions, and little patience."

"His hilt is unworn, hands bear no calluses, and retains all of his teeth. His mannerisms scream of a man who has had very little physical altercation. As well, his scabbard displays the tattered remains of an Emberwilde house military sigil, which are only severed when one is dishonorably discharged from their ranks."

"Excellent," Whisper huffed under her breath, pushing the last body into the brush with her foot. "Now I have neither." Her agitation was palpable since the static had resided, let alone her disapproval of Salem setting the bandits free. "In lieu of the situation now, what would you like to do?"

"*In light of,*" he corrected.

"What?"

"You are using the word 'lieu' improperly. You mean to say *'In light of the situation.'*"

Whisper tilted her head. "You think I'm stupid!"

"What?! No! I just... wait... what was the question...?"

"You think too lightly of what little restraint and self-control I have left, Salem..." she said as she huffed away.

Salem rubbed the bridge of his nose in bewilderment, well aware of the razor's edge he walked until she calmed down, but purposefully oblivious to the dangers that entailed nonetheless. "Restraint and self-control are the same thing..."

★★★

The jingle of gold and silver echoed in the massive stone halls as Duke Eywin's heavy velvet cloak skimmed the stone beneath his feet. He arrived at the large open space of his treasury, where intricately carved arches held the ceiling high aloft and rows of shelves, cases, and cabinets displayed the multitude of treasures and rarities in Lyre's protection. The latest of which stood in the center, with the Etrielle still imprisoned within.

Though the honeycomb stone was seemingly indestructible it wasn't too large, standing as tall as a man with twice the girth. It took the workers only a few days to free it from the surrounding stone, and a day for Lyre's Elite to transport it under cover of night. Since its arrival to the treasury, it had been under the constant surveillance of two Moths at a time. Even in the short while two Orbweaver infiltrators had already met quick ends at some of the several enchantments that trapped the room and halls. They knew where it was, but had no hope of reaching it.

"My lord Eywin," bowed Elder Waylander, his words laced with regret. All six Moths of Lyre's Elite were in attendance of the meeting.

The duke ignored his presence almost entirely. "What have you discovered?"

"The esteemed enchantress Ashissa of Realm Shén Shé has arrived, as per your request." He raised a hand to gesture towards a figure in a flowing hooded cloak of long, jet black fur. Behind her were two fiendish creatures, one on each side. They were both serpents, whose only vague humanoid characteristics were that they slithered upright and had two pairs of lithe arms. The light gleamed off the black scales adorning the majority of their body, but it was the white and coral markings and fierce green eyes beneath their hooded brows that projected the aura of ruination. They were Shén Shé malison, and the first the Moths had ever seen. Each of the abominations were outfitted with four dadao, four katar, two bows and two quivers, and was nothing shy of intimidating. Adding to the discomfort already thick in the air, it was a well-known fact that a Shén Shé malison was incredibly venomous and would coat every blade and arrowhead to ensure a quick and efficient victory.

The cloaked figure pulled back her hood to reveal a face of much more human likeness. Though she had no nose and strong serpentine traits in her skin, lips, and eyes, her facial structure was far more familiar. She, too, had black scales, with white and coral markings that danced and weaved across each other. Together they created a sharply pointed tribal design that stretched up from her cheeks, over her eyes, across the top of her head, and down her neck and back. Around her brow she wore a braided silver circlet that hung chains, charms, and bone past her shoulders. She was a Shén Shé pure blood, all of which were shamans. The Shén Shé believed that the pure blooded were smaller and lived shorter lives because their energies were condensed into unsurpassed intellect and spiritual connection, whereas the malison distribute their essence across their physical attributes evenly, tripling both their prowess and life span.

Though Ashissa had a physique similar to that of a human, the colder climate of Lyre was something she was not accustomed to and it showed in her slow steps as she approached the duke. Her two malison slithered behind gracefully, uninhibited by the temperature. Channeling small portions of essence into warming their blood allowed them to maintain dexterity in all climates, and was a lesson learned as a malison neonate. They were charged with the sacred duty of protecting the pure blooded and had to be efficient in all scenarios.

"I am Ashissa," she said with a smooth and delicate accent, her forked tongue flicked as she elongated the consonants of her name. The Shén Shé loved to study linguistics and the pure blooded could often speak several languages before becoming fully fledged shamans. Malisons, however, rarely ever knew more than their tribal tongue.

The duke tipped his head. He wasn't fond of things he couldn't trust, and though the Shén Shé were known for their honor their features often vilified them. "Thank you for journeying so far. Have you had a chance to examine the crystal before my arrival?"

She slowly turned to face the artifact. "Yes. It is as thought," she began. "It is honeycomb stone the dragon's glass."

"Does that mean the dragons buried it in the mountain then?" Waylander interjected.

"I don't care for its history, I just want it broken open," Eywin replied. "It doesn't matter who sealed it and when."

"Honeycomb stone is the hardest substance known, and yet there is also a powerful ward around it," Ashissa said. "A good question may be why the sword requires such extreme containment."

"Can you get the sword out?"

"Ashissa must study it longer. *If* the ward can be broken Ashissa will do it, but only a dragon knows the secret to breaking honeycomb stone. All Ashissa can do is try." she replied.

The duke was temporarily taken aback as she referred to herself in the third person, but her tribal accent was thick enough that it simply added to her foreign character. He also noticed she elongated her S's and mouthed each word slowly as she spoke, being very sure to articulate clearly to compensate for the fangs that folded along the roof of her mouth. "Let me know if there is anything I can do to make your work and stay more comfortable."

Ashissa pulled her cloak close to her body. "Perhaps if we move the stone to a smaller room, one with a fire. Heat will help Ashissa work more efficiently."

"I apologize, it is very cold this far north, and this damnable Whitewater Equalitarian Rule keeps me severely understaffed. I assure you, what few resources I have will be dedicated to your needs." Without hesitation, he waved a hand to the Moths. "Move the stone to the dining hall and light the fires immediately. Should our guests require anything more, see to it that they are satisfied."

"My lord..." Waylander interjected. "The dining hall has too many entrances, and is far too centralized to guard efficiently. Perhaps the war room instead."

"Fine," nodded Eywin, who then turned and left the room.

"This way, please," bowed Waylander as he gestured for the Shén Shé to follow.

Ashissa complied, her malison close behind.

8

SNOW LEAF AND THE SONG OF THE CAGED BIRD

A vibrant blue flower floated in a breeze and set down on the surface of a still pond. Massive trees wept above as their long branches hung like a bouquet of vines, each adorned with thousands of the beautiful blue blossoms. A petite woman knelt by the water's edge and watched her reflection distort in the tiny ripples. The air was cool and brisk, but she seemed unaffected in her vestments of light cloth and soft plant leathers. The water became still once again and she breathed deeply the loneliness that reflected within her. The features of the Setsuha were very distinct. Aside from their sharp eyes, they were a very lithe and fragile framed race, featuring hollow bones that made them incredibly light and agile. Though they didn't have wings, they had a distinct avian lineage. Fine, long feathers beautifully adorned their head like hair, usually accenting a darker color like black or brown with another, more vibrant one.

The Setsuha had lived on the mountain since the beginning of time, so the elders had said, and thusly the mountain was named by them as the Realm of the Snow Leaf. This ancient land of living fresh water rainforests was met with ocean to the north and east, the temperate and tundra of Whitewater to the west, and the dense serpentine jungles of Shén Shé to the south. For thousands of years, which was only a few generations for the

Setsuha, the elders had sealed off access to the realm through a combination of mundane wards and illusions. If any poor soul managed to get through, they wouldn't last long. The Realm of the Snow Leaf wasn't guarded simply by the Setsuha, but also by powerful and ferocious creatures that roamed its massive trees and hazardous terrain. The most namely amongst those were the fenwights. Spirit wolves nearly eight feet to the shoulder that could sense their prey through the earth and had such a strong connection to the trees that they were able to enter one and exit another anywhere in their territory. They are the guardians of the Snow Leaf and closest companions to the avian Setsuha. It was quickly learned that Snow Leaf was not to be bothered, nor conquered.

The woman stood and preened her black and gold feathers behind her ear with her fingertips. It was going to get dark soon and she had to get her basket of dremaera back to the village. The massive trees by the grove grew the sacred fruit from their large blue flowers.

Though it was much too hard and terribly bitter, it seemed a man named Salem Eventide, from the western border realm, wanted to turn it into some kind of drink. Something called 'wine' she was sure she heard him say. They had learned many new words since his arrival. It had only been a few years since the foreigner somehow wandered into the Snow Leaf for the first time and lived long enough to speak with the eldest of the elders. He was a dignitary of sort, representing the 'elder' of Whitewater, and through careful negotiation a deal was struck where they would provide him with a modest portion of dremaera in exchange for the protection of their borders.

A single fruit would temporarily imbue the user with the ability to visualize the strands of essence flowing off every living thing. Partaking in the fruit was a common ritual amongst the elders, allowing them to better understand the flow of nature's energy around them so they could find a deeper, more harmonic coexistence.

The light turned pale and the wind carried a faint misfortune that only a child of the mountain could feel. It was a foreboding. The woman turned to look into the grove of blue petals and stood incredibly still as she took it in. Something was restless, pacing in the darkness, hungry for something fierce. Blood. Fear. Despair. The malice brushed across her tongue, letting her taste the blood for which it called. Emerging from beside her with the sound of shifting earth and rustling leaves was a fenwight. A massive wolf with fur of mottled gray and large patches of green moss. He walked to the woman weightlessly, barely bending the grass beneath his giant paws.

"Hello Selva," she smiled sweetly in his presence. Though he stood above her shoulder now, she had known him since he was a puppy. When they were younger they would sneak out to the open groves and hide in the lemongrass. And though the elders would have thought she matured enough to forget such games by now, together they would still run off and play whenever the mood struck. He was her guardian and best friend, protecting her from the dangers of the living mountain and racing her across the meadows until she felt like she was flying.

Though Selva's eyes were soft and kind he approached with careful rigidity, dropping a shining piece of twisted metal at her feet. "Vaexa est'alara celys," Selva growled. It was Setsuhan formality to address her by her full name and status. The bulk translated to 'white diamond dove' and 'celys' signified her status as an elder.

Vaexa dropped to her hands and knees to examine the object closely without touching it. Though this item was twisted and nearly broken, she had seen an intact one before. Recently, Salem had told them it was a cutting tool called a kris, and warned them explicitly to avoid anyone carrying one. "Another?" Her voice brimmed with intrigue. As dangerous as they were said to be, she couldn't help but imagine how such an item was made and what it could be used for.

"Yes," Selva replied. "The mountain is devouring the body along with the others, but more continue to come."

"I wonder why..." The Snow Leaf was sacred to them for all the same reasons the westerners avoided it.

"His blood was foul and bitter," he said. "It is a sign his heart was tainted with evil intent. They are here to harm us in some way, I am sure of it."

She drew her attention back to the grove of petals and raised a blind hand, allowing Selva to place the bridge of his nose under her palm.

"Vaexa celys, we should hurry home. The trees are unsettled," he said, his slate eyes looking to the ground as he was sensing the earth around him.

Vaexa turned her gaze to the mist above them. Being atop the highest mountain in the world put them much closer to the ceiling, though it still seemed quite far off. "I think I saw a ripple in the mist... is that possible?"

"We have little knowledge of the mist, Vaexa celys. We fenwights are blind to anything not touching the earth. We have never seen the sky."

She was well aware they were blind and was more or less hoping he may have heard of movement in the mist from someone else.

The fenwight lowered to the forest floor. "Vaexa celys, I will take you home. Perhaps a question for the other elders."

The mist was clearly still, though she was certain something caused it to wake for but a moment. Reluctantly she broke her gaze and gracefully climbed atop Selva's back, clutching his fur in her hands. The massive wolf rose to his full height, took the basket of dremaera in his jaws, and disappeared into the vibrant blue curtains. The soft moss of the grove rose and slowly wrapped itself around the wretched blade left behind, beginning a decomposition exclusive to the Snow Leaf where everything eats anything.

A fenwight's dexterity was nearly unmatched in the realm and Vaexa barely swayed on his back as he wove through the trees. There were few things more invigorating than gliding seamlessly at great speeds through the labyrinth of weeping willows and feathered fronds. Riding a fenwight was a rare honor very few Setsuhans had ever experienced. Not only was the right reserved only for the elders, but most elders were far too cautious to risk the dangers riding presented. The relationship between Vaexa and Selva was very different though, and it worried the others to no end. They had raced through the trees thousands of times before, yet she would still catch herself smiling and holding her breath in the weightlessness of their jumps. They shared in the vigor of racing across the mountain together. Clutching the fur in her palms as their hearts skipped beats, closing their eyes as cool water from the streams and dew splashed on their faces. Oftentimes, when she was feeling restless or unhappy, she would sneak away from her duties and take a breathtaking ride at full speed, refusing to stop until they had run so far and so fast that she felt she was someplace new and undiscovered. She never was, however. She had run to all reaches of the Snow Leaf and knew every tree, cave, glen, and river better than anyone else. Countless afternoons were spent sitting with Selva by the river's edge watching the high grass of Whitewater rustle on the other side, or atop the sheer ledges of stone in the south, looking down upon the canopy of endless Shén Shé jungle. She had long fantasized of the freedom she would feel could she ever cross the border and enter the neighbor realms. But it was impossible.

To cross would be her death. There was a reason the Setsuha could live for hundreds of years. A coveted secret of eternal life for all but Vaexa. To her it was the curse that kept her eternally bound to the most beautiful cage in the world, as a Setsuhan could never leave.

She lost herself in her journey. Eyes closed, weightless. Before she knew it Selva knelt down and prompted her to dismount. She looked into the towering trees around her to see she was home. Llaesynd. It meant 'sky cradle', aptly named for the hundreds of bulbs that hung like ornaments. Each was made of woven plants and varied in sizes, from single nests and homes, to larger sanctuaries suspended between massive trees with a multitude of thickly woven vines. Some nests were built into the crooks of the branches, but the majority hung perilously, hundreds of feet above the earth. Each were connected with narrow bridges of vines, which was more than enough support for the Setsuhan's featherweight structure and nimble physique. In the short time she had been alive, by Setsuhan standard, she only ever saw one person fall. He died immediately, of course. His shattered body was a reminder that a Setsuhan is far too fragile to be careless. Every step should be planned. Know where you are jumping, know where you are landing. Vaexa hated it. Not knowing was as much freedom as she could get away with in her mew of fragrant blossoms and trickling streams. When she could get away with it, in the blind eyes of the other elders, she would welcome the invigorating spontaneity of recklessness.

"Thank you," she gently rubbed Selva's ear and collected her basket.

Selva bowed his head. "Vaexa est'alara celys," he said once more as he turned and slowly walked towards the thick trunk of the nearest tree. The sound of crackling wood softly met her ears as he walked into it, his body transforming inch by inch into a swirling dance of thin leaves. They softly settled onto the forest floor, and the fenwight was gone.

Just as she was about to proceed into Llaesynd, a powerful static flushed over her. She had felt this lightning across her skin many times in the past and had not yet determined its origin. She stood still and carefully examined her surroundings. Her vision vibrated with the essence in the air – it surrounded her, engulfed her. It was a random sensation that had come and gone for the last twenty years, and though others would likely feel uncomfortable in its static embrace, instead she could sense a belonging within it. Something positive. Something fulfilling. It had always been difficult to explain to the others as it seemed they were never privy to the experience. As quickly as it had arrived, it vanished, as it always did.

9

WEAVE AND THE WAR THAT RAZED THE DRAGONS

Salem sat huddled over a circle of small stones and twigs in a secluded patch of grass off the beaten path. They were making good time since parting ways with Swordhand and the other bandits, so far giving them four full days with no interruption.

Light smoke bellowed from a small stack of sticks as he softly blew on the tinder. Whisper sat across from him and watched as he worked. She thought it funny, in truth. A handsome man of noble attire in the dirt, bowing to tiny flame. For her it was perspective. No matter how enlightened, no matter what our title, we are humbled by primal necessity. Words she had learned within the monastery walls.

Though failing terribly, he was filled with temperance. At least, he seemed to be.

"Do you know anything about dragons?" she asked as she removed her wine from her shoulder.

Salem paused and took a calculated breath. "Before I came to Whitewater, I had much experience with the dragons. Why do you ask?"

"What kind of experience?"

She couldn't tell if his subtle impatience was due to the question or the fire. "Some friendly, some not. I was much younger then, before it became a tale soaked in blood, wrought with heavy hearts," he replied.

Whisper felt solemn as she watched his eyes grow distant. He readjusted the kindling and tried to light the fire once more – the flint sparked brilliantly in the pitch of the night.

"Is it possible we will ever see one?" she asked, letting her mind wander. Naturally, one would think she wanted to talk to it. In truth she just wanted to fight one, deeming them the most worthy opponent she could yet imagine. She had only ever seen sketches and paintings of the amazing creatures. Simply the thought of being in the presence of such awesome power weighed on her.

Salem stopped working and looked at her sadly. There was something forlorn within him that she couldn't place. "Dear Whisper..." he started, turning his eyes to the ground, "...there are no more dragons."

The dead of the night was a caustic quietude as she crashed back into her body. "There must be some still... right?" she said heavily. An anger began to stir. How could she claim her victory now?

"Two decades ago, the last dragon, Savrae-Lyth, died, ending the five year Dragon War the Fates waged."

She had heard of the Dragon War and had always felt dragons were far too cunning not to hide in the wake of extinction, but the Fates were a lesson long since forgotten from her time with the monks. She didn't like the idea that her destiny was at the whims and mercy of some invisible, otherworldly force, and chose not to pay it any mind. "Remind me..."

"You see, the Fates are gods that are all but immortal. Essential to the world, but not to mankind. They are driven by convictions. Powerful beings with one common goal: protect the world at any cost." He fixed the kindling once more. "Each fate may be brimming with power, but they are highly specialized, and still only mortal. It is because of this weakness they have created their own realm of existence on which to live. It is from there that they watch our world.

"It is because of their fear of death that each fate would choose a mortal and bestow upon them a portion of their remaining power. They are Instruments of Fate, and far stronger than the average enlightened. They are burdened with carrying out the Fates' commands. Creating political stability by assassinating a magistrate, or burning a village of innocents to the ground to prevent a war between realms. Whatever it takes to ensure the world continues to exist."

Salem continued to fight with the flint. He had almost gotten the fire to catch this time.

"I remember..." Whisper said, "The monks taught me about the Fates when I was much younger." She tilted her head and tried to recollect her lessons. "There are three. Origin Progenitus, Howlpack Sentinel Avelie, and Illy the Flux."

Salem nodded. "The Fates cannot see the future, but can predict the odds precisely, and use their Instruments to maneuver odds into favor."

"But why would they kill the dragons?" She didn't know who the Instruments were, but they were now the proxy for her glorious battle. Not only did they become worthy adversaries by wiping out her prior worthy adversaries, but they sounded powerful enough to have the aura she was searching for, making it personal.

"Well..." he started, "When you are born, a tiny spider called a fatespinner hatches from Origin Progenitus in a transcendental realm they call the 'Weave'. That spider then begins to build a web, and that is your timeline. Every living creature has a fatespinner, so you can imagine the complex interaction as millions upon millions of webs weave into each other.

"Each point where one fatespinner's thread fastens to the web of another is a waypoint. These waypoints are anchors that change the direction our destiny travels, due to the influence of someone else. Some webs can be small and secluded, barely touching any other strands as the creature lives out a life of minimal impact. Others are massive networks made up of hundreds of smaller webs, like King Liam Whitewater, for example.

"Howlpack Sentinel Avelie guards the Weave, while Illy the Flux studies and predicts the future paths of each fatespinner. They do this to avoid world threatening complications by devising plans to manipulate them if need be."

A soft red glow began to form as the fire began to take. Salem took careful breaths to nurture it, sheltering the flame with his hands.

"As for the dragons. They were the only creature for whom Origin Progenitus could not create a fatespinner. A dragon is born without destiny, devoid of any legible or predictable interaction or influence. As the realm's borders grew greater, there became more and more exposure between the dragons and mortals of the world, and eventually they began to notice that fatespinners were mysteriously altering their own courses without the interaction of a waypoint. People either inspired or manipulated by the dragons inadvertently began forging their own destinies, and without a waypoint to anchor the Fate's predictions their futures became illegible. What concerned the Fates most was how many fatespinners began dying. A handful of dragons had begun to kill. Some were protecting their territory, others were seeking to expand it. A few even sold their services as weapons to slay whole armies, while the rest flew further into isolation, never harming a single soul. Fatespinners began dropping from their webs in greater numbers and the Fates could no longer rely on their predictions with so many variables. It was then they decided the dragons had to be destroyed if they were to be able to guarantee the world's safety."

Whisper breathed deeply the cool air upon them. She felt sad, angry, naive. Like she was the last to hear news twenty years old, even though it was very likely few truly knew the origin of the war. The monastery hadn't prepared her for the world at all, it seemed. All of her teachings were to strengthen her virtues and cultivate wisdom, but since her plunge into the reality beyond their walls, she discovered she was completely oblivious to the workings of the world. "Don't let it get to your head, but you seem to know more about everything than anyone I've met so far," she said. "Were you a scholar before you worked for the King?"

"No, I was a doctor. I simply have a knack for being well informed." The flame was wavering and his attention began to wane.

Whisper sat and watched the tiny fire die in gray smoke and damp moss. She placed her index finger and thumb together and put the circle to her mouth. Air filled her lungs and, as she exhaled firmly, a jet of flame burst from her lips and exploded in a dazzling display of brilliant orange fire. Salem stumbled backwards and quickly clambered to his feet. He frantically swatted at the ash in his eyes while she laughed and basked in the warmth and glow. "I can breathe fire," she remarked, "Now you know a little more."

Salem squinted as the stinging subsided and his nerves cooled. He was nearly at his wits end, but still managed to feign temperance. "I have been building our fires for four nights, why would you wait to tell me this?"

"I don't like people knowing all of my tricks," she replied, "Besides, building your own fire build character."

He knew he would have said the exact same thing if their situation were reversed. "The flame is quite hot for such a simple technique. I am sure the monks quickly regretted teaching it to you." He finally regained his composure, and though he wasn't smiling yet, Whisper was sure he'd find it funny later.

He sat and tenderly nursed the sore side of his face, where he was struck a few days prior. "Between you and the bandits it is a wonder I have not died yet."

"Please," she rolled her eyes, "it didn't even look like he hit you. You don't even have a bruise." She wasn't a fan of weakness, especially from grown men, noble and barbarian alike.

"Of course he hit me."

Whisper shook her head in suspicion. "I don't know. It looked like there was contact, but I didn't hear anything. Usually there's a sound."

"Well, a single heightened sense oftentimes diminishes the others. Or perhaps you are just getting too old to hear properly."

Whisper took an apple from her rations and polished it against her robe. "You're right. It is a wonder I haven't killed you yet." She regretted holding her flame back and wished she had taken his eyebrows off. In her gut she was certain he somehow cradled the bandit's hit, which would have taken incredible reflex and skill to do. Hearing aside, she was confident in the sharpness of her eyesight and it happened only a few yards away. Salem was hiding something, she knew it.

"I have a theory," she said suspiciously.

"I like theories," he replied, trying to brush his irritation by prodding the fire with a stick.

She snapped her hand and let loose the apple, which firmly collided with his face and knocked him flat on his back. Had he the reflexes to cradle the impact he sure didn't use them, and she definitely heard it this time.

He sat up, flushed with fury, clutching the side of his face. "Wh... !? Why... !? The face!? Same spot, even!?" He took a deep breath and forced the emotion aside as best he could.

Whisper felt a little embarrassed but was far too proud to admit it. "Fine. I believe you now."

Salem shook his head in disbelief and gingerly touched the swelling.

"I honestly thought you would dodge or catch it."

"I am not an enlightened," he forced temperance with all of his being. So much, so, it pained him greatly.

"Not even slightly? You manipulate people so well. The first time we met there was something in your eyes that was unnatural. There must be something there, some cantrip you know or trick you use. Explain how you convinced the Setsuha to form the border treatise between the Realm of the Snow Leaf and Whitewater." She was adamant his charm and perception were too good to be natural, though if his weapons were truly his eyes she may have inadvertently disarmed him.

"The story of the Snow Leaf is complicated." He stood to excuse himself from the interrogation. Though often ill-advised at night, he needed to take a walk and drink some wine in solitude.

"Are all your stories tragic?" She felt a mild wave of empathy wash over her, but was still inherently tired of hearing him whine.

Salem stared into the fire, lost in the all-consuming radiance of the flames. "Dear Whisper. I collect them."

***

Alexander Tybalt sat at a table set before a small fireplace, awash in its warmth as he stretched his hand from the copious paperwork he had been tending. Before him lay two folded letters, sealed with his personal navy and white marbled wax and stamped with the crest of the Judiciar.

"May I enter?" spoke a ghostly voice from the door.

Tybalt nervously turned to see Vaughn Cross and brushed the letters aside. "Enter, chancellor."

Cross bowed his head and closed the door behind him. "Your estate is quite warm."

"Why are you here?"

"A friend can't say hello?"

Tybalt chuckled. "Are we friends now?"

Cross stood before the table and examined the papers until Tybalt tapped the surface to gain his attention and draw his eyes back to his. It was clear he wasn't welcome to peruse the documents, and he backed away to ease the nerves. "Are these the geomancer's contracts?" he asked as he pointed to the two sealed letters.

"Yes. They will be delivered with payment by tonight." Tybalt leaned forward on the table. "Why are you here?"

"I come with a concern."

"What kind of concern?"

"Though I can't yet be certain, I worry that there may be some... external influence within the military ranks. It cannot yet be determined whether or not it is related to the Orbweavers."

Tybalt seemed offended by the accusation, but was rational enough to know that regardless of whether or not he was Judiciar, there were far too many soldiers in Whitewater for him to vouch for. "On what grounds do you base this hunch?"

Cross approached and leaned with both palms on the table, being sure to keep his voice low enough that only they could hear. "I am trying to follow a money trail. Some of the soldiers are spending more than usual and it makes me suspicious."

"That's very thin."

"I'm aware. However, when I attempt to access the treasury records, I am always met with hostility by Fairchild. At a glance, it would seem we are at an unexplained deficit and I can't yet track where the money is going, if there is anything to track in the first place."

"If anything is awry, Fairchild has a hand in it, but what is it you want from me?"

"I will continue to search for a connection between Fairchild and the soldiers, but in the meantime I recommend either delivering your messages yourself, or having someone trusted do it for you."

"That's all?" Tybalt teased the idea of being part of Fairchild's demise.

"For now, yes. Information is something the Orbweavers have already, any opportunity to keep more from them will only weigh our advantage."

Tybalt nodded. "I will limit myself in this theory of yours, as I wish to remain a neutral party until there is something concrete to work with. Until then, ensuring the safety of my couriers is an acceptable request."

Cross nodded and stood back up.

"Be very careful, Cross. You may stir up more than you can handle, and if Fairchild becomes aware of your investigation against him your position on the council may be compromised."

"I mean to find the answers, whether it indicts Fairchild or not." Cross turned to the door and prepared to leave. "And if someone within the council happens to be involved, I am certain they won't outsmart me."

Tybalt acknowledged and watched as the door slowly closed upon Cross' departure, spilling a wave of cool air into the room.

"Agent Dask..." Tybalt called into the darkness behind him.

From the ichor of shadows, a slender figure clad in light combat gear silently emerged. "Aye, Judiciar?"

Tybalt leaned back in his chair, the wood softly creaked as he crossed his arms. "I want Cross followed."

★★★

The sweet wind across Vaexa's golden feathers was invigorating and marked the end of her and Selva's journey across the mountain. They already passed the sheer cliffs overlooking the Shén Shé jungles, and the aroma of lemongrass teased her senses from the grove ahead. The tall bunches of pale green blades beckoned to them and the moment they made the clearing she leapt from Selva's back and tumbled into it. The grass had grown almost five feet here, making it one of their favorite spots. The ground rumbled as Selva flopped onto his back, his tongue hanging from the side of his open mouth.

Vaexa hugged a bundle and breathed deeply, closing her eyes and losing herself in the fragrance. The earth beneath her shifted as she turned to lay on her back and stare into the mist. "Selva," she said sweetly. The grass was so tall she couldn't see his paws sticking up, but could hear his delighted panting. "What do you think the other realms are like?"

"I know they are not like Setsuha, so how great could they really be?" His voice rumbled the dirt beneath her and resonated through her chest.

"Salem Eventide says that Whitewater has a 'king', which is like an elder. Can you imagine? Only one elder for thousands and thousands of people."

"It sounds stressful."

"And he lives in a nest so big that a dragon sits on top!"

"It sounds lonesome."

"And Salem comes from an ocean, but it's made entirely of pink and white blossoms!"

"It sounds…" Selva paused. "Fragrant?" He wiggled to further bury his back into the cool dirt. "But it's not home."

"I know," she sighed. From the ground the grass looked like tall spindly trees reaching up to a sky they could never touch. "Wouldn't it be amazing to see though?"

Selva turned his head, knowing exactly where she was. "What's an ocean? Are pink and white types of colors?"

She winced, somehow forgetting Selva was blind and used tremorsense to navigate. "I took you to the ocean when you were a puppy, remember? We went to pick elmriss flowers? Nuith scolded us so badly."

"Ah," he recalled. "It was like an endless stretch of shifting fur."

Vaexa giggled. "Yes, I suppose for you it was."

Selva took a deep breath and let his tongue hang out again. "Vaexa celys, do you know what freedom is?"

Vaexa didn't answer.

"Freedom isn't just your ability to explore beyond the mountain, it's the spirit that makes you want to in the first place. Your imagination, your wonder. Freedom is sneaking out to ride a fenwight at full speed. It's sitting on a cliff overlooking a Shén Shé jungle and dreaming of its secrets instead of sitting in Llaesynd reciting knowledge you already know. It's clinging to a curtain of elmriss blossoms high above the ocean instead of letting physical fragility stunt your sense of adventure."

Remembering each experience filled her with spirit, bringing to surface the exhilaration she had felt.

"We can't leave the mountain," he said, "but I am freer than anyone anywhere else. Do you know why?"

Vaexa shook her head, knowing full well he could sense it.

"Because, whenever the mood strikes, we can roll in the world's sweetest lemongrass. A luxury no one else has." Selva wiggled back onto his feet and jumped all around her, his paws clearing the tips of the grass with every prance. He pushed his wet nose into her side and began to roll her through the grass until she started laughing.

"Freedom begins with a sense of spirit," he said as he jumped again, his tongue waving about. "And we have lots of it."

Vaexa stood and smiled, her head barely peering over the tallest grass to see him watching her mischievously. She leapt after him, laughing and playing while they took turns chasing one another. Her head would always be curious about the world beyond Setsuha, but in her heart she knew Selva was right. Freedom wasn't Whitewater. Or nests with dragons on them. Or oceans of pink and white blossoms. It was playing in the lemongrass.

10

WHITE SILK AND SOFT STONE

Lady Rhoswan sat on a stone bench alongside her glassy pond and sipped her tea. The morning air was both fresh and welcoming, and the light seemed to shimmer across her dress of white silk and peach blossoms. Pinned in her hair was a delicate pink lotus bloom. She placed the cup to her lips and finished her tea as her eyes caught Breon walking across the bridge, opening her lace fan and waving it to catch his attention.

"Lady Rhoswan." He bowed and brushed his graying hair from his eyes, then opened his ledger. "What would you have me do today?"

She folded her fan and placed her cup beside her, crossing her legs and adjusting her posture. "Please begin preparations for the Gala. Set the lots and decorate the gardens. We will hold the auction outside, weather permitting."

Breon wrote as she spoke and bowed upon finishing. "Yes, milady." He turned and immediately set to work.

She was fond of Breon, professionally of course. He was the eldest of her hired help, but he had the experience and drive she had not yet found in another. She noticed he was showing his age much more in the past months, though. Movements were stiffer, his attention would wander, his hair and scruff became peppered with silver.

Reluctantly, she stood and handed her empty cup to the nearest maid, tipping her head and smiling sweetly. The maid curtsied and wandered into the pagoda.

It was a beautiful day for a walk, and though her schedule was beginning to fill to the brim she decided to check Grove once more, just in case.

She approached the iron gate of Grove's stead and looked beyond, but nothing had changed since her last visit. She walked up the steps and knocked loudly several times, yet no one answered. Another sigh left her lips and she returned to the road, latching the gate behind her.

"Ah, Lady Rhoswan! I didn't see you there." A hefty nobleman approached her, cane in hand. It was the same gentleman she had seen the day and evening before, coincidentally. He tipped his hat to her as he always did and his eyes held their usual mischievous glaze. "What does a wren weigh?"

She smiled coyly once more and opened her fan across her lips. "A pound, of course." She reeled him in with her eyes and then turned to walk away.

The nobleman bowed and smiled nervously. "Aye. A pound." He stood upright and looked to the ground, flushed with the feeling he had done this before.

★★★

The warmth of daylight washed over the stone floors of Vaughn Cross' home in Whitewater – an artistic patchwork of gray and brown to accent the sleek curvature of the tables, chairs, and fireplace he had custom crafted to his standards. The scent of sweet orange and redcurrant wafted through coils of lazy steam as Cross carefully sifted the pulp and rind from his cup of tea. Though redcurrant was relatively abundant in the lower lands of Whitewater, oranges were an expensive and exotic import from the eastern shores of Emberwilde, where the air was warmer and sands were ocean-kissed. Many people of Whitewater had never seen an orange before, in fact, and Cross secretly loved having that which would leave others in awe, as though having money made him more interesting or cultured.

He closed his eyes and journeyed through the lighter notes that caressed his senses, only to be rudely interrupted by a hard knocking on his front door.

"What is it, Andus?" he called across the room, focusing more so on the color of his tea.

"Um... Chancellor. I came to inform you that the geomancers have arrived," the surprised voice resonated through the solid wood with authoritative clarity.

Cross traversed the room and lifted the latch, opening it to reveal a young, broad shouldered soldier. His silver half plate, polished and pristine, proudly bore the Whitewater crest on its shoulders, and draped across his back was cloak of white, trimmed in sapphire blue.

"Chancellor." Andus bowed his head. "How did you know it was me?"

Cross sipped his tea and straightened his posture. "Your knock," he began. "The undertone of half-plate told me you were one of the King's Cloister Guards, of which there are only twenty-two. Half are too old to knock with your vigor, others are too heavy to knock with your grace, which only left a handful of choices."

"So you guessed, sir?" Andus dared a smile. There was a fine line between professional and casual when it came to the presence of a council member and he was balanced just enough for Cross' taste.

"I never guess," he replied as he gathered his coat to leave. "Of my remaining choices, only you are left-handed."

Together they began to walk the cobblestone through the city, towards the outer walls.

"You have a very impressive skill, Chancellor," Andus complimented. An attempt to break the silence.

Cross wasn't one for needless conversations, always keeping his mind busy on something. He snapped back into his body as he realized he was being addressed. "Ah, well. Thank you."

"You know, sir, many of the Cloister Guards avoid you."

"I'm aware," Cross replied half-heartedly.

"They're intimidated, I think."

"As well they should be." Cross' eyes examined every home, alley, and passersby as they walked, taking in as much information as he could. "I am a man who loves to know everyone's secrets. Unlike Fairchild, I need no money, and unlike Tybalt, I need no authority. I need only look to see all and that should be terrifying."

"Much like the Voice of the King."

Cross stiffened at the mention of Salem and choked back the association. "Yes," he sighed, half rolling his eyes. "Much like the Voice."

Awkward silence fell upon them for the first half of their journey, both choosing to take in the bustle of townsfolk that scattered the streets amidst carts and carriages filled with fresh vegetables, meats, and hand crafted goods.

"Excuse me, Chancellor," a weak, elderly voice strained to be heard over their surroundings.

Cross turned to see an old man sitting in an alley with a chipped wooden cup. "Ah," he smiled as he approached and crouched to eye level. "How are you Bran?"

Behind clouded eyes, crusted with rheum, the elder smiled a vacant, toothless smile. "Still alive."

Cross reached into his pocket and withdrew a few pieces of silver. "What would you have today?"

Bran looked to the sky and thought, his head slowly swaying back and forth with the breeze of the morn. "Today... I would want a baked yam, with a glass of cool milk."

"You have simple tastes, my friend," Cross replied, noticing he had withdrawn far more silver than necessary for such a basic meal. However, with a soft nod, he reached out and placed the coins in the wooden cup.

Bran shook it, filled with delight, and listened to the coins rattle against each other. "I am a simple man."

Cross nodded and stood to leave when a young boy in tattered sack cloth and rags wrapped his arms around his waist. "Good day to you, young man."

The child looked up to him with deep brown eyes. "I practiced, like I promised!"

"Prove it." Cross began holding up a random number of fingers, allowing the boy time to slowly count them out and provide the correct answer. After a short test of basic math, Cross smiled and presented the boy with a small silver piece. "I'm proud of you. Keep up the good work, we'll be counting higher than ten next week."

The boy gazed upon the piece as though it were precious stone in his hand, losing himself in a bottomless fathom of possibilities only a child could muster.

In the wake of their gratitude, Cross turned and proceeded down the busy street.

"Sir," Andus trailed shortly behind. "You're teaching a peasant stray to count?"

"And read, too," Cross replied sharply. "Is the wealth of knowledge exclusive?"

"I... no... sir. I meant no disrespect. I was merely surprised." Andus felt slightly ashamed at his insinuation and looked to adjust the conversation. "And the elderly man? Who was he?"

"That is Bran."

"Yes, I heard that. Did he once have status?"

"He is a citizen of Whitewater." Cross looked over his shoulder before turning onto a side street. "A citizen of Whitewater doesn't need status to be important."

★★★

A fierce wind suddenly rose through Llaesynd, the nests swayed with the give of the vines. Vaexa stood at the entrance to Llaeilyer, the 'heart of the sky'. It was a larger, free hanging nest that acted as a reliquary and home to herself and the other three elders. It rocked in the wind and slowed to a stop as the air went still, once again filled with blood and malice. She couldn't help but raise her eyes to the sky to see if the mist was doing something unusual. However, night had come upon them and she could see nothing beyond the canopy.

One of the elders cheerfully gestured for her to enter. It seemed none of them felt the same turpitude in the air, as their greetings were both happy, formal, and oblivious.

"Vaexa est'alara celys." The male of the three smiled as he held his hand out to touch her forehead. The Setsuha were immensely sensitive and could feel intent through contact. The touch of the forehead was often used as tactile reinforcement for their greetings, to ensure motive was genuine and show they had nothing to hide.

"Rhys celys," she bowed and returned the gesture. Rhys was the only elder of male form and was named for the scent after the rain. The other two were Luseca and Nuith, named for the dawn and dusk, respectively.

Luseca was the eldest, shy of eight hundred, while Vaexa was the youngest at one hundred and fifteen. Despite their incredible ages, they all looked like adults of no more than twenty-five. This was one of the gifts of the mountain, near eternal youth. From the moment they gained life, to the moment they rejoined the earth, they would always be a beautiful, ageless, young adult.

Their life cycle was unique, as they were not born. They were created. To craft a Setsuhan, the elders would travel into the mountain and chisel one from whichever stone they deemed worthy. It would be meticulously detailed and refined over a series of days to ensure it was precise, after of which they would begin an ancient ceremony of life. It was a ritual that called out to the spirit of the mountain and it would respond by taking energy from itself and imbuing the statue with a soul. Stone turned to feather and flesh as the mountain would breath life upon it. The elders would then choose a name for the new Setsuhan and present them with a piece of stone from which they were created. This piece of stone was their connection to the mountain. Their lineage. Their being. Their heart. If they were ever to die, the heart would turn to dust.

The reliquary was where they kept their hearts safe. The stone hearts hung in little nests above their heads, one for every Setsuhan. The stones all looked very similar, as nearly all of them were of the same type, but to them each was incredibly distinct. Impossible to confuse one's heart with another.

Amongst the gray and brown stones there was a single, clouded, white crystal, swaying from the wind since past. It was a piece of selenite, and it was Vaexa's heart. Though it was beautiful, it was far more fragile than the others, which was why her elders would demand such precaution in her daily life. She was the most brittle of them all.

The number of hearts was restricted to the power of the mountain, therefore, only one hundred and fifty could ever exist at a time. Four of those souls were deemed as elders and were the only souls to retain the memory of how to do the ritual in their consecutive lives.

Though all Setsuhan are immune to poison, disease, and did not require food, water or air, they still had an expiry of eight hundred years exactly, at which time the energy within them would return to the mountain and the remaining elders would transfer the soul into a new vessel. Despite the energy being the same, the new body would retain none of the memories of the prior life, save for the ritual in the exception of the elders. In many cases their instincts and reflexes would be sharper, and their innate wisdom seemed to carry across the generations.

An elder whose time was nearing would set out on a journey, alone, to find a stone they felt a connection with and carve their new image in solitude. It was a tradition that would complete their cycle, bring peace to their finality, and prepare them for the next life. It was a journey that Luseca herself would soon take.

The elder prior to Vaexa had found a cavern of selenite and was in awe of its resonance. The others tried to deter her from crafting her successor from such brittle crystal, but she was assured that, in her new form, her sensitivity would be heightened due to the nature of the material. So far as Vaexa could tell, she was correct. Often times, she found herself feeling the intent of others even without contact and was the only one able to detect a fenwight as it traveled through the trees.

Tonight they were preparing for a ceremony of life they would perform in the coming days, but with the recent feelings in the wind she was unusually nervous. One hundred and forty nine hearts hung from the ceiling. This would be the twentieth year that the last heart had been missing. It was a phenomenon that puzzled them greatly, marking the anniversary of the death of Savrae-Lyth, Queen of Drakes and Ward of the Snow Leaf.

When Savrae-Lyth, the very last dragon, died, the one hundred and fiftieth Setsuhan heart mysteriously disappeared. What was even more unusual was that no one was able to recall who the last heart belonged to. He or she had somehow vanished from their memories and ceased to exist, leaving behind only the empty feeling that they had forgotten something important. The elders went through the process of creating a new one, but the ritual failed. Each year since, they try to reanimate the missing soul, but it would always be unsuccessful. Over time, this began to worry them. Speculation arose that the mountain was slowly losing power and had become incapable of sustaining their numbers. It was a terrifying theory the elders worked hard to keep under control.

Two other odd events happened at the same time as the vanishing heart. The first was that Vaexa's selenite heart had changed. A tiny striation here, a chip there. The changes were so minute that no one believed her, but she was certain it wasn't as it used to be. She could have confused it with another had it not been hanging in her nest, and were she not the only one with a heart of white crystal. It was terribly puzzling.

The second was the random static she would feel wash over her skin, blurring her vision. It was as though the air was vibrating around her and she could feel emotion charging through it, something familiar. She couldn't place it, but it brought her peace.

Hope was not lost. Soon, on the anniversary of the vanishing soul, they would try again.

★★★

Salem stretched his arms as his sleepy eyes adjusted to the morning light. A thin layer of dew dampened his coat and wet his lips. The soft moss bedding he slept in was very comfortable, surprisingly. It was a good night, save for the tenderness he could feel around his eye. Nothing quite like getting punched and then struck with fruit. With any luck it wouldn't have bruised much, but he was certain the damage was obvious. He poked his head around to see Whisper still curled up against a tree, seemingly alert and unconscious at the same time.

He quietly sat up and stretched his fingers towards his toes with remarkable dexterity, cradling his forehead on his shins as he loosened his back and legs.

He reached for a small leather pouch he kept in the lapel of his pea coat and opened it to reveal a set of six thin needles and one thicker, hollow one. Each was about the length of a finger at most. To his disadvantage, there were no reflective surfaces for him to work with and instead he closed his eyes and relied on inner sight to guide his hands. One by one he carefully removed the needles and pinned each into specific spots around his eye and cheek. A prior life of fine hands made the technique entirely painless and over the short time it took for him to trace his meridians and place the needles, he already began to feel the swelling subside. The bruising began to feel warm as it flushed with fresh blood, and in his mind's eye he knew the tint would be lightening by now.

He took the hollow needle and placed it in the center of the bruising, where it was the hottest. A thin trickle of blackish blood poured from the end as it traveled through the core. As the last drop fell and it began to turn red with oxygen, he removed it and pulled a soft piece of moss from the bedding on which he sat. The remaining needles were carefully removed and the moss was pressed over the wound. He gently tapped a finger along his ocular ridge, which immediately stopped the bleeding.

The flow of the three techniques made them all seem related, but in fact, they were each medical practices employed by different realms. The acupuncture was a high study of the western realm of Emberwilde, the bloodletting was a technique used by the Shén Shé purebloods in the far east, and the moss and meridian tapping were basic poultice practices of the herbalists of Whitewater.

He took his time and relaxed. The tenderness had nearly completely lifted and the cooling effect was comforting. They still had several days ahead of them, but only one or two in the forest. Once they were clear of the woods, the roads would become much more welcoming, and then Freestone. He smiled thinking of it. The blossoms above them, rich earth beneath, and the smell – oh, the smell. He had been many places and seen many things, but few could compare to the sense of sweet belonging one felt as they swam in a sea of a hundred thousand peach blossoms. The experience had become legendary on the lips of the realms and few places had such strong repute.

11

WILL OF THE RAVENMANE

The land was barren and hot. Nearly a rocky waste, were it not for the occasional oasis of fresh water and green trees speckled throughout the low mountain. These were the last cliffs in the south and it overlooked the desert beyond, which stretched as far as the eye could see until it eventually met the ocean. Emberwilde's southern border ended at the base of this mountain, as there was never any point in expanding further into the sand. Not far into the distance, nestled at the base of a rocky sheet, was a pillar of black smoke that rose from a village. Five hundred soldiers, each with a single blue feather in their hair, stood at attention and watched. Five rows of one hundred, each outfitted with lamellar of gold and red to reflect their clan colors.

"Brigadier General Phori." A man briskly walked through the rows of soldiers, the two red feathers woven into his hair signaled that he was a captain, and therefore commanded their full respect and attention. He bowed his head before a woman clad in half plate, sitting on her black stallion at the rear.

Her plate was a majestic gold with red trim, and hanging from the sword and sheath at her side were several red tassels and a single golden charm – a ruby flame glinted from it in the daylight. Red tassels were awarded as medals of honor, recognizing those who committed acts of incredible bravery and selflessness in the name of their malikah, who was also known as the Phoenix Queen by the tongue of other realms.

The golden charm signified she was from clan Salamander, guardians anointed by the malikah with the proud duty of keeping the southern border cities safe – usually from the tribal Baku that thrived in the barren desert beyond.

She had very slender facial features and black hair that hung in a multitude of thin, tight braids. Woven in were colorful glass beads and a violet plume that stretched over a foot long, marking her prestigious rank as a Brigadier General. She bore no shield, but instead held in her hands an elegantly curved, double bladed staff, with which she had a reputation for being unmatched.

Her burgundy eyes easily noticed the captain's approach. "Report. Is it a Baku raid?" She looked ahead to the smoldering village in the distance. She had seen the plumb of smoke from her posted city of Akashra, but received no calls for help. Her scouts had failed to return when she sent them to investigate, so she organized a fraction of her command and mobilized.

The captain stood at attention, rested a clenched fist in the open palm of his other hand, and bowed deeply. "No, general. There seem to be no Baku in the area."

She couldn't be too sure. The Baku were lion-folk of the southern sands, divided amongst several war tribes that scattered throughout. The largest and most aggressive were the Blademanes. Named for the males, whose thick manes of fur hung an assortment of sharp stones and bone. They were an ever vigilant thorn in the side of Emberwilde, but more often than not the tribes would just fight each other – establishing territory and enforcing their barbarism. They usually attacked in hoards head on, but it was much safer to assume all cats stalked on soft pads. One thing was for certain, though, and that was that Baku usually traveled in prides of a few dozen or more. If none were spotted near the village, it was very likely they had already moved on.

"Very well," she said. "Have your unit break off and take the village. I will take the remainder back to Akashra and establish contact with the others to warn them of a potential Baku tribe in the wind." Her orders were standard procedure in a situation like this.

"General, there is more."

She listened intently.

"We've spotted someone exiting the wreckage. At first we thought he was a Blademane, but..." he wasn't sure how to explain it to her. Instead, he handed her a retractable spyglass and pointed her far beyond the front ranks to a large spec on the hill in the distance. She opened the spyglass and placed it to her eye.

Marching towards her army was a single creature. Similar to a Baku's incredibly broad and muscular frame, but much bigger. The size of the creature astounded her. A standard male Blademane would average eight feet tall at best, and would wear lightweight leathers and harnesses to maximize their natural agility. What she was looking at was larger, perhaps twelve feet, and was clad head to toe in heavy plate as dark as the night itself. With its armor and at that distance she couldn't tell if it had the fur, claws, or tail of a Blademane, but the helmet definitely seemed like it would accommodate their lion-esque features. As he slowly approached, she noticed the air around him shimmered and waved, as though a tremendous heat was emanating from his obsidian shell.

"Ready archers!" she yelled into her ranks, which then echoed through her captains as they relayed the command throughout their units. All five hundred readied their bows and waited. "Hold!" she yelled once more. She was planning a safe distance interception to attempt a negotiation, or at the very least get a closer look.

The ranks parted as she rode to the front of her army and set out into the dry, rocky land ahead. She went far enough to keep herself under volley range and yelled to the approaching beast. He was still at least a hundred and fifty yards away, but she could feel the earth and stone tremble beneath her with every heavy step. This unsettled her horse greatly.

"I am Brigadier General Phori, Salamander to the malikah of Emberwilde!" He continued to saunter towards her. Its helmet covered his whole face, but now that she was closer, she could definitely tell it was a Blademane. The biggest one she had ever seen in her life. The onyx helmet shaped to protect his snout and jaws, while his mane poured out of the back. Thick, black fur streamed down his back and shoulders, with the glinting of several steel blades that swung from the tips. With all of her years defending the south from the Baku she considered herself an expert on the species, but they had always been tan, or a variant thereof, and had never had the skill to refine metal. Also, this was the first she had seen in armor. Alone, no less. There were many unusual things that didn't add up for her.

The Blademane stopped, and echoing across the barren stone was a deep, powerful voice. "You are who I am looking for."

"State your business," she replied.

"I am Agathuxusen, the unrivaled Ravenmane," he growled back. "The only of my kind."

She had never heard of a Ravenmane before, but it certainly explained the black fur.

"By order of the realm of Emberwilde I demand you explain the meaning of this!" Her horse had become unsteady again and was a hassle to control, but she was managing.

The Ravenmane tilted his head and slowly turned to look back at the burning village. The blades in his hair jingled as they tapped against his armor. "I was looking for you, and you found me." He turned his head back to face her. "I am an Instrument of Fate," he declared, "and my Fate would like to recruit you as her Instrument as well."

The Instruments of Fate were often the protagonists of fables told to children, and their strength in the Dragon War was a topic of deep study in their first years at the military academy. The men and women of Emberwilde were required by law to complete basic military training at the age of fourteen, earning a white feather for their hair to express their contribution to Emberwilde. Anyone who had not was forced keep their head shaved for all to look upon and shame until they did or died. As a realm where even the average citizen was a skilled soldier they were confident that if the Fates were ever to choose new Instruments they would likely be the first candidates. This was nothing like how she had imagined the honor, though, and was inclined to disbelieve.

"You lie," she yelled back. "It is a known fact that Fates keep only one Instrument at a time."

"My Fate has more power to give," he replied.

There wasn't a military official in Emberwilde that hadn't at least teased the idea of being chosen by a Fate, but none would have imagined an introduction like this. This monster was nothing like the Instruments she had read about, and she was certain that a Fate could only have one at a time. As much as she hated the idea, however, if this Ravenmane was actually an Instrument of Fate then she would have to try to believe that the burning village was a necessity in the grand scheme of things. "Should I choose to decline...?"

"You can't. She takes what she wants, and she wants you." His paws ignited in an eerie white flame that slowly danced off him like bundles of fine silk in the wind. "And should you hesitate, I will torture and maim everyone and everything you hold dear, until you grow mad with their cries echoing in your head and you wish for the silence to wash their blood from your hands."

"That doesn't seem like the deal of a Fate."

Though his face could not be seen, his smile could be heard. "I was only asked to deliver your power, how you accept it is up to me."

She had a terrible feeling of dread within her. He was quite far away and she could feel his power tingle across her skin already. Her sole duty was to Emberwilde, though, and surrendering herself to fable and threat would be dishonorable. "Turn back to the Baku lands, or we will fire."

The Ravenmane hung his head in disapproval. "I was hoping you'd say that."

He pointed a palm to her and fired a ball of white flame that struck her horse in the shoulder. The horse whinnied in pain and reared uncontrollably, collapsing backwards and sending Phori to roll through the dust. The flame seemed to roil in slow motion and moved as though it were fluid, eating through every inch of flesh and bone as slowly as possible. The stallion flailed and convulsed as it struggled to stand.

Immediately, the command was given to the archers to let loose their arrows and the sky was blotted as each row took turns releasing in cycle. It was almost impossible to see through the cloud of iron shafts that rained on the Ravenmane, but as the last row fired, a brilliant white flare stretched through the center of the ranks and engulfed over a hundred of them in sticky white flame.

Cries of agony pierced the air as the soldiers rolled in the dust, boiling to death layer by layer. Captains scrambled to reform their ranks and prepared for close quartered engagement.

Phori listened in horror and watched as the Ravenmane carelessly strolled through the countless arrows that littered the earth around him. She had watched every direct hit effortlessly ricochet, and as she stood and readied her double bladed staff at her side her army drew their swords and charged in tow.

The Ravenmane opened his arms wide and slammed his palms together, sending another blast of white fire that tore through another large unit of men. They bellowed horrifically, but the survivors charged onwards. They were oath bound to serve their realm and this was a threat they would die fighting if it would ensure the safety of the people.

Phori dashed towards him and speared her heavy blade under the ridge of his helmet, aiming for the soft tissue of the neck. She felt the blade sink into his flesh, though not nearly as deep as she had hoped. The Ravenmane growled and tried to strike her with the back of his fist. Fortunately, his large size and heavy armor made him slow enough that she could avoid getting hit, lest she be careless. She tore the blade from his throat and rolled under his swing, sending sparks through the air as she clipped his greave.

The rest of her army, only a few hundred now, had engulfed and engaged. Flecks of light flashed across his armor as their blows has no effect and with massive swings of his arms he scattered them through the air, several at a time. Anyone in contact with his fists instantly caught fire, and even the steel of their swords began to soften and bend from the heat when struck by his flaming gauntlets.

The Ravenmane's white fire began to flare brighter, and through his palms burst thick jets of liquid flame that rained upon them. He slowly arced his arms and turned, being sure to spare no man the searing wrath.

Hair burnt, flesh melted, and bones turned to ash. Bellows and screams were quickly silenced as soldiers choked on fire, and the sight and sound of the fallen army was harrowing to all that still stood.

Phori sprung towards the Ravenmane and tried to exploit any soft spots the armor was likely to have. Back of the knees, under the arms, under the helmet. The air dazzled with sparks that sprayed off his armor in brilliance, but she could not land a decisive blow. The few that managed to get through had barely caused any damage at all, though they would have killed nearly any other creature. The slightest bit of blood coated the tips of her blades, grimly reminding her that full force was still far too shallow.

The Ravenmane roared and drew his fist back, giving Phori the opportunity she needed to roll to his side and shove her blade into his armpit with all of her might. She felt it sink in a little further this time, but it left her open to a powerful strike as he swung his other arm. She managed to twist and shoulder the hit, but there was a terrible amount of force. The bladed staff slipped from her hands and stayed in his flesh while she tumbled across the sharp stone. The fire stuck to the pauldron of her armor and began to burn her skin beneath, allowing her to see it wasn't simply sticky flame but a thin liquid or gel that coated the point of contact, fueling or accelerating the fire. Quickly, she drew her sword and slid it beneath her bindings, shattering them with a single sharp twist. She shook the breastplate off before the fire crept to her hair and face, and watched the metal melt. The heat had damaged the shoulder of her silk undershirt, but her skin was fortunately unblemished.

The Ravenmane looked down at the bladed staff under his arm and pulled it loose. The iron immediately began to sag and droop as it liquefied in his hands – beads dripped down like candle wax. The few remaining soldiers feebly struck at his armor, but he ignored them completely.

"This power could be yours," his voice growled, trembling the hair on their skin.

"How could your Fate ruthlessly kill so many!?" She waved an arm to span the carnage. Most of the soldiers had finally died and turned to ash, stilling the air with solitude.

"Some die, some live," he started. "All for purpose."

"You're saying all these soldiers had to be slaughtered to convince me? I can think of much better ways they could have made their offer." She gestured for her soldiers to disengage, but as they pulled back the Ravenmane picked one up by the head. His hair immediately caught fire as he kicked and screamed in agony. Globs of liquid flame oozed from him and splattered across the stone.

"She doesn't just want you, she wants your rage!" The body fell lifeless in his massive paw, his feet and hands twitched as they swayed above the ground.

Phori's eyes grew dark. She was very good at controlling her emotions, but this merciless bloodshed was too much for her. "I accept," she started as she broadened her shoulders and faced him fearlessly. "Once I receive my gift of power, I will kill you with it."

Though she couldn't see beneath the Ravenmane's helmet, she knew he was enjoying himself. Her final reply was exactly as his Fate had predicted, word for word. He dropped the body and outstretched his paw, dispersing the flame and drying the liquid that fueled it. "I look forward to seeing you try."

Phori sheathed her sword and approached him. In his palm was a tiny white spider. "Seal your agreement," he growled.

She held out her hand and allowed the spider to climb onto her. It immediately burrowed beneath her skin, causing excruciating pain. She writhed as she felt it crawl up her arm, and screamed through clenched teeth. It finally stopped at her neck, where a black spider tattoo began to spread up to her ear. The formation burnt like a brand, but once the mark was complete the pain subsided.

She didn't feel more powerful. In fact, she felt weaker. "What did you do?" she asked as her vision blurred.

"You are now an Instrument. Your power will cultivate over a few days. When you are needed, you will be contacted." He leaned in closely. It was only from here that she could see the primal amber eyes of her new bane through the slits in his helmet. "And then, you and I will settle this."

12

SHIORI'S SECOND WISH

Rhys parted a curtain of vines and flowers before him and gestured for Vaexa to pass. They had wandered quite far in search for an herb called elmriss. It was a bitter little thistle that would occasionally bloom tiny red flowers, but it was very uncommon. The thistle grew on the other side of the mountain, where it partook in the salty breeze of the ocean spray below the cliffs upon which it thrived best. Elmriss was an important part of their ceremony and they wanted it picked as fresh as possible before they attempted to resurrect their last heart.

The moss beneath their feet was soft and supple with moisture, and the air was crisp and rejuvenating. Light gleamed in through tiny patches in the canopy high above. It was perfect.

"Be careful," Rhys said. "We are exiting fenwight territory and will be on our own if we run into trouble."

Vaexa nodded and kept careful watch in her peripheral. Fenwights had free reign of Snow Leaf, but could only travel through trees within range of their den. It was a fantastic advantage for hunting, hiding, and traversing the more crowded zones of the mountain, but losing it made them considerably vulnerable, especially in the thicker rainforest along the cliffs that faced the ocean furthest from their home. Though she wished Selva could have come with them to collect the elmriss, he hadn't been able to fit between the trees since he was a puppy. Even if he could, his size would be a fatal disadvantage in an ambush.

Few creatures in Snow Leaf were primal enough to attack prey head on. Through the millennia, they had evolved to be much more cunning, swift, and ferocious, always striking from any other direction but the front. It was important to always remember that the laws of nature in Snow Leaf were not restricted to two dimensions either, as oftentimes the fatal blow would come from above or below as well. The Setsuha had also evolved with the mountain though, and to them it was simply a natural precaution of life. They shared a strong energy and peace with nature, never needing to kill as they didn't need to eat and never being eaten as their flesh reverted to stone in death. This, of course, did not completely remove them from the food chain. Some creatures would kill to protect territory or young, while others just like the challenge of the chase.

"Rhys," Vaexa started, curiously.

He focused intently on his surroundings. They weren't far from their destination and the sound of waves pounding stone echoed in the distance.

"I felt the static again, a few days ago." She ran her fingertips across her shoulders and recalled the sensation of the electricity that had trickled across them.

Rhys shook his head, befuddled. The recurring static had perplexed him ever since she first told him, and likely being connected to the vanishing heart he couldn't help but remain invested. "Was the feeling the same?"

Vaexa nodded, though she knew he couldn't see her. "Yes. It carries such a sweet peace still, with the same hint of forlorn." She knew the feeling had to be connected, but still, no one other than herself felt it. It was widely assumed her soft selenite properties were much more attuned to energies, keeping her the only one sensitive enough to feel its subtleties. Some even speculated that the mountain was trying to communicate with her.

"What do you remember, from when the last heart vanished?" This question had been asked many times before, but she always sought to find something new in his usual answers. She was appreciative of his patience, as he never scolded her for being repetitious.

Vaexa appeared to be paying much less attention than Rhys as they walked, but in truth, the resonating selenite within her made her senses fiercely acute and gave her a very accurate understanding of the world around them. There were three hundred and forty two trees in her direct vicinity, twelve birds and eight nests above them, a small cluster of herbivores drinking far to their left, and a subtle change in the density of the forest floor led her to believe they may have walked over a burrow. She also knew the trees would end and they were about to reach the cliff edge.

"I see the cliff edge ahead," Rhys whispered as he proceeded. He then stopped and recollected the day the heart vanished. "It's discouraging. If we hadn't had one hundred and fifty nests made in the reliquary, I'm not sure any of us would have noticed someone was missing."

She knew what he meant. She, too, was filled with uncertainty when the event occurred. She knew every name of every Setsuhan, past and present. It seemed impossible that any of them could be forgotten.

The trees abruptly stopped at a sheer drop of rock that plunged into the blue waters below. The cliffs were incredibly high and to fall would certainly be death. Fortunately, Setsuhan's were born fearless of heights.

"I was terribly confused. Nearly incapable of remembering how many hearts we were supposed to have. There are times I catch myself wondering if we ever had the last heart to begin with and that the nest had always been empty." Rhys was letting some emotion seep into his words. The other elders tended to be much more objective, but that's what she liked about him.

She didn't believe this theory, though. Ever since that day, she could feel a memory tugging at the back of her mind. Something important she was supposed to recollect sat on the verge of clarity, but it never came. Whenever she felt the mysterious static in the air she somehow felt closer to the answer. It was almost a curse, living every day on the edge of revelation.

Sprawling the face of the stone below them were an array of tiny red flowers. The elmriss had bloomed and they were beautiful, creeping in long trains as they stretched to the water like a tattered curtain of crimson cloth. Together, they carefully scaled the stone and began collecting the thistle, placing the buds in a pouch of woven vines fastened to their hip. They didn't require much and were finished within a few minutes, but that didn't stop Vaexa from turning to face the ocean and admire the sparkling crests. She slid her hand beneath a cluster of vines and leaned further out over the perilous drop, looking straight down the rock to the waves and kelp below.

"Yato isn't out yet,"Vaexa said as she noticed the shadow of a dark cave halfway between them and the ocean.

Rhys squinted as he stopped and looked down. "You named the Llaezuke?" The word Llaezuke meant 'Hook of the Sky', and they were a rare and elusive creature. He and Vaexa had first seen the spindly legs of the one below two years ago, when it claimed the cave as its burrow. Since then they had only seen the shy creature once or twice, but knew he was there by the wispy strands of sticky, transparent thread that rose from the cave and danced in the breeze – waiting to snag an unsuspecting flock of birds.

"Of course I named him. He is special, because he is ours."Vaexa smiled as she swung herself around and began to climb back up.

"I'm sure *he* doesn't know that," Rhys chuckled.

They climbed back up with grace, as their light structure and sure footing made the perils of falling very unlikely.

"Do you believe that the spirit of the mountain is receding?" She was the first to the surface and crouched to help pull Rhys up.

He brushed himself off and secured the lid of his satchel. "I don't believe that," he said with conviction. "Look around you. How large and full the trees are. The bountiful wildlife." He looked out across the ocean to the wall of mist a hundred miles away. "Every day, I am in awe of this mountain. The roots have only grown deeper in our time." He smiled and walked back into the trees.

It was reassuring to hear his disbelief. She knew better than most just how healthy the mountain had become.

Together, they began their journey home. Moments in, however, a faint sound touched Vaexa's ears and she stopped, grabbing Rhys's shoulder.

"Wait," she said, listening intently. They both looked around but could see nothing. "I hear breathing."

Rhys crouched and pulled her closer. "Where?"

"There is something up ahead and another far to our right, where the other animals were drinking." She pointed as she spoke. The breaths were very soft and controlled, but deep, made with big, powerful lungs.

"How many hearts can you hear?" Rhys asked, worried.

Vaexa closed her eyes and focused hard on the one to her right. It took only a few seconds for her to catch its faint rhythm. "Two each."

Rhys's eyes widened. "Run!"

The moment they stood to run she heard a faint whipping sound. She turned her eyes just in time to spot a long, jagged spine spiraling towards her. Slivers of bark sprayed against her neck as she narrowly evaded and it plunged into the tree behind her. Then, they appeared.

The light shifted and refracted across the chitin plates that covered their body as they dropped their camouflage and reverted back to their usual matte blacks and greens. They were kin'nyi, a form of large panther, clad in bony plates that could bend light to render it almost completely invisible so long as it remained still. Fierce yellow eyes sat in the center of each side of their head, making their jaws, face and eyes horizontally symmetric. They were an apex predator that grew half as large as a fenwight, and were equipped with five tails, each with a pair of quills it would throw to wound prey.

She and Rhys were almost immediately separated. The kin'nyi knew exactly how to place themselves as to herd them in opposite directions.

"Back to fenwight territory!" Rhys yelled through the trees. He knew he was being pushed back towards the cliffs and desperately wanted Vaexa to escape.

He ducked and weaved through the dense trees as one kin'nyi closed in. He could hear the massive beast smashing through roots and branches as it tried to catch up. Rhys was smart enough not to give it a straight stretch on which to sprint and made sure to keep his patterns irregular. Kin'nyi were also excellent jumpers and climbers, limiting his methods of escape. His only hope was the cliff and he could see the light through the breach in the trees.

As the light began to wash across his skin, he dove for the edge. The kin'nyi screeched and leapt after him, massive claws outstretched. Rhys could feel a set of claws drag through the side of his face as he tumbled forward and slid feet first over the edge. He then hung hundreds of feet above the sharp rocks below by a handful of vines. The kin'nyi's hind quarters landed and skidded across the stone, but had so much momentum that it tumbled over the edge of the cliff as well. Rhys watched intently as the giant creature twisted upside down in free fall, tucked its arms and legs close to its body, and opened the chitin along its chest and stomach. To his astonishment, two long translucent wings stretched out and it began to glide upside down. They knew very little about the apex predator - enough to know to run, not enough to know if could fly.

Rhys squinted. When he was clipped by the claws he had lost a portion of his head, including his right eye. Fortunately, Setsuhan's did not have organs and the damaged flesh immediately reverted to gray stone. Though they were capable of feeling pain, damage to this extent was more numbing than anything, as the stone reversion deadened the nerves in the surrounding areas.

He watched the kin'nyi gracefully soar in a wide arc, high above the sparkling waters below. It was turning back towards him. He tried to climb the roots, but the damage to his head ruined his depth perception and he began struggle. Eventually, he turned to face his fate and stared deep into its large, unforgiving eyes as it drew closer.

Suddenly, a thin and wispy net and line shot up from beneath them and engulfed the kin'nyi. It was a Yato. Droplets of glue glistened in the light as they fused to the kin'nyi's chitin shell, and as the fresh silk began to cool it shrunk and constricted the giant creature. The kin'nyi thunderously crashed into the stone beneath Rhys and plummeted down the cliff face until the line became taut and it snapped to a halt above the ocean waves. Rhys watched below as the struggling ball of silk and rage was dragged up the cliff face and into the ominous crevice by a thin cable. In a matter of moments, it disappeared into the stone.

Vaexa tumbled through a small space between two large branches as the kin'nyi crashed into it, sending debris in all directions. It shattered the wood with its powerful jaws and proceeded to give chase. Vaexa was one of the most dexterous of the Setsuhan and she made sure to put her skill to good use by taking advantage of every small opening and sharp angle she could. Though the kin'nyi was incredibly strong, pursuing her through the route she was leading was creating more fatigue than necessary. Its evolved mind carefully calculated behind cunning eyes.

Vaexa veered off her course to avoid a quill that nearly clipped her. Then again. By the third time, she realized it had learned her method of escape and was steering her somewhere. Likely it was a more open space, but she couldn't be sure. With so many sudden changes in direction she had become terribly disoriented and had no idea where she was running now. Surely enough, she reached a large, open glade, and fell right into its trap.

She dashed across and nearly made it halfway when a large shadow briefly immersed her in darkness. The kin'nyi glided over her, upside down, on wings that chittered in the wind. It flipped back onto its feet and tucked the wings back into its chest to land, screeching violently. It knew it had her now. It veered its body down like a tiger, ready to pounce. Vicious claws dug into the earth beneath and it launched itself towards her, only to be struck violently from the side by a flash of mottled green and gray. She looked to see Selva with his jaws clasped around its throat. Together they slid and struggled across the glade, tearing the grass and soil to shreds. The kin'nyi raked at the Selva's flesh, cutting deep, grievous wounds that painted the grass crimson, but he wouldn't let go. The kin'nyi's tails whipped violently as they tried to land a clear hit and quills sung through the air in all directions, piercing trees and fenwight flesh alike. Selva whimpered as they bore deep into his ribcage, but still managed to find the strength to continue to crush its neck as it twisted and flailed. A sickly burning smell began to fill the air. Acrid. Caustic. Like that of singed fur. Eerie green saliva oozed from Selva's mouth. Vaexa had never seen it before, but Rhys once told her that when a fenwight breaks a tooth, the pulp, blood, and saliva mix to create an incredibly toxic venom. A venom that was melting the kin'nyi from the inside out, right before her eyes. It was a biological countermeasure for large, struggling prey that would almost otherwise be too much for a fenwights jaws to finish. The struggle began to subside and the kin'nyi cried before falling limp. Its hard chitin shell melted, twisted, and flexed at the point of puncture.

"Vaexa est'alara celys," Selva laboured as he dropped the body and staggered towards her, bowing his head so she could place her hand on his nose. He was grievously wounded and blood gushed endlessly into the chaos of dirt, grass, and stone.

She knew, on the surface, she wanted to cry. The trauma of being hunted. The terror of being so close to death without resolve. She knew there were tears of fear in her somewhere, but instead, all she could feel was sorrow. She wished with all of her heart that everything could be alright. That she could smile, rejoice. That she could hug Selva's nose in glee and proclaim how amazing he was. Her emotions were a scattered mess. Fear, melancholy, delusion. Perhaps another side effect of the selenite... maybe her softer, sensitive crystal wasn't stable enough to regulate such intense emotions properly.

Regardless, she looked into Selva's eyes and cried. "You saved me."

"Vaexa celys." Selva's right arm gave into his wounds and weight and his shoulder dropped. Slowly and deliberately, he nuzzled his nose against her and closed his eyes. "Never stop rolling in the lemongrass."

She watched in horror as his body thunderously crashed to the mossy floor. She wrapped her arms around his giant neck and held him, listening to the last few beats of his heart until his body grew silent. She buried her face in his fur and began to bawl. Endless tears, conflicted with breathtaking sorrow.

Rhys limped to the outskirts of the glade to the sound of her sobbing and watched from afar, the stone reversion of his wounds were heavy and unbalancing. He knew his life would soon be over, and lamented that Selva's was already lost. Vaexa alone would survive, but only in body. Her spirit was just as much a casualty. He had never imagined such a dark day. "Never stop rolling in the lemongrass."

★★★

A brilliant orange fire roared and crackled in the massive stone fireplace at the head of the duke's war room. The radiant glow flickered across the banners and tapestries that hung down the dreary slate walls in the giant, windowless space. The temperature was very comfortable for the Shén Shé pure blood and her two malison.

Ashissa was both impressed and appreciative of how accommodating the duke had been by keeping the fires blazing constantly since her arrival, and in the last several days, she had made very good progress on her work.

The honeycomb stone sat in the center of the war board, which spanned the majority of the room and allowed for upwards of forty seats, comfortably. Ashissa stood beside it with a calligraphy brush in hand. Her eyes were fully dilated, so large they were glossy black pools that scanned the outer surface of the multifaceted crystal. This was a technique the Shén Shé would use to see essence and she was using it to trace invisible markings that covered the stone. Without looking at the parchment to her side, she would brush a copy of the markings and designs she saw to inspect them later.

Her eyes constricted back to normal and she braced herself on the table. It required great focus and energy to hold that state for long periods and she had strained herself with overuse. A malison slithered up to her and held her carefully, in case she stumbled from the dizziness. Once she regained her bearing and was able to balance once more, he let her go and continued to guard the main entrance of the room.

She took the many pieces of parchment to the adjacent wall, where she had taken down all the artwork, scrolls, and curtains, and littered it with hundreds of pieces of paper, each with a multitude of unique symbols and pictures. She dipped her finger in a small jar of honey and dabbed the back of her most recent work, posting it with the rest. She then sat on a single chair that faced it from the other side of the room and deeply contemplated the whole collage.

There was a loud knock, followed by the opening of the doors. A cold draft spilled in as the duke entered with two Moths and the doors quickly closed behind them. He set his eyes on the papers strewn across the wall and carefully walked to Ashissa. Her forked tongue flicked out of her mouth to taste the air as he approached.

"Good evening," she said, not once prying her eyes from her work.

The duke nodded, though he knew she didn't notice. "There are so many," he said in awe. He knew nothing of enchantment or warding, or occult for that matter. "What do they mean?"

Ashissa shook her head softly. "Ashissa does not know what they mean yet, but she has noticed the curvature of these markings." Her words flowed slowly as she payed close attention to her pronunciation – her explanation was far too important to misunderstand. She stood and pointed to a grouping of symbols with long curves and bladed hooks.

The duke examined it closely, squinting in the low light. "It almost looks like Emberwilde script."

Ashissa nodded. "It is a very ancient form, the mother of Emberwilde script. Ashissa cannot tell exactly what it means, but it says something about Shiori Etrielle, and the sword being her *Second Wish*." She stepped back to look at the broader picture again. "Ashissa is now certain it is a ward, but its purpose is still unknown."

Eywin smiled. "The *Second Wish...*"

"What does *Second Wish* do?" she asked, not understanding the duke's excitement.

"In stories there are always three wishes. The first wish is always wealth, while the second is power." The words made him smile as he spoke. If this Etrielle artifact was powerful enough to merit the title of *Second Wish*, it could make all of his dreams come true.

"What of the third?"

"What?"

"What of third wish?"

Eywin waved a hand. "Who knows, the first two are the only ones that really matter." He turned to her, seemingly confused. "You said it was a ward? I was under the impression it was a fortification."

She shook her head. "The essence that coats it is not preventing us from getting in, it is actually preventing the energy of the sword from getting out. If this is true, one of two things may happen when a counter ward is created."

The duke took a seat and listened carefully, watching her lay her hands on the crystal. This was the first time he noticed that the pure bloods only had two fingers and a thumb.

"If the ward was designed to sequester, it could simply allow the essence of the artifact to radiate like a beacon. However, if the ward was meant to fetter, releasing it could release enough energy that the honeycomb stone could crack, or even explode." She gazed at the beautiful sword within. "Ashissa dares say that the power this artifact could potentially hold may be more than enough to flay herself and anyone else in the vicinity with shrapnel."

The duke took a deep breath and considered his options. His desire was fiercely strong, but it wasn't his place to demand she risk her life for his gain, not when she wasn't a citizen of his realm with an oath to his King.

She flicked her tongue into the air again. "Ashissa knows what you want to ask."

He shifted in her presence. Shén Shé were discomforting enough without knowing they could taste emotions.

"Ashissa and her people live for learning and exploration. She will risk her life to free *Second Wish...*" she started, "but in return, a copy of each codex in your great library will be donated to the Shén Shé so they may have their own library, whether the honeycomb stone claims her or not."

It was an outrageous request, as their library contained thousands of texts, but a large payment of knowledge was better than money, property, or the originals. She being a snake, his natural instinct was that she was lying about the risk, to trick him into paying significantly more. However, he kept reminding himself of their honorable reputation and that she was the best at what she did. There was no guarantee that hiring someone else would get the crystal unlocked and she seemed confident she could do it.

"That is a very steep request..." he began.

"Ashissa's life is not cheap. Your library is too far away and too cold for the Shén Shé. Having the texts to create our own would be the greatest gift Ashissa could give her people, in exchange for the greatest gift she could give you. It is true selflessness."

He had no grounds on which to argue. It was the least selfish request imaginable and gave him no room to bargain. "Agreed," he said as he stood. "I will have a decree formalized, to seal our arrangement."

She bowed gracefully as he turned to exit the room.

"How long do you think it will take?" he asked, placing his hand on the door. The two malison watched him very carefully. It seemed the lack of trust went both ways.

"She has enough information to begin a counter ward. To be safe, she would like to try to replicate the original first, to be more assured of its nature."

"How long?" he asked again. His patience was thin with her heavy request and it instilled in him an expectation of swift fruition.

"Within a week, Ashissa assures. Wards are fickle and exact, like elaborate locks that require a precise key to open." Her features remained cool, as not to reflect the slight irritation that grew within her. Shén Shé pure bloods didn't like to be rushed, especially when their lives hung in the balance. However, she had just placed a price on hers and as heavy as it was, he agreed she was worth it.

13

NECTAR DRAKE

"Where are we?" asked Whisper. The trail began to wind, growing ever narrower as they pressed onwards. It was definitely not a merchant route and she was certain Salem had lead them off course.

"I wanted to show you something since we are in the area." He gestured up ahead to reveal a grove of trees with brilliant gold and violet leaves, guarded by branches of thickly wound bark that formed vicious spines and hooks. "We are currently traveling on the King's Low Road. A route designed to be hazardous with speed." He ducked beneath a low hanging branch of spiny bark. "The tightly wound paths, thick with overgrowth, thin enemy hoards that might give chase."

Whisper caught her robes on a few branches so far, breaking finger length tines as they stuck in the fabric. "The trees here are very unforgiving compared to those everywhere else in Whitewater."

Salem looked to the rich color of the leaves that warned of their disagreeable disposition. "All of these trees were once 'sweet grove', thousands of years ago. This region then became a nesting ground for Verdigris Dragons, who loved eating the bark for the sugary sap they made." He reached out, carefully broke a tine from a branch, and placed the severed end to his tongue – it was a sweetness like no other. He then tossed the tine into the brush. "Over centuries, the sweet grove grew these long thorns to better protect themselves. Now they are called 'bittersweet grove'."

"Did the Verdigris starve then?"

"No," he replied. "Of all of the dragons, the Verdigris were one of the most adaptable. As the bittersweet grew sharper, the Verdigris grew smaller. After several generations their wings turned into flexible tails and their bodies became narrow and lithe, like salamanders. This helped them scale the trees and harvest the nectar without harm. The bittersweet then ceased evolving more defenses, as the dragons had grown so small that even with their voracious appetites for nectar, the bittersweet were no longer in danger of being overeaten. It was for this insatiable hunger and evolution that the Verdigris Dragons became known as Nectar Drakes."

"Then the Instruments killed them." The abrasion in her voice could have easily been mistaken for anger, but Salem was sharp enough to know it was anxiety, imagining her strength measured to one.

"Actually..." He pointed into the bittersweet, a pair of tiny eyes hung from a branch by two slender tails that stretched from lithe little shoulders. It was scaled like a dragon, but its body was incredibly slender, like that of a serpent. "The Verdigris evolved so far from their draconian roots that they were no longer considered dragons in the eyes of the Fates. All boundaries can be traversed when survival depends on it."

Whisper watched it keenly as it suckled on a broken tine with six clawed hands. Their presence then startled it, causing the drake to retract to the branch and contort its dexterous little body between the multitude of thorns. A unique strategy, using the tines of the branches to deter larger mouths from trying to eat them.

"Their eyes are very beautiful," she said, noticing the glimmering pools of green that formed an 'X' across their irises.

"A trait exclusive to the dragons, in fact." He smiled. "The pools of color in the eye are called lacunae and almost always form a design in the eyes of dragons. More often than not, males have the 'X' design, while females have a blossom. A quick and simple way of determining a dragon's gender without offending them."

"Why did you show me this?" she asked. Though she found it very interesting, the moral undertone eluded her.

"I simply wanted you to know that the magic is not gone. Though the last of the dragons died with the Queen of Drakes, Savrae-Lyth, life found a way to press onwards. No matter how big, no matter how powerful, the capacity for adaptability can be a most powerful tool – even for a dragon."

"Savrae-Lyth? You briefly mentioned her before."

"Most dragons had the ability to transform into different forms and Savrae-Lyth was fond of the Setsuhan body for its grace and delicate nature. She was very beautiful, powerful, and fiercely protective of her kin. The most fearless, the most feared. Laying claim to the entire realm of Setsuha, uncontested."

"She was that much more powerful than the other dragons?"

"Like the Verdigris, she also evolved, breaching what was thought to be her maximum potential and transcending even further. She became the first of her kind. A new evolution of dragon whose renown grew as the world's only Halo Drake. Savrae-Lyth was near ageless and underwent this transformation many millennia ago, whilst Shiori Etrielle still walked the world. Naturally, Etrielle was astonished by Savrae-Lyth's accomplishment and they became inseparable allies, right up until the day Shiori Etrielle disappeared from this world.

"Savrae-Lyth was a Queen because she changed the race and was feared most for the power of her eyes. A technique she only mastered in her latest year, known as the Gaze of Brittle Chains. They say she could look at anyone, anything, and see its exact weakness. It was a terrifying power that made her invincible."

"But the Fates defeated her..."

Salem paused. "The Fates fear that which they cannot control, but even more so, they fear that which can kill them. The Fates had a multitude of reasons to want Savrae-Lyth dead, but kill her they did not."

Whisper was confused. "You said she died, though. The last dragon."

"Yes, that is true. However, Savrae-Lyth could see her own weakness as well, and that was her love for her kin. When the Fates rallied the realms against them, they were too scattered to mount a proper defense and most did not want to harm the humans in the first place, choosing to defend their territory rather than expand an offensive line. Some fought and died, others retreated and were hunted down, while the last few transmuted and evolved to avoid the scouring. Savrae-Lyth was the very last dragon to die, within her own nest at the top the great Snow Leaf Mountain in Setsuha, by tearing her own broken heart from her chest."

Whisper was astonished at the thought. "I can't imagine the courage necessary to do something like that. To rip your own heart out..."

"Not courage, but despair."

She hung her head as she tried to fathom the image.

"As I have made clear, my dear Whisper. The world has endured many tragedies and I collect them all."

★★★

"Do it again," Cross commanded sternly to the pair of geomancers, each knelt on the stone streets before him. Their adornment of rusty brown cloaks and cast iron medallions made them stand out as practitioners of the earthly energies.

"My deepest apologies, Chancellor, but there is nothing here," one replied. Though they were dressed alike, the two were only vaguely familiar with each other, having graduated from the same academy but enlightening at different times. The elder of the two knelt slightly farther back than the younger, whom was actually more experienced. Both were heavy headed and damp with the sweat of their labours.

Cross reviewed their written report once more and recollected the last few hours he had sat and watched them work. Much to his dismay there was nothing immediate that stood out as unusual or miscalculated. Nonetheless, he could not contain his suspicions. "I said to do it again." He folded his hands, as he often did when containing his anxiety, and pierced them with certainty.

"We cannot," the youngest replied. "Geomancy is not like other forms of thaumaturgy. When dealing with earth and stone, a practitioner must exert significant spiritual force. Especially when sensing the depth to which the Judiciar had requested."

Cross closed his eyes and focused his breathing. He was well aware it was no fault of theirs, and that, perhaps, there truly was nothing significant about the location. However, he could not bring himself to accept that he did not have an edge over Salem in regards to the investigation. "Fine," he said begrudgingly, waving them away. "Get lots of rest, I may employ you to do it again soon." He abruptly turned and signaled for Andus to follow him.

"Where are we going, Chancellor?" Andus asked as he hurried to keep with Cross' ambitious pace.

"We must speak with Fairchild to negotiate a second contract."

"Sir, I highly doubt the royal treasurer will allow the expense once he sees the report."

"Very true," Cross replied, pausing a moment as a dark figure briefly crossed his peripheral and disappeared through the crowds, stalls and alleyways.

"Are you alright?" Andus asked, peering out to see what had caught the Chancellor's attention.

Cross studied the streets carefully with absolute certainty he was being followed, but could find no trace of his pursuer. "It's nothing," he replied, breaking his focus and returning to his mission.

Before long, they entered the castle walls and came upon the rosewood arches of the treasury, fragrant flowers draped overhead through a lattice-work of woven bark. The foyer was of moderate size with a single wooden reception counter and featured elegant furniture and vibrant flora to keep visitors comfortable.

"May I help you Chancellor?" asked the bookkeeper tending reception. Her voice was both light and melodic, far from the normal scribal women of vinegar and chalk.

"Pay me no mind," Cross said, bowing his head as he approached. "I must speak with Victor Fairchild immediately." He didn't give her any time to consider before he marched past and disappeared around the corner, leaving her flustered as she quickly sifted through the schedule for the day.

Heavy doors swung wide on smooth hinges to reveal Fairchild, adorned head to toe in his usual array of flourished silks and sparkling gemstones. He stood at the foot of a tall bookcase with an open ledger in hand. A pair of small, circular optics sat at the edge of his nose as he continued to read the contents. "What is it?"

Cross folded his hands and decided to get straight to the point. "I need to withdraw from the royal treasury to employ the geomancers a second day."

Fairchild turned to meet his eyes, head tilted down, peering over the edges of his glasses with curiosity. "Why, pray tell?"

"They have exhausted themselves and need more time for results."

A grin crept across Fairchild's face as he slowly closed the ledger and carefully slid it back onto the shelf. "As I understand, they have finished, and found nothing. Care to revise?"

"Can't we both be correct?" Though Fairchild was often at odds with the Judiciar, he and Cross were professionally neutral at best.

Cross sauntered to the escritoire and began fidgeting with the objects on top of it. Blank parchment, ink, books, and a small chest of iron and abalone that was to hold the monetary intake for the day. He peeked beneath the lid at the velvet within, though the chest was empty. "How would you know the results already?" The lid snapped shut as Fairchild approached and made his irritation clear.

"My money hears further than your ears, I suppose."

Cross took a step back. "I strongly feel there is significance to the site. Allow me to fund them for one more day."

"I'm afraid I can't do that." Fairchild feigned concern and twirled one of his rings around his finger. "Without permission from either the King or Judiciar I can't allow you to squander this city's funds on hunches proven wrong."

"As Chancellor, I have the right to withdraw funds and contract for the sake of Whitewater's economic growth," Cross replied, catching Fairchild's attention. "My intentions are to construct a trading post with a dual level cellar to keep goods cooler, and I need geomancers to accurately survey the area to let me know if the foundation will be stable enough."

Fairchild sat down and leaned back into his chair, staring Cross down, waiting for weakness. "A trading post?" he asked in disbelief.

"Yes."

"I don't believe you."

"It doesn't matter what you believe. What matters is what my application reads."

Fairchild thought carefully over the matter. In truth, were a formal, economically oriented withdrawal to be made, only Cross could be held accountable should it be proven the money was used otherwise.

"Fine," Fairchild agreed. "You may apply for one geomancer. Standard for surveying."

Though it wasn't ideal, it was better than leaving empty handed. "Thank you. I will return with the paperwork shortly."

14

IVORY, THE UNWOVEN

Night had fallen upon the Emberwilde city of Akashra, and since her altercation with the Ravenmane, Phori had returned to her home to rest her aching body and heavy heart. The pain of the tiny spider crawling beneath her skin still lingered, the new brand on her neck felt numb, and she was overwhelmed with the discomfort of feeling like she didn't belong in her own body.

As she lay her head to sleep, vivid dreams of the Ravenmane setting her army ablaze tormented her. The heat across her skin, the smell of molten flesh and steel, and the cries they made. She tossed and turned while sweat dripped down her brow and soaked her hair, her skin burning to the touch. Her eyes opened to the still of the night and dim glow of the embers in her little fireplace – hours must have passed. She climbed out bed, her wet silks stuck to her skin and cooled in the surrounding air, giving her chills. It was a terrible feeling. She was incredibly feverish and sensitive, going from sweltering hot to cripplingly cold in seconds. She draped the moist blanket around her shoulders to cut the chill and threw a few small logs onto the dying coals - pulling a sliver of burning wood to light a lantern.

The streets were completely silent and Phori assumed it must still be very late. The guards on the street had already changed shifts, making it well past midnight at the least. She used the lantern to light her path and shuffled into the kitchen for a cup of water.

The chills managed to subside with the warmth of the blanket, but the slightest movement created breezes that threw her into shivers over and over again. She set the lantern on the counter and reached up onto a shelf with shaking hands, fumbling a clay cup that tumbled from her grasp. She panicked as she felt it slip and watched as it slowly fell. Her panic turned into confusion as the cup continued a slow, floating descent, as though time had slowed. She looked to the flickering lantern light and jumped at the loud popping of coals in her fireplace. Time was certainly normal, yet the cup continued to fall.

Cautiously, she outstretched her hand and delicately grabbed the cup. Her thumb stroked the rough edges of fired clay as she examined it closely, but there was nothing unusual about it. She placed the cup on the table and stared at it, as though it were to perform for her in some way, but nothing happened. It had been a very long day, and she was beginning to think her fever was to blame for her delusions. She dared think of what a fool she must look like if anyone were to see her just now. She began to laugh nervously until the sound of groaning wood met her ears. Immediately she became on high alert, scanning the darkness for the source. There was nothing. Only faint shadows danced across the empty room to the carnal hymn of crackling flame.

She heard the groaning wood once more and she lowered her face to the table. The surface moaned like the hull of a rocking ship, but she could see nothing. Suddenly, a small crack stretched across the finish, directly beneath the clay cup, and in an instant the whole table collapsed into two halves. The sound startled her most, filling her home with a resounding crash that caused her to jump. Her nerves began to ease in the silence to follow. She took the lantern and investigated closely, shining the light directly on the scraps of wood that lay strewn across her dining room floor. The cup had somehow broken the table, and what was even more absurd was that it continued its descent through her floorboards into the cellar beneath.

She quickly rushed to the cellar doors and unlatched them, dashing down the musty steps into the cold storage below. Vegetables and other goods best kept cold filled the wooden racks to either side and a small wine rack held a few bottles. One of which was a beautiful amber that proudly held the pride and joy of the Scarlet Ribbon Estate. There were no peach trees in Emberwilde, so the brandy was an expensive import.

Carefully, she approached the hole in the ceiling and shone the lantern to the floor beneath her. There sat the cup, wedged a few inches into a fissure of cracks that spread across the stone. She was focused so intently that the last thing on her mind was her fever, dropping the blanket to her feet. She reached out and touched the edge of the cup. Somehow it was still intact, and even remained that way as she pried it from its crater.

The cup seemed normal by every means. Felt like clay, looked like clay. She examined it closely and tried to figure out what happened, but she was at a loss for answers. As her mind flitted with confusion, the cup began to lift from her palm and float in the air, much like when she first dropped it. She was breathless, completely mesmerized. She gently tapped the base and watched it twirl weightlessly before her.

"Everyone experiences something different," a woman's voice chanted behind. It was deep, rich, and confident.

Phori turned to see the shadows of the room stretch towards the center, where they wrapped and twisted into a pool of ink. The ichor began to rise from the ground and form into a beautiful woman. She had long, raven hair that spread into a thick train behind her. Upon her head she wore a crown of pure ivory, intricately carved and ornately crafted. Her pupils formed the silhouette of a black spider and a design of white web stretched across the most vibrant blue eyes she had ever seen.

The dress she wore was exquisite. Its collar wrapped around her neck and branched out into a web of shimmering silver thread that glistened across her collarbone and fastened to a gown so rich with shadow it swallowed all other color in the room, leaving only her brilliant blue irises to contrast sharply. As the dress flared past her waist, it slowly began to unravel until it hung like tattered cloth. A roiling, ivory cloud formed beneath her, hiding her feet and making it look as though she were floating on the wispy strands of broken fabric that waved hauntingly beneath her.

Her skin was perfect and unblemished, and as she held her hands together, a heavy bangle hung on her wrist. Two platinum wings spread from a flawless diamond setting and wrapped around her wrist to join at the tips. It sparkled brilliantly in the lantern light, and though it was hard to see, there was a unique and distinct rune suspended within the diamond. It was pristine and beautiful, but nothing she recognized.

"Who... are you?" Phori's fever was getting the best of her and the cool air was throwing her into a fit of restless and uncontrollable shivers.

The woman waved a hand and spindly shadows lifted the blanket from the ground, wrapping it around Phori and hugging her tightly.

"You may call me Ivory," she said softly. "You are my new Instrument."

Phori was confused. "There is no Fate named Ivory."

The woman laughed sweetly. "Ah, yes. Well, you're the expert on reality and what can and cannot exist, aren't you?" She seemed playfully chaotic, tilting her head and delicately dancing her fingertips against the wall. Tiny fractures began to spread with every gentle tap, and what looked like glittering sand seemed to trickle out.

Phori was taken aback. There was no reason in her mind that there couldn't be powerful beings out there that mankind had never heard of. "My apologies. Ivory," she replied humbly.

"Forgiven." She outstretched her hand and the shadowy spindles delicately pulled the floating clay cup towards her. "As a Fate, I cannot predict what abilities unlock in my Instruments. I just simply know they will be useful." She smiled as she watched it turn in the air. "It's always so exciting, seeing what develops. Like opening a gift!"

Ivory was filled with a glee that shone through her vibrantly webbed eyes, but kept a very mature and womanly demeanor. Phori wasn't sure what to say. Her reality was fuzzy at best and she half wondered if she was hallucinating from her temperature.

Ivory sighed longingly. "We often forget the joy and enlightenment, or fear and futility that only uncertainty can bring. Always knowing, always seeing. It takes the spontaneity out of life, strips us of revelation, fills vibrant existence with lack of appreciation." Her eyes grew sad as she spoke. "These moments... these rare moments where I do not know the outcome... They remind me what it's like to live again."

Phori collected herself. "Forgive me, Ivory. I was raised under the impression a Fate could only have one Instrument at a time and Aga... Agathux... the Ravenmane said he was your Instrument already."

She laughed and touched her lips. "That's true. A Fate normally makes one Instrument with their excess power, but I am much more powerful than the ones in your books and can afford to have a few more," she winked at her and smiled. "Which brings me to why I am here."

Phori brushed aside her illness and focused intently. This she needed to hear.

"There is one more Instrument I wish to collect for my grand plan," she started. "I will require you to recruit her."

"I will not murder the innocent like your Ravenmane did," she said sternly. Better to put the foot down early.

Ivory nodded softly, "Certainly not." She graced the back of her hand to Phori's cheek and pouted playfully. "As a matter of fact, the woman I am having you get is an outlaw. By bringing her into our fold you'll be saving lives."

Phori had a long list of criminals at large, but few were women, and even fewer seemed worthy of Ivory's attention. In her gut, though, she had a feeling she knew who Ivory was after. "Fever."

Ivory looked impressed, but she was a Fate and definitely knew she knew. The praise was simply good behavioral training. "Excellent. I chose you for more than your looks and leadership."

Fever was a black widow, per say. A woman of very sensual appeal that would use her body and charm to seduce her targets, and then poison them with a signature blend that would throw them into a fierce fever, spiking their body temperature so high they'd die by morning. The name Fever was coined twofold – for her body and her venom.

"How could I possibly convince Fever?" she asked. There were many ways to enlist the aid of the wanted, but she needed to know what leverage she had at her disposal.

"Ah" she chuckled and waved a hand. "Offer what most outlaws seek – Freedom."

"But she is already free..."

"Then make it so she is not."

Phori nodded, though she didn't hold much faith in the plan. "Today your Ravenmane murdered many good men under my command. I'd like to know why you would allow that."

Ivory pursed her lips and placed her index finger over Phori's to silence her. "The loss of your soldiers' lives is tragic, and I would not have allowed it if there was any other way. The truth is, when the time is right, I will need you to fight the Ravenmane. I will need you to win, and to do so you will need the rage. This may be the single most important waypoint of your future."

"You said you were embracing uncertainty, yet you seem to have strong opinions of my future." If Ivory truly was a Fate, she would have access to the Weave, making clear all matters of destiny.

"I have chosen to break my bond to the Weave, my child, and with each day my ability to read the flow of time has slowly faded. In turn, I am experiencing the overwhelming joy of the unexpected, yet I will always remain cursed with a small burden of foresight. I do not know how, and I barely know when, but you will fight the Ravenmane to an undetermined outcome. I will need your victory, but I cannot guarantee it."

Phori liked the idea of vengeance upon the Ravenmane, but wasn't entirely keen on feeling manipulated, even though that was entirely what Fates do.

Ivory's eyes seemed to soften. "I'm sorry to nudge you in this direction, as I aspire to be a purveyor of free will, but I truly need your help to save this world. So long as an Instrument is in my charge they are forbidden to raise a hand against each other. When I no longer need his services and am certain you are ready, I will arrange for you to settle your vendetta with Agathuxusen. Until then, I know it's difficult, but please trust me. A murderous Ravenmane, a Brigadier General, and an assassin might not be the saviors this world wants, but they are exactly what this world needs."

It wasn't ideal, but Phori could sense a profound truth in Ivory's words. "What is your plan?" Phori asked, pulling her lips away from Ivory's finger.

"A restoration of true freedom to the people, by banishing the lie of freedom that has oppressed them," Ivory replied with a sweet smile. "An oppression the world is barely aware of." She reached out and held the clay cup, which began to turn into a fine sand of white diamonds that poured through her fingers. "The Fates will control Elanta no more. Destiny should belong to the people, as it is their right to choose, not follow. Together we will return to them the freedom they don't know they don't have."

15

WAYLANDER

"Now watch very closely." Casamir brushed the dark hair from his eyes and fastened a pair of round safety glasses over them.

Katya took a step back and held her hands nervously as she watched her brother approach an object viced to a workbench. This wasn't the first time she was called to the Great Library's engineering wing to witness the unveiling of one of her brother's engineering prototypes. It was in her experience to fear the worst. Ever since Casamir began to show signs of struggling with the enlightenment process, he had become more and more adventurous with his designs. She feared he was already giving up on himself and began searching for ways to compensate for the disadvantage.

"Okay, this is the 'high tensile compression bands with retractor' test." He slipped on a pair of heavy leather work gloves and reached for a brass pin inserted into the device. The object was about a foot long, half as wide, and crafted from steel with a complicated brass gear and band system. "Here we go." He carefully grabbed the pin and pulled it out, immediately backing up in case something went wrong.

The gears within whirred and from each end shot a cable that embedded itself into a set of bookcases at each end of the room.

The speed startled Katya. "By Fate!" she said in shallow breaths.

Casamir looked surprised. "I didn't think they would reach that far... and with that velocity." He took the gloves off and marked his findings on a piece of parchment.

"The sages are going to be upset," she said, inspecting the damage done to the nearest bookshelf. "What is this even for?"

He didn't raise his head from his writing, but answered her nonetheless. "This prototype only had light weights on the cables, the final product will have either blades or bolas, I haven't yet decided."

"But... why?"

Oblivious to her question, his face scrunched as he pondered something else. "It's only supposed to fire one side at a time, for some reason it did both. I'll have to look into that."

The gears within the device began to autonomously wind and the cables snapped taut, pulling both bookcases forward and sending them crashing to the ground. Still embedded into the wood, the cables continued to reel, hauling the shelves across the floor with a noise so dreadful they clutched their ears to block it out. The racket finally ceased as the shelves met the workbench, where they slowly lifted to a stop and dangled. The gears within ground and slipped as the weight and angle were too much for it to lift, and with a loud crash that echoed throughout the room the gears shattered, the cables went limp, and the shelves collapsed to the floor.

Katya was at a loss for words as the terror of her father's scorn filled her mind.

Even Casamir was quiet as he looked upon the damage until he turned to his sister and smiled. So proud, so oblivious, so stupid.

***

Elder Waylander crouched on one of the castle's overhangs and stared off into the dying lantern lights of Lyre. Hundreds of feet down, patrolling the cobblestone, were the duke's night watch.

"You've been distant as of late," a man spoke from behind him, his voice deep. Waylander turned to see another Moth, the largest of the six, Rowan Bastet. Bastet crossed the rooftop with the soft steps of a much lighter man and stood behind Waylander. The cool wind ruffled their adornment of scarves and cloaks.

Waylander looked back out to the city and admired the Great Library from this vantage point. It had been built larger than the castle, with several amazing spires and towers that reached into the sky. It was a testament to the skilled hands of Whitewater's best stonemasons and architects, and an awe inspiring symbol as crisp and rejuvenating as the arctic air. "I love this city."

Bastet nodded. He had lived in Lyre for most of his life, but was actually born in the western realm of Emberwilde. His tanned skin and red tinged eyes were a solid sign of his roots. "If I may, there is some concern amongst the other Moths, both for Lord Eywin and yourself."

Waylander hesitated. "After the Dragon War, I swore an oath to protect the Duke of Lyre and the great city itself, under the rule of Liam Whitewater."

"We all have," replied Bastet.

"And if protecting one means betraying another?"

"It is a very broad oath, I'm afraid." The burly westerner knelt along the edge and looked down. "In times of conflict, perhaps it's important to remember where the power of the oath lies. I recall Salem Eventide once saying *'True conviction requires sacrifice.'*"

Waylander nodded as he thought it over. It was Whitewater that honored him with privileged position, not the duke, thereby making his convictions of loyalty to the King more important than anything else. "What are your thoughts on the *Second Wish*?"

Bastet took a hesitant breath, clearly not sure how to answer. "I'm inclined to agree with you, objectively. The Orbweavers showed their hand by involving Eywin, the right course of action would be to destroy it."

Waylander sighed. "It's true." The tactician in him played briefly with the idea of assassinating the Shén Shé to prevent the seal from being broken, but feared the political repercussions that would ensue. If the Shén Shé ever had a reason to go to war with Whitewater, they would be a force most formidable. "We need to protect Lyre, even if that means defying the duke."

"Be careful Waylander. Any decision you make has an enemy behind it and the other Moths may not share your interpretation of the oath."

"This weapon will be our ruination and Eywin means to wield it."

"I know," Bastet nodded, "but sometimes there is more honor in unwavering loyalty to your commander, whether it leads to greatness, or beyond the mist."

"*I* am your commander, Bastet," Waylander replied sternly.

There was a silence as he analyzed his prior words. "True," he stood and excused himself. "And that is why you have my blade, Elder Waylander, but Lyre has my life, and the King, my oath. May we continue to share our values."

Waylander nodded as Bastet took his leave and vanished from the rooftop. He had no intention of making enemies of Lyre's Elite, but knew that stopping Eywin from destroying Lyre was more important, whether it marked him a deserter in their eyes or not. He reached into his cloak and revealed a scroll cylinder with the seal of Lyre's Elite. It was time to notify the Whitewater Leviathan.

16

FREESTONE, THE OCEAN OF BLOSSOMS

There it was, their very first peach tree. It was one of thousands that lined the horizon like a fortress wall, and as they entered into the thicket it was as though they had stepped into another world. The breeze was thick with an enchantment and beauty more supernatural than Whisper could have ever imagined.

Though Salem had been here before, it never ceased to amaze him. He looked upon his companion and reveled in her wide eyes and held breath.

Whisper had never felt so peaceful in her life. The road led far into the distance and disappeared into the trees, making her feel that it stretched eternally. For the most part, it nearly did. They had only reached the outskirts of the Scarlet Ribbon Estate and still had a few miles to walk before they would reach the city.

Salem smiled. He loved seeing people in this moment. It was the one thing he knew to be consistent, the one thing he knew that could bring to surface a man or woman's innermost adoration regardless of how buried beneath hate, sorrow, or abandon they were. There was no other place in the world quite like what he and Rhoswan had built here – a window into the goodness of everyone.

"You would not believe, but these trees are less than five years old. A testament to the richness of the soil in Freestone," he said with pride as he led the way. Between the blossoms in the trees he caught a glimpse of what appeared to be a large messenger raven flying towards them, high in the sky and far in the distance. He directed Whisper to its presence. "If you please, dear Whisper."

She focused her sharp eyes on the bird as it flew by. Though only Salem knew it, there used to be a very wide variety of vision types, though most were only accessible by the dragons, which depended on their type and region. Infrared, essence sight, ultraviolet, emotion. Some of the eldest had honed their skill so well they claimed to be able to see through dimensions with enough meditation. It was around that time the Fates began to seriously consider destroying the species.

Whisper had none of these advanced eye techniques, but she did have the two most basic ones. Telescopic, which allowed her to flex her lenses to magnify her vision, and Accelerated, which processed the information to her brain faster than normal, allowing her to see fast moving objects with complete clarity.

"It's a messenger's raven, with a scroll tube. It has a strange crest on it. Some kind of butterfly, I think," she said.

Salem pondered, calculating the direction it had come from and where it was heading. "It must be from Lyre, heading to the King."

"Is that unusual?" she asked as she strained to see the tiny black blur in the distance.

"It is, in fact. The Duke of Lyre is a highly ranked official in the realm. He is a man of fierce tradition, but is duke to the King only out of convenience and nothing more. If he were to send a message he would do so by messenger, bearing the crest of Lyre."

"Should I kill it?" Whisper asked excitedly.

"No," Salem replied, though he gave just enough pause that she could tell he had thought about it. "This will be a secret I will have to pass on, unfortunately." It pained him not to know and the desire to pry the raven from the skies and read the news, before the King himself, was an incredible temptation. He was certain the 'butterfly' on the message was actually a Moth, sigil to Lyre's Elite. If so, something very big was happening. Something that required no intermediary between Moth and King. He immediately drank the remaining ounces of wine he had left in his bottle to ease his nerves and continued to travel down the path.

Whisper could tell it pained him not to know something. "I've never seen a man drink words like wine."

"Addictions come in all forms," he replied.

"At least there's one good thing to come out of being a monk."

Salem chuckled. "You claim a lack of addiction? Dear Whisper, you are an addict. In fact your addiction is far worse than any other."

"What addiction?" she retorted. "I drink wine because I like it. You drink because you seem to need it. You poison your body far more than I do."

"I was referring to revenge," he said, shaking the bottle to get every last drop before slinging it. "It is the poison of the heart, of the soul. Your first moments amidst the trees of Freestone have been the first your jaw has not clenched, and even as you sleep you stir, swear, or even cry. Drinking consumes me in large portions of my day, that is true, but revenge consumes every moment of your life."

"It's a life purpose! You would have me forget and move on?"

"The problem with revenge as 'life purpose', is that it is no way nurturing. Your cup has been so full of the emotion that once you have your moment, once you have had your revenge, that cup will empty. And so will you."

Whisper was clearly upset with him, but by allowing some silence she began to understand the point he was trying to make.

"Dear Whisper." He stopped and turned to look her in the eyes. The gentle wind caused the blossoms to rustle and dance above them, raining soft petals of pink and white silk. He reached out and took her hand in his. "There is a beautiful world, of beautiful things. I wish you to fill your heart with them, even a little, because that would fill mine as well."

Whisper was flushed with an unusual nervousness as her face grew hot. For the first time in her life her eyes saw nothing but a man before her. The trees, the road, the blossoms, all faded into the background and melted into the haze. She was standing in the most beautiful place in the world, and she couldn't see it.

Feelings like this were a new, complex combination of delightful and uncomfortable. She slowly removed her hand and stuttered with her words.

"I'm... sorry," she said softly. "I truly sully the name of my fellow monks by letting my emotions consume me."

Salem tilted his head and eased her with sympathetic eyes. "If you think the monks care about their name, then you truly miss what it is to be a monk."

They walked in silence for the next hour, passing more and more merchants and civilians along the way. There were many palanquins and carriages escorting the wealthy through the beautiful trees, as well as commoners with blankets and picnic baskets, playing soft songs beneath the shifting canopy above them. Taking in the breathlessness of their homeland was a common activity, and why wouldn't it be. Whisper looked forward to being outdoors every day while here.

As they neared Freestone the sweeping tiled rooftop of the Scarlet Ribbon Estate slowly came into view. A tall, grand pagoda of rich reds and soft cream, surrounded by an old rock wall, accented with green moss and flowing vines. Standing in the circular entrance was Rhoswan, conversing with a client as they held a bottle of brandy in their hands. She briefly looked up to see them and a coy smile stretched across her lips. She finished her conversation and picked up the front of her dress as she walked the few steps to the cobblestone.

"I'm so happy you made it in one piece!" she chanted, hugging him sweetly.

"As I am surprised I did." He chuckled as he held a hand towards his company. "This is my dear Whisper, one armed escort commissioned to keep my pretty face safe." As he turned to Whisper, his eyes and tone turned playfully stern. "I bruise easily."

Whisper looked away and tipped her nose to the air, ignoring his petty whining. It was just an apple... this time.

He then gestured to Rhoswan. "And this, is the esteemed Lady Rhoswan, White Haired Witch of Freestone."

"A pleasure," she said, pressing her palms together and bowing her head lightly. She then leaned in closely as Salem joined her side and they began to walk to the Estate. "She is a mistborn, Salem." She looked at Whisper's demonic eyes and leaned back to Salem. "Is this the one who killed a horse barehanded?"

Salem chuckled awkwardly and looked back to see that Whisper wasn't listening. "Something like that. Actually, I have enjoyed her company greatly, but she can be more trouble than her worth in weight, I promise you that."

Rhoswan shrugged. "She's just your type, actually." She then turned her head to Whisper, who followed in tow. "So, *dear* Whisper, is it? You must be special, he never calls anyone *dear*."

"Really?" Whisper asked. She had assumed it was an endearment he shared with all the ladies and it intrigued her to know that it was exclusive.

Salem cleared his throat and quickly changed the conversation. "Let us show Whisper the distillery."

Rhoswan smiled mischievously and complied. "This way please."

They entered the estate foyer, immaculately decorated with expensive stone carvings, vibrant hanging lanterns, and rows upon rows of wine and brandy on soft pillows displayed behind glass. Whisper was filled with an awe and wonder she hadn't felt since her first time in Whitewater's Great Hall. Though nothing could compare to the white marble and ocean blue honeycomb stone, the intricate detail of the rosewood woodwork in the Scarlet Ribbon lured her eyes to marvel as closely as possible. As expected the staff were very well dressed and they stopped everything they were doing to bow deeply in Rhoswan's presence. Exquisite silks, humbled in the radiance of their White Haired Witch.

Rhoswan led them through a pair of doors that opened into the production area – a vast and open hall with lofted ceilings and hundreds of oak casks. From one of the many rows, Breon slowly approached.

"A pleasure to see you, ambassador," he said as he bowed his head.

Salem nodded back and examined the elderly man as earthy notes subtly met his senses. He couldn't help but notice how much Breon had aged since they last met. His hair was falling out, skin was paler, and his fingers seemed to creak with the weight of the ledger he held. Quite possibly the result of working for the meticulous Rhoswan Gray. Even his clothing seemed dusty, and crumpled in his other hand was a burgundy kerchief – few elderly were seen without.

"Mr. Breon," Rhoswan chimed. "You will recall Salem is shared owner of this estate and will be referred to as Master or Lord."

Salem chuckled and waved a hand. "No no, please. Ambassador is fine. You do most of the work here anyways, I will keep the title from where my efforts earn it best."

Rhoswan forced half a smile in hopes of softening the irritation in her narrowed eyes. She didn't like being corrected in front of her inferiors. "Mr. Breon, please have the girls ready a guest room."

"Yes, milady." He bowed and followed the casks to a rear exit.

"Why only one room?" Whisper asked. She was sure she wouldn't like the answer, but was open to being surprised.

"You will be staying with Rhoswan while I am at my clinic in the city," Salem smiled.

Whisper was expecting him to enforce her role as his personal protection by making her stay with him and was strangely suspicious that he waived the opportunity to make her uncomfortable and test her limit. In a very unexpected way, she felt let down. Perhaps she was beginning to enjoy the banter.

"Will you be staying long?" Rhoswan asked.

"Until after the auction for certain, though I will be stepping out a day or two at a time," he replied. "Then we will be off to Snow Leaf, to collect this year's dremaera."

Whisper caught herself holding her breath. She hadn't thought they would go to the Snow Leaf and was awash in the excitement of it. After all, this was a realm cut off from the world for millennia, where only one man had ever tread and survived.

"Well, if you need any assistance in your investigation, I will see what resources I have access to," Rhoswan offered.

"Actually..." he began. Rhoswan leaned in closely as Salem spoke under his breath. "I need to know what is happening in Lyre."

★★★

The afternoon light shone in through the woven reeds of the reliquary, Llaeilyer. An incense pot released sweet and smoky aromas into the air. Rhys lay on his back and watched the hearts sway above him while Vaexa rested in soft bedding on the other side of the room. He had taken his heart from its nest and held it in his hands, feeling the notches and grooves with his fingertips. Admiring its weight, reconnecting with the earth from which he came. Luseca, the eldest, glided to his side and placed a gentle hand on his chest. The light seemed to make her vibrant green plumage glow.

Rhys and Vaexa rested in silence since narrowly escaping with their lives from their encounter with the kin'nyi. He had suffered significant damage to his head, losing both an ear and an eye. There was only one thing he could do now, and that was to set out on his own journey to find a new stone from which to carve his successor and relinquish his life to the core of the mountain. His wounds had reverted to his original stone and the weight was far too unbalancing for his light frame. Without assistance across the thin bridges of Llaesynd, he would surely lose balance and fall to his death. This was a flaw of their race, as they were incapable of healing or repairing their wounds, no matter how insignificant. They could only rebuild from scratch.

"Rhys celys," Luseca said as she bowed. "How are you feeling?" Physically, she knew he was fine, despite the obvious. It was his mental state she was referring to. Completing a life journey tragically early required resolution.

"Luseca celys. Thank you." They placed a hand on each other's foreheads.

"I will be leaving on my journey soon, to search for stone," she said, smiling. She was almost at her maximum age and needed to create her successor as well.

Rhys sighed and seemed to reminisce. "You've lived nearly eight hundred years... That's beautiful." He looked into her eyes and smiled. A complete cycle was a thing of pride.

"I thought that, perhaps, we could go together. For the initial journey of course, until we find you the stone you want. Then we can part ways." Traditionally they would venture alone, however, it was only the act of carving the stone that demanded solitude and attunement.

Rhys knew he was in no condition to run into the woods on his own and he felt guilty placing the fenwights in danger given their recent sacrifice. It was a good idea. "I would appreciate that. Thank you."

Luseca bowed her head and stood. "We will leave in the morning."

As she exited, Llaeilyer rocked gently, swinging the hearts in their tiny nests even more so. They were entrancing to watch.

This would be one of Rhys's last days amongst the Setsuha and though he knew his soul would carry on, he also knew his memories wouldn't. The faces he had grown to love. Luseca. Nuith. Vaexa. Had he lived a full life, perhaps his regrets wouldn't have been so overwhelming, but he was still young by all standards and there was much he had wished to accomplish in his time.

He decided to close his eyes and rest until dawn. There would be plenty of time for reflection as he carved, and for now, he just needed the strength to get him started.

***

When Vaexa awoke the next morning, they were gone. The emptiness lingered heavily, sapping her of the strength needed to begin her day. She had preparations to do, grinding the thistles into powder so she could create ink. Her measurements had to be absolutely precise, as she had barely enough resource to accommodate the unsuspected third ritual they would be doing within the week. Though it was difficult, she had to choke back her sadness and be a priestess.

Nuith entered Llaeilyer and placed her hand to Vaexa's head. "Veaxa est'alara celys."

"Nuith celys," Vaexa reciprocated.

As quickly as the softness had cushioned her, it was taken away. "Get up child!" Nuith slapped Vaexa lightly on the leg. "You do your elders no honor in mourning."

Vaexa slowly sat up and stretched, preening her golden feathers first, then her black ones. She always knew Nuith to be fussy and excessively motherly, always scolding her for not being careful enough, or slapping her with a reed to remind her not to slouch. In this case, she would have likely lectured her on the importance of tidy appearance, had she left her feathers the way they were. Nuith was the perfectionist of the group and never missed an opportunity to give someone a piece of her mind.

She could remember, many times, laughing with Luseca and Rhys as Nuith groaned on about little things. "*I thought I was the old lady here,*" Luseca would whisper. It was cute every time. Nuith knew they teased behind her back, but she was a proud Setsuhan and didn't care in the least.

Vaexa sat on the floor with her ingredients laid out in front of her.

"I have finished the ink for the first ceremony," Nuith said as he approached her. "You will make the other two."

Vaexa solemnly acknowledged and placed her dried thistles into a mortar and pestle.

"Sit up properly, child!" Nuith squawked.

Vaexa straightened her back and continued to grind the plant into powder, when she felt a cold object placed on the crown of her head. She stopped and dared not move. "What is that?"

"It is the first batch of ink," Nuith answered as she released the stone bowl and let it balance on Vaexa's head. "We only have enough for three, so don't drop it." She then proceeded to the exit of Llaeilyer. Nuith knew Vaexa had incredible dexterity and could be trusted to balance the bowl perfectly, should she not get careless and start slouching again.

"I won't drop it," she said patiently. She wasn't in the mood for the nagging, but recognized that Nuith was just trying to keep her mind focused.

17

HUNT FOR FEVER AND THE WEIGHT OF A NAME

Phori dismounted her horse and set foot in the city of Valakut for the first time. It was a burgeoning place where the streets were lined with merchant carts calling at the passersby, and where guards patrolled with ruthless efficiency. The buildings and minarets were very square in concept, with tall, pinnacled arches and domed roofs. It was a very common, ancient form of architecture in Emberwilde, though many people tried to place modern or conventional twists on it.

Hundreds of people bustled in robes around her, each stopping to examine the newcomer. She knew she stood out.

When she awoke from her fevered encounter a few days prior, hung on her armor stand was a suit of obsidian scaled mail. The joints and shoulders flared to emulate flames and the edges were trimmed with ruby to further concrete the visual. It was sleek, vicious, and probably cost more than she could have ever imagined. Barely an inconvenience for Ivory, as it seemed she could transmute diamonds from nothing with a brush of her hand. Alongside her new attire was also a two bladed staff. The shaft had the weight and feel of black granite, etched with designs from one end to the other, while the blades were like nothing she had seen before. At each end was a platinum chakram that pinched to a point at the tip, giving it a teardrop shape. It certainly had the weight to deliver a fatal blow, the curvature of the blades were perfect for carving, and the points were ideal for precision strikes in soft zones. A marvelous instrument of death she couldn't help but admire.

The weapon on her back made her stand out even more so, and people hushed and whispered as she passed, leading her horse in tow. The only comforting thing about her look was the violet plume that hung from her rows of braids, a reminder that she was one of them, and a high ranking one at that.

Two guards approached her and held a fist to their chests in salute. "Brigadier General," one of them greeted. He had never met her before, but most officers in Emberwilde were familiar with her reputation and weapon of choice. "What brings you to Valakut?"

"I am looking for Efrit-ali mirza." Mirza was a form of royal rank that denoted being a noble prince. Most of the major cities were large enough to have several and Valakut was no exception. The skyline was full of massive palaces, their golden domed roofs glimmered in the daylight. She had no idea which one belonged to Efrit-ali, but Ivory had left a small card with her gifts that read his name. He either knew the woman she sought or was a target. Either way, she needed to find him.

The guards were more than helpful, giving her clear directions to his palace and offering their assistance in any matters otherwise.

She kindly declined and excused herself to wander the streets and admire the vendors. She sifted through rows of silks and wools, perused the fresh produce, and watched as quick meals were prepared for hungry customers. The people we quite fearful of her, so she politely purchased a bag of walnuts, though the merchant begged her to take them free of charge. It pleased her to see how many citizens of Valakut bore the white feather in their hair, expressing their completion of basic military training and proving their willingness to serve their realm. Too many times had she passed through a city of shaved heads and mourned their weakness, knowing that one day a Baku raid could claim them while the war council ponders saving those who choose not to save themselves.

As she strolled the streets to her destination, she would occasionally crush the shells in her hand and eat the nuts, all the while practicing her new power. The last few days, she had been trying to hone the new ability she saw affect the clay cup. It seemed she could use her essence to adjust the weight and density of an object and was training it by making the walnut heavy to hold, brittle enough that she could crack it open and then floating the contents weightlessly to her mouth.

Since first learning of her power, she had trained the application to become much more reflexive and exercised it daily by continuing to focus on keeping her weapons and armor lighter, without making them brittle. By the time she had reached Valakut from Akashra, she was able to sustain all of her equipment, as well as her horse's gear. This allowed them to make much better time in their final stretch.

She arrived at the massive archways that led to his palace. It was a truly amazing stead, showcasing sandstone sculptures, long waterways, and green, leafy trees. Oftentimes, the mirza would employ local soldiers or mercenaries as personal protection and this mirza was no different. Stationed on either side of his entrance were two officers of the realm, low ranking ones at least.

They each saluted Phori as she approached.

"I have business with Efrit-ali mirza," she stated.

"Yes ma'am," one said, entering the building while she waited with the other. He seemed nervous in her presence. The lowest ranking were often uneasy around her, but she was certain her new armor wasn't helping. Awkward silence passed for what seemed like forever and the absent soldier returned to his post and gestured for her to enter.

The foyer was grand indeed. White marble floors held massive pillars that stretched to the lofted ceiling above. Natural light seemed to enhance everything on the inside, as the gleaming white surface highlighted all of the silver, gold, art, and curtains of red silk. Standing before her was a middle aged man dressed in noble silks, with a thickly groomed beard and mustache. A white feather adorned his hair, marking him as a civilian who had completed basic military training. Down the hall behind him she noticed nearly a dozen women disappearing around the corner as they left the mirza's presence, each adorned in a variety of colored silks and golden jewelry. It was very common in Valakut for nobles to have multiple partners based on their wealth and status, and Efrit-ali seemed to have more than average.

"Brigadier General," he saluted. "How may I be of service?"

"You are Efrit-ali?" she asked as she scanned the room. There certainly weren't many places to hide should her target be here already.

"Indeed, I am." He seemed reluctant in her company. Nobles tended to offer food, drink, or comfort while in the presence of a highly ranked military official but he clearly wanted her business to tidy up quickly.

"Are you familiar with the criminal, Fever?" she asked.

"Certainly. You would be hard pressed not to find a posting on each corner." His curiosity had been roused and his eyes momentarily shifted as he recollected the many women in his palace, most of which wore decorative veils to cover their faces.

"I am going to be forward in asking if you know where she is." She was fishing for his reaction more than anything.

He was appalled by the insinuation that he was housing her knowingly. "Absolutely, I do not!"

Phori bowed and apologized. "If that is the case, then I feel your life may be in danger. I hereby charge myself with the protection of your wellbeing."

"What? You can't just hire yourself, I have plenty of guards." He hadn't taken well to her so far and would definitely rather take his risks with his hired help than have her follow him around all day.

She pointed to the weapon on her back and tilted her head to bring his attention to her feathered rank. "I can, and for several reasons. Pick your favorite." She stepped up, uncomfortably close, and bathed him in her fearsome aura, crushing his desire to contest. "Have you met any new women lately?"

He swallowed hard in her presence and stuttered in thought. "No, not in a while. I only arrived home from a visit to the capital last night."

This news was double edged. It meant Fever was probably not hiding within the harem, but it would force her to take a much stealthier approach to her assassination now that it was obvious she was being tracked. A sharp eye would have to be kept, as Fever's reputation was far too renowned to let Phori's presence discourage her from claiming her mark. For now, it was a waiting game.

★★★

Elder Waylander's stride up the Great Library's stone steps was both graceful and silent, a flourish of cloak and scarf amidst the flickering candles that led the way to the upper floors of engineering. He arrived to an open workspace with several benches and shelves for scholars to work at, and heard the voice of his son, Casamir, coming from the furthest end of the hall. Not to his surprise, Bastet was also here. He was a close family friend and often shared and defended Casamir's love for ingenuity.

"Father," Casamir bowed, a little embarrassed. He knew that if his father was taking the time to visit him while he was studying it was out of concern rather than interest. His father, though impressed in his own way, preferred more focus be placed on his meditation and application of energy, as to enlighten quicker. "Why are you here?"

Elder Waylander looked to Bastet and gestured for him to give them some privacy, to which he respectfully complied.

"I'm sorry about the bookshelves..." he began, certain the sages had spoken with him about the damages. "It won't happen again, I promise."

Waylander had still not spoken and instead approached the worktable. He examined the device as the gears and coils were organized from smallest to largest, running his hand along the edges of the steel.

"It's... um..." Casamir was very hesitant to explain it to him, not really knowing whether his father was expressing interest or disappointment. "High tensile bands, with a retractor. I designed it to be compact, though it would make a very interesting siege weapon at larger scale I think."

Waylander silently turned away and traveled further down the table, where blank scrolls of paper laid. To the touch, it was certainly different than anything he had felt, a strange combination of fibre and something silky.

"I call those 'Wet Glyphs'," he began. It was something he was very proud of and felt it would have significant application. "It's a paper designed to hold a single, precast enchantment. When you place the Wet Glyph against a surface, the stored enchantment transfers over."

Still no words were spoken, though Waylander spent more time looking the paper over. It would be hard to deny its usefulness.

"I thought it would save time channeling sigils, allowing a quick arsenal of precast enchantments to be used for tactical advantage. It would speed application and reduce energy usage when attrition is key."

Waylander looked to the end of the bench. A sheath fitted with a small brass halo, attached to a mess of copper wires and cranks lay abandoned. "And this?"

"Oh… that…" Casamir stuttered, clearly embarrassed. "That… explodes. Often." He laughed nervously. "It's not supposed to, of course. It just… does." It was a prototype weapon augmentation that would infuse an electric charge with the first strike from the sheath, but he was struggling to store the energy without consequence. As badly as he wanted to explain it, he was certain his father would have no opinion.

Waylander sighed and turned to him. "I don't want you to think I'm not proud of you, son." He gestured to the items on the workbench, namely the Wet Glyphs. "These ideas of yours are truly, very good."

Casamir sunk a little. Though it was an off compliment, it was hard to accept when he could feel the disappointment to follow.

"It's just that I am beginning to feel you have given up on your quest to enlighten."

"No..." Casamir replied shamefully. "I just... I feel I'm making more of a difference this way."

"I know in your eyes you look at these inventions and see future, but when I look at them I see fear. I see a young Waylander burdened with a destiny of greatness, who is too afraid of the commitment that entails. A young man, compensating for his fears of realizing himself by making his name that of *things* instead of spirit."

"I haven't been able to sense anything, in all my study. I don't know if I *can* enlighten. I don't know if I am capable of being the Waylander the world expects me to be. Why can't this be enough? What can't I be enough?"

"I am a Moth. Your grandfather was a Moth. His father was a Moth, and his father, and his father. You are the flesh and blood of six generations of honored greatness and are every bit as capable of reaching enlightenment as we were." Waylander approached Casamir and tried to place a hand on his shoulder, only to have him pull away.

"Maybe I can enlighten. Maybe I can't," he began, a fire burning in his eyes. Desperation, pride, and shame, all mixed together in a rousing brew of unusual self-confidence. "But either way, I don't need it to be worthy of *honored greatness*."

Waylander was a patient man of much experience, and allowed a moment to settle before continuing to speak. "You cannot be a Moth without enlightenment."

"I don't need to be a Moth to protect Lyre and I don't need to enlighten for my oath to the King to hold merit." It had been a long time since he had stood up to his father, but he knew he was a man of objectivity, if nothing else.

"We don't enlighten because we have to. We do because we want too, because we are the few who have it in their blood. It is a gift the world yearns for, yet only few truly receive. It is not gained from our needs, but our desires. You've lost your desire and until you find it you will only be using half the potential your bloodline can access."

"I *desire* to serve Lyre without enlightening."

"No, you *need* to prove that you can." Waylander turned and proceeded towards the stairs, stopping at the archway. "Something big is coming, son, and the world needs us to be Waylanders."

★★★

Cross delicately ran his fingertips across his waxen seal of white and red, being careful to mind his footing in the darkness of the fading city street lanterns. Andus had accompanied him once again as he made the journey across the district from the royal treasury to the cottage of the youngest and most experienced geomancer. The sealed parchment, freshly written and crisply cornered, held his written order. Cross had taken care to write it, as Fairchild had to approve and sign it as well. The suggestion of a trading post was a clever manipulation of his economic power, though he was well aware the King may not share his pride should he realize the abuse. He sneered as he imagined the confrontation and convinced himself Salem Eventide would have been praised had it been his idea. The idea of favoritism sickened him greatly.

Before long, the last of the daylight subsided, leaving only the yellow glow of lantern light to guide the way. The streets were slowly growing bare as the last of the merchants finished packing up their carts and wheeled them home, either by mule or the strength of their own shoulders.

Even as the evening grew more and more still with every footstep, Cross' eyes honed with more attention than usual. Since the first sighting of the shadow in the corner of his eye earlier that day, he had noticed it twice more. Though, the last sighting was before he had his writ signed and nothing had caught his eye since. Strange as it seemed, whomever was following him seemed to have given up surveillance, leading him to believe they found what they wanted, or had new orders to pursue. Either way, he wasn't terribly worried about it, but rather curious as to who cared enough to have him watched in the first place.

His focus quickly brought his eye to a small grouping of lights. Torches and lanterns held aloft by a group of people over the rise of the next hill. Within moments, the women and children fled into their homes, while some of the men dashed towards Andus in panic.

"Help!" one cried as he approached.

Andus laid his hand on the hilt of his sword, a silver gladius inlaid with the Whitewater crest in sapphire shell. "What is it?" He quickly began to run towards the crowd of people, half plate clinking, but not encumbering.

They arrived at the crowd, who parted to reveal the young geomancer Cross wished to rehire, hanging from a rope anchored to one of the gables. Blood streamed down the hanging man's face from a spider carved into his forehead, and nailed to his chest was a piece of bloody parchment that read, "We're coming."

Cross, wide eyed and breath taken, fought to collect his scattered thoughts and manage his shock as he watched the man's feet dangle and sway with the breeze.

Andus quickly turned around and dashed to the nearest street lamp, where he formed a sigil at the base that glowed the cool blue brilliance Whitewater was recognized for. In a matter of seconds, streams of energy burst from the glyph, traversed the length of the pole, and streamed a constant pillar of blue light into the sky. An illuminating signal to the other cloister guards and patrols.

"He hasn't been dead long..." Cross spoke to himself, noticing the blood still had some warmth, the body lacked rigor, and the sign had been nailed through his chest while still breathing. He pulled himself away and quickly burst through the door, taking in every room with every sense. Immediately, he caught the pungent scent of fresh ash and noticed a small copper bowl that slowly smoldered with a dying heat. He examined it closely, finding the cooling ashes of burnt paper and a small glob of wax that pooled in a filthy mess at the bottom. He blew on the wax to cool it down and carefully plucked it from the bowl, still soft and malleable. "Interesting..."

"What have you found, Chancellor?" asked Andus as he entered and secured the rooms to ensure no one else was inside.

"Wax," he replied. He then turned to Andus with grim realization in his eyes. "We must get to the other geomancer!"

18

LOVELY PSYCHOPATH AND THE ORDERS OF ORIGIN

Salem sat on a stone bench alongside the pond and accepted a piece of parchment from Rhoswan. The garden was still busy with preparations for the Gala, but the bench was private enough to have a delicate conversation about Grove.

"This is the report from the captain of the guard," she said as she released the letter. She had already given him the details of her findings thus far and wanted him to piece together the captain's investigative report. Or lack thereof.

Salem scanned the words and noted how fresh the ink was. "He just gave this to you."

"Shortly before you arrived," she replied.

He examined the folds and seal as well. "He has feelings for you, also."

Rhoswan wasn't surprised at the attraction, though she was at his conclusion. She knew better than to ask and remained quiet, knowing he would tell her anyways.

"The creases are crisp, the seal has been tidied, and the paper is free of dirt and smudging." He held it to the sky and allowed the light to permeate. "He took a great deal of care in writing this. Washing prior and allowing the ink time to settle before sealing it."

"He probably had a squire write it," she smiled coyly, attempting to debunk his theory out of pure bemusement.

Salem smiled back. "Please. No squire spells the word 'stead' without an 'a'." He gently folded the report and handed it back.

"Your mind is still sharp, I see."

An awkward laugh left his lips. He knew it was a compliment, but no one could really understand the curses that came with a process that never slept. He held a fresh bottle of wine from his sling and stared into the grass beneath his feet. "My mind is manageable at best, I dare say." His words had a very subtle hint of inner turmoil, which he immediately drowned with a drink before corking the bottle and letting it hang from his shoulder. "Barely. Though the drinking helps slow me down."

Salem held his fingertips together and rested his head on his thumbs. "I assume by the broken seal that you have read the report?"

She nodded.

"Well, Whisper and I will take a look. Not to discredit the good captain, I must simply see for myself." He arose from the bench. "She will return with the details. Save for the Gala, I will be unavailable in the evenings this week." He bowed his head and walked towards Whisper, who stood on the bridge and watched a bright orange carp lazily swim beneath her.

Rhoswan grew solemn as she watched him walk away. She knew his business and could already feel him detaching. He had done this in the past, the same time every year, and this was no different. Even the birds grew silent in his wake. Some things never change. Some ghosts never fade. Some demons are never slain.

A few long minutes passed and the wind began to slow. Trees began to blur as time trailed to a stop, leaving the Lady Rhoswan Gray alone on the stone bench.

A chattering began to arise from the trees and emerging from the temporal beyond was a man of uncontested power. His body was grotesquely deformed, with a multitude of bulges beneath his flesh, head to toe. He crooked over with the weight of a silken egg sac attached to his back and walked in short, ginger steps. This was the first Fate, Origin Progenitus, father of fatespinners, and the living nest from which they were born. He had only appeared to her twice before. The first was the acquisition of her power, as he chose her to become his Instrument. The second visit was the first and only thing he had ever commanded her to do, which she could only imagine he was checking up on.

"Have you been keeping a close eye on Salem Eventide?" he asked. Even as he spoke the power that blanketed her was immensely heavy. She recalled it being much more suffocating the first time though, which led her to believe her power had grown since his last visit.

"Yes, my Fate," she replied. "Though I still don't know what I'm looking for. Everything he has done has been to the benefit of the realm and its relations."

"Nothing unusual?" As he spoke, the occasional infant spider would break from the nest and crawl across his body.

"No, still overconfident and self-destructive. More so this week, as it is the anniversary of some loss." She pondered a question she dared to ask. "If Illy the Flux watches the Weave, why do you need *me* to watch Salem?"

The clouded eyes of Progenitus paralyzed her as he stared her down. "The purpose of an Instrument is to maneuver the Weave as necessary. By keeping you close to Salem, we are using you to softly influence him, whether you realize it or not. The Weave is a very busy, ever evolving creature. Your eyes on Salem allow Illy's eyes to focus on other endeavors."

"I apologize, I did not mean to bring Illy's capability into question. I was merely sateing a curiosity." Rhoswan felt a little embarrassed. She knew her role and felt their power. It was a bit foolish to expect information she hadn't yet earned. "Oh, he did come to Freestone with a mistborn though. Whisper."

Progenitus lazily swayed his head, giving the impression he was thinking, though she couldn't be sure. "You will watch both very carefully until I approach you again."

"It would help to know what I'm watching for. I don't understand why Salem is of such interest in the eyes of the Fates."

"He and his mistborn are of paramount interest, that is all you need to know. Under no circumstance are you to let them leave Freestone until I contact you next. Is that understood?" The egg sac rustled slightly and a fleshy tumor or two showed signs of something crawling beneath.

As appalling as his appearance was, his role was pivotal in the continuity of the world and was a genius in her eyes for creating the fatespinners in the first place. The synergy, energy, and intellect required to have made that a reality was awe inspiring, even at the cost of the form his power had produced.

"Yes, my Fate. They will not leave, lest you permit."

The soft chattering that sounded when he approached met her ears once again and slowly grew louder. As it permeated her head and grew unbearable, her perception of reality began to shake and distort, until, in a single instance, the sound disappeared and the trees rustled with the gentle breeze once more. Origin Progenitus was gone and time continued as though nothing had happened.

Salem stopped and turned his head to spot her over his shoulder, his eyes half closed with an air of suspicion.

"Is everything alright, Salem?" Rhoswan chimed politely.

"Yes," he replied as he turned to face Whisper at the bridge and continued walking. "I thought I heard someone say my name."

★★★

Salem and Whisper journeyed into the city together, admiring the sights as they walked to Grove's stead. The streets were lined with shops and cottages, all small buildings of wood and clay with thatched roofs that added much to their character. The people greeted Salem politely as they passed by. It seemed everyone knew who he was. Being in his company washed her in waves of adoration, as though she were of incredible importance simply by association. It was not the kind of attention she was used to and it embarrassed her a little.

Shortly before their arrival, a flock of beautiful women approached them, giggling bashfully as they curtsied. They were in lovely laces and fine cotton dresses, not quite of noble quality, but fancy by commoner standard. Whisper felt withdrawn by their presence, for reasons she wasn't quite sure of. What felt like irritation in the presence of their femininity slowly transformed into a thing of mild envy. She had never owned a dress before. Dresses were for women, and she was a warrior, though a softness within her would reveal itself once in awhile.

The woman at the head of the group was a pretty young blond, with curls that cascaded down her lace trimmings. "Ambassador Salem," she sung sweetly. They were certainly nervous in his presence and could barely stand the shimmering of his emerald eyes.

"Please, no need for formality," he smiled humbly.

Impatience churned within Whisper as she watched his charm envelope them. *Stupid girls and their stupid dresses.*

"There is a festival tonight, an opening celebration before your Gala," she shied. "We would be honored to have your company."

Whisper rolled her eyes and looked away.

"I apologize," he tipped his head gracefully. "As you can see, I already have company." He held out his arm and gently placed his palm on Whisper's back.

She was at a loss for words as the heat rushed to her cheeks. She was both surprised and relieved at his refusal, but equally confused. He couldn't be serious, could he? For the faintest moment, she wondered what she would wear.

The ladies looked upon her with an expression she hadn't seen before. Esteem. "My apologies," she bowed, embarrassed. "You have the most exotic and exquisite eyes I have ever seen, milady."

What was this? A compliment? What felt like a genuine one, at that. It was the first time anyone said that something about her was *exquisite* and it paralyzed her. She wanted to tilt her head and express the bashfulness she felt inside, but what came out was that of confusion and disbelief. "Thank you."

The young women curtsied once more and excused themselves, shuffling into the distance with their racing hearts and flushed skin.

Salem continued onwards to Grove's, they weren't far now. Whisper followed a few steps behind, arguing with herself the validity of his words.

Fortunately, he cleared the air first. "I apologize, dear Whisper. I will be preoccupied tonight." In truth, he could have simply declined the request without bringing her into it, but as he did with Rhoswan and her reputation as the White Haired Witch, perhaps he wanted to establish belonging for her. The seed was planted amongst the people of Freestone and before long, maybe she would be revered as *their* mistborn also.

Whisper veiled her disappointment with contempt. "That's fine," she lied. "I wouldn't have gone anyways."

He hid a smile as he approached the iron gate and unlatched it. His eyes took in every bit of information available, though it was exactly as Rhoswan described. The porch was clear, the door was sealed, and it appeared no one was home.

Whisper stood at the top of the steps and waited patiently as he remained motionless before the door. He held his fingertips together and seemed to be lost in thought. "Dear Whisper," he began. "Tell me what you think."

She didn't know where to start, other than the obvious. "Well..." she shrugged, knowing that if he was asking, there was probably something to find. She used her sharp eyes to carefully look over the doors and windows and examined the portions of interior she could see through the glass. Something had caught her attention. "There are boxes inside. Unopened parcels."

Salem nodded. "And what do you hear?"

Once again she wasn't great at listening, but she tried her best to focus. One by one, layer by layer, she slowly filtered out the conversations of the passersby. Then the footsteps. Finally the rustling of the leaves. All that remained was a constant clicking. It was very faint. "I think I hear a clock."

"Precisely." He smiled and praised her with his eyes. "I believe that someone has been inside the house within the day, as the clock has been wound." He traced his fingers across the edges of the door frame. "Whomever is within is not Grove and does not wish to draw attention to his absence. It explains why the parcels have been brought inside, but remain unopened." He stepped back from the door. "You will have to break it down."

She seemed surprised and looked at him suspiciously for reconfirmation. "You don't mind? With all of these people around?"

"It will be fine," he assured with a grin.

Hesitation briefly swept her, but his assurance was all she really needed. With a swift heel kick, she smashed the door open. As her foot connected, there was a brief flash of green that rippled across the surface before shattering like glass. She had seen a barrier exactly like this before when she infiltrated the Orbweaver sect in Whitewater.

Shockingly, Salem began to yell to the masses. "Guards! Guards! This woman is breaking into this house!" He pointed and hollered into the streets as guards patrolled in pairs further ahead. "Quickly! Arrest her!"

"What are you doing!?" she panicked, staring into him, both flustered and perplexed. She didn't know whether to snap his neck or flee the scene. Or both.

He met her nervous eyes and smiled cleverly.

"What's going on?" It was only then she began to notice that no one on the streets was paying them any mind. Even the guards sauntered by, ignoring them completely.

"I noticed after I opened the gate that there were tiny sigils hidden across the property. They are engraved into the cobblestone, trees, and fencing. A barrier to mundane perception, disallowing anyone on the outside to see or hear anyone on the inside."

Occult and the infinite uses it held never ceased to amaze her.

His attention returned to the interior of the house. "It means someone very skilled has gone to great lengths to shroud his movements." He entered into the small mudroom and briefly examined the other rooms at a distance before heading straight to the study. Whisper strafed into the adjacent rooms to ensure they were clear and then rejoined him when she was certain the floor was empty.

The study was small and cozy, with rows of shelves containing old books and texts, all ordered and organized meticulously. Salem was examining a particular section on the writing desk that was missing a codex. "Grove was an accomplished enchanter and had several volumes of techniques he would sell to the realm. These are the originals." He gestured to the leather bound ledgers, worn with experience that adorned the escritoire. "However, one is missing from this set, and this room." There was an empty space where two ledgers leaned against each other. "The originals are valuable and it would appear Grove was particular about order. I highly doubt it was misplaced."

"So, we need to find the ledger?" she asked, catching a faint smell that lingered in the air.

He didn't answer and tilted his head as he caught the scent as well. It was the pungent smell of decay, though subtle. They both began to scour the house for the origin.

Whisper tracked it first. She was much keener to the scent of blood and followed it to a cellar door hidden behind a cabinet. "I've found something," she called. Salem arrived as she slid the obstacle from their way and opened it.

Death filled their nostrils and choked them as they rushed to cover their mouths. The odor was intense, but not nearly enough to discourage them from their investigation. Salem lit a lantern and descended into the darkness, while Whisper trailed behind him. Though he didn't seem it, she could assume he was nervous. Doctors often confronted death, but not quite like this. There was an unmistakable danger here and though she should have been worried, instead, she was overflowing with the excitement of a potential confrontation.

At the base of the steps, engraved in the center of the stone cellar floor, was a large glyph with five pink crystals encircling it. Far in the corner was the source of their anguish a body, chained to the floor by the ankle, rotting in a bed of molding straw. Salem cautiously approached and examined it. He had been dead for some time now and at his feet lay two books, a quill, and dried ink. Upon closer examination, one was the ledger that was missing from the set in the study and the other was a curious edition titled *Envied Emerald to the East*. He picked them both up and briefly skimmed the pages for relevance.

Whisper looked at the many facets of the pink crystals. They sat, ever so peacefully, in what seemed to be an exact distance from each other.

"These seem familiar for some reason," Whisper said. She slowly extended a hand to touch one and felt a gentle hum vibrate the air. Within an instant, a pulse of dark energy exploded outwards and hurled her across the room. The stone wall buckled under her force and crumbled over her shoulders as she fell to a knee.

Salem rushed to her aid as the crystal powered down. "Are you okay?" His concern was somewhat flattering.

"Yes. It was nothing." She didn't have to act tough, it truly wasn't bad. The blast was sheer concussive force and nothing more. It would take far more punishment before she would come close to bruising. Much to her chagrin, though, she stood in a pool of her wine as it soaked her sleeve and dripped to the floor; shards of her clay jug lay broken at her feet. It was a heavy thing to lose a personal possession when you have so few to begin with.

Salem analyzed the crystals at a distance. "This will be a very big problem."

"What does it do? Besides that." She stood and brushed the rubble from her robes. Grumpily, she unfastened the remainder of the shattered jug from her shoulder and let it fall to the ground.

"I am not sure, yet. Perhaps our answer will be in this ledger." He wound it shut and secured both books firmly in his hands. "Unfortunately, it seems primed and impregnable with our meager skill."

"What does that mean?" she asked.

He sighed and nervously ran a hand through his hair. "It means that, whatever it is supposed to do, it is ready to do it, and there may be no way to stop it."

★★★

Vaexa carefully hung three strips of fabric, soaked in a blessed water, to dry in the warm air. Droplets pattered the floor as she hummed contently. She was in her own little world and managed to find a smooth pace at which to get her work done. The whole day passed in what felt like an instant and she was already working by the glow of luminescent moss they often cradled and cared for in small gardens built into the walls and ceilings. Were it not for her abnormally heightened senses, she wouldn't have heard Nuith enter Llaeilyer.

"Silly child," Nuith laughed and shook her head. Vaexa was still balancing the bowl of ink on her crown as she finished her chores.

Nuith liked to fuss about most things and Vaexa knew it. Had she removed the bowl earlier, thinking that her trial was complete, she probably would have been scolded for assumption. In balancing the bowl until instructed not to, she would only be teased for lacking common sense, and that was far more tolerable. Nuith rarely gave praise.

She felt the bowl lift from her head as Nuith placed it on the floor, alongside the other two. Everything was coming together nicely. The ink was thick and rich, the water was blessed, and the prayer strips were drying. As well, the other daily chores and duties were completed. Though it would never be said, Nuith was impressed. It wasn't as though she didn't care, she just had her own ways of appreciating the hard work of others.

"You may rest for the evening, child," she said softly. Vaexa knew it was her way of complimenting her efficiency and that she had earned some time to herself. "All that is left, is to wait for them to finish."

The most common place for the elders to carve a new Setsuhan was at the top of the mountain. For as long as they had known, the mountain had a chasm at its tip that led straight down into an unexplored abyss, and they believed it led to the heart. This made the stone at the breach sacred and had always been first choice. Save for her situation, of course. Luseca and Rhys had likely climbed the cliffs and were chiseling their successors from the mouth. In the overall, this made the process easier. Once they were complete, Vaexa and Nuith would join them at the peak, enchant the new vessels, and watch as Luseca and Rhys leap into the darkness to relinquish their energies back into the mountain. If all went according to plan, their souls would immediately enter their new forms and a new life cycle would begin. If they were lucky, the last heart would join them in their rebirth as well, but they were beginning to lose faith in the idea. Reattempting each year was becoming a tenacious formality as the hope dwindled. For most of them, anyways.

Nuith bustled quietly about Llaeilyer and fixed her nesting as she prepared to sleep. Vaexa lay at the other end of the room and watched the hearts sway above them. She felt lonesome. Something within her chest was begging for the static to return, but as she lay in wait nothing happened. Whatever it was that caused it, it wasn't listening to her quiet prayer and left her feeling incomplete. It was a feeling she had periodically ever since the last heart vanished, as though her body needed the lightning to remind her she was alive. Perhaps it was why she was so reckless or why she rode so fast. A passive means to fill her body with the electric feeling only adrenaline could bring, to supplement the random occurrences that hooked her like a drug.

The anxiety slowly wrapped around her, squeezing her chest, and all she could think of was sneaking away for a ride with Selva. His sense of spirit was enlightening, and without it she was sinking like a stone. She sat up and peered around in the dim phosphorescence. Nuith lay still as she rested at the other end, and Vaexa carefully rose, as not to wake her.

***

Crickets filled the evening air as Phori lounged on a soft chair alongside the mirza's bed. He had been incredibly reluctant to her proposal of watching over him in the night, but was powerless to contest. The chamber held a bed that would have likely had many of his women in it with him were it not for her presence. Though the majority of the palace was fashioned from marble and stone, his room was made of rich woods, giving it a darker, more comfortable mood. The dim candlelight shimmered across curtains of satin and cast shadows from the fronds of large, exotic, potted plants.

She had been waiting here for hours, thus far. Driven to the brink of madness as the mirza snored incessantly on his back. The whole house was asleep and she pondered other ways she could catch Fever without having to remain awake until then.

Another hour passed and she presumed there were only a few more until dawn. The soft cushion of the chair was beginning to claim her and her eyes slowly relaxed. She was caught in the weightlessness of comfort. Drifting away, anchoring herself only to the sounds of the room. Immediately, her eyes shot open. The mirza's breathing became labored and she quickly stood to examine him.

Beads of sweat began to form as he panted in his sleep, mouth wide open.

She was at a loss for how this could be. No one had entered and Fever couldn't have made her move in the brief moments she closed her eyes. She began to search the room when she heard the faintest sound. A drop of something landed in the mirza's mouth. He shifted and smacked his lips, continuing to sleep. Her attention darted upwards, where she saw a string hanging from a tiny hole in the ceiling. An inexpensive yet highly technical assassin's technique, where a cotton strand would be lowered and positioned above a victim and poison would be carefully poured down the thread to drip directly into the mouth.

Upon sight of the string, she heard soft feet dash above her, retreating to the marble halls outside. She quickly pursued and filtered through her options, though she wasn't sure she had any. It would be far too difficult to give chase while Fever was in the ceiling, which led her to a terrible idea. She stood at the open stretch of hall and placed her hand against the wall, channeling her energy up to the marble above. This was a gamble, as she wasn't sure if she could affect the single portion of stone without affecting the rest of the mansion.

She envisioned enforcing her will through the stone. She imagined the gossamer threads of her intent sprawling from her open palm, demanded they traverse the stretch of hall, commanded them to tear the ceiling asunder. The mark on her neck began to burn, the whites of her eyes blotted with red as vessels burst within. A deep growl rumbled through her throat to drown the sound of her grinding teeth. Finally, she could feel it. The assurance her energy was where she wanted it, the confidence she could snap the marble with sheer force of will. Her hand clasped shut and the ceiling came crashing down before her in a spectacular rain of powder and stone. Every muscle in her body told her to collapse from the strain, but amidst the debris, staggered and surprised, was a woman clad head to toe in dark fabric.

Without hesitation, Phori rushed in to engage her, swinging her bladed staff so only the flat of the blades would connect. A flash of steel caught the ambient light as the woman parried with a small dagger in each hand. The combination of force from the staff and unstable footing sent her tumbling backwards.

The woman tried to spring to her feet, but her hand was pinned to the floor beneath the weight of her dagger's hilt. Phori had channeled her energy through her strike, and as the woman parried, the density of her dagger had been adjusted. She viciously struggled to lift the hilt from her hand as her fingers grew numb, but was unsuccessful.

Phori harnessed the staff to her back and towered over her catch. She was furious with herself for not being vigilant enough to prevent the death of the mirza, but managed to push her wounded pride aside enough to remain fairly objective. "Fever?"

The woman stopped struggling and seemed to admit defeat. She hung her head and pulled the hood from her face with her free hand. Sinister blue eyes, supple red lips, thick, wavy, golden hair. Everything Phori had expected. Even her voice sung like a singing bowl. "A Brigadier General. My my, I certainly have been sinful."

Phori crouched before her, giving enough distance that she couldn't be reached in case there was something up her sleeve. "You have caught the attention of a Fate, and she would like you to be her Instrument."

Fever winced as she struggled with her hand and then allowed a smile to stretch across her lips. "You don't 'eem happy about that, love."

"Is it that obvious?" Phori sneered as she outstretched her palm, a tiny white spider formed from translucent threads that pulled themselves from the air itself. "I'd be content in leaving you here to lose your hand and watch you squirm before the Phoenix Queen. Prosecuted for your travesties, suffering your castigations." She had decided to refer to the malikah as the Phoenix Queen in case Fever wasn't from Emberwilde. It was uncommon for someone with their lineage to have blue eyes, but it wasn't unheard of. "Fortunately for you, you have a higher calling."

Fever delighted in Phori's moral struggle and felt inclined to take the offer simply to bask in it further. Sparing her hand was also a very good incentive, mind you, but the bulk of her desire to comply was for the infamy alone. Being a taboo whispered on the lips of Emberwilde was invigorating, but one on the lips of the world, justified and honored by a supreme being... she would be immortalized.

"I accept." Her voice was a melody of entitlement and conceit as she reached for the spider, all the while not breaking eye contact with Phori. Provoking her. Challenging her. Waiting to see who would blink first.

The spider crawled onto her hand and bore into her palm. Phori grinned and prepared to watch Fever's smug expression change with the intensity of the brand.

The spider crawled beneath her skin and traveled down her collarbone to her side, but instead of bellowing in grievous agony she broke into a sweat that flushed her skin with color. Her face grew red with the intense pain, but from her lips were short breaths and moans of ecstasy. Sweat dripped across her brow and dampened her hair as she clawed beneath her shirt. She lifted the fabric from her stomach and watched intently as the mark of the black spider stretched across her left ribcage. The spindly legs stopped left of her breast and she sighed in deep relief. Her eyes rolled into the back of her head as she smiled, biting her lower lip and resting her fingertips on her chest.

Phori shook her head in disbelief and begrudgingly lightened the dagger to release her hand. She hated Fever even more so now and added the murderous masochist to her growing list of scores she needed to settle.

Fate or not, Ivory's plan to put destiny back in the hands of the common man was raising questions. An Emberwilde official, a renegade Baku, and a psychopathic assassin, hardly the conventional ingredients to saving the world, and Ivory still had much of her hand yet to show.

★★★

The cool evening air briskly licked Vaexa's skin and carried with it the soft aroma of the lemongrass grove. It was a long walk she was used to riding, but the solitude brought her a little peace. In the darkness the tall grass was a spiny silhouette in which to lose one's self, and that she did. She wandered to the grass she and Selva had pressed while playing and collapsed to her knees, clutching the sweet bundles to her face. She hadn't cried all day, but the sorrow had been building. She curled into a small ball and wept.

'Why?' She pleaded softly. Life was barely worth living without Rhys, but a world without Selva... It was a fate worse than death. Who would she race with? Who would she explore with? He was her friend, her companion, her love. He taught her to play, nurtured her spirit.

She turned onto her back and continued to clutch the bundle of lemongrass to her chest. The sky was empty. A dark stretch of absence far beyond the soothing scent of lemongrass. It was exactly how she felt. A ghostly reminiscence of what she had, set before the infinite abyss of nothingness. She could still hear Selva's voice.

"Never stop rolling in the lemongrass" she whispered. She held the bundle tighter and continued to cry. *How could I ever again?*

19

DIAMOND IN THE ROUGH, LAMENT OF DELRIS

Lady Rhoswan delicately swept a lock of hair behind her ear and admired the warm glow of a stone lantern as it shone across the surface of her pond. A chubby white carp, speckled in black, lazily broke the water and submerged again.

She had changed into a shimmering dress of a similar black and white pattern, trimmed with tiny feathers and long sleeves that hung around her bare shoulders. It was an evening of celebration mere days before the Gala, and she wanted nothing more than to turn every head. As she prepared herself to depart from the pagoda, sipping a half glass of peach brandy, a figure on the bridge caught her eye.

Whisper, sullen and irritated, carried a Whitewater soldier over her shoulder. She hadn't seen Whisper since she had reported Salem's findings earlier that afternoon, after of which, she had promptly vanished.

Whisper flopped the soldier's unconscious body onto the soft grass and adjusted her stained sleeve, red wine from her broken jug.

"Oh my…" Rhoswan stood at the soldier's side and peered down at him. "What happened?"

Whisper gave a soft brush of her hand and waved off the concern. "I asked him to help me train. He'll be fine."

"Does something trouble you?"

Whisper looked down into the pond and carefully collected her words. "I've learned more about the world this last week than I had in eighteen years at the monastery," she began.

Rhoswan laughed softly. "I learn something new every time Salem and I meet as well."

"May I ask... what are your opinions of the Fates?" Whisper seemed genuinely invested in the topic and eagerly open for the perceptions of another. "In the Monastery, I learned that the Fates watch over us to protect us all from ourselves, but Salem told me they also chose to destroy a whole species simply because they couldn't be controlled."

The Lady Rhoswan gently nodded and swirled the amber liquid in her hands before passing it to Whisper. "Please, taste this and tell me what you think."

Whisper pressed the glass to her lips and took a sip. It trickled over her tongue and warmed her palate with perfect undertone and depth. "It's amazing," she replied, passing the glass back.

"This has been hand crafted from a simple peach," Rhoswan explained as she gestured out to the endless flowing stretch of blossoms. "People of the world are like peaches. Some of us are sweet, some sour, and some rot from the inside out, but with care and cultivation the future of these peaches may be that of exquisite, immortalized refinement. I am like a Fate to my groves, choosing which will be used and for what. I nurture them, protect them, and craft their potential."

"But do they need to be? Perhaps a peach simply wishes to be a peach." Whisper struggled with the cuteness of what she was trying to say.

"Unprotected they are devoured by birds. Untended they nest wasps. Uncultivated they grow wild. And unpicked they simply fall to the worms. I like to believe that a peach in my grove is far better than a peach with no one to care for it."

"I suppose..." Whisper took a deep breath. "I suppose I'm just unhappy with the idea that I have no control of my life. I can't be the greatest fighter, I can't find purpose, and I can't even find the man who took my family unless it's what the Fates decide *they* want for me."

"The Fates decide what's best for all of us. If they were to deprive you of the future you want, it would only be because attaining it would have strong negative consequences. It's the concept of *your future* versus *your best future*." Rhoswan sipped the last of her brandy and held the cup aloft until a maid came to claim it.

"And people just... trust?"

"Faith," she nodded. "It is what keeps our future's bright and allows us to find meaning in hardship."

Whisper nodded as she let Rhoswan's perception settle. As much as she despised the idea of faith, she warmed with the feeling that everything she had gone through would somehow serve a purpose she was not yet aware of, something that would make her life better. Heavy thought was something she was not yet used to and was quickly making her tired. "Where is Salem tonight?"

Rhoswan shifted uncomfortably. "I'm afraid he has prior engagements this evening. Best not to bother him."

Whisper crossed her arms and sulked slightly. A small part of her figured he had gone to the festival with some pretty young thing, though she couldn't shake how he rejected the young woman's proposal earlier that day. Since then, she found herself disoriented. A nimbus of unusual emotion. Perhaps it was the loss of her wine jug, the irreversible staining of her robe, or that the so called pride of Whitewater's military spent more time unconscious than he did awake, but something accented a feeling that sprung forth without control.

"Is there a woman in Salem's life?" She regretted the words the moment they slipped from her mouth.

Rhoswan carefully smoothed the wrinkles of her dress. "You mean to ask if he is in a relationship? No, he is not."

Whisper didn't know what to think, but since she had already professed interest, she figured she may as well continue. "I don't understand. I've seen him flocked by many beautiful women since Whitewater and yet he expresses no interest."

"Salem is a man of... distraught origin, best not to understand, but accept."

"Distraught?" she huffed. Distraught was having your family murdered. It was emerging into a foreign world, alone, after eighteen years of isolation. It was being branded a monster for being different. She was certain he had no entitlement to the word. Not with his noble clothes, wealthy estate, and prestigious status. "The man has everything and could have anyone."

Rhoswan neither smiled nor laughed at her childish ranting, but instead, approached her with heavy eyes and placed a hand over her heart. The irrational emotions quickly fled with the warm connection and she took a deep breath.

"You have to ask yourself this," Rhoswan began, "Why would a man who could have anyone, choose to have no one?"

The words continued to cycle through her head, over and over, even as she took her leave and strolled the streets of Freestone to ease her mind. Everyone was aflutter with excitement as they sang and socialized, dressed in handsome suits and pretty dresses, noble and common folk alike. Beautiful music resonated amongst the happy smiles and drunken laughter, but she couldn't bring herself to care.

As she ventured further from the bustle of festivity and the joyous people grew fewer and further apart, she arrived a small house. Candlelight flickered through one of the windows. Before she had set into town, she had convinced Rhoswan to tell her where Salem lived, and it wasn't what she expected.

It was much smaller than she imagined, with an old sign at the gate that used to advertise it as a clinic. A single story home with an attic and yard of simple grass. A large bittersweet grove draped brilliant violet and golden leaves over the walkway. She hadn't seen a single bittersweet since Salem first showed her days ago and it was truly astonishing to be in the presence of.

She was ascending the steps when she heard the loud crash of shattered glass pierce the air from within the home. Immediately, she rushed to the doorway and threw it open. The strong scent of patchouli immediately struck her senses. It was the same smell she recalled in her encounter with the demon summoner, Kalen, back in Whitewater.

From the hazy darkness of the corner, gently licked by the light of ambient flame, Salem sat in a chair with his head slumped. She briefly noticed something white shimmer against the light as it vanished up his sleeve, but even with her eyes, the motion was too quick and fluid to catch what it was.

"Why are you here, dear Whisper?" His voice was slow and slurred, tangled in drunken misery and burdened with despair. The darkness of the room seemed to wrap around him, pulling his shoulders towards the floor.

She carefully checked her surroundings to be sure he hadn't fallen victim to an Orbweaver invasion. The interior of his home was professionally set as a medical clinic, with comfortable chairs, a padded table, and shelves of equipment and supplies. There was no bed, but it looked as though he may have slept on the examination table from time to time.

Whisper entered the room and closed the door quietly, being careful to avoid the flecks of shattered glass that spread to the doorway from a broken bottle of liquor that bled down the adjacent wall.

"Is... is everything alright?" she asked as softly as the jaded could. 'Supportive' wasn't something she had much experience with.

Salem didn't raise his head to look at her, but instead reached for another bottle of something dark and pressed it to his lips. "I asked you why you were here."

"I remembered where I saw the pink crystals before," she said as she sat in a chair across from him. "It was in Whitewater. They were laying on the floor when I confronted Kalen. The same time and place I first smelled this smoke too."

"Chthonomancy," he replied gruffly. "In Grove's cellar, I caught the hint of musk and patchouli amidst the blood and decay. A very common combination in the vile art." Even though he could manage complete sentences, his eyes pressed in long drawn blinks as his head gently swayed. He feebly attempted to gesture to a small stone bowl of patchouli on a trivet. The mossy smoke rose in thick plumes from the smoldering resin.

She shrugged her shoulders, this was the first she had ever heard of such an art. "Is that like necromancy?"

"Similar." He reeled as he drank again, this time from a small square bottle that definitely didn't look like it was for imbibing. Streams of the liquid slid down his chin and dripped onto his clothing. "Necromancy is the dark art of the undead. Chthonomancy is the blood art of damnation." He lazily swung his hand and gazed into nothingness with eyes half open. "Demons, devils, and the such."

Though she was interested in the new pieces of their puzzle, she struggled with ignoring his present state. She had always recognized his reliance on wine, but had never expected a man of such control to, well, lose it.

"Why are you drinking like this?" She gestured to the cold atmosphere of his clinic. A world apart from the celebration beyond his walls.

The shadows of the room seemed to shade his eyes as he straightened his back and continued to hang his head low. The candles dimmed and a cool emptiness brushed across them, gently crushing the wind from her lungs. The stillness was nearly maddening as it wound with forlorn and tribulation, reminded to breathe only by the low, ominous sound of his voice.

"A blissful hallow harrowed, my feral fervor frost.
Recant, the eyes that pulled you in.
Obliterate the lost.
To rob you of our life, and thieve my love, my word, my name.
A rake upon the coals, a bleeding heart of wax and flame.
A tome of pages, burnt to ash, a long forgotten verse.
The silver blaze of power cannot balance with the curse.
The solitude of quietus, a thistle in the breath.
Eternal, faceless wandering;
a ruin, worse than death."

A heavy silence forced a deep breath. The candlelight remained on the verge of extinction.

"A Snow Leaf verse, written by a Setsuhan named Delris," he said softly, the glass groaned against his fingers as he clutched the bottle tighter. "Right after he…" His voice trailed off. "It sounds incredible in the original Setsuhan dialect."

"What happened to Delris?" she asked.

"I am sorry, dear Whisper, my stories are tragic."

"I understand not all stories are happy, especially yours, but I am more than strong enough to hear them." She had never wanted to help someone like this before.

He raised his head and met her with emerald anguish. "It is not *your* spirit I fear breaking under the weight of the words, dear Whisper."

'Why would a man who could have anyone, choose to have no one?'

The words resounded in her head as she looked into his glossy green eyes. On the surface he was absent and withdrawn, but deep beneath, he roiled with torment and crawled across broken glass. *'Having something close means having something to lose, and some people have lost too much.'*

★★★

The Lady Rhoswan stood at the entrance of her pagoda and smiled as she watched a nobleman cross her bridge with a small wooden box in his hands. Placing her palms together she bowed. "Welcome."

The nobleman bowed in return and presented to her the small wooden box she had seen so many times before. "Lady Rhoswan, what does a wren weigh?"

She carefully lifted the lid to gaze upon the polished silver bars within. "A pound, of course." The sheen of the silver glistened in the red light of hanging lanterns to each side of her. She closed the lid and accepted his gift, holding it out to her side until one of her servants took it. "I am honored you would choose to spend your night at my Aviary in lieu of the gala celebrations."

"I have traveled nearly all of Elanta, milady, and there is truly no night better spent than in the company of your birds."

Rhoswan laughed coyly and looked deep into his eyes. "I am but an emissary between desire and reality."

His lips stretched into a large smile as he looked beyond her and saw many beautiful women approach from the foyer of the pagoda – giggling in wait. Their light, airy gowns covered enough to remain classy, yet showed enough to inspire the imagination.

"Please," Lady Rhoswan began sweetly as she turned and gestured for him to enter. "My birds await you."

20

IVORY'S DELIGHT AND THE ENVIED EMERALD TO THE EAST

The dry heat of arid mountains quickly cooled with the evening winds, bringing the salty scent of the ocean from far below the sheer western cliffs of Valakut. From her window on the second floor of the inn, Phori rested her elbows on the sill and allowed the evening to rejuvenate her spirits. Though she removed her armor, she had yet to remove the silks and wear something more comfortable. The cooling air tingled her skin and fueled her procrastination further.

"How much longer now?" Sung the sultry voice of Fever from behind, who was fixing the waves of her golden hair in the sheen of polished steel.

Phori hung her head and sighed. The grace of the evening, the freshness of the ocean, the orange groves far in the distance, all lost in her overwhelming frustration with this... convict. "She is coming," she replied. "I can feel her approach."

The shadows of the room began to sequester the ambient daylight and drown all color with a scale of grays. Phori hadn't noticed it during her first encounter with Ivory, but as she continued to watch out the window, time began to slow to a stop. Birds in flight hung frozen in the sky, while chimney smoke lingered like ghostly strands of tangled gray silk.

Fever's sultry eyes glistened with excitement and intrigue as she watched the shadows pool and could barely contain her glee as Ivory ascended from the ichor of darkness. With no regard, she immediately approached and ran her fingers along the purity of white ivory with which she was crowned, slowly making her way down to the intricate silver threads that wove the web across her chest.

Phori averted her eyes at the subtle eroticism Fever was known for, though it seemed Ivory loved the attention.

"Welcome, my Instrument," Ivory said, smiling. The webs across her irises were joyously pristine in what little light remained and contrasted vividly against her form. A graceful figure in shades of gray and white, with eyes so blue they suffocated all desire to look away.

Fever took a step back and curiously examined the wispy threads that swayed in the cloud beneath her dress, wondering to herself whether Ivory was truly floating. "You are exquisite," she sung softly.

"Let's get to the point," Phori interjected. "What do we do now?"

Though she imagined Ivory would look upon her sternly, instead, she met her with eyes of clever delight. She then turned and melted into a stream of shadowed smoke, traversing the room only to reappear at the table a few short feet away. "I am so elated!" she flirted as she rested her elbows on the surface and leaned towards them both. She began to walk her slender fingers across the grain, turning each groove into a river of tiny diamonds. "You may not know it yet, Fever, but you have a fantastic power."

Ivory disappeared in a stream of smoke once more and appeared behind Fever, resting back to back and leaning her head on her shoulder. Her long hair swayed and caressed Fever from head to toe, as though it had a mind of its own. "You are my new favorite."

Phori crossed her arms. She truly didn't care who was better than the other, but rather, she knew Ivory was playing and basked in the tension. "I must return to my post in Akashra in the morning."

It was tormenting how both Fever and Ivory's eyes gleamed with amusement at her rigidity. "Now, now," Ivory chanted. She spanned the room once more and appeared beside Phori, gently caressing her arm with a scroll of vellum sealed with the blazing red crest of the Phoenix Queen. "You trusted me and did exactly as I asked. I believe loyalty deserves to be rewarded."

It had been a very long time since she had seen such a seal. The malikah's High Court was the highest of governing bodies in the realm of Emberwilde, serving as the first and final word of law between the Phoenix Queen and every other living creature within her influence. Oftentimes, her orders would be passed down through her superiors until they reached her. An order directly from the Court was exceedingly rare.

Both bewildered and curious, she slid her finger beneath the wax and rolled the scroll open, only to shake her head in disbelief. "This is a summoning. To Obsidian."

Ivory smiled amorously. "Also known as the Palace of Roiling Cinder, home of the Phoenix Queen herself, and war chamber to the greatest and most powerful generals in Emberwilde in times of war, of course."

Phori continued to read in silence, allowing every word to betray all logic with disbelief. "I'm to serve as general to an army of Obsidian. How is that possible?"

"I am a Fate, love." She gently brushed her hand along the edge of vellum, and like that of all-consuming flame the lambskin slowly crumbled into a handful of white diamond sand that rained at their feet. "Through me, all things are possible."

Phori gazed endlessly into the multitude of tiny facets as she cradled a small pile of the diamonds in the palm of her hand. "But why?"

Ivory swayed to the window. "There is a hunger in the mist beyond Elanta. A hunger that will soon attempt to consume us all."

"What do you mean?"

"Soon, though I do not know exactly when, this hunger will fall upon the world. The chaos that will ensue will be pertinent in my plan to free the people from the dictations of the Weave – an unexpected and necessary chaos to distort the lawful order of the Fates. Though I intend to use this to my advantage, it is not actually in my interests to have Elanta suffer. It saddens me deeply to say, but the great city of Valakut will fall to ruin when the hunger comes. Nothing would put me more at ease than to have one of my Instruments at the front of Emberwilde's greatest army."

"Valakut will fall? If that's true then we must begin evacuating the civilians immediately!" Phori was abhorred by the sudden news and still wasn't certain she believed it.

"We cannot," Ivory replied. "The demons in the mist will strike several cities at once. If even one were empty or over-fortified they would become suspicious and we would lose our advantage."

"You expect me to sacrifice one of Emberwilde's greatest cities to maintain an advantage?"

"Yes," she replied. "This world's freedom is neither cheap nor free. When the demons blindside the people of Elanta, the Fates and their Instruments will be forced to intervene. They will be divided. They will be confused. They will be vulnerable."

Phori shook her head. "You have given me crucial military intelligence that could save thousands of lives. To keep this to myself is dishonorable to my malikah, let alone treason to my nation. Generals don't become generals because they turn blind eyes to conflict."

"You're wrong," spoke Fever, who stood in cold, stern stillness. "Having the grit to sacrifice the few to save the many is exactly what makes them generals in the first place."

"And what would you know?"

"More than you'd think." It was clear in her eyes that Fever knew something Phori did not, but amidst the overwhelming new information it was of much lower priority.

"Forgive me, Ivory, but I'm not certain I am fit to be your Instrument," Phori began. "Your plan leaves me with more questions than answers and I find the lack of clarity to be disconcerting. You speak of war, and not just one but two. It is a travesty to even think of sacrificing innocent lives when there must be another way."

The shadows flexed as Ivory basked in the inner turmoil. Moral struggles like this didn't exist for Fates, and it was fascinating to watch Phori unravel. The deep brilliance of her blue eyes contrasted so sharply against the gray of everything else that it hypnotized the room, commanding their full attention. "A war will come whether you want it or not, because if we wish to claim our destinies from the hands of the Fates, we must do so when they are most distracted. By interfering needlessly, you will endanger the people of Emberwilde, but most importantly, your Queen. My plan is carefully constructed to preserve as many people as possible, but my grace is not free. It requires a sacrifice of pride, not flesh."

Honor bound, Phori was perpetually defiant.

"You claim to be unfit as my Instrument because your heart wishes to protect your people, but that is the exact reason I chose you. You would raze any village to save your realm, slay any man to protect your Queen. You even chose to give yourself to me, an unknown entity of unfathomable direction, simply to save a handful of soldiers from the Ravenmane." Ivory pulled them in close with a smile. "You are exactly what Elanta needs, General Phori, and we will save more lives together than you will alone."

Phori averted her eyes and focused intensely on the groves in the distance, allowing herself time to think of how accepting her new position could help her protect her malikah. War was coming, making foresight and alliance crucial in the preservation of her people, and a force influenced by a Fate was something formidable.

"I will go to Obsidian to serve my Queen, but only because I feel it is the best strategy. I will contemplate your plan as I travel and decide when I arrive," Phori replied sternly. "Whether you want me as your Instrument or not, I reserve the right to protect my honor and seek wisdom within myself."

For the first time, Ivory stopped smiling, as though it were a rebellion she had not expected.

"I may be a vessel of your power and I may be important to your plan, but know this, and know this well, I serve only my malikah."

Ivory pursed her lips and tilted her head, noticing in her peripheral as Fever took a half step back in the tension. "The choice may feel like yours to make, but remember, so long as we Fates exist you have no free will. I have predicted your future, I have influenced your destiny, and no matter what you do you will fulfill your waypoints as I have seen them. So contemplate if you must. Refer to your inner wisdom, but know in your heart that you do not get to choose your path. No one in this world does. To break the shackles that bind the world you must accept the shackles that bind yourself. Be my Instrument, as together we will ensure no mortal will be forced to be something they do not want to be ever again."

★★★

Whisper was silent, and the most uncomfortable she had ever been. Helplessness was a feeling she dreaded, and at that moment she was drowning in it. It filled her lungs as her body ached.

"I'm sorry Salem," She stood awkwardly, determining whether she should leave or remain in silence. "I think I'll be going," She quietly walked to the entrance and pulled the door open a crack, when his hand pressed against it from over her shoulder and she turned to face him. His arm held most of his weight as his dizzy body drifted close to hers, until his forehead rested gently on her shoulder.

"Sometimes, you make me feel like I can move on," he said.

Her skin became hot and flushed, and though her normal response would have been to push away, instinct closed her eyes and let her fall into it. She wrapped her arm around him and gently rubbed his back.

"Wait," he said quietly as his mind and body flickered back into reality.

At this point, she wasn't sure if they were having a moment or if he had blacked out and was resting on her to keep from falling.

"You said there were pink stones amongst the Orbweavers." He seemed on the verge of a realization, but she couldn't help but feel robbed. "The crystals in Whitewater, they were laying on the ground?"

She crossed her arm and held her shoulder as she leaned against the door. Salem turned and walked to the examination table, laying on it as his eyes went blank with thought.

"Yes," she said, a little wounded. "They weren't set up like the ones we saw today, though."

"Something had been troubling me since that day you confronted Kalen in Whitewater." He shifted, dropping the bottle and placing his hands on his head to help him concentrate. "The circle required to summon that demon required time, of which he would not have had when you burst in. This led me to believe someone informed him of your arrival ahead of time, someone with quick access to the warrants and decrees of the King."

Whisper entered the room once more and sat down to listen. Though she was uncomfortable, she was interested in hearing what he had deduced.

"However, when I read the incident report, there was no mention of the crystals found in the wreckage."

"They were there, I saw them." She felt defensive, as though he were offhandedly accusing her of lying.

"I trust you. I believe someone took them before the sweep, or even during, perhaps."

"The commander and a unit of guards were there the whole time."

"Precisely!" His eyes were still fogged and drowning as he struggled to keep his focus. "It means whomever warned the Orbweavers was also in a position to take or hide the stones without being noticed. The Orbweaver mole must have been someone from that unit." He stared at the ceiling with cutting intensity. "Or there were multiple moles, but we will assume one and build from there."

Whisper thought carefully of the events that transpired that night, when she recalled something unusual. "The scout," she started. "Agent... Dask, I think it was... He had gone ahead to secure the grounds before our arrival and only appeared to report at the last minute. The commander scolded him for being late."

The deeper Salem delved into his theory, the more sober he seemed to become. "Dask certainly has the skill to get away with such acts, should he be our Orbweaver insider. However, he was also hand chosen by the Judiciar, which might implicate Alexander Tybalt as well. If the cultists indeed infect so highly in our ranks, it could explain how they are frequently several steps ahead of us."

"If Dask and Tybalt took the crystals, then they could have set them up and activated them by now, like the ones at Grove's." She wasn't sure what her revelation meant yet, but it couldn't be good.

Salem gracelessly sat up from the table. "The ledger." He slowly slid off and staggered across the room to the disheveled escritoire, shuffling through stacks of papers and books. He returned and opened the leather bound ledger from Grove's cellar.

"This particular volume we found highlights the fundamentals of energy and their cyclical nature in high concentration." He seemed so focused, but she had no idea what he was talking about. The pages within were a collage of calligraphy and unusual sketches.

"I really don't understand," she said.

"Enchanters were going missing because the Orbweavers needed them to design the ritual necessary to prime the crystals. With the research in this book, I think I know what they were doing." He stood and ran his sticky hands through his hair. "This whole time I assumed it had something to do with dark arts, but, in fact, they were making a containment glyph. Primed to absorb and seal extreme amounts of energy."

"What good does that do?"

"According to his notes, a high enough concentration of contained energy would result in a funnel effect. To what end, I am not yet sure." He closed the ledger and placed it on the table.

"Maybe the other book you found has some information we can use."

Salem shook his head and failed to conceal the twitching of an eye. "Much to my irritation, I have no idea what that book is, or why Grove had it."

Whisper stood and collected the book from the chaos of Salem's desk. "Envied Emerald to the East," she read aloud, opening the book and examining the first few pages. "It's just a bunch of poorly written text about the jungles in Shén Shé."

"Exactly. Nothing about energy, occult, or anything pertinent to our investigation."

She shuffled further into the book, when something of interest caught her eye. "Did you notice some pages have unusual letters?"

Salem hopped down and staggered to her side, looking over the page with absurd scrutiny. "I don't see anything unusual."

She pointed to one of the letters, in one of the words. "The edges along this letter are smoother than the others and the shade is slightly darker."

Even with her pointing it out he still couldn't tell. "It is amazing your eyes can perceive such minute detail." He smiled and claimed the book from her. "Excellent work, dear Whisper!"

Awash with pride, she couldn't help but smile.

"I will need you to go through the whole book and mark which letters stand out."

Her smile quickly fled.

"But first, we must send a raven to Whitewater immediately, to warn them of the potential Orbweaver spy and let them know the circle could be active somewhere in the city."

Salem shuffled to the door and fumbled with his coat as he awkwardly tried to thread his arms into the sleeves.

She wanted to demand he stay and rest, but didn't want the terrible chore of reading the book for him either. A little exercise seemed in order, and at the very least it would keep his mind on the case and off the bottle.

***

Luseca peacefully sat on a stone and gazed into the misty sky. This far up the mountain, the thickly treed landscape turned into a cool, desolate rock face. It had been nearly seven days since she and Rhys left Llaesynd, and after helping Rhys find a stone he liked she quickly found one of her own not far off. Since completing her sculpture she traveled to the top of the mountain, where they would complete the ritual.

The process of carving her successor was both deep and revealing, allowing her a very clear recollection of her past and all the people she held so dearly. So many lives had been touched, so many experiences were had. She laughed, remembering Vaexa's spirit, Rhys' wit, and Nuith's fussiness, and cried as she came to terms with never seeing those faces again. She felt a strong appreciation and connection to the mountain and allowed the subtle energies that flowed across the trees and stone to guide her hands.

Though she avoided interrupting him, she was certain Rhys would finish soon and was waiting patiently for his return. Under normal circumstances, they would return to Llaesynd to say goodbye, but given Rhys' condition they thought it would be easier to remain on the mountain and have Vaexa and Nuith join them after a week's time. They were sure to say their farewells before they departed.

While carving, she had entered into a meditative trance and therefore lost track of how many days passed. Though it only felt like a few, she knew it had to be close to seven by now. Until someone broke the ridge and joined her company, it was just her and the last heart.

The last heart was a statue, of course, carved from the sacred rock of the chasm at the top of the mountain. They carved it twenty years ago, after his or her disappearance, and have been using it as the vessel each year they attempted to bind the soul.

Were it to work, he would be lithe and tall, with sharper eyes and features than usual. They also shaped his plumage to flow longer, stretching to the small of his back. She wasn't sure why, but Vaexa had demanded it – apparently she just couldn't picture it any other way. Vaexa also strongly predicted he would have black, white, and violet plumes all tipped with gold, which was a combination never encountered before. They had no control over the color of the feathers and no Setsuhan had yet received three. The idea of four fell on deaf ears as they laughed away her naïve prediction.

A soft sigh overtook her. She both loved and envied Vaexa's freethinking soul, unfettered by tradition. Where even the laws of nature were molding clay and anything was possible.

As hours passed the sky grew dark and as the last bit of light began to fade, in the distance she caught sight of three beautiful faces. Nuith held a woven basket of materials in her hands, while Vaexa helped Rhys ascend the rocky path towards her. It was fortunate they bumped into him on his way back, as it looked like he was struggling with his footing.

How time passes so quickly. These were to be her final hours.

21

RIFT IN THE GLASS

Though it took longer than she would have liked, Whisper managed to help Salem navigate the bustle of the celebration and arrived at Rhoswan's pagoda. Being amidst the high energy of the crowd, it seemed he slowly began to get his bearings. She shamefully didn't mind being the shoulder on which he balanced, though.

Rhoswan had given the majority of her maids the night off to enjoy the celebration, keeping behind a select few to manage her estate. They were still in the process of arranging the gardens for the Gala and seemed to be behind schedule. Fortunately, they had begun arrangements a few days early to ensure there was room to avoid the necessity of improvisation.

Together, Whisper and Salem ascended the staircase, a solid, rich red wood trimmed in etched silver, leading them to the floor on which Rhoswan kept her office and raven's perch. Generally, it was Breon's responsibility to handle their scribing, but he was nowhere to be found.

"Master Eventide," one of the maids curtsied. She immediately tried to help him stand, oblivious to Whisper's territorial irritation. "You should lay down."

"I am fine. Where is mister Breon this evening?" he asked as she placed his arm around her shoulders. He tried to evenly distribute his weight, but

Whisper pulled his hips closer and took most of it, ensuring the maid felt her efforts moot.

"Mister Breon is unwell and has retired early this evening to recover," the maid replied. She quickly realized he did not need her and stepped aside.

Salem stopped before the office and leaned in the sliding doorway. "What is wrong with him? Why was I not informed?"

"He was very pale and disoriented," she started. "Lady Rhoswan was explicit in telling us not to bother you tonight."

"Fair enough," he shrugged. "My dear Whisper will serve as my scribe then. We will be in the office."

The maid curtsied once more and exited down the stairs.

The office was as elegant as it was meticulously organized. Rows upon rows of ledgers lined shelves that spanned the length of the wall behind the escritoire and rich wooden furniture with pink silk cushions accented the flow of the room. A soft rustling of feathers could be heard from the raven's perch, just outside the shuttered window.

Whisper fetched fresh parchment and a sumi, a solid stick of ink comprised of tree soot and tendon glue. She ground it in slow circles on an ink stone until a thick liquid.

Salem opened the shutters to examine the large raven in its mew and spoke aloud the contents for Whisper to write, being sure to keep it short as not to weigh the raven down with excess parchment.

> *Liam Whitewater, King of Whitewater.*
>
> *I am certain there are Orbweaver informants within your city guard.*
>
> *Watch both Dask and Tybalt closely.*
>
> *Confide in only your most trusted. Be on watch for rose crystals, used in occult. Extreme caution, they are using 'chthonomancy' to enforce their goals.*

"What an absurd word," she fussed. "Spell it for me."

"C – H..." Salem reeled slightly as he fought to focus his wandering mind. "I think there is a T in there someplace."

Whisper cringed at the 'Cht' she had written, as it simply didn't look right. "'Blood magic' then?"

Salem was still muttering random letters to himself.

"Blood magic," she said aloud as she wrote the words.

Though chthonomancy was the formal and traditional name for the art, it had grown far too esoteric a word for people to recall. Practitioners were scarce and completely unheard of in many of the realms of Elanta. The practice quickly fell to the commoners tongue, as blood magic, aptly named for its rituals requiring the sacrifice of life energy to function.

Whisper finished the note and sealed it in the canister along the raven's back. Its midnight wings quickly disappeared into the darkness of the night beyond as it fled to Whitewater.

"Come, dear Whisper." His eyes grew stern as he turned and approached the doorway. "We have one more piece of business with which to deal."

***

A strong blend of jasmine and mint danced around rows of flickering candles. While the fireplace in the duke's war room produced more than enough light to work by, the candles were necessary for the counter ward. Though the heat of the room warmed her blood comfortably, the guards tending the fire were sweltering beneath their armor.

Ashissa spent the last few days attempting to recreate the wards that sealed the honeycomb stone, but was unsuccessful. In fact, she felt no closer to understanding it now than she had prior to her experiments.

Moments earlier, they received the duke's paperwork, with a sealed approval of payment. The documentation was formalized and placed in a secure scroll case for her malison to protect. Immediately, preparations began at the Great Library to fulfill the request.

She was still unsure of how to release the ward, but what separated a Shén Shé pure blood from the other shamans of the world was adaptive instinct. Her plan was to attempt attuning to the honeycomb stone and allow its energies to synchronize with her own. Typically, it was dangerous practice to allow foreign energies to mix with your personal flow, but she was confident in her experience and wanted to yield results without weeks of written study.

Hours guided her well into the night as she worked to decipher the seal. She stretched her pupils across her eyes and engaged her spiritual sight once more, tracing the faint glow of energy that crawled across the surface in thin lines and symbols.

This was what she did best and was the cornerstone of her reputation. Synchronizing energies was akin to having a conversation. You speak with it, ask questions, and feel responses.

She was close and she knew it. An anxiety began to churn within her and her motions became more and more instinctive as she began to bond with the essence within the ward. Her hand began to trace the lines without her as the flow quickly took control and led her body. Unusual words in a language she did not know began to flow from her mouth.

The two Moths on duty watched in awe as the invisible sigils slowly began to appear before them, while the malison disallowed it to distract them from the door to the room. Its slow flowing fire was entrancing and the room grew brighter with the golden sheen that radiated across it.

Duke Eywin had chosen to be present at this moment, but was fortified at the other end of the room, forced to peer above the edge of a slate table turned sideways at the behest of Lyre's Elite. He was most unhappy about the arrangement, feeling it was undignified to cower in the presence of greatness, but the Moths were very persuasive in reminding him the Second Wish was of no use in the hands of a dead man, no matter how brave he is.

Suddenly, the door burst open and the remaining Moths stormed in. The two malison reflexively drew all of their curved, heavy dadao blades, and were battle ready at the slightest confrontation. The dadao's steel gleamed with menace against the glow of the room.

The Moths, in turn, drew their weapons as well. "Stop this at once!" commanded Elder Waylander as he held a decree adorned with the waxen seal of the King. "By order of King Liam Whitewater, the Second Wish is to be immediately placed into the custody of Lyre's Elite and Eywin shall be alleviated from his role as duke until further investigation."

If Ashissa heard it, she chose not to comply, as the golden aura continued to reach out and began to flow up her body.

The two malison maneuvered backwards and positioned themselves between the Moths and the pure blood. To this point, it could only be assumed there was a significant language barrier between them all, and Waylander wasn't certain they knew to stand down peacefully.

"What is the meaning of this!?" duke Eywin scolded. "What have you done!?"

"Bastet, please escort the former duke to his chambers and see that he does not leave," Waylander ordered, and as swiftly as the words left his lips, Bastet traversed the room and locked one of the duke's arms behind his back, leading him towards the doorway.

"You'll pay for your treachery! Every one of you will be a head upon a pike by the end of the day!" He dared not struggle as he knew he would get hurt, and chose to leave without any further resistance. Already, his mind was beginning to formulate a way to convince the King of his innocence.

With the former duke out of the room, the malison could taste the tension decrease as they licked the air. Waylander gestured to the other Moths to sheath their weapons. "Stop," he said sternly. There was no way he could be any simpler with word or will.

The malison watched him with stone cold eyes, measuring his motivations and intent through the flux of heat that radiated across his skin. In combination with the body chemicals they could taste and the heartbeats they were sensitive enough to feel through the floor, they too began to sheath their swords. One began to speak in tribal tongue to Ashissa, though it was clear to all of them she was unable to hear.

The enchantress' body began to float off the stone as her unusual chants grew louder and more ominous. They echoed throughout the halls and the honeycomb stone began emanating brilliant golden flame. Light bled as thick, luminescent liquid from her eyes.

The malison addressed her again, with no answer, and reached out to grab her arm.

Waylander squinted and shielded himself from the blinding incandescence as the chanting reached its climax, and moments later, a fissure tore across the glassy surface of the crystal so violently it reverberated through the halls like thunder and showered the war room with razor sharp shrapnel. The brilliant golden aurora burst violently outwards in a halo of pure, earthshaking force that streaked across the entire city of Lyre and continued well into the distance in all directions.

22

BLINDING LIGHTS, BINDING PATHS

The faint sound of soft knocks resonated through a small, wooden home. Few candles and a fireplace lit the living space, wherein a hunched elderly man slowly shuffled to answer the door. Over his shoulders draped a dark knit that kept him warm, though the home was certainly not cool by any stretch.

"Master Eventide?" The old man bowed his head as the door presented Salem's green eyes and violet sheen. In his hands he held a little stone bowl with nothing in it.

Whisper greeted from behind with a tip of her head and remained on the cobblestone.

"Mr. Breon," Salem said softly as he stepped into the home and closed the door behind him. "I have brought a few medical supplies to aid you in your recovery."

Breon smiled through thin, pale lips. His complexion was quite sickly and he carefully walked on shaky legs to a chair by the fire. "Thank you."

Salem smiled as he pulled his pouch of medical needles from his lapel pocket. "I hear the preparations for the gala are going very well. It was wise of you to allow a few days of lenience." He crouched before the fire and used an iron scoop to fetch a small coal, placing it in the empty stone bowl.

Breon pulled the bundled knit to his neck and fought a fevered shiver.

"I apologize, Mr. Breon. I realize you are cold, but I will need you to expose your upper back and shoulders please." Salem put the bowl on a side table and placed a small, tan cube on the charcoal.

"I'm terribly sorry for the timing of my illness, master Eventide." Breon's guilty words seemed to burden him as he allowed the blanket to fall to his elbows and unfastened the buttons on his night shirt. "I hate to disappoint yourself and Lady Rhoswan at such a crucial time."

"Nonsense." Salem stood behind him and placed a warm hand on his pale flesh. Breon's skin was both cool and clammy, flushed of most color. With calculated hands he began placing the thin needles in key points along his back. "What are your symptoms?"

Breon fought a shiver, though he was mere feet from the fire. "Dizzy, mostly. My joints ache and I feel disoriented at times."

Salem finished placing his needles and walked around the chair to crouch before him. "How long have you felt this way?" he asked as they locked eyes.

"Not long," he replied. "Perhaps I have just overworked myself with the gala."

Salem reached for the stone bowl and held it between them. The tan cube was, in fact, plant resin, and had begun streaming thick tails of smoke that coiled and slithered before them. A plume of the incense reached Breon's nostrils and he watched carefully as his pupils began to dilate.

"An interesting concoction, would you not agree?" Salem asked, refusing to break eye contact.

Breon appeared to have no idea what he was referring to. "It is unusual, indeed. It will help me feel better?"

Salem chuckled. "Not in the least, though it has certainly helped ease my own nerves." He placed the bowl back on the side table and leaned in closer. "It is a peculiar blend of patchouli, sandalwood, and musk. A combination you are certainly familiar with, as your eyes betray you."

Breon remained silent as his expression slowly transitioned from frail and naïve, to cold and deliberate.

"There you are." Salem met him with equal eyes. "Chthonomancy requires a sacrifice of personal vitality. The price, of which, you have clearly been paying in amplitude."

He stood and turned his back to Breon, gazing into the lantern light of the streets as it distorted through his imperfect windows. "That, of course, was the most obvious clue, as you were unable to hide it. There were many more subtle signs. A brief glimpse of your kerchief, stained burgundy by staunching the wounds from which you bled yourself. The faintest scent of resin, stuck in your hair, though you changed your clothing. And the powdered stone on your shoes, from engraving the glyph on the cellar floor of Grove's stead."

Salem could hear Breon struggling to move his arms with no success. His placement of needles paralyzed both of his shoulders, leaving him completely defenseless.

"You were fortunate I was away from Freestone for so long, as I would have caught you much earlier. Much to my dismay, you have completed your project for the Orbweaver's. However, I believe you can tell me how to disarm it."

"You're too late. I was only taught to create it, not destroy it." Breon continued to struggle, channeling his will into his arms, begging them to move.

Salem turned and approached him, reaching beneath the blanket and withdrawing the kris Breon had been trying to retrieve. It was a beautiful dagger, with a solid steel handle and wavy blade. They were a favorite amongst demon worshipers as an efficient and intimidating tool of bloodletting.

"Kill me if you want, I have served my purpose." Breon forced a brave face, though fear and self preservation flickered in his eyes.

"You have not yet served *my* purpose." Salem examined the fine edges of the blade. "As a doctor, you should know, I have all the skill necessary to keep you in severe pain for as long as possible. Should you lose consciousness, I could easily bring you back to the hell, of which, you have wrought."

Breon swallowed hard, thinking carefully on his next actions. The job was already completed, and to his knowledge could not be stopped. Holding onto menial information would be senseless when the cogs were already in motion. "What do you want to know?"

"There are three questions for which I require answers." Salem touched the tips of his fingers with the kris as he counted them out. "Where are the other circles located? Why were they created? Who made you create them?"

The skill of reading eyes was something Salem was renowned for and in the present circumstance Breon didn't want to risk suffering for lies he could not feign true. "I don't know where the other circles are, but I am certain the largest cities have one. Freestone, Whitewater, and Valakut for certain."

Salem listened intently. So far as he could tell, he was telling the truth. "What of Setsuha and Shén Shé?"

Breon shook his head. "We tried, many times, but no one could get far enough beyond the borders."

"Who chooses the targets?"

"I have dabbled in blood magic for many years now, but a few months ago a strong communion took place between all practitioners and the demons in the mist. They said we were chosen to rule as kings in a new world order, and to prepare for their arrival we needed to perform select rituals at select locations."

Salem listened carefully while brushing his thumb along the edges of the kris. It was truly quite sharp. "Go on."

"It was the first time in history all blood magic users converged, and we called ourselves the Orbweaver Sect. We have a unified purpose, but it wasn't until we were approached by a Fate that we knew how to fulfil the wishes of our demon lords. She was explicit in saying she was only an emissary between our worlds and did not know the techniques we needed. Instead she told us which enchanters in Elanta would know, where to find them, and where to place the circles."

"A Fate?" he choked on the words. "They clearly neglected to inform you of how much life energy the request would require. Is it worth being an old and feeble king in your new world?"

"I don't know what the circles are for, in the grand scheme, but I do know that the demons are coming to crown the loyal and thresh the weeds of this world," he smiled, ignoring the question. He didn't feel the need to explain his contentment with short term power versus a lifetime of weakness.

The door to the home burst open and Whisper appeared before them. "Salem! You need to see this!"

He dashed to the doorway and gazed in awe as a wave of golden light stretched across the horizon, charging towards them at a blinding rate.

Citizens in the streets and participants of the festival, including Lady Rhoswan, all stopped and stared into the nexus of brilliant energy. Tense with the indecision to panic or watch.

"What is it?" Whisper asked. As it swept towards the city, her eyes began to understand how large the wake truly was, as it seemed to tower hundreds of feet high the closer it became.

"From the north." Salem recalled the raven they saw on their travels and the suspicion it had brought him. "It is from Lyre."

The human eye could not accurately gauge how quickly the wave of energy was falling upon them, but in a blinding instant that forced the city to its knees, the golden wake washed across their flesh and bone.

Breaths were forced from their lungs as windows shattered and buildings shook within the turbulent force. It was a tempest of wind, light, and essence that seared across every surface in near heatless flame.

Salem was thrown back through the doorway and crashed into a small table set against the wall. He raised a hand to shield his eyes from the bright light and flailing debris, only to see the silhouette of Whisper standing firmly in the door. Her hair and robe waved violently in the wind, but she didn't move an inch.

What had started as a force that pushed them back abruptly changed direction and began to vacuum towards Grove's stead, in the center of the city, where the golden energy shaped into a massive tornado of rumbling ire. The ambient wind began to subside, allowing the survivors to stand safely and watch in dread and awe.

Whisper shifted her eyes to the ceiling of mist and gestured for Salem to look. It was a breathtaking phenomena that balanced on the knife's edge of beautiful and damning, as the canopy of thick mist that had always been their ceiling began to funnel into the vortex and slowly lowered upon them.

Salem turned to Breon, who lay conscious and motionless on the floor. Broken glass scattered across his frail body. His breaths were growing shallow as life became fleeting.

Salem rushed to his side and plucked the needles from his back. "Who was it? The Fate. Which Fate means to disrupt the Weave?"

Breon's pupils swam like lazy fish in all directions. "Ivory."

Whisper could see the dread suspended in Salem's eyes.

"You fool!" He shook Breon violently. "Have you any idea the ruination you have set upon us!"

Breon's eyes rolled into the back of his head as one last smile crawled across his lips. "I never will."

***

A small flock of blue birds playfully flitted through the trees and along the rocky terrain of Emberwilde, welcoming the dusk as the light slowly faded away. In tandem, they swooped and weaved in an aerial dance, when a surge of chaos betook them. Their pattern broke as each flew in random directions, flailing through the air as they all collided into branches and stone, which shattered their frail, hollow bones.

A sinister chuckle sung over Fever's soft lips as she held an open hand to the space where the flock of birds once frolicked.

"It that necessary?" Phori was very agitated and had been since their initial encounter. Together they were walking into the mountains east of Valakut with their horses in tow, as per Ivory's latest orders to travel to Obsidian.

After her and Ivory's contest of will, she was excused, leaving Ivory to grace Fever with both equipment and information on her new strength in private. So far as she could tell, the power seemed to break the sanity of a creature, though she couldn't know for certain and Fever refused to explain.

Fever adjusted the top of her new attire and examined her bust. It was a sleek, strapless dress of deep scarlet, with an intricate silver patterned spider that stretched across the back and wrapped its legs to connect on the front. Loosely hung from her wrists were shimmering bangles of silver and gold, each bearing a row of black diamonds that seemed to absorb the light, rather than reflect it. Her slender legs flashed through the draped skirt of hi-low hem with a sensual allure even Phori couldn't help but notice.

"You're just jealous I'm not playing with you." Fever pouted playfully, still adjusting her cleavage. "I could, if you like."

Phori clenched her jaw and pushed onwards, hoping with all her heart that whatever orders Ivory had given to Fever didn't involve her coming to the Palace of Roiling Cinders as well.

"Awww, come now," Fever teased. "No need to be tense around me, I know just how hard to bite before it hurts." She smiled at the back of Phori's head, knowing she could feel it trace through her beaded hair. "You know, I've seen you before, at your inauguration some five years back."

Phori recalled the date, but not her. Her malikah, the Phoenix Queen, had come to her posted city of Akashra to award her with a red tassel for the sheath of her sword and promote her to brigadier general by weaving the violet plume in her hair.

"Such a celebration it was." Fever was coiling her golden curls with her fingertips. "It was quite a victory that earned you that fancy trinket and hollow rank, if memory serves."

"What would you know of the tactics of war? We defended our homeland from the surge of Blademane Baku." Phori felt defensive, though she wasn't sure what Fever was fishing for yet.

"Why did you close the gates and leave the smaller villages to fend for themselves?" she asked.

"A sacrifice had to be made, to protect the heart." Phori could recall the day clearly.

The Blademanes had cleverly stalked through the southern borders of Emberwilde and divided into several smaller prides to avoid detection from scouts. Somehow, they had heard the Phoenix Queen would be traveling through Akashra and planned an ambush. The Baku were found by mere accident, but when the information finally reached her ears she didn't have enough time to fortify the surrounding villages or mount a preemptive assault. With such an important figurehead within the gates of Akashra, she couldn't risk keeping them open in the event they were overrun, so she ordered them shut until reinforcements arrived.

The Baku came and began to raze the unprotected border villages in order to draw them out, but she could not risk any harm to the malikah. Soon thereafter, reinforcements arrived from the north and they were able to safely exit the stronghold and dispatch of the horde, but the damage to the villages were extensive.

"Many devoted people died that day. In terrible, terrible ways," Fever's voice held a hint of disdain and malice.

"Were you there?"

"I was."

"And you are alive. You may not have been had I not sealed the gates."

Fever tousled her hair a little. "I was not on your side of the wall."

Phori wanted to assume she was bluffing, but as she met her eyes, an anger and loss that could only be truth poured from Fever's dark expression. "Impossible. There were no survivors."

"There was one," she started. "My family and I hid long enough to avoid the brunt of the invasion, but a rogue Baku tracked our scent."

The darkness seemed to coalesce around her black diamond bangles as she delved into the memory. "I watched it eviscerate my father and run down my mother as they tried to draw it away from me. I heard them scream. I watched the terror in their eyes. I drowned in hopelessness and fear. That is, until it turned its eyes to me and I felt no more."

A dark aura began to churn lazy serpents of black smoke, that slowly swayed and writhed in the air around her.

"All I saw was red and by the time I regained my wits, the Baku lay mutilated at my feet. I was soaked in blood and in my hands I held the broken trowel I used to gore it. Most women would have panicked, but I felt something else. Something different, something powerful, something broken. The pleasure began to define me and the beast within me tasted its first blood, and liked it."

Phori was unsure of what to say, but regardless of this woman's loss, it was her sworn duty to protect the malikah and she did not regret the decision she had made. "The people of Emberwilde live to protect the malikah, your family included. Their deaths were not in vain."

"This story isn't about them, it's about you and me," Fever sung. "Had you not left me out there to die, I would not have learned the resolve to kill so many men."

"The sooner we part ways, the better. I don't keep murderous company."

Fever laughed. "Murderous company!" She drew her attention to the violet plume in Phori's hair. "How many people have you murdered for a feather?"

"Deaths at my hand were for the sanctity of the realm," she snapped.

"Killing men in the name of your Phoenix Queen doesn't absolve you of your sins." A sultry smile sharpened her eyes as she examined her nails. "Not only are you a murder, but you are far more a monster than I could ever be. At least I know what I am, killing for money, killing to live. But you, you twist your conscience to fit your ideals when all you've done is kill in the name of another, and for a feather no less. A feather to show the world just how good, selfless, and obedient a killer you truly are. It's foolish to believe that your actions are without consequence, after all, it was *you* that made *me*."

"Shut your mouth! I have mourned every life I've taken in duty, but you... you enjoy it, and that is no fault of mine."

"Certainly, I do, but I have only taken a handful of lives compared to your genocide." Her smile was a drop of ink on fresh parchment, creeping towards her, engulfing all that was light. "You are a brigadier general, Phori. That isn't a position one gets without spilling blood, especially in the name of an ideal. Then, you train more men and women, who, in turn, train more. In the end, you are cornerstone to a monument of corpses that litter the land."

Phori stood silently as she tried to keep calm. Lashing out would only please her more.

Fever continued to pick her apart. "You sit on your horse, at the rear of your lines, or behind your high walls, and you watch. Supervising the bloodshed in the name of your Queen. Placing your price on the lives of the people, when we all deserve walls for refuge. People die when your soldiers bear arms, people die when they don't. However, you are naïve to the fact that every life lost in your command is a soul for which you are accountable."

The wind gently rustled through the trees as the tension between them wound, and deep within Phori's eyes was a faint spark of realization that lightened the blinders she had placed on herself. Fever caught the look and stepped in for the final blow, placing her hands delicately on Phori's shoulders, pulling intimately close and brushing her lips against her ear. The serpents of smoke and shadow slowly crept around her throat and lightly licked her flesh.

"How many people have you murdered?" she whispered again, kissing her lobe before withdrawing slowly.

Tears welled behind Phori's eyes. She promised herself she would not let Fever get into her head and she was failing. A military official of her rank was expected to be objective to loss of life, but she was still human, and she had allowed all of those battles to build behind a floodgate within her.

"Countless," Phori admitted as she turned and fought to retain composure.

Fever simply smiled and let her cutting eyes play in the torment she inspired. "One day, when it will make you suffer most, I will take from you something you love. I will make you watch, like I had to." The dark aura extending from her bangles began to subside and the ambient light returned to its normal fading dusk.

Phori nodded, as a small part of her claimed responsibility. It astonished her how much more complicated her life was since she had become an Instrument. Between Fever's grudge, and her own with the Ravenmane, it was now only a matter of whose collar Ivory removed first.

Phori forced herself along the stony path to Whitewater, when something caught both their eyes.

Through the trees, overlooking a gorge to the north, a brilliant golden wave of light stretched across the horizon, charging towards them.

"What is that?" Fever pondered, watching it approach with great speed.

Before they knew it, the blast of energy rolled over them with incredible force, throwing Fever to the ground. Phori quickly grabbed the reigns of both horses and increased the density of her armor, turning her into a solid pillar of unmovable obsidian.

As quickly as the wave had come, it also passed, and a massive thundering could be heard in the distance behind them, from Valakut.

"Hurry!" Phori ordered as she normalized her weight and mounted her horse.

Fever climbed to her feet and brushed the debris from her dress in time to see Phori's steed disappear down the path they had just taken.

Phori carefully maneuvered through the inclines and trees until she reached a stone clearing that overlooked Valakut in the distance, where she was astonished to see a massive tornado of gleaming energy that stretched from the center of the great city and funneled into the ceiling of mist.

"It wasn't supposed to be this soon!" she argued, imagining the panic of the people. Her plans to convince the council to evacuate Valakut before the demons claimed it disappeared with the rest of the city and she welled with desperation. Perhaps the idea of forging her own decisions truly was hopeless.

Shortly after her arrival she heard the hooves of Fever's horse behind her.

"This is where we part ways," Fever's voice sung.

Phori couldn't take her eyes off the city. "What do you mean? You aren't coming to Obsidian?"

"No," she replied. "Ivory told *you* to go to Obsidian. She told me, when I see the wave of light, I am to travel to Lyre as fast as I can."

She didn't care and raised a silent hand to shoo her away.

"Good talk," Fever chimed as she reared her horse to leave. "Play again soon."

★★★

The edge of the chasm was all but intimidating, regardless of its near endless plummet into darkness. Were anyone to accidentally fall in, there were no ledges on which to grab and save yourself, but instead, just a cylinder of smooth walls that dove into the heart of the great Snow Leaf mountain.

It was here where their predecessors gave their lives to the mountain, and where Luseca and Rhys would give theirs once more.

Rhys didn't seem saddened at all, as Vaexa led herself to expect. The process through which he carved his successor and came to peace seemed to have given him all the resolve he needed.

"You are nearly a different man since I last saw you a week ago," Vaexa said sweetly as she placed a blessed prayer strip on his chest. A second strip was placed on each of their newly carved forms as well, to guide the spirit to its new body.

Rhys smiled and softened his remaining eye. "Though my time was short, it was beautiful."

She could only imagine the difficulty he was having with his stone reversion and in a small way found peace with him being freed from his crippled form.

"Hurry up child! He'll have lived out his full cycle by the time you've finished." Nuith didn't handle emotional situations well and managed to channel her discomforts into even more fussiness than usual. They all knew she was keeping a strong face, guarding herself from the tears she would later shed in solitude.

"I think it's time," Luseca's soft voice calmed them all. She stood on the ledge and peered down into the void. "Come, Rhys." She extended her hand to help him perch with her.

Vaexa knew this was it. As an elder, she was familiar with this great leap into the heart, but had not seen it in her current lifetime. It was turning out to be a very emotional time for her, as her chest became heavy and tense.

"You have been wonderful," Luseca started, nothing but strength gleaming from her eyes. "We love you."

Both she and Rhys extended their arms to their sides and closed their eyes.

Nuith held Vaexa's hand tightly as they watched the two slowly lean forward. Time felt like it began to crawl, allowing them to experience every shimmering feather, every waving cloth. It was as their heads passed the horizon and their bodies had leaned past the point of no return, that a flash of light distracted Vaexa's gaze.

A thick wave of bright energy stretched as far as she could see along the horizon, which, being on one of the largest mountains in the world, was endlessly far. She squinted as it drew towards them with great speed.

Rhys and Luseca completed their descent from the ledge. Nuith watched them free fall into the abyss until Vaexa distracted her with a nervous tug of her hand.

"What's wrong child?" she asked as she raised her head and looked into Vaexa's worried eyes, locked on something behind her. Nuith turned to see the golden wake only moments before it engulfed them both. The earth shook beneath their feet as the energy seared across their skin and Nuith began to lose her balance.

Vaexa was momentarily blinded and then torn off her feet as Nuith's hand, still in hers, pulled her violently to the ground. Her vision slowly normalized amidst the torrential onslaught of wind and rubble and she saw Nuith hanging perilously over the edge of the chasm.

"I have you! Don't let go!" Vaexa yelled over the howling wind as Nuith clawed at the surface of the stone with her free hand. Fortunately, only half of her body was in the hole, and the grip was quite tight.

With a loud thundering that shook the whole mountain, the wind began to vacuum into the chasm, violently dragging them both further into the mouth. Nuith slipped completely, and now freely hung by the hand of Vaexa, who lay her body out as flat as possible and dangled partly over the edge.

"Let go child!" Nuith cried.

"No!" Vaexa strained with all of her might, but she wasn't strong enough to pull her to safety.

"Don't be silly!" she scolded, placing a stern hand on her hip.

"Now isn't the time..."

"Neither of us have successors, and we can't trust Rhys to have better taste in his new form than his last!" Even at the peril of a near infinite free fall into a chasm from which no one had ever survived, she could be a nag. "He's not allowed to help carve my new form, do you hear me child? You keep him away! The boy has a terrible sense of detail!"

"Be quiet and let me think!"

Vaexa concentrated on her grasp and disallowed Nuith to release her grip. Their fragile structure made them incredibly lightweight and keeping her grip wouldn't be so difficult had the suction of air that continued to siphon into the mountain been weaker.

Deep within the hole, golden light shone as a brilliant cyclone of energy began to spiral towards them, sending tremors through the stone that made it more difficult for her to keep hold. She winced under the strain and begged the mountain for benevolence.

It was then that she felt it. The tingling of gentle lightning danced across her body and filled her with hope. The aura she frequently experienced had returned, though she couldn't see its source.

As the cyclone nearly swallowed them whole by bursting from the top of the mountain, an incredible force grabbed Vaexa's cloak and pulled both her and Nuith out of the chasm and clear of the path of razing winds and light.

Together, they huddled and shielded themselves from the flailing stone and dirt as the tornado reached high into the sky. The mist began to funnel downwards and descend upon them.

Vaexa frantically looked around to spot her savior, but the aura was gone. The electric sensation of belonging and warmth was quickly replaced by the malice and turpitude she had felt from the mist before, and as her world grew hazy from the blanketing fog that was swallowing them whole, the shrill screech of something vicious echoed from above them. Something big.

***

Metal on wood resounded through the emptiness of the streets as Andus banged on the door of the elder geomancer, but there was no answer.

Cross gingerly stepped through the hedges beneath the shutters, which were closed and locked. "The door is barred from the inside," he said as he tried to shake the window open.

In the intermittent silence, the soft sound of struggle caught the attention of the Cloister guard, who quickly drew a glowing sigil on the center of the door. Cross watched carefully as Andus channeled into the glyph and then molded a hole in the wood like soft clay, allowing him to reach in and remove the wooden bar that locked them out.

Together, they burst through to find the elder dangling from the rafters by a rope around his neck, exactly like the other. His feet flailed weakly in the air as his consciousness began to flee. Behind him was a figure, a mere silhouette of darkness on darkness. The faint glow of flame highlighted the leather gloves of his hands as he lit a folded piece of paper with a hot coal.

Andus drew his gladius and rushed in to confront the shadow, while Cross hurried to the elder and wrapped his arms around his legs, using as much of his strength as he could to lift the hanging man and give him a chance to breath.

Warm droplets of blood trickled down Cross' face from the crude spider brand carved in the man's head, which streamed down his cheeks like crimson tears. "I've got you," he labored. He could tell the elder was very weak and frail, but holding on just enough to make it through, perhaps.

Dazzling arrays of sparks flashed and faded as Andus clashed with the assassin, who seemed to be wielding a pair of jagged kris, one in each hand. Despite the brief illuminations, the figure's face could still not be seen, as though the shadows were bending to assist his anonymity.

Whether a curse of logic or curiosity, the slow burning of the mysterious paper pulled at Cross with intensity. He watched in horror as it slowly turned to ash and fought with whether to let the old man go so he could retrieve the remnants before there was nothing left.

"Andus!" he cried out, "Put out the fire!"

Beads of sweat trickled down Andus' temples as he chanced a glance, only to be quickly placed back on the defensive. More sparks burst in rapid succession as he parried. "I... can't get to it," he replied, being sure to keep his focus. Whomever this shadow was, he was very agile and difficult to see. If there was any chance of survival, he would need to remain vigilant.

Cross looked up to the elder; blood soaked eyes, heavy and hurt. The anxiety within him mounted and in a snap decision that seemed to last ages, he let the old man drop and made for the paper. The elder's mournful groans and gurgles weighed him like a stone as the rope went taught and heaved back into his throat.

"What are you doing!?" Andus called angrily.

Cross ignored everything and threw the flaming fragments to the floor, wincing in pain as the fire singed his fingertips. Carefully, he began padding the flames out, trying to keep all remaining pieces intact.

"Forget the paper and help him!" The combination of divided attention and the assassin's skill allowed a kris to slip by, wedging itself between the seams of armor in his shoulder. He ground his teeth in pain and quickly raised his sword to block the second kris, which was inches from his eye.

Cross looked to the elder as his kicking slowed and noticed a faint glow through the shutters that grew with golden intensity. "What, by fate...?"

The shutters burst inwards and a great golden wind razed through the cottage, sending them off their feet to tumble across the floor. The weight of Andus' armor helped to weigh him down and minimize his fall, while the mysterious assailant was hurled through the air and sent crashing through the shutters of the far room, disappearing beyond. The violent wind of brilliance and warmth continued to subdue them, pushing all but the cast iron stove to the far reaches of the room until it finally subsided and flooded the cottage with the darkness of nightfall.

Cross squinted, brushing at his eyes as he tried to clear the dust and dirt. The golden flash ruined his night vision, leaving him to search his vicinity with the pads of his hands. "Andus? Are you there?"

A shuffling moan replied with a rustle of furniture as Andus pulled the kris from his shoulder and attempted to stand. The chilling, unhallowed moan of the barely dead, or worse.

Cross fumbled uselessly as he gathered his bearings, until the soft blue glow of a sigil illuminated the room. The gentle light revealed Andus, who had drawn it on the floor with his blood.

The room was in a shamble of broken clay and debris. Shutters hung lopsided on broken hinges while vases, dishes, and décor littered the floor in looming display. Off center to the room lay the geomancer's body, whose rope had snapped from the rafters with the force of the wind. Between the hanging, wind, and falling, the elderly man didn't have a chance of survival regardless of their efforts.

Crumpled in Cross' hands were the fragile remnants of the burnt paper. Carefully, he examined the damage he had done in trying to protect it and realized the edges he tried to keep intact had crumbled to dust.

Andus stumbled to the body of the geomancer, whose neck had been twisted and broken from the force of the pull. "What's going on here, Chancellor?"

"I'm not certain yet," he replied as he tilted the paper to gather more light, "but it is definitely Orbweaver."

Andus looked over the spider that was carved into the elder's forehead and proceeded to scour the window the assassin had flown through. Broken wood, patches of thatch, and the dissonant cries of neighbors were all the evening would give him. "You sacrificed a citizen of Whitewater for that."

Cross paid his righteousness no mind and replied with such facts that only the logistically inclined could understand. "He would have died regardless of my influence."

"From the blast, of course, but you didn't know that would happen. You chose to let him hang."

"The Orbweavers sent a professional to execute the two geomancers and destroy evidence of something. Had we saved the old man for a day, they would have killed him the next."

"That's cold."

"That's truth." Cross shuffled closer to the light.

"By that logic we should just hand the city over and surrender! If we save it today they'll just destroy it tomorrow, right? Why try anymore?" Andus paced as he contended with his fury, and given the situation no court in Elanta would have condemned him for expressing his disapproval with a member of the High Council. "What's on that letter better have been worth it."

Cross held the paper to the light to reveal the burnt remnants of a message. "Trust me, Andus. This changes everything."

Andus grew quiet and gazed out into the distance. Several new signal beacons stretched into the sky, barely illuminating a whirlwind of monumental proportions. "By Fates…" he gasped.

Cross dusted himself off and staggered to the window. The low rumbling could now be felt like the hooves of a thousand wild horses. His eyes widened in wonder. "The hovel," he whispered. "I knew something was there."

23

DEMONS IN THE MIST

The mist blanketed Freestone so thickly that one could not see more than twenty feet in any direction. The haze was disorienting for more than just restricted vision, but also the psychological effect it seemed to have on everyone within it. People became flighty and lightheaded, as the air seemed rich with something intoxicating.

Whisper and Salem slowly navigated across town in the darkness. They tried to light a lantern, but there was a cold moisture to the air that made it near impossible to create a spark. So far as they could tell, no one else had any luck either. Every torch, candle and coal was extinguished in the tempest of brazen light.

Fortunately, Salem was very familiar with the streets and seemed to know where he was going. Panicked civilians cautiously scurried to their homes and closed their shutters. Holing themselves inside until someone came bearing news.

Whisper shook her head in attempt to shrug the feeling of weightlessness and tried speaking to keep level and focused. "Who's Ivory?"

Salem took long, forced blinks to steady his mind and honed the majority of his attention on the streets ahead. "A forlorn Fate. She was once the Great Taker, un-weaver of that which is woven."

"A forlorn Fate? I don't understand, I thought there was only Progenitus, Avelie, and Illy," she replied.

A man stumbled into the streets before them and began to vomit in the gutter. It seemed the mist affected some worse than others and she could only imagine how the elderly and children were coping.

"Originally, there was a fourth. Ivory, the Unwoven. She monitored the deaths of the fatespinners and, in some cases, orchestrated them for the good of the Weave. Death is an important part of the cycle of life and Ivory ensured that both energy and soul transitioned smoothly from one cycle to the next in a form of universal, metaphysical balance." More people began collapsing on the streets and he stopped to inspect them, they were unconscious, but alive, at least. "Whether it is a plea for life, a prayer for salvation, or a respect to the lost, Ivory is whom they beckon."

"What happened to her?"

"She became bored, perhaps. Once all the dragons were slain fatespinners no longer died mysteriously, forming a spite for the monotony of predictability. Or maybe she began to lose her objectivity, feeling an attachment or compassion towards souls she would tragically have to kill, choosing to disavow herself as the harbinger of death. Regardless of her reasons, she abandoned the Weave and ventured into the mist ⊠ the only remaining *unknown* in the eyes of a Fate. To my knowledge, she was never seen again. Ever since, Howlpack Sentinel Avelie has kept careful watch to ensure Ivory never regained access to the Weave and Illy the Flux bore the responsibility of Ivory's old duties in addition to her own."

Whisper watched a woman bramble and stagger foolishly, only to stop and stare into nothingness and then burst into a fit of horrific screaming. The woman frantically began clawing at her hair, tearing it from her head in handfuls of brunette curls.

"Quickly!" Salem ordered as he dashed towards the frantic woman, drawing two needles from his lapel.

The woman didn't try to defend herself and, in fact, gave no apparent notice as Whisper used both hands to restrain her, being very careful with her claws, as not to cause her harm. Salem carefully placed the two needles and the woman's screaming tapered as her breathing slowed.

"Where did you learn to do that?" Whisper gingerly released the woman and tucked her arm back beneath her robe.

Salem gently sat the woman against a building and cradled her head until she lost consciousness. "In the jungles of Shén Shé."

She had heard of the Shén Shé, but little. Most common folk spoke of their monstrous appearance rather than their culture and referred to it as the 'Realm of the God Snake'. Apparantly that's roughly what it meant.

Salem looked around nervously. "We need to get to the pagoda and rendezvous with Rhoswan."

Through the fog, from down the street, they could hear several sets of rapid footsteps and panicked breathing. Salem stood and focused on the hazy void as they approached.

"Please, someone!" cried a woman in the fog. She was almost upon them.

Salem and Whisper both readied and within moments three figures fled through the mist, running at a full, albeit staggered, pace. The three seemed to pay them no mind as they dashed past and disappeared down the road, their hollers faded as the distance spread.

"It's like they can't see us," Whisper thought aloud. "Do you think they're hallucinating?"

"Shh," Salem hushed her, raising a hand. He could hear a faint humming in the direction from which they ran and focused as it progressively grew louder.

A deep seeded uneasiness pitted within him and bursting from the fog was a massive insect, the size of a carriage horse. Its six legs bore bladed filaments and protruding from its face were two long chitin spears, one beneath the other. Its faceted eyes locked onto them and it swerved to impale him.

As Salem dove to the ground and felt the wind brush past his neck, Whisper pressed her thumb and index finger together and placed it to her mouth. With a deep breath she forced a jet of flame from her lips, which immediately caused an unexpected burst of searing hot light that blinded them both.

Heat flushed across their skin as their clothing caught fire and the smell of burnt hair took the air as the explosive flame scalded every inch of them.

The insect careened out of control as its wings melted and veered it into a building, while Whisper and Salem rolled along the cobblestone to snuff their burning vestments.

Moments later, several more insects plummeted from the mist on singed wings and caused incredible collateral damage, crashing into the roads and structures.

Salem lay in astonishment, his coat left smoking. Much to his surprise the air was easier to breath, for now.

"That's never happened before..." Whisper ran her hands through the tips of her damaged hair and noticed Salem had somehow managed to spare his coiffure and eyebrows.

"The component in the mist that is causing psychosis appears to be flammable under certain intense catalytic conditions," he said as he watched an insect attempt to clamber to its legs. Its body began pulsing and twitching as it struggled to get away and then it collapsed. "The creatures may not be able to breath without it, which would explain why we have never seen them breach our world before." Though the explosion was substantial, he had little reason to believe the mist of the over-world had been affected. "There must be some form of ratio between the gas of their world and the air of ours that fuels such volatility to your particular flame."

"How is my fire different than any other?"

"Because normal flame oxidizes a combustible fuel, whereas your flame is conjured by agitating the flammable elements already present within the air itself. When you use your technique you must be igniting the flammable elements within the mist as well, creating a blend of fuels that creates an amplified exothermic chain reaction."

"Should I do it again?" she asked, climbing to her feet and readying her hand.

"No!" He quickly stood from prone and placed his hand on hers. "For now, the gas is gone. It will likely return, but we cannot ignite it again. That blast would have continued until the mix ratio changed. For all we know that could be the whole city. Anyone simply inhaling at the time of ignition would have died as the flame entered their lungs."

Whisper was in disbelief. "You mean, I may have killed half the city?"

Salem awkwardly examined their surroundings and noticed the woman he had rested against the building, she lay breathless with charred eyes wide open.

Whisper had been in a significant amount of confrontation over her few short years since leaving the monastery, but always with someone who deserved it. This was the first time she killed someone innocent and the guilt pierced her in the heart she thought she never had.

She stood, paralyzed. Lost in the smoking ruin of this once sleeping woman, flooding her mind with all the other men, women, and children that smoldered lifelessly in the dirt because of her.

He held her shoulders firmly and forced her to look into his eyes. They brimmed with enough compassion and strength to bring her to focus. "This was an accident and though you may have been a catalyst, you are not the source. You are not to blame for this, Ivory is. Say it."

The words swam in her head, slowly anchoring, one by one. "Ivory did this."

"Yes. Ivory. Now, we must get to the pagoda. We will run, while the air is still fit to breath. Understood?"

Whisper nodded as her composure began to normalize and any remnants of anguish that remained were quickly soothed as Salem cupped the back of her head and touched his forehead to hers. It was a moment of stillness that felt as beautiful as it was tragic.

★★★

With the psychogenic gas burnt from the air, Salem and Whisper were able to make decent time crossing Freestone, despite the darkness. Much to their chagrin, they passed over a significant number of charred civilian corpses who had been caught trying to flee the festival at the time of the explosion. Amidst them, hundreds of the monstrous creatures lay strewn among broken trees and shattered stone.

Lady Rhoswan's pagoda was a welcome sight, though her winery appeared to have taken some damage. Several of the large insects had scraped the ceramic tiles from the roof as they fell from the sky and one larger creature had crashed through the building completely, leaving a blemish of splintered wood and glass in its wake.

As they crossed the bridge, a familiar voice called to them. It was Rhoswan, signaling to them from an open window on the second floor. "Come in, quickly."

They entered the foyer of the building and closed the door firmly behind them. An acrid stench caught their nose as Whisper glanced over the room and she quickly realized every paper door, red lantern, and flower petal had turned to ash. Her sense of guilt returned as she recalled how resplendent it had all once been. Now, just a tattered ruin of ash and cinder.

"What's going on?" asked Rhoswan as she descended the staircase. Though her silk dress was ruined, she handled it no less delicately than if it were new.

"Breon," Salem began, catching his breath from the run.

Whisper hadn't even broken a sweat, nor did she have to regulate her breathing.

"Breon delved in chthonomancy," he continued, "and created something to capture the excess energy within that shock wave. The result being that massive tornado over Grove's stead, which is suctioning the mist over the city, perhaps even further."

"Breon?!" Rhoswan was shocked, and were it not for her trust in Salem she would have argued wholeheartedly. "What's chthonomancy?"

Salem hung his head. It was beyond him how so few people knew of the practice considering how dangerous it was to the realm. "Believe it or not, there is a problem much greater than the mist itself."

Whisper took a seat and remained withdrawn from the discussion. Anything to do with their situation, she had nothing to contribute.

Breath quickly fled Rhoswan's chest, drawing Whisper's attention back. "Ivory?" she gasped. "Are you sure?"

"He would have no reason to lie. Also, a pandemic of this scale could only be orchestrated by someone of great conviction and resource," he replied. "I am still unsure as to what it is she is trying to achieve."

"What should we do?"

"The aurora came from Lyre, that is where Whisper and I will go. The Orbweaver cultists built the crystal circles in anticipation of the wave of energy. If what it came from was powerful enough to create such a force we can be certain it is something of interest to her. She will make a move, but unfortunately she is a step ahead." Salem gestured for Whisper to join him and prepared to leave.

"Wait..." Rhoswan pleaded. With all of the commotion, she hadn't time to compose herself and speak with less desperation. "Stay a day or two at least, help me help the people of Freestone."

"Are you mad?" he argued. "Those who survived may need to evacuate, and with yourself and the King's guard you have all the help necessary. My skills are better used determining the origin."

Rhoswan wasn't sure what to do, though she knew for a fact if she didn't find a way to keep Salem and Whisper in Freestone, Origin Progenitus would be furious. "You owe it to the people!" she yelled sternly, allowing herself to shy her gaze and appear weak. "I'm afraid, Salem. Please, it doesn't have to be long."

He appeared both torn and frustrated, unsure for the first time since Whisper had met him.

"Salem..." Whisper approached, clearly wanting him to consider.

He looked to Whisper suspiciously. "Why?"

She sighed and thought it over. "For the first time, I feel guilty for my actions. I need to help, to ease my conscience."

His jaw clenched. "So be it." He turned back to Rhoswan with a fierceness in his eyes. "If anything goes wrong, you take Whisper and lock yourselves in the aviary."

Rhoswan tilted her head sternly and flashed him a look of pure frustration. She had gone to great lengths to ensure only select nobles to whom she had gifted the ornate wooden boxes were privy to the knowledge of her other business. Though she knew she could never hide it Salem, she didn't appreciate him mentioning it in front of Whisper.

"There's an aviary?" Whisper chimed curiously. Though she hadn't been in Freestone long, she had well acquainted herself with the pagoda and surrounding area on tactical and territorial instinct. Not only had she never seen an aviary, but she also didn't understand how it could possibly fortify them from the demons of the mist.

"Just a place to keep my wrens, love."

★★★

Loose shale slipped and crumbled down the slope as Vaexa and Nuith hurried down the mountainside. They weren't sure if they were being pursued by the creature they heard echo above them, but knew the treeline would be their only defense.

A bellowing screech roared through them as the beast descended from the sky. Though their eyes were adept at low light conditions, it was Vaexa's sensitive hearing that gave away the creature's position through the mist and urged her to strafe hard to the left, narrowly pulling Nuith from its jaws as it scooped a mouthful of stone.

She couldn't believe her eyes as she peered behind to see its lengthy body slither back into the air and disappear in the haze. It was nearly ten feet thick and long enough that she could see no end to it. The body was a writhing worm-like larvae, which adorned an eyeless face and triangular mouth that split into three toothy sections. She was unsure as to how it was moving through the air since she could neither see nor hear wings, but was in no position to sate her curiosities.

The creature howled again as it coiled back and closed in behind them.

Vaexa could feel its hunger crawl up her back and as they wove into the trees, and the creature razed a massive section of earth before returning to the sky.

Together, they crouched in the darkness. It was Vaexa's assumption it was tracking them by vibration as it had no eyes or ears she could see. Her theory was simple – if they didn't move and didn't speak, maybe it wouldn't see them.

She could hear it drift in circles above them as it searched, and eventually it drew its attention to something else and maneuvered to chase it. Moments later, it was gone.

"We have to get to Rhys and Luseca," Vaexa whispered, examining the trees and attempting to gather her bearings. Once she was certain of which direction to go, she grabbed Nuith's hand and pulled her along.

"A great curse has befallen us," Nuith cried. "The mountain is angry."

"The light didn't come from Setsuha. If the mountain is angry, it's not at us."

"Keep your voice low, child. You'll draw it to us." Nuith cautiously looked around, though she could barely see anything through the fog.

"I'm speaking just as loudly as you are," she argued.

"But you're speaking *more*."

She forced her irritation from her shoulders and decided to keep quiet.

Somehow, they managed to trace their way back to Rhys's carving and expected him to be waiting there. However, dread betook them as they came upon the statue, still solid stone.

The prayer strip remained fastened in place and the small channeling glyphs drawn across it seemed intact.

"I... I don't understand..." Nuith held her hands to her mouth as tears began to form. She gently caressed the surface as her mind reeled in disbelief. "This can't be..."

The mountain had claimed his soul but not returned it. A tragic and unexpected break from the traditions of millennia.

Vaexa's sensitive body was overwhelmed by the despair flowing from Nuith and it caused her to burst into an uncontrollable fit of tears. She didn't know what happened and loss was overwhelming.

She immediately turned and fled into the darkness leaving Nuith to quietly plead for her to return. All went still, and Vaexa had vanished.

She dashed through the trees recklessly, driven by anguish and blinded by tears. Eventually, she reached a grove with a small waterfall pouring into the center. She trudged through the icy water, waist deep, until she reached the bank of the other side. It was there she saw Luseca, solid stone and statuesque.

Vaexa dragged her feet towards her, feeling heavy for the first time in her life, and rested her forehead on Luseca's. The waterfall continued to crash down and droplets of water began to bead from her golden feathers.

The stone was cold. Lifeless. Foreboding. She was a Setsuhan who could feel everything and for once, felt nothing.

She bawled, begging the mountain to return them to her. She prayed, implored, beseeched. Offered anything and everything to have Luseca place her arms around her and tell her everything was alright.

In the end, only water and wet stone sung her soft lament.

24

ONUS OF INSTRUMENTS

With the morning light came hope in the tattered city of Freestone. The vacuum effect of the golden tornado had pulled in the remaining mist that blanketed the city and contained it within itself as it continued to funnel into the sky. It wasn't long until the people bravely set foot out of their homes and began to assist the royal watch with removing the alien bodies that littered the streets.

Whisper graciously assisted as well, dragging the strange insects in pairs to the outskirts of the city to be burnt.

"They're much lighter than they appear," she told Salem as he examined one closely.

"The musculature around the base of their wings and gravely under formed legs lead me to believe most of their life is spent flying. It stands to reason their structure would have to be built lighter." He maneuvered his way to the long, spear-like proboscises at the front of its head. He took a minute to look it over very closely and cross sectioned a piece with a dagger.

"Why does it have two mouths?" she said curiously.

"I think only one is a mouth, the bottom."

This confused her even more. "Then the top is a stinger, maybe?"

Salem shook his head. "No. The diameter is much wider than expected and the muscles seem peristaltic." He stood and took a deep breath, allowing his mind to consider the possibilities. "While the bottom is clearly the mouth, sucking the fluid from the victim, the top may be to fill the body with something. A digestive fluid maybe, or perhaps to lay eggs. Either way, it is grim, even to my limited imagination."

Whisper grimaced with the image and continued to work. The insect bodies were hauled by cart and piled high, forty by Whisper's count, and once all collected she was given the honors of setting them aflame. A single, long, sustained breath of flame was more than enough, and as the townsfolk returned to contend with the dead of their own, Salem and Whisper stayed behind and watched solemnly.

"What an unusual thing to find beyond the mist," Salem stated, recalling all of the fables, stories, and theories of what magical worlds laid behind the haze.

Whisper only nodded as the fire entranced her.

"Thank you, dear Whisper," he said softly. "Were it not for your grace, I may have died last night."

She was flattered. "I wouldn't be a very good Ward of the Voice if I couldn't save you from a hoard of massive, flying, body drinking insects, right?"

He looked to her with eyes that seemed to want to smile and cry at the same time. "I meant before that."

Her mind went to his hovel and the first time she saw him there, slumped in his chair, drunk on surgical spirits, and hiding something white up his sleeve. She desperately wanted to ask him what secret he was keeping, but didn't want to interrupt his moment of humility. Who knew if she'd ever get this opportunity to revel again.

"You saved me from myself and that is no mere feat." He bowed his head and turned towards Freestone.

With a simple smile, she followed close behind.

***

Rhoswan gently touched the crumbling bouquets of flame kissed flowers that were displayed in her garden. Obviously, the gala was not going to happen this season, and the beauty that once was haunted her deeper than she would like to admit. A small fortune was lost between the damage that was done and the sales they would have had.

With a heavy sigh, the light began to dim once more and time slowed to its usual stop as the chattering of Origin Progenitus crept from the trees beyond.

"My Fate, can you explain what's happened here?" she asked, trying not to sound desperate for answers.

Progenitus seemed hesitant and even remorseful in his own strange way. "It is a great tragedy to have lost so many lives to something so unexpected," he began. "One of three artifacts was found near Lyre. An artifact meant to be lost and warded to prevent its presence from being detected, even from myself."

"What is this artifact and how can the Fates not even see them?"

"They are Shiori's Three Wishes, sealed and hidden for, and by, Shiori Etrielle herself."

Rhoswan shook her head in surprise. "Shiori is real?" Stories of the Immaculate Artisan were always interesting to hear, but she never truly believed that a single person could have created a whole world. To her, Shiori was just a symbol of the simplicity in the grandeur. A reminder that no matter how different everyone was, we were all crafted from a single vision. She heard an abundance of rumors involving Shiori's three wishes, but none of them depicted the wishes as actual *artifacts*. If the fables were actually true, then the artifacts would be unthinkably powerful. "Her three wishes…"

"Etrielle explained them once in a very early codex, several millennia ago. The first is of wealth and was banished into the mist where it would be useless. The second is of power and was buried beneath a mountain and encased in honeycomb stone to keep it from anyone's hands but her own. The third was entrusted to her closest ally, Savrae-Lyth, the Queen of the Drakes, always to be in her safe keeping but useless without the first two wishes."

"What is the Third Wish for?"

"I don't know. Etrielle's only recorded words were 'What all Third Wishes are for.'"

Interesting as it was, Rhoswan's attention was divided between her personal losses. "Well, as you can see here, something big has happened. Salem knows the source is Lyre and is pushing very hard to leave as soon as possible. I don't know how much longer I can keep him here."

Several spiders emerged from the nest on his back and scurried into his hair. "You needn't worry. Avelie's Instrument, Howlpack Shade and his many wolves, have been informed of the situation and are on their way to Freestone."

"Shade?" she whined sternly. "I don't need his help." It was clear in her voice that she and Shade were not on good terms. "He's a selfish, paranoid recluse. Please don't make me work with him."

"I agree completely. He is not a man I would choose as an Instrument, but Howlpack Sentinel Avelie did and you will respect her decision and his role. In truth, the situation is much bigger than you know and you will need his help."

"What are we supposed to do?" she asked, daring to imagine a situation that would require the influence of two Instruments at once.

The chattering began to grow louder as the spiders churned beneath his skin. His clouded eyes rose to hers and the ominous caress of thousands of tiny crawling legs seemed to march across her skin. "You will kill Salem Eventide."

25

WRATH, UNFETTERED

It was several days of hard riding but the cool mountain winds of Lyre could finally be felt as Fever stopped at a breach in the trees. In the distance she could see the massive walls surrounding the city and the ancient spire that towered in the center.

She was less than an hour from the gates and still had no idea what it was she was supposed to be doing, but veered her horse to continue. It was then she noticed the darkness in the trees that formed into an all-consuming void that twisted and contorted, until it coalesced into a portal before her.

"Excellent timing," Ivory's voice sung from the darkness. "I have someone I would like you to meet."

Fever steadied her horse's nerves and watched intently as two massive hands burst from the vortex and grasped each edge. A large helmet pressed through the ichor with strain, as though the portal were a thick liquid that adhered to its heavy black plating. Its body towered above her as it forced itself through and stretched to its full height. The portal was far too small to comfortably accommodate it. The last of the darkness peeled from the armor and receded back into the shadows, eventually returning everything to normal.

Fever was at a loss for words and struggled to keep her horse calm in its presence, as it towered no less than fifteen feet high.

"His new name is Wrath," Ivory's voice resonated in Fever's head.

"He's a leviathan. A true leviathan." Fever was in awe of the massive creature. It was well known Liam Whitewater was the only true leviathan left since the war. Giants that were thought to have been eradicated nearly a century ago, though the occasional rumor arose from time to time.

"Yes, he is, and my fourth Instrument."

"Fourth?" she replied, shocked. It was unheard of for a Fate to have enough power to support more than one Instrument without severely sacrificing their own fortitude, let alone four. Up until now, she had only known of herself and Phori, and was already impressed. It was a moment of revelation, as it put Ivory's true power into complete perspective. She either had the strength to make it work, or was crazy enough to stretch herself dangerously thin.

"Yes, and once I have the Second Wish, more will come." Ivory's voice was light and pleasant, only slightly fatigued with the extreme amounts of energy she was sustaining.

Wrath barely moved as she and Ivory conversed, and turned his head to inspect the landscape. He didn't seem familiar with his surroundings at all and even examined the grass and trees with incredible focus.

His armor had a multitude of lines and pathways engraved into it, which periodically flashed a stream of blue energy and effectively covered every inch of his body. He had no other equipment on him, though she could only be so surprised. A leviathan, an Instrument of Fate no less, probably didn't need a weapon.

"This is incredible, where did you find him?" Fever asked.

"That isn't important. What matters is what he will do."

Fever and Wrath turned their attention to Lyre and examined the bastion city from afar. The walls towered over fifty meters high, were several meters thick, and bore a reinforced gate, barred by an additional iron portcullis. The twin doors were quite large as to accommodate the arsenal of siege equipment within. Several watch towers perched along the wall, each with a sufficient number of murder holes for their hundreds of archers to snipe through safely, and even if one should somehow manage to bypass the gate and volleys, it was well known Lyre had more soldiers than any other city in the realm.

Fever knew in her heart what Ivory wanted them to do and dreaded the words before they even sung in her head.

"In Lyre, somewhere within the castle, there is a sword of platinum and gold known as the *Second Wish*. You and Wrath will enter the city and claim it in my name," she said gleefully. "Kill everyone or kill no one, I don't care, but there is one target you must be sure to eliminate."

Fever listened carefully. She wasn't sure how they would get in *without* having to kill everyone, but it was nice to have options. She was sure she could sneak by, but Wrath was ridiculously conspicuous.

"There is an enchantress," Ivory explained. "A Shén Shé pure blood named Ashissa. I can't sense where she is, but I know she didn't die in the explosion. She is an ambassador and is within the castle somewhere. It is paramount you take her life."

"As a Fate, why can't you tell where she is, or manipulate it so her death is guaranteed?"

Ivory seemed irritated by the question, as sound as it was, but forced admission. "I no longer have access to the Weave and therefore can neither manipulate nor read it. All of my predictions herein are based on my own intuition and experience."

Fever smiled, her eyes glistening in awe of her Fate's power. "But you're Ivory, the Unwoven. You are the physical embodiment of death itself."

Ivory's eyes softened with the flattery. "You are not wrong. My whole life has been dedicated to refining my specialty, but without access to the fatespinners my power no longer has infinite range. I am too far away to kill the enchantress, and cannot risk getting closer as I am still mortal." She outstretched her hand and gently ran the back of her nails along Fever's cheek. "I am trusting you to claim the sword and kill the Shén Shé pure blood, in my name."

***

Whisper stood before the brilliant tornado of energy that continued to roil in the city of Freestone. Salem had given her the time she needed in order to sate her conscience and she wanted one last close look at the phenomenon that triggered it all. The churning of mist within was nearly silent and only being this close could she feel the low rumble of its power. So far, no one had dared attempt entry. If the barrier did not consume them, the creatures within surely would.

"Are you all set, dear Whisper?" asked Salem as he approached with a horse in tow.

She glanced at him and the mount, allowing a smile to fill her. The idea of riding a horse was exciting. "If I'd known you wouldn't make us walk to Lyre I'd have agreed to leave sooner." She approached the beautiful creature and ran a gentle hand between its eyes.

Salem shrugged slightly. "My mistake for not deducing the horse would be leverage."

There was a softness and wonder in her eyes he hadn't seen before and it saddened him to see it vanish as she instinctively reached for the wine jug that no longer hung on her shoulder. "I'll have to get a new one, I suppose," she sighed.

He nodded politely.

"Before I forget," Whisper began as she pulled her hand into her sleeve and fetched something from within a pouch of fabric sewn inside. She revealed the book they had gathered from Grove's, *Envied Emerald to the East*, with some pieces of parchment placed between the pages. "I read over the book and noted all of the unusual letters."

"What did you find?" he asked, carefully accepting it and removing the loose leaf.

"Nothing. The book is just about the jungles along the eastern coast and doesn't seem to have anything to do with... well... anything."

Salem carefully looked over the letters she had copied down. They truly seemed like hundreds of random characters. If it was a hidden code of sort, it would be very difficult to decipher without a key. "Excellent work, dear Whisper, and with such haste. I am truly impressed." He smiled with his eyes.

"May I ask a question?" she began.

"Asking before asking?" he seemed playfully surprised. "Who is this respectful woman?"

She smiled sweetly at first, but grew serious as her question approached. "Do you think an Instrument killed my family?"

Salem seemed to genuinely consider the possibility. "Why do you ask?"

She drew her attention back to the swirling mass of energy and felt the power across her skin, probably better than anyone else could. "We've seen many things and it feels like the Instruments might be the only creatures powerful enough to create the aura I'm looking for."

He nodded as she shared her thoughts. "I agree. Since the passing of the dragons, it is likely an Instrument may be the only one capable of such energy, however I cannot be certain. We should count our blessings neither of us have met one. The influence of a Fate and their Instrument can be fatal under the right circumstance."

A soft voice interjected, "But always for the greater good."

The Lady Rhoswan approached them, wearing yet another adornment of fine navy silks – a long sash of vibrant orange cloth wove behind her back and draped over her arms.

"I suppose so, though one could argue the dictations of three powers that be." It was unclear as to whether or not Salem truly didn't like the idea of the Fates making all of the decisions for the world, or if he was simply playing devil's advocate to keep everyone's eyes on both sides of the coin. Either way, it didn't seem as though Lady Rhoswan shared his perspective.

"One can argue all they wish, I suppose," she said with an air of sadness.

"Is everything alright?" he asked, noticing she was not her usual self.

Rhoswan forced a smile. "It's complicated, I'm afraid. Perhaps we could speak in private?"

"Of course," he obliged, handing the reigns to Whisper. "I will return shortly."

"And Whisper," Rhoswan spoke as Salem prepared to leave, "It was a pleasure meeting you." She turned to Salem and hooked her arm under his, leading him across town towards the pagoda.

26

WYRMSONG

Soldiers scrambled as they loaded a row of four ballistae along the walls to each side of Lyre's main gates. In the distance, the leviathan Wrath approached with footsteps that shook the earth.

"Ready!" their commander yelled as they wound the massive weapons and locked a jagged harpoon into each. "Hold!" Under normal circumstance, he would only line the walls with archers, but given the size of what approached he preferred to be safe and ready their siege engines as well.

A reinforced door to the side of the main gate opened and through it rode a messenger bearing a blue and white banner, on which displayed the royal crest of Whitewater.

The messenger rode to safe distance of the titan and then stopped to deliver.

"You are in the territory of Lyre, Realm of Whitewater!" he began. "By order of the Duke of Lyre we command you to cease your ascent on the city and return from where you came!"

Wrath paid the warning no mind, or perhaps didn't understand it. Fever watched from the treeline and wondered if he even spoke their language. She had only just met him, but since then he had been completely silent and would stare at her blankly when she tried to converse. He seemed to understand her through hand gestures and she decided to let him lead the assault so she could sneak in behind. She wasn't certain he could handle the front line, but he seemed willing enough. She wasn't about to risk herself.

"This is your last warning!" the messenger cried. Though some of the distance had closed, Wrath was clambering very slowly. "Turn back or be labeled an enemy of the Realm!"

Wrath tilted his head forward and began to pick up speed, shaking the ground with each massive step until he was in full charge.

The messenger reared his horse in terror, realizing the titan was capable of significantly more speed than anticipated. He crouched low on his horse and began to dash for the gate, but the horse struggled with the tremors as Wrath closed in, and stumbled into the dirt, hurling him from the saddle. He painfully tumbled across the rocky terrain only to raise his head in time for Wrath to trample over him. Even from the ramparts his splatter of blood could be seen.

The commander turned to his men and hollered so loudly his voice began to crack. "FIRE!"

Rows of archers took turns filling the sky as each ballistae fired in tandem. Iron shafts ricocheted and snapped against Wrath's armor and the cold iron harpoons crumpled and shattered as they barely interrupted his charge. Before they could load a second round he crashed into the portcullis and gate, shaking the wall on which they stood. The stone quivered so violently several soldiers lost their balance and fell the fifty meters to their death.

Wrath buckled the gates with his first blow, but the portcullis buffered most of the hit. He latched onto its thick iron bars and with one swift feat of strength tore the whole mesh from the stone. The chain draw used to raise it from the other side came with, ripping the winch and gear system through the wall and tearing a huge fissure that rained mortar upon him.

"Soldiers, ready melee!" the commander yelled down to the hundred men he had positioned on the other side of the gate, while other commanders began rallying hundreds more. Had he thought the gates could be breached he would have readied a thousand. It was astonishing how a single creature could have pried several tons of iron from the stone, but he was in no position to let his nerves take over. In fact, he knew his leadership was needed now more than ever, as his soldiers below had just witnessed something supernaturally monstrous effortlessly tear through their defenses. The staggering apprehension was palpable.

Wrath cast aside the mangled ruins of the portcullis, trembling the ground as the weight fissured the earth. A low growl rumbled through his helmet and he took a few large steps backward, lowering his head to the gate once more.

"Brace!" yelled the commander, readying his troops for the titan to breach. A panicked hush fell upon the rows of soldiers as they braced their spears in the cobblestone, ready to receive the charge. Sweat dripped from beneath their helmets and wafts of cold breath suspended as the seconds drew out. Then the foreboding came to fruition and time began to flow faster than they could manage.

The leviathan burst through the gate with thundering footsteps, sending splintered wood and shrapnel in all directions. Both gates buckled off their hinges from the force and began to collapse inwards as Wrath stampeded through the ranks.

No soldier, no spear, could slow him down as he crushed them beneath his feet. The two towering doors plummeted behind him, instantly killing those who couldn't evade quickly enough.

Hundreds of soldiers in broken ranks swarmed on him to break his rush, but none could divert his path as he ran straight for the castle.

"This is an absolute slaughter, commander!" cried one of his lieutenants.

The commander called into the remaining ranks. "Pull back to volley range! Wheel the ballistae to the castle." He turned to the lieutenant and proceeded to descend the wall. "When he hits the outer courts, he will meet the Cloister Magi. That should buy us time to strike him with wyrmsong. Go!"

"Wyrmsong, sir? We've never used it inside the gates before, we run the risk of razing our own city."

"It may be the only weapon powerful enough. That's an order!"

The lieutenant gave a sharp nod and rushed into the fray.

Wrath spared no one in his path as he ran to the castle, reaching the courtyard with blood slicked across his plating. He didn't slow as he smashed through the decorative stone archways that marked the perimeter of the castle grounds, but tripped and dredged through the grass and tiles as something managed to catch his foot.

He turned while prone to see a glowing lash that rose from a glyph on the ground and ensnared his leg. Beyond it, a cloaked figure knelt with his hands firmly planted, channeling his power into the entrapment.

Though Wrath didn't know it, the city of Lyre was guarded by several enlightened enchanters known as Cloister Magi. They had only one job, for which they were well trained, and that was to protect the castle.

Wrath clambered to his feet and raised a fist to crush the magi, when a second lash wrapped around his throat from behind and forced him back. He grabbed the lash and fought it, nearly tearing it apart, when a third, fourth, and fifth flew in from all directions, ensnaring his remaining hands and leg.

Surrounding him were four more magi, whom all knelt with palms down and focused everything they had into holding him still.

The soldiers rolled the ballistae within close range and carefully loaded the wyrmsong shot, which were large bolts with a row of glass spheres in it. The liquid inside was relatively harmless on its own, but each sphere contained a fluid that would ignite an intense, explosive heat were they ever to come in contact with each other. Wyrmsong was a prototype ammunition developed by Lyre's top alchemists for melting holes through stone walls, and no other realm had yet replicated the formula.

"Ready!" their commander called as they adjusted the angles with hand cranks.

Wrath frantically tore and thrashed at the bonds, but they were barely enough to hold him.

Suddenly, the daylight by one of the ballistae suppressed and clouded, as though something were absorbing the luminescence. The near invisible flash of a smoky serpent snapped through the air and shattered the ammunition, which exploded in brilliant violet flame and created a chain reaction that ignited the stash of nearby shot.

Shock rumbled through the earth and intense fire stretched in all directions as the explosion engulfed the surrounding soldiers and sent the others into disarray. It was an inextinguishable liquid flame that dramatically spread along the surface of water like oil, which the soldiers quickly realized as they frantically tried to douse their melting comrades.

"Fire!" the commander ordered to the few remaining engines that had not yet burst into flame, but there was no response. Instead of obeying his orders and laying waste to the leviathan they began stumbling in all directions, screaming and yelling in complete disorientation. "What are you doing!?" He tried to reform their ranks, but they didn't respond.

He rushed in to pull the lever himself, but in the corner of his eye he caught a glimpse of Fever as she allowed her shadowy aura to free some of the light it was devouring. Darkness roiled off her bangles like noxious smoke, which stretched into a dozen writhing serpents, six to a side. A smile crept across her supple lips and she raised a hand to point at him. Instantly, the six serpents that danced from her black diamonds burst forth, shattering the ammunition. The flash of wyrmsong washed over the commander with such intensity it felt cold as ice, searing every nerve in his body before consuming him whole.

Fever basked in the screams of the suffering as they crawled through the dust, begging for death. Their cries filled her with a joy she couldn't explain and the power she felt flowing within her sent glorious shivers up her spine. She turned to the five Cloister Magi, knowing full well they were completely helpless. The focus they required to entrap Wrath made them oblivious to their surroundings. An opportunity she couldn't help but exploit as her serpents crept through the air and violently wrapped around each of their throats.

The lashes binding Wrath immediately dissipated as their concentration broke, but much to Fever's dismay they weren't fighting back as much as she hoped. One by one, her serpents sunk their fangs into their necks and they began to kick, flail, and force muffled screams of agony.

Wrath saw the pure ecstasy in her eyes, but it was impossible to tell if he cared. He seemed to take a moment to gaze upon the wall of violet flame, burning so hot the shattered stone arches began to droop and ooze like magma. Though he hadn't thought he could be defeated by mortal means, he seemed to recognize how close he had actually come to death. Being powerful certainly didn't mean he was immortal, which was a mildly deflating revelation.

He turned his attention back towards the castle, lowered his head, and began rebuilding velocity.

★★★

"Hurry brother!" Katya cried as she watched Casamir gather as many of his blueprints as he could.

The Great Library was a chaotic mess of scholars and sages, all scrambling to the point of nearly crawling over each other to either escape or hide. Many fortified themselves within the innermost halls of the academy, while everyone else gambled on a safe journey home to their loved ones.

"I almost have everything," Casamir hurried to her with a dozen scroll tubes in his arms. "Take these and I'll bring my prototypes."

"We don't have the time," she replied, accepting them anyways.

"One more minute. I'm almost ready." He dragged a locked chest from his work area and opened it, placing his latest invention inside with the others. "Okay, okay." The chest was hardly light, but the adrenaline gave him the strength he needed to lift it and hobble out.

"Will father be alright?" she said in worry as they ran down a fleet of winding stairs to the lower floors. "He doesn't have to protect the duke anymore now that Eywin has been relieved. Can't he just come home to protect us?"

"No," he replied sternly. "His oath is to Lyre and I assure you he will be on the defense with the rest of Lyre's Elite."

"I'm worried." Her mind recalled the massive creature she witnessed storm through the city. A force that lost no momentum regardless of how many men it trampled.

"You needn't, each Moth is a master enchanter. By now, they will have secured themselves deep within the treasury."

They arrived at the front gates. Soldiers were attempting to coordinate the evacuation of the common folk, making it very difficult to move. Together they pushed through the crowds and scurried along the large stone walls that protected the inner cloisters. They began to make good time as traffic thinned, when Katya stopped in her tracks. "Look! What is that?"

Casamir drew his attention to a woman with a large spider design on the back of her scarlet dress, ascending the castle from the outside as a dozen strands of shadowy serpents hoisted her along the stone like massive spiders legs.

Fever anticipated the front halls would be fortified the heaviest and decided to climb through a spire at the rear of the castle to avoid the brunt of the trouble.

It was unlike anything they had ever seen before and couldn't help but stand in awe as she scaled the wall.

Immediately, Casamir dropped the chest and began to open it. "Run home, Katya!"

"What are you..."

"Now!" he ordered fiercely.

She knew he was going to do something stupid. Whether it was for the sake of the family name, the city, or simply pride, she was certain there was no stopping him. With great apprehension she turned and fled.

From the chest he pulled his latest invention, of which he still had no name since its 'successful' testing the other night. After realizing the few flaws it had, a second pin system was placed to allow him to fire each side independently and the front cable was outfitted with a set of heavy steel bolas. Carefully, he pointed the device at the woman and pulled the first pin.

With a recoil he did not expect, the bolas fired and crashed into the stone above her, catching her attention. It was a miss he wasn't sure he could afford as her eyes met his and gleamed something sinister. The cable quickly began to retract and he nervously watched the gears whirl as he begged it to reload faster.

The light around him began to fade and as he looked back up he had just enough time to shift as a smoky serpent ripped through the tender flesh of his face. The pain seared up across the right side and he could feel the wound cauterize as his eye was torn from him.

He fell to a knee and bellowed in pain as the device clamped the bolas back into their sockets. Panicked and dizzy, he scrambled to aim and fired a second shot, which wrapped around her arm as she shielded her face. In his desperation he had miraculously scored a hit and with his free hand flung open a Wet Glyph from within the chest. As the paper rolled open to reveal a lightning ward, he pulled the second pin and fired the rear shot through it, embedding the barbed anchor into a wall several meters behind.

Fever glanced in wonder at the cable that wrapped around her arm, when the Wet Glyph began to spark. In mere seconds the glyph flared and electricity began to arc up the cable, washing her in full convulsive burn and agony.

Fever bellowed as the electricity seized her every muscle and before she could use her serpents to sever the bond, the device abruptly retracted and tore her from the wall. Her body flew through the air, past the wounded Casamir, and crashed into both the wall and scroll, which exploded in a vibrant display of lightning, sparks, and debris.

The stones of two floors collapsed upon her and for a sacred moment, all seemed still amidst the settling dust. Seconds passed in silence, until the shadowed serpents began to heave the stone and rubble aside. With the last large piece finally pushed away, Fever arose, more fearsome, volatile, and insane than ever. Though she was masochistic enough to have enjoyed the near electrocution, she was not a fan of embarrassment. Her aura churned with incredible malice, but to her frustration Casamir was nowhere to be seen. Her head tilted as her primal urges to hunt began to take over, when Ivory's voice echoed through her head and her brand began to burn slightly. *'Kill the Shén Shé first, then do as you wish.'*

Brimming with anger, she stepped out of the wreckage and walked back towards the castle. She would be certain to claim his life for this.

27

ASSASSINS

The Lady Rhoswan played lightly with her hair before allowing it to drape down her shoulder, breathing deeply the warm spring air. The once beautiful collage of pink and white blossoms clung as curled bundles of black along the multitude of brittle branches.

"Will it all be the same again?" she asked Salem, still cradling his arm.

"Flame, though destructive, has a way of turning old life into the foundation for the new," he said looking out across the barren groves. "The ash will rejuvenate the soil and the trees will return more hardy and vibrant than ever."

"That's excellent," she replied softly. "The brandy in the storage cellars and casks in solera were barely damaged. They should compensate our losses assuming we can recover sooner than later."

"The trees here will not produce for at least another year, though I will collect dremaera from Snow Leaf soon."

"I will bring in plums from Blackthorne for the time being, until peach brandy is viable again."

Salem nodded as he briefly glanced her over. Frayed hair tips from overplaying, slight chapping of the lips indicated frequent licking, the flexing of her jaw, and the faint aroma of mint, which was commonly used to treat headaches. The Lady Rhoswan had all the explicit symptoms of stress induced Bruxism. "Yet, there is something else that ails you greatly. To be fair, you have an adequate list from which to choose."

She was careful not to make eye contact with him, as she knew he would read the betrayal behind her eyes. "There is a matter of business you and I must still tend."

He looked to the pagoda and scanned the surrounding property ⊠ quiet, solemn, and desolate. Neither maid nor guard wandered nearby and only the sound of the wind could be heard through the trees. Attention turned to minute fibers of black and tan hidden amidst her dark dress, what appeared to be wolf fur. He gently placed his hand on hers as they approached the pagoda, feigning concern for a chance to feel her pulse. "Is something awry, Lady Rhoswan?"

★★★

Whisper was lost in thought as she pet the beast before her. She hadn't even seen her first horse until after leaving the monastery. They had a mule, but it hardly qualified. There was something awe inspiring and majestic about the creatures, so powerful, humble, and vigilant. She liked to think that one day she could have her own, though she would be the first to admit it was a responsibility she could not yet afford. Keeping Salem safe was trouble enough, between the Orbweavers and his own self destructive habits.

It was a new feeling to her, this peace. She began to feel it more often the closer she allowed herself to feel for Salem. Well aware of his demons, there was something alluring about the turmoil that hid in the shadow of his heart. A gritty, yet comforting reminder that though they seemed so different on the surface, their hearts had something to share. His words from the other night echoed in the back of her mind. *'Sometimes, you make me feel like I can move on'*. She hadn't realized it until now, but they were the exact words she had been looking for to express how she felt as well.

Relief washed over her as the revelation set in. In twenty years, she finally met the one person who challenged her to feel whole. As though the world truly had a place for her, without her having to carve it herself.

Difficult as he may be at times, things seemed easier, and it was a flow she could get used to succumbing to.

She caught herself smiling, and for some strange reason tears strained behind her eyes. An odd feeling of wanting to cry but not committing. The joyous pain of the tears were there, and even though they didn't yet fall, knowing she had them made her feel more human than ever.

As she reveled in the flush of foreign feelings and basked in how much brighter the world seemed in the light of revelation, the tiniest motion caught her eye. It had to be a mile away, camouflaged within the dizzying legion of barren trees, but something only her keen eyes could catch had briefly shown itself.

She squinted to compensate for the distance, and with a force that surged through her body, the long shaft of an arrow penetrated her chest. The shot was so instantaneous it had yet to hurt, and the confusion of what just happened brought her pause. She carefully ran her fingertips along the entry wound, sanguine warmth began to spread across her wrappings. The arrow pierced the right side of her ribcage breaking through the bone and damaging her lungs. Inches to the left and it would have struck her heart.

The moment her mind finally collected itself the second arrow came, and in an attempt to deflect, it pierced through the scales of her mistborn arm as she threw off the shoulder of her robe. The velocity at which they flew had incredible stopping power for the range she was certain they were being shot from. Either the bow or arrows had to be reinforced with enchantment of some sort, as no mortal man could ever strike with such precision and force from such a distance.

She quickly mustered her strength and funneled her anger, mounting the horse and pursuing the source with as much speed as possible. It was beyond her who this person was, but to nearly kill her with one well-placed shot was worthy of her wrath. Blood poured from her wounds and it would only be a short time before she would be defenseless without treatment. The pain began to catch up to her and the bouncing of the mount was borderline unbearable. Were it not for her inner fire and familiarity with revenge the agony would have likely crippled her completely.

Another arrow nearly struck her, but as she quickly closed they became easier to spot, and easier to dodge. The anger was brimming and the thirst for blood was thinning her eyes into slits. A sudden shift of her head and the fletching of another arrow cut her cheek as it flashed by.

She was almost at the treeline when she caught glimpse of the next shot. There was little to do but hold her breath as she watched it plunge into the chest of her horse, collapsing them both into the dirt. The horse crashed head over tail in a mass of rigid, flailing limbs, throwing Whisper from its back. Though she plummeted head first she managed to throw her demonic arm in front and used it to curl her body into a series of painful rolls. The sound of cracking bone chilled her as the tumble crushed her claws and wrist, but as she slowed enough to roll to her feet, she continued to maintain her speed and dash into the trees. It didn't matter anymore, whoever attacked her was as good as dead. She would need only one hand to rip his throat out, and only one lung to laugh about it.

★★★

Ashissa arduously forced her eyes open to see the red velvet canopy above the bed in which she lay. Her bones ached as her head drifted around the room, noticing two royal guards posted by her door. She carefully tested each of her limbs by wiggling her fingers and toes, and then elevated each as slowly as possible. By her assessment, she had taken some severe bruising and lacerations as the honeycomb stone fissured, but fortunately nothing seemed broken.

"Where are Ashissa's malison?" she asked one of the guards as she gently pulled herself to a seated position.

"They insisted on guarding the hall, enchantress," he replied. "Master Waylander has suggested you remain here and rest. This is one of our most fortified rooms."

"Why would Ashissa need fortification?" she wondered.

Both guards hesitated, but were interrupted as a massive thundering echoed through the castle halls. Portraits that hung against the stone shifted, and some had already fallen.

"What is happening?!" She struggled to the side of the bed and stood on shaking legs. The majority of her body was bandaged, and the majority of her bandages were encrusted in blood.

"Please," chimed the other guard. "You'll open your wounds. You should lay back down."

She shot him a look to remind him of his place and staggered to the window. Thick plumbs of smoke rose from an inferno of violet fire that blazed in the outer cloister as thousands of soldiers scrambled to organize their ranks.

"What is this?" She watched in horror as a titan donned in obsidian plate stepped into the fray, swinging the castle doors as a weapon. With each massive arc, tens of soldiers buckled within their steel shells and flew several meters through the air.

"The castle is under attack. We strongly recommend you remain calm and stay in this room. The castle halls in this section are too narrow to accommodate the leviathan, he should not reach us here."

"Do you know why? How long has Ashissa been unconscious?" Her mind was a fluster of adrenaline and, what she imagined was, visinnia, an herbal extract often mixed with warm water, which was poured across the body to numb the skin. She was regaining some of her feeling, but it was an unusual sensation that prevented her from moving gracefully.

"You have been healing for several days now. As for the leviathan, no demands were made, but he ran straight for the castle."

"And Second Wish?" she asked sternly, tracing a finger along her chest. As she made the motions, a glowing emerald energy began to follow her hand, drawing a symbol as it moved along.

The guards couldn't avert their eyes as their curiosity overtook them, but did muster a delayed response. "Still sealed, I'm afraid. The honeycomb stone fractured, but not enough to release the sword."

"Ashissa believes he comes for Second Wish. The ward kept energy contained, invisible to those with strong senses. Now that Ashissa has broken it, great powers will draw to its calling."

The symbol on her chest was complete and glowed vibrantly. She took both hands and thrust her fingers into her ribcage, releasing a seam of green light that tore from her hips to her head. With all of her might, she pulled the seam apart and peeled herself from her own skin.

The guards were dumbfounded, their minds, a mixture of abhorrence and reverence. They stood silently as she pried herself from her shell, containing their judgment as the husk crackled in their ears. After a long minute, she stood before them, anew. Her scales glistened in the light and even her wounds seemed less severe.

She rotated her shoulders in their sockets and delicately touched the minor wounds that remained. The sensation of pain was welcome, as she shed the skin that held the visinnia and no longer felt inhibited by the numbness.

One of the guards broke form and smiled in amazement.

The sound of steel rattling outside the door interrupted, and bursting into the room was a malison, who quickly sealed the door behind him.

He began speaking to Ashissa in their tribal tongue and braced the portal with all four of his hands.

"What is he saying?" asked one of the guards, readying behind the malison.

"He says a woman of shadow ambushed them and killed Ashissa's other malison."

She slowly backed to the window as everyone grew silent – the crackling of the fire and distant bellows of the troops below kept the stillness maddening.

The room began to darken as the firelight receded, and from the seams of the door poured an inky smoke. It immediately coalesced into a dozen indistinct serpents that lashed blindly in the room, constricting everything they could wrap around.

Both guards and the malison were quickly ensnared and the snakes buried their fangs into their flesh. The guards swiftly spiraled into a fit of screams as they dropped their weapons and stumbled to the floor, curling into a fetal ball.

The malison, however, remained completely calm. Intense concentration narrowed in his eyes as he held the door firm, and he barely moved as all twelve serpents slowly coiled around him and sunk their teeth in succession. He twitched as each one painfully pierced his skin, but continued to hold his ground.

He began to speak incredibly loudly. His words were slurred and distorted, but after he sloppily formed his first sentence he carefully spoke a single word, over and over ⊠ begging her to run.

She quickly snapped out of the paralyzing shock and hurried to trace new symbols on her palms and feet, shifting her attention back and forth between her work and her malison.

With a startling burst that caught her off guard, the umbral snakes snapped taut and worked together to pull the malison into the door. Wood creaked under the pressure, and the malison's breath labored as he began to shake from the strain. His arms soon collapsed and the trap snapped shut, utilizing all of the tension that had built to violently thrust his body through the door and into the hall.

Fever stumbled into the doorway and wearily braced herself on the frame, sweat fell from her brow as she panted for air through a sinister smile. The dizziness wasn't nearly enough to quell the blood lust that lurked in her eyes.

She was still new to her power and had not yet trained enough to sustain it for as long as she had, especially against foes as strong and resilient as Shén Shé. The complete exhaustion had almost taken her, and she was certain to lose consciousness were she to push herself much further.

Ashissa stood across the room, bewildered with dread, and Fever mustered her last remaining bit of strength to swing her hand and send a destructive flail of serpents to whip across the room. The bedposts were instantly severed in a dramatic display of fragmentation, and gouges of stone turned to dust as the vipers ripped through the walls.

With the incredible reflex she would not have had if she hadn't shed her skin, Ashissa arched backwards and tumbled out the window, narrowly avoiding the serpents as they fiercely shredded the sill.

A dread clutched Fever's heart as she realized she failed to execute her mark, and the anxiety quickly relieved her of the deleterious smile she had worn so elegantly. She quickly recalled they were near the top of the spire, where the sheer drop was several hundred feet. She rushed to the window, praying she'd see her target splattered across the cobblestone. Instead, she spotted the Shén Shé pure blood descending the wall, slithering along the stone on glowing palms and pads.

Ashissa completed the glyphs on her hands and feet, which allowed her to adhere to the castle walls and skate across its surface in wide strides.

Fever readied to hurl a lash of shadowed serpents when a glow of green light caught the corner of her left eye. She turned only to see the final flare of energy that lit a sigil quickly and cleverly drawn on the stone of the sill. Though Ashissa had scribed it hastily in her retreat and hadn't the time to make it as potent as she could have, it was still more than enough to ensure Fever would not pursue. The sigil burst into a noxious green mist that washed across her. She quickly snapped her head backwards as the corrosive mist boiled the skin around her left eye and filled the air with the acrid smell of burnt hair. Fever writhed in agony as she clutched her face. She reacted quickly enough to save the rest of her body, but as she watched the green fog devour the surface of the sill she couldn't help but imagine the horror it had made her face. Her bellows of rage slowly became those of fear, tears swelling as her fingertips gingerly touched the blisters that began to bubble. Nothing mattered anymore. Her power, her Fate, her mission – all lost in fear of her monstrosity as she curled up and wept.

28

ELDER WAYLANDER, RISE AGAINST

"My lord, I wish you'd reconsider. This is no place for you right now." The captain of the guard knelt in a bed of gold coins before the duke. Since the Second Wish had fissured, it had been moved to the royal treasury for safe keeping.

"Nonsense!" said Eywin, shifting in his seat as he feigned comfort. It certainly wasn't ideal, but the treasury had thicker walls than any other room in the castle. "The Second Wish must not leave my sight."

Coins jingled as tremors rattled through the copious amounts of chests and treasures that lay strewn about. Under normal circumstance, the treasury was well organized, but the leviathan's footsteps were so invasive stacks and shelves began to topple over in the course of the raid.

The captain nodded and rose to his feet. "Be ready," he ordered to Lyre's Elite, who were just arriving to the chamber. "We can be certain the titan will try to breach."

"What is he doing here?" Bastet scolded as he pointed to the former Duke of Lyre.

"He has not yet had his trial, Moth," the captain argued. "He may not be the current duke, but he could regain his title and it is our responsibility to protect him until then."

Bastet looked to Waylander with agitation, which was waved away as he ordered the doors to be sealed. "He may stay in this room, but our focus will be to the Second Wish."

Waylander divided the Moths into three smaller units and assigned them tasks. One unit began trapping the door with a warding seal, which surged and crackled like lightning as it scrawled across the heavy wood and iron. The second began a circle of warding glyphs that surrounded the Second Wish, sprouting glowing vines that wrapped around the crystal and locked it down. Lastly, Bastet crouched on the floor and carefully placed enchantments on their blades, turning them ghostly translucent.

The tremors grew louder and more intense, raising their attention.

They had all seen what happened in the cloister with the magi and knew it was only a matter of time before the majority of the militia would be designated to evacuating citizens and controlling the wyrmsong. By this point, he could assume the titan was roaming freely and uncontested within the castle walls, making them Lyre's last line of defense.

"Time?" Waylander asked as he pulled his ghostly sword from the enchanted pile, faint white symbols glowed eerily up the flat of the blade.

The lightning ward was stretching across the doors and growing ever brighter as the Moth's focused all their efforts into making it as powerful as possible. "Nearly at full charge, sir."

***

Wrath clambered through the castle halls, seemingly lost. The soldiers had broken their offensive against him and began tending the wounded, though a handful of Lyre's most evasive trailed a safe distance behind, keeping a careful eye on where he seemed to be heading. So far as they could report, the leviathan didn't seem to have the slightest idea where to go.

Servants and maids screamed in terror as he smashed each door down in passing, peering inside and moving on to the next. He noticed the guards following him, but didn't seem to pay them any mind.

Wrath turned a corner and proceeded down a hallway much narrower and less decorated than the ones prior, when he heard the clang of steel falling upon stone. He stopped and turned to see Fever, bracing herself against the wall as she shook fresh blood from a curved dagger.

"Can't have them following us, love," she labored between heavy breaths. Tied across her head was a piece of torn silk, possibly from a tapestry. It hung across and concealed the left side of her face.

Wrath stood motionless as she approached him, sliding her hand along the stone to steady her balance. The overuse of her power caused her tremendous strain and she fought with dire effort to remain focused. Her feet began to drag as she neared and the fatigue quickly buckled her knees, sending her in a stumbled fall.

Immediately, Wrath fell to a knee and carefully caught her with his massive gauntlet, cradling her fragile body across his palm and fingers. Her vision slowly cleared and she felt herself softly propped back to standing.

"Um... thank you…" She watched as the massive creature held out a hand to assist. Bewilderment betook her, but she was of no use in her current state and used both hands to steady herself against his palm. It was a kindness she had not expected, but it could not have come at a better time.

He crouched as the ceiling began to descend and continued along the hallway, smashing in each door at a time.

"Why aren't we killing them all?" she asked between the roars of shattered wood.

The leviathan neither responded nor acknowledged she was speaking.

"Can you understand me?"

He smashed open another door to an empty room.

She allowed some time to pass and noticed her strength had begun to return. It wasn't much, but it was enough to take the numbness from her limbs and center her vision.

"Are we going to smash open every door here?" she chirped. The repetition was quickly growing tiresome. "We'll be here all day if this is all you're..."

Suddenly, as Wrath's fist slammed into a pair of reinforced doors, an explosion of blue light and crackling energy blasted them through the adjacent wall. It happened so quickly that Fever's body violently whipped about, but Wrath managed to twist his torso enough so he could shield her from the bulk of debris.

Pebbles and shards shifted beneath their bodies as they clambered from prone. Her ears rung as the room wobbled and spun. She felt Wrath nudge her to safety and noticed the air shift as the lines of energy along his armor grew brighter. Whether it was real or a trick of the eye, the subtle arcs of the blue electricity seemed to flow along his armors leylines. He lowered his head and growled, bursting towards the doors that had just rebuked them.

The air was a blinding flash of blue lightning as the seal on the door exploded once more, but this time Wrath was prepared, and firmly planted his feet to resist the knock back. His rage brimmed with each ferocious strike as he assaulted the door over and over again, filling the hall with such resonant thunder and lightning she had to close her eye and cover her ears.

She maneuvered to the corner of the room and could no longer see him, though the constant flashes were far too disorienting to keep her eye open anyways. From what she could gather with muted senses, the lighting from the door was having little effect on him, or at the very least, he was angry enough not to care. Eventually, the door shattered under his force as the glyphs' energy expended their last bit of explosive resistance.

"Attack!" cried Waylander as the Elite sprang in to overwhelm the titan, their ethereal blades held tightly in their grasp.

Generally, Wrath's strategy was to stand and bear an attack, relying on his armor and resistance to thwart any potential damage. However, searing pain startled and staggered him as the Moths effortlessly plunged their blades into him.

Waylander watched the leviathan's hubris very carefully as he drove his sword into the titan's throat. The blade slid its full length, until the hilt clanged against the obsidian plate.

Lyre's Great Library attracted some of the top minds in the fields of alchemy and enchanting, which gave them a great advantage by recruiting scholars and funding research in a variety of fields, foremost being realm defense. This provided them with an arsenal of unfathomable weapons and technology, including wyrmsong, lightning wards, and his personal favorite, the specter glyph.

When a specter glyph is channeled, it gives the weapon a gossamer visage that cuts only flesh and passes through all other materials. Something invaluable when fighting a creature with such reliance on armor.

Wrath fell to a knee as Waylander stepped backwards, but quickly noticed the other Moths were struggling to remove their swords. The air became thick with static that vibrated along every hair on his head, and he stopped in his tracks as the swords began to crackle and glow. Some Moths continued to pull, while the others released their grasp. Regardless of contact, brilliant blue lightning, like that of the glyph prior, burst from the leylines of his armor and arced across them all.

Waylander flinched backwards as the remaining five elite soared off their feet at the behest of the blinding flash. Some quickly arose with only mild burns and scarring, while the rest moaned and wailed. One clutched at his face as both of his eyes boiled and burst from their sockets.

One by one, Wrath pulled the swords from his body. Each blade was simple, mundane, and bloodless, completely devoid of the specter glyph that gave it its lethality. As each sword slid out, the leylines across his armor shifted from lightning blue to a ghostly white.

Waylander watched in awe as he realized his dilemma. The leviathan's armor was able to absorb and discharge energy. Too thick to pierce with normal steel, but able to devour enchantment. Also, his body was able to survive being struck with all of their blades, including the one he drove into his throat. There had to be another ability he didn't understand. It was a predicament that kept bringing him back to wyrmsong and realized it was possibly the only weapon they had that could kill it, but was far too volatile to use within the castle. Then, Wrath pulled the last sword from his chest and groaned; the blade, soaked in blood.

Interesting... Waylander took a wide step and hurled a second sword with all of his might, planting the blade firmly through the eye slit of Wrath's helmet. The titan flailed and angrily smashed the stone archway and floor, bellowing a low, loathsome howl.

"Everyone must leave, now!" he yelled.

Former Duke Eywin simply crossed his arms in reluctance.

"Never will I retreat," he said stubbornly. "If you feel the need to abandon your city, you are free to run with your tail between your legs."

Waylander bit his lip in frustration and quickly turned to his Elite. "We haven't much time before the titan recovers. Take the wounded to triage immediately!" The Moths seemed hesitant to leave their commander behind on the forefront of battle, but recognized his word was absolute;

respecting his judgment above all else. He looked to Bastet. "Evacuate the families of the Elite immediately. Get them to the capital and report to King Whitewater." He scooped a bag of coins from the treasury floor and tossed it to him. "I leave them in your guard, Bastet. Until I catch up."

"What are you doing?! That doesn't belong to you!" Eywin scolded.

Waylander paid no mind and instead nodded to Bastet to gesture for haste. "Former Lord Eywin," he began, "the continuation of the legacy of Lyre is a sound investment, well worth a few coin." He watched as the elite formed a sigil on the far wall that turned it to sand and allowed them to escape. "Besides, there is a strong chance you may not need it anymore."

He picked a rogue coin from the stone and held it close to his mouth, whispering soft mysticism.

Wrath finally withdrew the blade of the second sword from his helmet, much to Waylander's disappointment it was bloodless. Rage flushed his movements with such intensity it buzzed in the air like a plague of locusts. He roared and lowered his head to charge, when the single gold coin bounced beneath him. He paid it little mind and readied, when the coin released a massive explosion of flame and shrapnel that staggered him backwards, but then vacuumed into his leylines, turning them red.

As the bedazzlement cleared, he found the Moth kneeling before him, having just completed a sigil on the stone beneath their feet. Wrath raised a fist to crush him, the ruby leylines lit his gauntlet in flame, when the stone suddenly transformed into fine sand. Together they plunged through the floor and into the lowest castle room below.

Waylander, having landed first, quickly tumbled to safety as the titan crashed down above him.

Wrath landed flat on his back with incredible force and immediately began to feel himself sink as liquid granite began to fold over his body. He turned his head to see the Moth with glowing hands, channeling essence into the stone and turning it to quicksand. As he discharged the light the sand reverted back to solid stone, leaving Wrath strewn prone and partially encased within the floor, both his arms and legs completely consumed.

Wrath struggled, cracking the stone as his tremendous strength slowly began to free him.

Waylander quickly pieced together all the information he had gathered so far and tried to form his next course of action. The armor could absorb energy and utilize the last enchantment it assimilated, but willingly, explaining why the spectre enchantment didn't take effect once it was eaten. As for the leviathan's body, it took damage, but only from one sword. Closest to the heart. Though the other swords seemed to hurt him, they left no signs of lethality.

Wrath's ruby leylines burst into flame to keep Waylander at bay while the stone fissured little by little.

It would hurt, a lot, but now was his only chance to strike. Waylander withdrew a long, thin knife and quickly formed a spectre glyph along its edge. The ghostly gossamer sheathed the blade and gave it translucency. He took a deep breath as he looked into the flames before him and leapt onto the stone that wrapped across Wrath's stomach.

The intensity of Wrath's blaze blistered his skin and caused his clothing to smoke, but it was too late to turn back. He raised his knife and buried the blade into Wrath's heart, twisting it to be sure. Wrath bellowed in agony. The flames from the prior leylines subsided and the armor turned translucent, eating and using the spectre glyph. Wrath dropped a few inches as his armor no longer braced the stone at his back, which now gave him more room to escape if the strike to the heart didn't stop him. Waylander could now see the tender flesh and breastbone of the leviathan through the armor, coated in a ghostly blue mist that lingered between its skin and gossamer plating.

The nexus of wispy blue fog that crept across the leviathan's skin began to climb the blade and caress Waylander's hand.

The mist was cool to the touch as it trickled along, but soon shifted into a searing pain as it began eroding his fingernails, converting the matter into tiny particles of energy which syphoned into the armor. He watched in horror as the mist moved to the flesh of his fingertips, vaporizing and absorbing the energy there as well.

He tried to pull himself away but it was as though his arm was tethered in place, fighting a vacuum that wanted to pull him in piece by piece. Waylander grimaced as the flesh of his arm dematerialized a layer at a time, and quickly drew another glyph on his own shoulder. With a blast of flame the rune exploded, severing his arm from his body and allowing him to fall backwards to watch his lost limb succumb to the titan's unusual aura. First his skin, then muscle. To the very last moment, he had the liberty of seeing even his blood and bones devoured by the mist, until nothing but cloth remained. The essence of his severed arm eerily wafted into the shell until it was completely consumed.

The mist danced back into Wrath's armor and the leviathan turned its head. The translucence made his features fuzzy, but he could tell Wrath was smiling. Somehow it didn't seem malicious, though, more like he was enjoying the challenge Waylander had presented and was impressed. With the help of the spectre glyph in his armor he now had more room to escape the stone and maneuvered to free an arm, grabbing the hilt of the dagger in his chest. He slowly pulled the dagger out, inch by by inch, and let it fall to the ground with a clang. Not a drop of blood along its edges, not a scratch on his body. He then rubbed the 'wound' as though the pain was true and lingered.

The fire rune had cauterized the severity of Waylander's wound and he staggered to stand as his cloak smoldered in tatters along the right side of his body. The dark mark of the large, black spider brand of the Fates stretched across his side.

With a grunt, Wrath pointed to Waylanders mark and then lifted his forearm. Even with the lack of detail, the brand was large enough to be clearly seen through the armor. The same, sprawling black spider.

Waylander turned to draw another sand transmutation glyph along the closest wall. As it crumbled before him, his weary eyes looked back to Wrath, who was now nearly freed from the stone. "You have won this time, Instrument, but in the name of my Fate, Illy the Flux, I will not rest until I have my justice for this day."

***

The streets of Lyre were a bustling chaos, the likes of which Casamir had never seen before. Soldiers amassed in the cloister as they contained the wyrmsong with a barrier of powdered counter agent, but struggled with getting close enough to deploy it on the flames to extinguish them. The wyrmsong had been pushed back from its incredible expansion, but the ground was far too molten for them to approach any closer without risk of spontaneous combustion.

Triage and medical centers overflowed with the wounded, and the bodies of hundreds of soldiers were being excavated from the path of wreckage.

Those with homes and stores surrounding the cloister were taken to a safe distance and the homeless filled the streets with only their most valuable possessions in hand. Civilians in other sectors, though urged to stay in their homes, conglomerated to watch the travesty in awe, ready to leave at a moment's notice, though the order had not yet been given.

He passed frantic mothers that hurried their children into their homes, and frenzied merchants that loaded their carts down with goods they meant to secure as far away as possible. After pushing and weaving through the masses, he finally came upon his home.

At the door sat two small trunks filled with belongings as Katya hurried to gather all the valuables for evacuation. Though the rest of the city seemed absolutely manic, seeing Katya's stone cold focus was somewhat soothing. Casamir dropped his box of inventions and braced himself against the wall, catching his breath and regaining his wits.

Katya heard the box hit the floor and turned sharply, only then noticing her brother reeling as he contended with the wound on his face. She immediately rushed to his aid and thoroughly examined the damage to his eye. As a nearly enlightened third year student of medical alchemical botany, she had the experience necessary to treat the terrible wound. This particular injury was not one she had much practice with, but he trusted her with his life when it came to herbal remedies and poultice application.

"Katya, I will be fine. We have to get out of the city," he tried to gracefully brush her aside, but she had more of her father's fire than any of them.

"We're not going anywhere until we dress your eye." She quickly left the room and returned with a bowl of water and fresh white cottons. "Come, sit."

Casamir carefully padded his way to a wooden chair that stood by the doorway and sat. Running through the streets seemed easy with the adrenaline coursing through his veins, but now that he was beginning to calm down the world was starting to spin. "There may not be much time, we need to go immediately."

He looked to the basin of water as Katya finished pouring a small vial of black liquid into it. The dirty water splashed and stained the edges as she wrung a soaking cloth. "This will hurt, brother."

He nodded.

She took a deep breath and begun to cleanse the smallest portion of the burn that begun at his jaw, remaining vigilant even as she felt his body tremble.

The burn sizzled and boiled as the dark liquid trickled over it and Casamir ground the tips of his nails into his seat to contend with the pain.

Katya continued to clean the wound despite the creaking of the wood. "Do you think father is coming back?" she asked calmly, hoping conversation would distract him a little.

He forced heavy breaths through clenched teeth. "I... I don't know." There was a mild relief as she stopped to soak the cloth again, though he could still hear the wound fizzle. "I saw the woman walk away from a fully charged lightning ward Bastet had put on a Wet Glyph for me. I dare think of what the titan could walk away from."

"Giants were once a common creature in the realm, in the generation of our grandfather and the fathers before him," she begun. "Yet they were wiped out, so they must have vulnerabilities."

He shook his head. Not so much in disbelief, but in being reminded that his younger sister had more level headed leadership than himself. Were he not his father's first born he could imagine she would have been the one to don the title of Lyre's Elite, and he to wear the healer's vestments.

She loosely wrung the cloth to keep it sopping. "If it can die, father will kill it."

"If it can, yes."

"Everything dies, brother. Even the Fates are mortal." She turned to him and held his head with her free hand, preparing to clean his eye where the damage was the most severe. "Be sure to yell, if you clench your teeth you may break them."

Her gaze was piercingly intense, but the confidence gave him assurance of the peace he would find in the aftermath. Casamir swallowed hard and accepted what was about to happen. "Do it."

29

THE ORBWEAVER INFORMANT

King Liam Whitewater sat upon his throne and wrapped his fingers around the orbs of onyx-marble. Seated before him were the remainder of his High Council, and to his right stood the tall silver shaft of a massive war maul, resting on the flat of its head. It had been the King's weapon of choice for decades, and though it shone with virgin brilliance, it had spilled more blood and shattered more bone than all of his cloister guards combined. To him it was simply a tool to enforce his right and claim, but to both soldier and survivor it was known as 'Wood Cutter', for its reputation of severing whole family trees. Salem always disliked the name as his logic could not overlook the fact that a war maul had no sharp edges and could not actually cut anything, but the name brought awe to the people, courage to the armies, and fear to all who opposed, so it was worth overlooking.

"Have you been in good health?" Fairchild asked Cross, whom he noticed was sitting quietly in his chair, hands folded over a wooden box upon his lap.

"I was unharmed in the assault," he replied. "Andus is recovering well, in case you were concerned."

Fairchild feigned empathy with an undertone that irritated like an itch beneath the skin. "Oh, of course. Though, he is a soldier, trained for that kind of... confrontation. My concern is for your mental well being. It must have been very traumatic for you."

Cross took a breath and closed his eyes, letting the words fall from his back.

"Tell me more about this tornado of mist," Whitewater interjected.

Tybalt rose from his seat and bowed his head while Fairchild rolled his eyes at his military etiquette. "Your majesty, the tornado has engulfed a portion of the perimeter wall and lower district."

"How interesting," Cross sneered. "Right where the hovel of Orbweaver cultists was, correct?"

Tybalt ignored the comment and continued to explain the situation to the King. "Several creatures breached the mist, but were quickly destroyed by elites that hurried to the area."

"The mist has receded slightly since?" The King asked.

"The diameter has shrunk since its first arrival, but it has since stabilized. Though it spins, there is little current that pulls inwards and it seems relatively benign now. Nothing has gone in or out since its first appearance."

"I see." Whitewater wrung his hands on the orbs of his throne. "I want a full regiment to keep it secure until we know more. No one goes within thirty yards without my expressed permission."

"My apologies, my King," Cross stood slowly. "I also have an urgent matter in need of attention."

"Explain," sounded the Leviathan.

Cross spied the others in his peripheral and approached the dais with the wooden box in hand. With a soft creak, he carefully lifted the lid and withdrew the seared remains of the note he had found and handed it to the King.

Whitewater's crystal eyes scoured every remaining word of the message, being certain to gather the full weight of the script. "This note seems very clear in its intent to threaten the geomancer's with the health of their families."

"Indeed," Cross began. "Andus and I risked our lives to secure this remnant, which was nearly destroyed by the Orbweaver assassin we encountered earlier. The note clearly expresses that the geomancer was to inform the King that nothing was found by investigating the earth beneath the ruined hovel. In return for their compliance, their immediate family would be spared a gruesome visit."

"These cultists are a blight!" Tybalt was clearly frustrated by the situation, wrenching his hands as though to wring an Orbweaver throat. "The geomancers obeyed the demand and in return lost their lives."

"Much of the note is burnt. It's possible the exchange of their life for their families was part of the initial demand as well," Cross stated.

"Or, it's your fault, Vaughn Cross," Fairchild chimed, toying with the weight of golden rings upon his hand.

"How so?"

Fairchild placed his fingertips together and rested his weight back into his chair, smiling softly as he relaxed. "Perhaps the Orbweavers truly intended to leave them be after they obliged, until you decided to push for a second contract. They may have felt their hand was forced with such little time to act and chose to eliminate them, rather than make another bargain."

Cross knew it wasn't absurd to think they had been executed in response to his haste, but certainly didn't want to give Fairchild the satisfaction of knowing he had considered it to be the most likely theory.

Fairchild shook his finger in the air as he came to a realization. "We came to the decision to hire the geomancers and then contracted them for the following morning. Only a half day passed between our verdict and their original contract. Wouldn't that mean the Orbweavers were aware of our plan almost immediately after we came up with it...?"

"No one else should have known. That information was privy only to the King and High Council," Tybalt replied. "It's possible they could have found out after the letters of commission were delivered that night."

Cross nodded. "It's a small window of time between then and dawn, but possible. Who delivered your contracts?"

Tybalt placed his hand on his chest. "I delivered them myself, to be certain."

A shadow tinted the ridges of Cross' eyes as he agreed with Tybalt and turned to present the King with two other pieces of evidence.

Whitewater held out his hand to receive a scroll of vellum and a small blob of wax while Cross signaled to the far guards to approach, one to each side of Alexander Tybalt.

Tybalt looked over his shoulders and quickly grew stern. "What is the meaning of this?"

Cross gestured for the King to open the scroll as he stood aside the dais and began to address the rest of the council. "This burnt message was of such significance that the Orbweaver assassin rushed to destroy it before myself or Andus arrived at the scene. In the assassin's haste at the home of the first geomancer, he not only set fire to the paper, but tried to destroy that which the paper came in." He gestured to the blob of sealing wax he found amidst the ashes. "Once the wax melted and mixed with the ash, it became gray and unrecognizable. However, by cutting it into smaller pieces, I have determined the color is a mixture of both blue and white, exactly like that of our Judiciar."

Fairchild slowly clasped his hands and rested them upon his mouth, eyes overwhelmed with a combination of joy and intrigue.

"Are you accusing me of having written that note because of the sealing wax?" Tybalt began. "That's absurd. Anyone could make that combination."

"You are correct," Cross replied. "I am accusing you because of the hand writing."

Whitewater's eyes slowly rose from the scroll and crushed Tybalt with betrayal. "This is a report you wrote earlier and the script from the message is identical to this sample of your hand."

Tybalt, appalled and overwhelmed, attempted to stand and defend his name, only to have the guards press his shoulders back into his chair. "Your Grace! It wasn't me. There must be a mistake."

"I am afraid there is not." Cross turned the burnt message over to reveal the faint black markings of something barely noticeable. "If you look closely, on the backside of this paper are the faint words of commission, from the ink that had not yet dried before you pressed this extra note in with the contract you delivered."

Tybalt struggled for words, but chose to silence himself and brush away the air of desperation that was filling his lungs.

Cross continued his train of thought. "After we decided to hire the geomancers, you wrote their contracts, placed this message inside, sealed it, and delivered it. Unbeknownst to myself, it worked, at first ⊠ blackmailing them into giving us false reports upon completion of their work. Then, I noticed I was being followed in the streets, which was how you were informed of my plan to hire the geomancers once more. You panicked, as you knew I would work quickly and had whomever was once following me execute both geomancers in such a gruesome manner that it would discourage any and all other cooperation from the citizens of Whitewater in the future. At the same time, you had your assassin be sure to destroy all evidence that could implicate you. Had it not been for Andus and myself, the last message would have turned to ash, leaving behind only the sealing wax, which, as you said earlier, would have been thin evidence in the first place."

"Your Grace," Tybalt pleaded softly, "I assure you, I had nothing to do with this travesty. Please. I will go willingly to the cells, but I beg of you to reconsider all evidence pertaining to this. Perhaps if Salem Eventide could examine..."

The halls echoed with the crash of wood and iron as Cross hurled the small box down, smashing it to pieces against the marble and honeycomb stone. For but a moment, his eyes strained with rage as his pupils constricted and his lips pursed to contain his voice. "Salem Eventide will not...!" Snapping back into his own body and mind, Cross caught himself yelling and forced his heart back into his chest. He cleared his throat, crossed his hands, and continued sternly. "Salem Eventide will not be necessary for this investigation."

A dramatic pause befell them as Whitewater thought to himself, before waving a hand and commanding Tybalt be taken to a cell. Though he remained silent thus far, he had a terrible aura of disapproval that wound him tightly, as though at any moment he would snap and bury Woodcutter in Tybalt's chest. "Is there anything else?" he asked Cross as he watched Tybalt rise and allow himself to be shackled.

"No, your Grace. With the Judiciar gone, the Orbweavers should have significantly less access to confidential information, making it easier for us to maneuver them into a corner."

Fairchild watched carefully as Tybalt was escorted past him, smiling with the corners of his eyes. "Take care, old friend," he said with an undertone of chauvinism and delight.

Cross adjusted his posture and wore his pride like a badge of honor, addressing the King with a vigilance only a victor could adorn. "Your Grace, your kingdom will be without a Judiciar for now. I wish to offer my service for the role, until you find someone more qualified."

Whitewater leaned back into his throne, not once taking his eyes off Tybalt. "No."

Immediately, Cross appeared deflated, as though he was absolutely certain of the King's approval. "But... I assure you..."

"I said no," the King's voice thundered, commanding the purity of silence. "You have many responsibilities and our economics is crucial to me. I cannot afford to have you dividing your attention as such. I will act as Judiciar until my Voice returns, then he will fill the role until I have chosen someone."

"You will give the position to... Eventide?" Cross fought to contain his anxiety, though both Fairchild and the King knew it was there.

"Do you have a problem with that, Chancellor?" Whitewater pulled his gaze from Tybalt for the first time since the accusation had escalated and met Cross with supreme authority.

"No..." he swallowed hard. "Eventide will make a fine judiciar. I am pleased that my hard work has been to the benefit of the Voice."

The King stood to his full height and prepared to descend the dais. "Watch your tone," his voice resounded with intolerance, "or I will give him *your* job as well."

The heavy doors slowly swung open as the guards escorted Tybalt from the grand hall, and as they closed, Cross caught the dark leathers of agent Dask watching as the former Judiciar was taken away. The agent's cold eyes then affixed to his as the space between the doors narrowed, and in the final moments of abalone and alabaster, a clever smile crept across his lips.

30

DECEIT, FOR THE GREATER GOOD

Salem reached for his wine and poured a small cup. Together, he and Lady Rhoswan stood before the pagoda in silence.

"Is this about money?" he asked, still assessing the extent to which her deceit would play out. Though he had little evidence of it, he knew something was wrong.

"No," she replied, still not meeting his eyes. Her attention was elsewhere, staring into the shadows of the Scarlet Ribbon Estate, whose once glorious visage now lay in partial ruination since the burning of the mist.

"Whatever it is that ails you, I am certain we can overcome it together," he said softly.

"I'm very sorry Salem," she began, turning to capture his mind with the glyphs of her eyes. "But this is bigger than you or I."

Just as she was about to lock her eyes to his, all went black and she clutched her face to ease the burning. Salem had thrown his cup of wine into her face to avert the gaze and she could hear him running away. "Don't kill him!" she ordered desperately into the unknown. "I must speak with him first!"

Salem dropped the bottle of wine and began to dash back towards the tornado, hoping to grasp Whisper's attention before it was too late. The road ahead seemed barren, when a figure cloaked in a large wolf's pelt appeared from the shadows of the Estate. Another caught the corner of his eye, brooding from the rooftops. The head of the pelts hung over their own as cowls, shadowing their features and gracing them with fearsome presence.

Without pause, they dashed in to capture him, but much to their surprise their fantastic speed somehow wasn't enough. With remarkable agility, Salem slid and tumbled beneath their advances and dove through the half open window of the nearest cottage.

The two wolves looked to each other with an air of confusion and branched off to quickly pincer him in. Yet, with a single pass of the building, Salem had already exited and bounded up the next, disappearing over the ridge of the rooftop.

Salem's breaths came easily as he delicately dashed over the thatch and tile, running along the thin branches of trees that connected the rooftops of Freestone to keep his stride. Knowing full well he had gained some distance, he slid off the roof and latched onto the edge to stagger his drop, landing gracefully to the road below.

The wolves seemed close in tow and he continued his retreat through the abandoned streets. Much to his own surprise, one of the two wolves intercepted his path ahead. Salem strode weightlessly up a series of crates and carts in attempt to bound over him, when the whirling of cord caught him off guard and a bola tethered his legs together. He awkwardly plummeted to the stone, but managed to gracefully roll to stand.

The wolf, both calculated and cold, tried to grapple him with no success. Even bound at the feet, Salem would weave, duck, and tumble his way around capture, until the second bola came from the side and wrapped its weights around his wrist, staggering him in the process. The two wolves had more than enough reflex to take advantage of the small opportunity and tackled him to the ground.

Salem lay prone beneath the weight. Their eyes could now be seen beneath the cowls they adorned. Gruff and grisly men, with chilling demeanor and the chins of killers. The closest wolf rose a fist and wound for a big hit.

Salem threw his hands ahead in surrender, eyes wide. "Not the face! Not the face!"

★★★

The breeze of another arrow brushed Whisper's hair as it struck the tree beside her. Her assailant could now be seen poking out from behind cover to riddle her with arrows. It was a man, clad in wolf's' fur from head to toe, with a simple bow. A bow far too mundane to have struck her from such range. From what was now such a short distance she could tell his quiver was running low and a tinge of fear seemed to strain his eyes as she approached.

He quickly attempted to notch another arrow when she breached the trees and forced her fingertips into the soft flesh around his throat, crushing his windpipe in her hand. Rage filled her heart, which bled her quicker and labored her breaths. She moved the body aside to catch the glimmer of another arrow and shielded herself with the corpse.

Another damned archer, she cursed to herself. The searing pain of another shot struck her shoulder from behind, dropping her to a knee. *Two.*

Immediately, her aura began to flare and she curled into a tight, fetal ball. The nexus of lashing energy began to whirl and surround her like a dome, churning violently and creating a tempest that began pulling everything into it. It was a powerful technique for fighting multiple enemies, though it was taxing on her body and she was unable to move while employing it. The cyclone grew greater and more virulent by the second, and peach trees began to tear at the root as they succumbed to the wind.

From the inside of the sphere Whisper was barely able to see through the mess of lashing winds and debris that encircled her, though before long three bodies of wolf's fur helplessly flailed within, having been pulled off their feet and sucked inside. With a deep breath that agitated her wounds, she placed her fingers to her lips and exhaled an intense flame into the cyclone, engulfing her with fire and setting the cyclonic dome ablaze. The orange flare was brilliantly blinding, overwhelming all senses as it disintegrated everything caught within her trap. The jet of raw flame continued to pour from her lips until every last ounce of air was pushed from her lungs and she was forced to stop. Her aura began to settle and as the flaming winds dropped, all that remained was the ashen snowfall of that which was once solid.

"Avelie was right," spoke a man's voice from behind her, heavy with a confidence only experience could forge.

Whisper wiped a bead of sweat from her brow and winced as she turned to see who addressed her, but there was only the desert of forlorn trees at her back. "Who are you?" she called.

"I am Howlpack Shade, Instrument of Howlpack Sentinel Avelie." His voice turned to a whisper that seemed to travel from one ear to another, as though he were stalking around.

She had exerted herself quite badly and strained to keep balance, when the glint of matte steel flickered under her jaw. She quickly spun and struck the blade from the wolf behind her, who had nearly slit her throat as the eerie voice distracted her. She was learning by this point that their tactic was to pull her attention in one direction and strike her from her blind spots by other means. This known, she instinctively turned to catch another wolf in mid leap, sword drawn to drive her into the dirt. A simple side step and she evaded the blade, sweeping the wolf's legs and crushing his face into the ground with her palm.

Whisper continued to check her blind spots after each confrontation and surely enough, every new attack led to another until she was desperately combating five wolves simultaneously. With every block, with every tumble, and with every sound of crushing bone, a smile crept further across her lips. The pains of her wounds were subsiding and a vicious strength began to weave into her she was winning, and enjoyed every moment of it.

"An Instrument of Avelie," she called, her reflex in dealing with the other wolves had smoothed around the edges and required less focus. "My, my, aren't I the fortunate one!"

There was a quietude in her head as she hurled the last wolf through the grove.

"Be careful what you consider fortune," the eerie voice replied.

She dashed towards the fallen body of the last wolf as though to punish him further. Instead, she quickly pulled the dagger from his belt and spun, hurling it into the grove until it struck a flame kissed peach tree. The curled edges of singed blossoms and leaves fluttered to the ground.

The faint outline of a strange creature refracted in the light as the blossoms fell and it slowly stood, dropping the enchanted camouflage that allowed it to blend into the grove near-seamlessly. Before her stood a broad man cloaked in a dark, heavy dire wolf's pelt. The pale white skull, which he used as a helmet, sat upon his shoulders, dark eyes peering through.

"I underestimated the potency of your senses," he admitted. Though she couldn't clearly see his features, he had the cool, calm voice of a calculated hunter, with eyes to match.

"And I thought you'd be smarter," her sinister smile returned as her eyes grew sharp, rotating her shoulder to loosen it up.

"Little girl, you don't even..." the air quickly left his lungs as she appeared before him and drove her fist through his stomach with such force it splintered the bark of the tree at his back and rained upon them more singed petals and leaves. Before a single blossom could touch the ground, she clutched the dire wolf's skull, plunged him into the earth, and followed with a heavy foot to cave his head.

Shade, bewildered by the overwhelming surge of power and speed, managed to tumble enough to avoid the brunt, but not quickly enough to avoid her heel as it clipped the edge of his helmet and shattered the bone of his dire helmet. He swiftly rolled to his feet and tore away the rest of the skull, which had fissured so deeply it was more hindrance than help. The heavy pieces of broken bone fell to the dirt and the faint flicker of dancing shadows was all that warned him as a wave of flame poured over his skin, engulfing him in an inferno of orange and red at the lips of Whisper, whose eyes glinted with gleeful ruination.

The stream of glorious fire poured from her lips as she blew through her fingers and if not for the acuity of her vision, she would have nearly missed the faint, dark streak that shot towards her through the current of flame. She immediately stopped her fire and staggered backward, jolting her head away as she caught an arrow just as it graced her lips. The arrowhead cut shallow slits that tinged her mouth with trickles of her own blood.

She took a moment to gather herself, astonished Shade managed to fire an arrow directly through the path of fire to her mouth, nearly burrowing it into the back of her throat.

He slowly rose before her, smoldering as the oils of the dire wolf pelt seemed to provide some limited resistance. In his hand he held a rustic bow of warped wood, reed and antler, and with his other he unfastened the pelt from his shoulders and allowed it to fall behind him. He was a man of long, unkempt hair, dark features, and a bristled jaw. Light armor of leather and hide wrapped his body, a quiver of crimson fletchings hung low on his back, and on each side of his harness was a short blade sheathed in tusks. Despite the ferocity of her attacks, he seemed relatively unharmed, though impressed.

"It was a mistake to think my wolves could handle you. You are prey worthy of my full attention." He adjusted the grip on his bow and flexed his fingers as he prepared to quickly draw an arrow at a moment's notice.

Whisper discarded the arrow she had caught and pressed her fingertips to her lips to inspect the cut. She had suffered significant damage from her prior encounter already. A broken wrist, punctured lung, and an arrow to the shoulder and forearm, yet she had never felt better. Before her stood an Instrument of Fate, scourge of the dragons, and potentially the one who orphaned her so long ago. No wound could steal her excitement in this moment.

"You can't win in your condition," he stated confidently, as though she would consider agreeing with him.

Whisper crooked her head from shoulder to shoulder and met his eyes with unwavering resilience. His skill of preference was clearly with the bow and she could only fathom his mastery over it. "Killing a creature from stealth and range doesn't make you a warrior."

"You're right," he replied. "It makes me an assassin."

31

DIAMOND DUST AND THE FALL OF LYRE

"Are you okay?" Fever crawled to the edge of the hole in the floor and looked down upon Wrath as he pried his arms from the stone and disbanded the spectre glyph that had given his armor its ghostly appearance.

Wrath remained completely silent as he clambered clumsily back to his feet and shattered the remainder of his entombment.

"You will not take it!" Eywin stated valiantly, sword drawn and pointed towards the weakened Fever.

He was on the other side of the hole and of little threat to her, but were he to find a way across she wouldn't have the energy needed to defend herself.

"Who do you represent?" he asked. His eyes were affixed with the unwavering intensity only a mere few possessed, until the drawing of shadows caught his gaze. Fever noticed it as well and together they watched as the darkness pooled and rose to form Ivory in all her slender beauty and grace ⊠ her iconic webbed dress, platinum diamond bracelet, and ivory cloud at her feet.

Her hand formed at the tip of the blade and the simple touch of her fingertips to the steel began to infect it. White crystalline lines stretched from her touch like webs that crawled towards his hand, though he released the sword before it could touch him. The veins turned the steel both white and brittle and as the blade struck the ground it crumbled into a mass of tiny diamonds.

Ivory smiled warmly, though the frigid intensity of her eyes sung a different song. "She hails to me."

It was clear he had no idea what he was dealing with, but knew better than to underestimate. "Know that you have raised a hand to the Whitewater Leviathan, whose justice will be swift in light of your attack on the fine city of Lyre."

Ivory laughed softly and waved a hand as if to shoo him. "Your 'king' can keep his precious city. I've come for the Wish." Her jovial expression slowly faded as she noticed it still imprisoned within honeycomb stone. In a single graceful swoop she glided across the floor and wrapped her arms delicately around it, teasing the edge of the fissure with her fingers as she mourned its containment. "Soon you will be free."

The white veins began to spread from her hands and crept along the surface with little avail. Though the ward was broken, the substance was still too hard to affect, even for her. The enchanted vines that tethered it down, however, fell to diamond dust nearly instantaneously. The faintest glimmer of frustration and wonder crossed the corners of her eyes as the veins clung to the honeycomb stone but did not deconstruct it. Nonetheless, she softened her gaze and released.

"That is the sword of Shiori Etrielle, creator of the known world. Its power will reject your corruption."

Fever thought that perhaps Ivory would laugh at his remark, but instead she clenched her jaw and grew stern. "You are an insignificant speck who doesn't even know how much he doesn't even know." Her eyes studied the sheen of the platinum and gold. "The power of this weapon would have devoured you whole to the touch." She followed the artifact all the way to the tiny fabric ghost charm that hung in frozen suspension from the ornate chain on the hilt, its little eyes sealed shut. "Only I am powerful enough to wield a weapon Shiori Etrielle made for herself."

Wrath's head and shoulders appeared through the hole in the floor as he climbed up from below. "Take the Second Wish to Sabanexus," she commanded.

Wrath gave a single nod, approached the honeycomb stone, and hauled it over his shoulder.

"King Whitewater will find you and your life will be forfeit," Eywin warned. "The Phoenix Queen, the Shamaiyel, there is no reach nor realm where you will be safe, for the moment you claim that sword, you will be the enemy of a world united."

"Believe me," she begun. "Your kings, queens, and snake lords will be far too busy soon enough." She delighted herself with her secret plot involving the seals that funneled mist over the realms and breathed easily knowing the one Shén Shé enchantress most capable of disbanding her enchantments had been executed by her Instrument.

"My fate..." Fever began nervously.

No explanation was needed as Ivory met her eyes and saw the shame. All the joy, all the enlightenment, vanished from her victorious smile as Fever's failure sunk her ambitions. The rage and intolerance was palpable as Ivory grew viciously stern and pierced her with eyes so unimpressed they drowned in icy madness.

"I'm sorry my…" Before Fever could finish, Ivory lifted a finger and began to approach.

Ivory delicately lifted the fabric draped across Fever's face to inspect the damage, and though an anger churned within her there was still a glimpse of remorse in her eyes. The damage was grotesquely extensive and she was certain to never recover her former beauty. "The Shén Shé enchantress did this?"

"Yes." Fever looked down to her feet in shame.

As much as Ivory wanted to punish Fever for her failure, she couldn't help but feel a massive price had already been paid. "You fought bravely," Ivory said softly as she lowered the cloth and placed her hand on Fever's shoulder. "You have made a great sacrifice in my name and I am thankful. I promise I will do everything in my power to rectify your loss."

Fever wasn't sure what could be done, but if there was a method of recovery Ivory was her best chance.

"You will go to Sabanexus also," Ivory ordered gently, "Wait there for my return." She gently squeezed her shoulder and Fever's body collapsed unconscious. Ivory then turned to Wrath. "You will take her and protect her at all costs."

Wrath turned his head sharply as he emoted strong disagreement, and for the first time a low rumbling voice of ancient guttural language shook the rubble as he spoke.

Eywin was familiar with many languages, but this was the first of its kind to him. Its deep grunted utterance and heavy tribal undertone was synonymous with giants and other large, barbaric races long since lost. This only helped him conclude even further that the massive beast was, in fact, a true Leviathan, impossible as it seemed.

Ivory forcefully replied in his native tongue, saying something Wrath clearly didn't approve of, but he no longer felt the power to contest. He growled as he turned from Ivory and gently cradled Fever.

Ivory waved a hand and created a portal akin to the one Wrath first arrived through. He roughly tossed the Second Wish through the vortex in silent outburst and crouched to squeeze himself and Fever in afterwards. The shadows latched onto his plate mail like sticky fibers as he forced onward, until they completely disappeared and the vortex closed behind them.

Ivory viciously turned to the Eywin. "I had planned to leave Lyre to its wyrmsong and underwhelming morale, unfortunately I need the Shén Shé to die. Due to the failure of my Instrument, a new unfortunate destiny will befall this ancient city."

"You will not get away with this, by the Fates I assure you."

Ivory laughed. "Do you hear that?"

Eywin listened closely, but couldn't hear anything.

"There are no howling wolves or chittering of spiders in these halls," she laughed, "No Instrument to prevent your demise, no Fates personally washing your city in salvation. Either they cannot see or do not care, and your streets continue to burn."

"The Fate's see everything, and everything happens for a reason," he replied valiantly.

Ivory smiled. "The gaze of the Fate's can be avoided if you know how, and sometimes bad things happen for no reason whatsoever." Ivory opened her arms and prepared to channel a brilliant amount of energy from the winged platinum bracelet she wore, which began to glow a near blinding silver light as the power stretched from the large flawless diamond and crept across her body. Emanating from the roiling ivory cloud that shrouded her feet were a dozen of the white crystalline veins, which began to branch outwards and consume everything they touched.

The duke tried to evade backwards, but the veins split and spread at an alarming rate. Before he knew it, the whole room turned white with tiny diamonds. Flecks of the glittering gems fell like glittering rain in his last few living moments.

The veins quickly crawled up his body, reaching into his eyes, nose, and mouth. It was a cold burning he had never experienced before and the feeling of both flesh and bone succumbing to the crystalline conversion was so foreign that it was uniquely uncomfortable rather than painful, like that of a sleeping limb.

"Your Fates fail you," her voice sung. "Only I am worthy of your worship, but I'll settle for your fear."

★★★

The lovely Katya brushed her brown curls from her eyes as she finished dressing Casamir's grievous injury. He slowly regained consciousness and bobbed his head as he collected his bearings. The fibrous texture of torn cloth teased his fingertips as he gingerly traced the dressing.

"Escape..." he strained under low breaths. "Katya..."

Katya looked out the doorway into the crowds of people rushing to leave the city, all bound for the capital. "The roads will be very crowded. We may have to use the duke's low road."

Casamir gradually recovered his coherence, able to sit upright and adjust his remaining eye to the light of the room. The pain was more intense than anything he had ever imagined, but whatever Katya had dressed it with afterward was numbing it to a tolerable level.

"We need to get to safety," he began as he attempted to stand.

Katya helped him up and held the brunt of his weight as he found his balance. "The whole city is being evacuated to Whitewater."

Casamir nodded, his center of gravity stabilized. "Do we have horses?"

"Plenty," she replied. "The streets are too crowded, so everyone is leaving them behind."

He nodded. "We'll travel to the duke's low road then."

The low road was a narrow path that traveled alongside the city walls and branched through dense forest to many of the main routes. It was meant as an escape route for the duke in the event of an emergency and is only accessible through a gate in the castle's outer cloister. The Lyre's Elite were amidst the few privy to the knowledge of its existence, so it was bound to be clear for horses to traverse.

"Come brother." Katya gestured as she led him towards the doorway. "We will go to the stables, but we need to leave now."

Though he was still fatigued, he was a Waylander, and he pressed forward through the doorway and into the world.

It was astonishing how many more people flooded into the streets, all pressing for the nearest bastion gate nearly a mile away. Carts sat abandoned as swarms of the frantic engulfed and bodies of the trampled could be felt underfoot. Together they fought the current of desperation and took to the side streets for better maneuverability. Though they were quite full as well, there was a bit more forgiveness when it came to people carelessly bumping into Casamir's fresh wounds.

Though the initial leg of their journey was both slow and complicated, it wasn't long before people became fewer and further apart. The masses were all charging the gates, while they were going to the one place no one else dared ⊠ the castle.

Horses cried and tugged at their tethers as they shifted in their stables. Nearly every one of them was left behind, so they had their pick of the duke's finest geldings.

It was then they saw it. Crystalline veins that began to spread across the outer walls of the castle.

They both stopped to watch as it rapidly traversed the stone like ivy and drained every bit of color, turning the massive structures white as bone. Katya caught herself holding her breath. Perhaps it was the astonishing beauty it beheld as the surface shimmered amidst the blazing wyrmsong, or the suffocating sense of dread that prevented her from averting her eyes. Regardless, the world around her dimmed and muffled as her focus drew to the breathtaking ruination of one of the realm's most coveted cornerstones.

The structure became immensely brittle and the towering spire was the first to collapse in on itself. Floor by floor, stone by stone, the castle crumbled into white diamond sand that tumbled in droves. She expected the ground to tremble beneath its mass, but felt nothing as it weightlessly disintegrated. A cloud of fine crystalline dust began to expand towards them and shrouded nearly everything in its path. She caught a brief glimpse of more veins as they spread towards the gatehouse and inner cloister walls before the line of sight was lost.

"It's spreading! Go quickly!" she yelled to Casamir as she struggled to mount her horse. She had planned to place a saddle first, but there wasn't enough time and she was forced to ride without.

Her first few attempts failed as the horse grew restless and wouldn't stop shifting. Frustration and panic began to overtake as she troubled herself by checking on the cloud, which was rapidly expanding towards them. She tried once more and nearly pulled herself onto its back, but slid off and fell onto the thin layer of straw beneath.

"Katya!" she heard him call her name. It was the first sound she heard since her senses shut down and it seemed to snap her back to reality. She turned to see Casamir atop a black gelding, reaching out for her hand. One fluent motion was all it took to clutch his arm and allow him to pull her up, where she sat behind and held as tightly as she could. The power and agility of a duke's steed was remarkably obvious as they accelerated much quicker than she had imagined, nearly throwing her to the ground once more.

"It's catching up!" she cried as she chanced a glance behind her. For the briefest moment she saw something else as well, but the wind flicked her hair into her eyes. A lithe figure gleaming forest green light from its hands and feet jumped an inhuman distance from a rooftop and disappeared beyond the other buildings. A squint later and it was gone.

"The gate is open!" he called back to her. It was most fortunate for them someone had already been there to raise the door, not just because they wouldn't need to dismount and burn precious time, but for the hope that it had been opened by their father, who may have defeated the leviathan and escaped the collapse of Lyre. The open portal would allow them to keep their lead on the cloud. However, the low road would run alongside the wall before branching outwards, which would give ample time for the ruination to catch up.

The hooves echoed loudly as they raced through the tunnel and breached the light at the end, which opened up into thick wilderness. The low road turned sharply before a drop and they nearly slid from the ledge as they veered the horse. Though the fall would be no more than two stories, at their speed it could have been fatal had they lost control.

The towering wall alongside may have hindered their sight of the cloud, but the fear of being engulfed lingered heavily.

"We're almost at the first branch!" He had only traveled the low road once before and recalled an exit would appear shortly, though he couldn't remember where it led.

She held his body tightly, perhaps with more strength than she intended, as she watched the narrow path ahead. The dense trees were but a blur while the wind stung her eyes and as the tension torqued her nerves to their peak, she caught a glimpse of the same forest green light on a portion of wall ahead. Before either of them could speculate as to what it was, the wall burst as they passed and showered them with blinding sand. The force of the blast was more than enough to push them over the edge, but something hard also collided into the horse with such velocity it violently jarred their mount off its legs completely. It was a moment of slowed time. A disoriented and weightless world devoid of all sight, sound, and smell.

She could feel the sand against her face, the lonesome wind as she spiraled through the air, the hard, unforgiving surfaces of the forest beyond, and then she felt no more.

***

The dissonant cries of the soldiers were a muffled susurrus amidst the damp drear of cobwebs and dust. Rays of soft light streamed through cracks in the old wood and windows as Ashissa's black scales glistened like midnight water, her forest green runes flickered dimly on her palms and pads.

How dare the human raise unhallowed serpents to Ashissa and her malison, she thought to herself angrily, recollecting the events that transpired shortly before finding refuge in the open attic of an abandoned home. *Shamaiyel shall consume both her and her tainted snakes!*

Though her essence churned with such disgrace against her brethren, one wouldn't know beyond the cold blooded demeanor they wore with such objective principle. Behind the ruthless cunning, the Shén Shé were known well for one more trait ⊠ steadfast doctrine towards their serpentine god, Shamaiyel, who is depicted as a massive nine headed serpent with feathered tongues of blazing green flame and scales of lambskin leaves. Any slight towards serpent kind is a slight to Shamaiyel, whose wrath is that of cunning rather than strength. Tales often involved Shamaiyel whispering deceptions into his transgressors, driving them to devour the goodness of their lives before he devours them in turn. To the rest of the world it was mere tribal folklore, but to the Shén Shé it was dogma.

The dull throbbing of her partially healed wounds ached beneath her new skin. The deeper lacerations hadn't yet repaired and she had felt more muscle tear as she fled the tower. She gently placed a hand to her stomach and examined the blood of pale violet, allowing the cool fluid to glide between her fingertips. The largest cut reopened in the escape and she applied her best efforts to resourcefully dress the wound. Fortunately for her, the wound wasn't fatal anymore, and the time she had taken to wrap her torso in old linens helped to staunch the blood loss.

What a tragedy it was, having to abandon the great city of Lyre before perusing its renown collection of ancient texts and tomes. She argued with herself to infiltrate its depths as the city ran rampant, but was certain that the current crises would have activated some very serious lock down protocols, raising the risk much more than comfortable. Regardless, her demands for written texts was approved and she could leave knowing they would meet their end of the bargain at their earliest behest.

The potent potion of anger and remorse was a combination she struggled to conceal beneath her stoic visage, though her eyes told tales for her. She slid to the window on her glyphs and peered towards the castle. The wyrmsong had raised thick pillars of roiling smoke, an intensity of heat that could be seen as the air flexed along the inner cloister.

What unusual enchantment is this? she asked herself as white crystals began to engulf the castle from the inside out. Her eyes were not very sharp at determining detail over distance, but the collapse of the spire was unmistakable and the taste of powerful energy filled the air. The massive cloud of crystalline dust burst outward as the building silently crumbled and swallowed whole that which surrounded it. At first she thought it a blessing from Shamaiyel. Swift justice brought upon the shoulders of those in need of penance. She dared smile in sweet retribution when she noticed it spread to the surrounding homes, much faster than she imagined possible.

Quickly, she turned and dashed across the old floorboards, bursting from the far window with arms wide open as she braced herself to land on the next building. Ceramic tiles worn pale with weather and mold cracked beneath her feet and hands as she landed hard and began to stride across.

Her eyes quickly assessed the terrain as she tried to formulate a swift plan of escape, and proceeded to build great speed as she leapt from rooftop to rooftop. Were she able to use the straights of the roads she would be able to reach top speed, but with so many pedestrians, carts, and other various obstacles it was unlikely she would have the opportunity.

Her arms and legs were growing numb from the bumpy ridges of the tiles, but the taste of destructive power was growing more and more palpable. It would catch her very soon, but she refused to take her eyes off the wall. Only a few more houses before she would reach it, and the anxiety of feeling so desperately close forced her to keep a cool head.

Every aching muscle in her body strained as she burst off the last rooftop. The cool emptiness of the cloud was so close it tickled the pads of her feet as the tiles crumbled into tiny diamonds.

Time began to slow as her focus honed on the palms of her hands, mid-flight. As she fell from the air and plummeted headfirst towards the thick stone barrier with arms outstretched, emerald energy began to channel through her hands, and the glyphs she had drawn to give her the ability to glide reformed into a new design.

She forced her eyes closed as she connected, though she could feel the stone transmute to soft sand at her fingertips. The multitude of tiny cool grains trickled against her scales as she burst through and the weightlessness of success elated her, until the concussive force of something solid interrupted her path and sent a terrible pain surging through her body. An agony drowned only by the cracking of bones, though she wasn't sure if they were her own.

The last few conscious seconds played out much longer, a nauseating vortex of both confusion and dread. Her breaths grew labored as she felt the cold of the earth creep upon her, and her last moments flooded with despair, bloodied and clawing desperately at the coffin of her mind.

32

AVIARY AND THE QUEEN OF THE DRAKES

Salem awoke amidst the cold, damp musk of a cellar, with two wolves on either side of him. As his vision steadied from the hit to the face he had suffered, the pain was beginning to throb across his eye and nose. Both his hands and feet were bound in silk rope as he sat on the floor, propped against the wall broken, dirty, and tired.

"I don't know what to make of this," spoke Lady Rhoswan from a seat at the other end of the room. In her hands she held a white crystal and placed it alongside the other possessions they relieved him of. She sifted through the few belongings. "Coin, needles, book, flask of dremaera..." She picked up a vial of something dark and smelled the contents. "What appears to be black dye." She placed it back on the table. "Who are you?"

"Salem Eventide, Voice of the King of Whitewater, need I remind," he looked to the wolf on his right, though he didn't look back. "And here I thought *I* got hit in the head."

"Believe me," she began, "I am unhappy with this situation"

"Far be it from me to call you a liar."

"I don't want to bring you harm, Salem. I have always admired your help, and you have always been supportive of myself and my ambitions. What we have built here, together, is beyond words."

"I am pleased to hear these bindings and bodyguards are to protect me."

Rhoswan fiddled with the objects on the table once more, feebly deducing why he would have some of the unusual items he did. "I have been ordered to kill you, you know."

Salem would have been surprised were it not for his present condition. "By what authority? Are you an Orbweaver? Emberwilde spy? Or has the good King Whitewater gone mad?" he tried to gauge her reaction to each suggestion, gaining no information in the end. "Are you, too, a vassal of Ivory?"

She shifted the edge of her robe to reveal her thigh, upon which she bore the black spider brand of the Fates. "I am an Instrument of Origin Progenitus."

There were few things that would catch Salem off guard, and hearing the news forced him to recollect all the interactions they had together. He sifted through memory after memory, putting together the pieces to the puzzle he could now see, and realized she exhibited no sign in the time they had known each other. She had covered such a great secret well and he felt foolish for not considering the possibility or delving deeper into the history of her enlightenment.

"So, the Fates wish me dead then," he pondered. "Do they not realize I am helping them with their latest dilemma? My organization against the Orbweavers would be a strike against Ivory and her rebellion."

"This isn't about the Orbweavers, or Ivory."

"Then what?"

"The wolves tell me they chased you along the rooftops. Hardly the skill of a royal dignitary, is it?"

"We are not all born into politics, Lady Rhoswan. I had a life before I served the King." His blend of compliance and farce kept her patience shifting.

"Yes, a doctor, right? And before that, you would have me believe you were, what? A street performer?"

Salem chuckled and shook his head as though it weren't a bad idea. "I am delightful..." He could tell she didn't care for his jokes, perhaps it was what made him want to make more. "Progenitus wants me dead because I am athletic? Come now."

"Progenitus wants you dead because you have no fatespinner."

The hesitation was palpable as Salem scoured the room, taking in as much information as he could.

"No fatespinner," she said again, examining the dye once more. "There hasn't been a creature without a fatespinner since the dragons, if I'm not mistaken."

"The implication being that I am a threat because the Fates cannot control my destiny? Or better yet, that they think I am a dragon?"

"Whoever or whatever you are, Ivory has begun a war and you are a wild card. The Fates cannot afford unpredictability in times like these. Especially from a man of such influence."

"Ivory's war is a poor excuse to hide behind. I have committed no crimes and have explicitly shown that my efforts are to the benefit of the realm. That aside, if I truly have no fatespinner, how is it that they know of my presence in the first place? Convenient I should appear to them now, no?"

"The Fates have been aware of your presence for five years now. In fact, I was chosen as an Instrument specifically for the purpose of keeping you close."

Salem didn't know how to respond. Typically, one would feel offended at the idea that all of their connections were under false pretense, however he was certain the feelings and friendship they had developed over the last four years was genuine. "I thought of you as a true friend, you should know."

She looked away to hide the tears she wanted to shed. "Believe me, Salem, this breaks my heart. I have always been a woman of business and you were one of the very few I could call friend. Perhaps the only one who truly understood me, even. Spying on you was a mission, but becoming close was not."

He sighed heavily. The will of the faithful was something that did not break easily and he didn't have the time to convince Rhoswan sparing his life would be a better option, especially knowing that Progenitus would probably punish her horribly if she did. His mind assessed his predicament, understanding the only reason he was still alive was because she intended to kill him more humanely. Nervously, he looked over the room once more for a route of escape, but there was only a single door at the top of a wooden staircase. It was only then he realized where he was. "This is the aviary..."

Rhoswan stood and delicately crossed the room, crouching before him. "What makes you say that?"

He gathered his thoughts and quickly responded. "By scent of ash we are still in Freestone, redwood supports tell me we are in an estate, and undertones of blossom tell me it is yours. There are old, worn chips and drag marks along the floor, which would lead me to believe this used to be a cellar, before you removed the shelves and barrels to make room for the narrow slats you use for beds."

She smiled. "You're a sharp one, more so when you're sober, but if this were my aviary then where are my wrens?"

"Do not play me for a fool, I am well aware of where your power lies. Your patrons pay you a weight of silver, then you lock their minds within a palace of their desires. Providing them the beautiful, nay, legendary brunettes you refer to as your 'wrens'." He looked over the room once more. "Hardly the atmosphere of a pleasure house, yet I suppose your clients are not conscious by the time you store them here for the night."

"You will see the aviary soon enough," she said sadly, making her plan apparent.

"Though my thoughts may be overwhelming at times, they are my own. I prefer you stay out of my head." Salem was beginning to worry, gently writhing his wrists at the bindings in hopes of some give.

"Powers that be want you dead, Salem." Her words seemed heavy with remorse. "Though I don't understand, it is your destiny. Please, in respect to your contributions, allow me to place your mind in the aviary. There you will not feel pain, but rather drift away peacefully amidst your last heavenly indulgences. This is the best death I can offer you and I do not wish to see you suffer."

Salem seemed to consider it. Despite his struggles, his bindings were quite tight and there was very little hope of escape under the conditions. Even amidst his demise, the concern for himself was but a shadow to the concern he had for Whisper. "What of my dear Whisper?" he asked. "You expect to use your inception to place false memories of my passing? She is far too smart for that, you know."

There was a dooming pause as Rhoswan allowed her gaze to fall. "Whisper is marked for death as well."

She expected to see terror, sadness, or something similar when she rose to look at him, but was awestruck with intensity as his eyes locked her in place. They weren't that of a man in his last moments, but piercing daggers of emerald that reflected a cold and relentless confidence. "If you so much as lay a finger on her I will spare you no quarter."

She was at a loss for words. Certain he had no tricks at his disposal and shocked that his wrath ran so deep. "There is nothing I can do, it is being dealt with as we speak."

"Know this," he began. "You have chosen your side, and though I truly admire your conviction, I expect you to know I have convictions of my own. Of which you will feel in full force for your actions this day."

"You would punish me for Whisper's death?"

"Do not seem so surprised, for you are, in fact, punishing me for no death at all. Your Fates wish to kill me for being born. You best believe that, should I escape, they and all they employ shall be held accountable for their actions."

She looked to the wolves and nodded, cuing them to restrain his head as the glyphs within her eyes flared once more. "It's for the greater good."

"No!" Salem yelled, struggling violently against them to no avail. "I will not let you hurt her!"

The two wolves held him down and pried his eyes open, forcing him to look to the Lady Rhoswan, whose emblazoned pupils wept with what she had to do.

He flailed, twisted, and fought with every ounce of strength he had, yelling for help, calling for vengeance. Everything but begging. "I will not lose another!" The words tore from his chest in desperation before his eyes dilated and his body fell lifeless locked away to die in silence.

★★★

Salem sat atop a pair of marble steps that led into an airy building of silk and orchids, the sweet aroma of peach blossoms graced his senses. The scent reminded him of Freestone in its prime, and despite his inner turmoil it somehow soothed him with nostalgia.

"Welcome, master Eventide," chimed the lovely voice of a brunette woman walking through the lush grass and gardens that surrounded him.

She was possibly the most beautiful thing he could imagine, and he figured that was the point. Trapped within his own mind his force of will was interjecting with realistic thought, which dulled the sense of belonging that most men would have easily succumbed to.

"You are not real," he stated, examining his inner world.

"I feel real," she replied. Her playful eyes paired the flirtatious curl of her smile as she gestured for him to enter the building.

The overwhelming urge to yield continued to surface, as though Rhoswan's power was not simply that of hypnosis, but was somehow encouraging him to indulge and enjoy. It was only then he realized he was standing, unfettered and unwounded in the aviary. He gently touched his face where the wounds once swelled and felt nothing but the enhanced sensation of touch against his skin. It was a very dangerous world and he fought to keep his priorities straight.

He ignored the wren's suggestion and wandered into the grove until the building disappeared behind him, losing himself in a cloud of perfect fragrant blooms. The trees bore beautiful fruit that hung so juicy and full the branches sagged, tantalizing him at every glance.

"Hurry inside," the wren's voice sung once more. "I brought some friends." He turned to see the woman standing at the top of the marble stairs beside him, with two more beautiful wrens behind her. His mind would not allow him to leave the area, and in any direction he wished, it seemed he would always end up here.

"I cannot," he declared as he remained focused on Whisper. "There is someone I must save."

The wrens smiled and held each other lovingly. "You are weary and she will be here shortly."

He thought hard on his predicament and finally tapped into what little frustration the illusion would allow. "No." he shook his head in disbelief, knowing there had to be a way out. "I must get to her."

A hand gently took his and filled him with belonging. It was a petite Setsuhan woman with hair of black and gold feathers, eyes as sharp as his own. "Delris celys," she said sweetly. "We are finally together again."

Salem withdrew his hand and looked away, refusing to make eye contact. "Vaexa est'alara celys. You are not truly here."

"I am in your thoughts," she replied, "as you are in your thoughts. That makes me as real as you are."

"Go away," he begged, walking back into the grove.

The softness of a hand clutched his once more and he turned to confront her. "I said go..." He stopped as he saw Whisper before him, wearing a beautiful robe of black and blue, her eyes filled with tears.

"Come Salem," she pleaded. "I can't bear to be without you any longer."

"I... no... no, I cannot."

"I have been blind," she mourned, pulling herself in close to hold him. Her head rested against his chest. The fragrance of her hair was intoxicating. "All along, you were right in front of me."

He held her for a moment and then gently pushed her away. This place was even more dangerous than he had first anticipated. His initial thoughts were that he would simply have to find a way to escape his mind, but it would seem the desires of his heart and soul would fight him on it. He closed his eyes and tried to focus, but the familiar scents grew stronger. He held his breath, but the sounds lured him in further. Regardless of which senses he suppressed the others would compensate and it was making his situation dire.

"Don't you love me?" he heard Whisper ask.

"Don't you miss me?" asked Vaexa as well.

The feeling of desperation began to overwhelm him, and instead of contesting he decided to embrace it. He opened his heart to the frustration and fear, and within moments the pleasures subsided enough to allow him to refocus.

He opened his eyes to find himself alone, surrounded by the falling of blossoms as the wind cooled and the trees withered ever so slightly.

Suddenly, the ground behind him shook as something crashed through the trees, shattering the delicate branches and sending a snowfall of colorful petals adrift. As he turned, a great dragon towered before him. Four powerful legs sunk claws into the soil, a long bladed tail whipped effortlessly through what trees remained, and all shimmered as light crossed her opalescent scales. As striking as it was to be in the presence of a dragon, this one hypnotized him. She bore massive wings that stretched out into two pairs, and all four glistened a multitude of vibrant color and design. Wrapped down over her eyes and under her throat was a brilliant golden blue halo of blazing fire. Though one would think the flame covering her eyes would make her see nothing, he knew well enough that she could see everything.

A pair of wings folded over the lower half of her body, while the other pair cloaked and concealed her head. With a swift and graceful motion, a woman's hand outstretched and pushed the wings aside, which simultaneously shifted into a cloak of vibrant feathers that hung from her shoulders and trailed the full length of her previous draconian form. She transmuted into the figure of a Setsuhan woman, whose long golden plumage flowed beneath the blue flame that continued to blaze around her head and across her yes.

"This is quite a predicament," she spoke, her voice both powerful and disciplined. The first sound to bring him relief.

He instantly bowed to a knee. "Savrae-Lyth, Queen of Drakes."

"You needn't bow. I am only here in spirit."

He refused to rise. "You are my Queen, even in my dreams."

The winds gently ruffled the feathers of her hair as she looked around. She raised a hand to her face and motioned as though pulling away a mask, dispersing the halo of flames and revealing her eyes to him draconian pupils in pools of scarlet, with petals of silver to form a blossom that flexed as she focused. "There is still work to be done. Now that the Fates are aware of you, plans must go ahead quickly."

"There are complications," he replied. "Ivory the Unwoven has rebelled against the Weave and is making moves to plunge the world into chaos."

Savrae-Lyth seemed agitated at the new development. "Ivory," she thought aloud. "After they betrayed Shiori Etrielle and sealed her away all those years ago, I suppose it was only a matter of time before they would betray each other. The only thing greater than her madness is her sense of entitlement."

"Is Shiori still safe where she is?"

Savrae-Lyth nodded softly. "For now, though she is still bound and helpless until the key is ready. How is Whisper progressing?"

"She is very powerful, but undisciplined. Unless something drastic changes, she may take some time to mature."

"See to it she is ready as soon as possible and be careful not to reveal her nature to the Instruments. As it stands, we have an incredible advantage. So long as the Fates remain divided, they will not have the power to defeat

Shiori a second time. And if Ivory is creating chaos in the mortal world, Illy's eyes will be overwhelmed with irregularities in the Weave. Now is the time to prepare, for if everything goes accordingly there will be a three way war between Ivory, the Fates, and Shiori Etrielle. All for the destiny of the world."

"What would you have me do about Ivory?"

"Leave her. Unless confronted we will stick to our original plan. For now, the Fates will all fight each other. Should they become aware that we intend to return Shiori Etrielle to rightful rule, they could rally together to stop us. Discretion is of the utmost importance, now more than ever."

"Of course." He bowed his head once more. "Unfortunately, it would seem I am trapped here. Do you know how I might escape?"

The Queen of Drakes looked over him with a hint of sadness. "This is a very strong enchantment," she began. "It materializes one's primal desires and uses the heart and soul to reinforce the illusion. The stronger the want, the stronger the hold."

"I do not know if I can force apathy," he replied.

"You care too deeply, not only for our cause, but for..." she thought of both Whisper and Vaexa at the same time, "...others. Yet, there is another way."

"Please, anything." His fealty flattered her.

"This illusion is fortified with your pleasures. The fastest counter agent would be to overwhelm you with your ails."

Salem pondered what this meant as she opened her hand and revealed an array of electric fluxes that danced between her fingers.

"Your mind is too complex and our time too short to work with your emotions. If you wish to escape we will have to inflict grievous physical pain to break the enchantment. Enough to wake you, but not enough to kill you, for if you die here within your mind you will die in the real world as well."

Salem swallowed hard and met her with fearless intensity. "I must do what is needed, for you."

"No," she replied, slowly approaching him. "You must do what is needed, for Whisper."

He nodded as he prepared himself, setting his second knee to the ground and bracing his hands on his legs. "True conviction requires sacrifice. Once we free Shiori Etrielle and restore her rightful rule, the Fates will pay for their treachery."

33

BITTER FRUIT AND THE IRE OF THE SNOW LEAF MOUNTAIN

The quietude of the night broke with the crashing sound of clay and wood as Cross flipped the edge of his table, scattering a candelabra and bowl of oranges across the smooth stone of his home. Shallow breaths and clenched fists accented the feral nature of his eyes beneath his hair.

"Salem... Eventide..." he growled as he reached for a cup and prepared to hurl it across the room, only to be interrupted by a knock at his door. The hour was growing late and the company surprised him enough to stagger his rage. The weight of the knock was both delicate and cumbersome soft hands and heavy rings. "Go away Fairchild."

Surely enough, his sinisterly pleasant voice replied as the door creaked open. "Now now, I am simply a friend willing to hear the tales of your tribulation." He looked over the room as he entered, plucked an orange from the floor, and held the rind to his nose. "I like what you've done here. A few wrinkles in the pristine brings out your humanity."

"Get out of my home," Cross commanded sternly.

Playfully offended, Fairchild entered further and helped himself to a chair in the sitting area. "Well, as Judiciar, you certainly do have the right to... oh my... that's right, you're still just a Chancellor."

"You've come all this way simply to rub this in my face?"

"Actually, I want to know why you care so much?" Fairchild began to delicately peel the orange, tiny spritz of oil took to the air and scented the room. "I had no idea you had such a passion for leading our great military."

Cross sighed heavily and ran his fingers through his hair, brushing it from his face. "I…" he shook his head and rolled his eyes to the ceiling. "I suppose I don't actually care that I am not Judiciar, but I care that Eventide is."

Fairchild chuckled to himself. "The discord between you two is more entertainment than even *my* money could buy."

"I simply wish the King would recognize my skill."

"And you feel demonstrating the responsibility of both roles would earn his respects?"

"I suppose that's what I thought. I presume you are here to convince me otherwise."

Fairchild finished peeling the orange and took his first bite of the exotic fruit, wincing slightly at the acidity. "What a terrible fruit," he said, setting the rest on a side table and holding his hands out, pondering what to wipe them on. He stood and crossed the room, choosing a common cloth over the silk of his expensive vestments. "I believe you would be a fine Judiciar."

Cross seemed suspiciously surprised. "You do?"

"Certainly. You have something to prove and everything to lose. Two things Eventide does not."

Cross shook his head. "It doesn't matter anyways. The King has made his decision."

Fairchild struggled to wash the stickiness from his hands and expressed his disapproval quite clearly. "Be patient," he began, "Salem is not faultless. He will make a mistake."

Cross took a deep breath and imagined the opportunity when another knock sounded at his door. He looked on in silence and intrigue. They knocked again.

Fairchild folded his hands and tilted his head, carefully studying Cross' reaction. "Don't you recognize it?"

Cross turned his head to Fairchild and spied him sharply. The latch of his door lifted and the hinges softly creaked as they let themselves in.

★★★

Vaexa knelt before a pond of crystal water and cried, her head buried in her hands. From beyond the trees, a fenwight watched in mournful silence. It had been several days since the mountain consumed both Rhys and Luseca without giving them back and the mist that funneled down from the mystical blast had receded back into the ceiling along with the demons within. Since that fateful hour, she had been coming to this pond to cry and vent her frustrations.

The people of Setsuha were in despair. The halo of energy that engulfed them had caused several deaths and grievous injuries, and with the mountain refusing to give them life, their emotions concerning the finality consumed them.

She looked into the water and watched her reflection through the ripples of her fallen tears. What had she done that merited such an ending? They were a race of peace and connection, always treading softly as not to disturb the flow of nature, always respectful of how their energy affected those around them. Aware of intent, aware of emotion. She'd heard of the travesties of mankind against the leviathans, and then the dragons. The constant wars between Emberwilde and the Baku. Even the Shén Shé, though peaceful, ate meat and hunted life within their jungles. The Setsuhan's had never done anything of the such and it frustrated her to know that her people were suffering needlessly.

She hoped dearly that, in the next week, when Salem Eventide came from Whitewater to collect the dremaera she would get more answers and insights from the world beyond. She had only spoken to him once before, as he immediately refused to do business with her. The elders had her removed from negotiations for reasons she was not told, but it seemed her presence made him uncomfortable. Now that Rhys and Luseca were gone, she would have her opportunity to speak with him directly and hear some of the wisdom the others had claimed he was renowned for.

The ground shook as a loud sound startled her, drawing her eyes to a massive fenwight as he lay prone in the moss. She immediately stood and ran to him, placing her ear to his ribcage and listening to his labored breaths and slowing heartbeat.

"What's wrong?" she asked frantically, placing her hand along the bridge of his nose. She could feel him dying, the blood growing cold and his mind going dark. "Please! Don't leave me!" It was happening all over again.

In a matter of moments, his eyes rolled back and the moss began to crawl up his fur to digest him.

The world spun as she tried to collect herself, backing away in horror at the spontaneity of its death. She held her hands to the feathers of her head and panicked, tears swelling behind her eyes as she wanted to scream. Immediately, she turned and dashed into the trees, recklessly bounding full speed back to Llaesynd. As she neared, the distant cries of fellow Setsuhan's could be heard and it weighed her heart ever further.

She breached the foliage to find herself before a crowd, all frantically looking over someone in terror. They immediately parted for her, revealing a Setsuhan sister who lay in the grass with eyes wide open. Her flesh was reverting to stone before them, though she was uninjured.

"The mountain is taking her!" The crowd was crying.

For no reason at all, her life force was being sucked away and all they could do was watch.

"Was she hurt at all?" Vaexa asked.

The crowd shook and trembled. "No, celys," replied one. "She was in full health. It just... began."

First Rhys and Luseca, then the fenwight, and now the Setsuhan. Vaexa dared think that the mountain was not just taking them, but taking everything. Whether it was angry, or dying, they could not know. All that was clear was that the era of peace was done, dawning one of fear and darkness.

Suddenly, her body filled with pain, something they were very unfamiliar with. The surge of intensity was enough to drop her to her knees, clutching at her chest as it consumed her. It was unusual, as though it were an enhanced form of the static she would feel at random times, and it tore at her from the inside out. She expected to begin turning to selenite at the behest of the mountain, but strangely the pain continued without reverting her. A confusing sensation, both foreign and familiar, but a sensation that she somehow felt was not her own.

The crowds back away as she bellowed, watching her curl into a ball and fall to the ground. She was still only a child, the most innocent and connected of them all. The mountains ire would spare no one, it seemed.

★★★

The blue pillar of light stretched into the Whitewater sky to alert the night watch, and Andus hurried to its source. He had been cleared for duty since his latest altercation, though he was nursing the blade wound to his shoulder. The healers of Whitewater were very skilled, but the run still aggravated it beneath his pauldron. As he neared the beacon, crowds were beginning to gather in the grey smoke and eerie glow of a burning building set against the dark of the night.

This can't be… He slowed his pace as he looked upon the home, brilliantly ablaze. The few nightwatch that had arrived before him were frantically trying to control the fire with enchantments; moist fog, cones of sleet, and the shifting loose earth. The city of Whitewater had such frequent rainfall that the skill of firefighting was rarely practiced, but they were successfully containing the fire and slowly pushed it back.

"Is there anyone inside?" Andus called out, but everyone was too busy to respond. He marched to the nearest soldier and roughly pulled him by the shoulder. "This is the home of Vaughn Cross! Do you know if he is inside?"

Beads of sweat dripped down the soldier's face, his focus divided. "I haven't seen anyone, sir."

Andus quickly ran to the back of the house, giving wide berth to the heat of flame that desperately tried to jump to the next buildings.

"Chancellor!" he yelled, squinting as he peered through the dance of orange flames within. "Are you in there?" Through the flicker of fire he caught a glimpse of a body hanging by its neck from a rope in the rafters. His heart stopped as he watched it sway, lifeless and dark. The rope then broke and the body fell out of sight. "Damn, damn, damn," he chanted frantically while tracing a sigil on his palm. There was no safe way into the blaze. The only thing he could do now is try to quell the fire enough to enter.

The crowd of civilians watched in horror. The heat against their skin, the burning reality that their city was falling to the Orbweaver sect. Many covered their mouths in dismal awe, others held their own shoulders to close themselves off from the rest of the world - but only one, cloaked in shadow behind the crowd of frightened eyes, played with the heavy gold rings that adorned his fingers.

34

HOWLPACK SHADE, THE LEGENDARY DRAGON SLAYER

The air held a tension that forced both Shade and Whisper into slow, deep breaths. The darkness finally settled in and shadowed them into ever graying silhouettes against the collage of sinewy trees that stretched like bony hands. It was a winding moment, where muscles slowly tensed and focus honed.

"I have a question," Whisper spoke through the stillness.

Shade twitched at the sound of her voice, barely able to control his reflex at the false start. He tilted his head slightly in compliance, as to gauge her reaction to his body language. Though he knew his night vision was excellent, he suspected hers was even sharper and used the moment to see if she could notice the finite mannerisms he employed. Surely enough, she responded immediately.

"Have you killed a dragon before?"

His eyes smiled in such a way that the light seemed to fade further. "Little mistborn, I have slain more dragons than any other instrument in history."

"Well, Instruments only started killing dragons twenty five years ago, right? So that's not *that* impressive." Whisper was trying to goad him, but in truth she could hardly contain her excitement. This was to be her biggest challenge yet and the anticipation made her welcome every bit of fatigue she knew she was to feel. The anxiety began to overtake her and in the fraction of time it took for her to commit to her impulses, she dashed forward to close the distance, only to stagger in her approach as Shade quickly drew and fired two arrows at her dominant leg in one fluent motion. She dodged, as he was certain she would, but it gave him the time he needed to stride back and launch a decisive attack.

The arrow he notched began to glow a vibrant yellow light that streamed through the air as it soared towards her heart. Whisper waved her hand to create a sudden burst of wind that veered the arrow off course. As the iron shaft burrowed deep into the bark of a tree, the air burst as a pillar of brilliant golden lightning engulfed it whole. Layer upon layer turned to ash as the earth crystallized in the dazzling show of sparks.

Though Whisper was aware of the spectacle, she wasted no time in using the flash and thunder to close the gap. She was confident her eyesight was far more accelerated than his was, making her less affected by the visual disorientation and reduced her need to adjust. Much to Shade's dismay, she was right. In the mere moment it took his eyes to conform to the sudden shift from light to dark, her silhouette stood before him, giving him no time to react.

The first of many hits cupped his ear, ringing his senses and toying with his equilibrium just enough to allow her other strikes to land unhindered. Sharp pain from an elbow sung across his eye and as he tried to step back he could feel her clutch the leather harness that crossed over his shoulder, holding him in place. The dull force of her knee drove into his stomach and momentarily took his feet off the ground, right before a familiar and malevolent orange light flickered.

Whisper took a deep breath, brought her fingers to her lips, and rained down another torrential storm of fire point blank, nearly engulfing him as he clumsily leapt to safety. The heat kissed the right side of his body with such intensity he was certain he suffered a radiating burn beneath his armor.

He focused hard to shake off the burning pain and wiped away the stream of blood that dripped from a cut above his eye.

She crouched low and dug her feet into the dirt, and as she lunged towards him he instinctively reached to his quiver, only to grab fletchings that crumbled to ash between his fingers. In his narrow escape from her fire he neglected to think she was aiming for anything other than himself and was surprised to see she had intentionally washed over his arrows to render his range useless.

The trees spun around him as Whisper collided, sending him tumbling through the fertile soil, kicking it up in curtains.

Whisper's instinct was to close in and finish him while he tumbled, but she forced herself to stop. Though she was connecting with all of her strength, something seemed awry and it made her suspicious. No man, Instrument or otherwise, should be able to withstand the force of such direct hits. Unless she hadn't been making direct hits at all. Her playful demeanor slowly receded and allowed her to seriously assess the last half minute of their engagement, which lead her to a lack of ease.

Shade tumbled to a stop and clambered back onto his feet, spitting dirt from his lips and tossing his bow aside. "You are much smarter than I thought you'd be," he admitted, feebly brushing at the soil that streaked across his arms and chest.

"And you're faster than *I* thought." She had finally come to resolve her suspicions. "I haven't been making direct hits, have I?"

Shade smiled grimly and wrapped his hands around the hilts to his side. The ring of thin steel sung as his short blades left their sheaths of bone.

"Every time my strike connects, you shift your body in such a way that you absorb or redirect the brunt of impact and avoid your vital organs. The only solid, significant damage I have done so far was the knee to your stomach because I held you still."

"You're pretty sharp," he waved the tip of a blade at her, "but there's still one more thing you're missing." The blade whistled in the air as he spun it between his fingers. "I've already won, you just don't realize it yet."

***

Warm red blood spattered across the pink velvet petals that fell from the peach tree above as Salem hunched over and trembled, watching the blood stream from his eyelids and drip off the tip of his nose.

The electric grasp of Savrae-Lyth shot another immense surge of pain through his body, bursting vessels in the whites of his eyes and cracking his teeth with sheer strain.

The silence amidst his heavy breaths was haunting as she watched him with the same crippling sorrow that made her tear her own heart from her chest in life. She had been torturing him for hours, it seemed, and was only just beginning to see some progress. With every bellow, flourishing blossoms would wilt and fall. With every drop of blood, bark would curl and crack.

"More..." he labored between sticky lips.

The Queen of Drakes hung her head and struggled. "Perhaps just a short break."

"No." He reached out and grabbed her arm, smearing streaks of red across the lovely silks she wore. His nails had torn off from clutching his fingertips into the earth with such intensity. "I have to do this."

She crouched softly to wash her sadness across the dizzying turmoil of his eyes. "If you die, our war is lost."

Salem placed a hand into his lapels and shakily withdrew the white crystal he always kept with him. "The war is lost if I wait." He held the crystal to her and stared into it. "Twenty years," he said. "The weight of a world, the right to freedom, the heart of a man, and the will of the dragons. Two decades of preparation, two decades of study, and two decades of sacrifices... all die if I do not save Whisper."

The sorrow in her chest ached across her shoulders as she held her hand to his face and caressed his skin. Her mourning rooted deep, and with eyes welling in tears she gave a heavy nod and filled the air with his agony.

***

The fluttering of burnt leaves in the wind softly resounded as Whisper watched the glint of steel flash before her eyes. Her head shifted just enough to prevent Shade from raking it across her pupils. Now that she had neutralized his range, his attacks became much more oppressive, pushing her back with an onslaught at the edge of twin blades. With each swing he grew more fearsome, and she could feel the wind cut closer to her skin each time she weaved.

Strange as it was, it seemed he was increasing in speed somehow, narrowing her escape a hair's width at a time. With one wrist broken, it would be difficult to disarm him of both swords without taking damage and she began to hone her focus with the grit of necessity.

"Where has all your fight gone?" he toyed. "Was it the monks who taught you to back away so skillfully?"

It was clear to her he was trying to shake her resolve, but she quickly shut him out.

"Or perhaps it was Salem Eventide that taught you such weakness." He knew for certain they were close and spared no word in claiming his victory. "He's going to die, you know."

Whisper staggered and caught the flat of a blade in her good hand, while guarding her vitals by allowing the other blade to slide through her scaled arm. Her hand trembled as she struggled to hold the one blade still, and fought with clenched teeth as he twisted the other through her arm.

For the moment, they were at a physical deadlock, though the contest of wills had only just begun.

"That's a pitiful trick," she scolded.

"Poor, naïve mistborn girl. Rhoswan Gray has betrayed you both."

"Shut your mouth!" She turned the blade with her hand and drove it through the opalescent scales of her other arm, aligning both swords side by side. She wrapped her hands around both guards and locked them in place. The air began to flicker as the anger within her brimmed and the lashing strands of brilliant corona flexed from her growing aura. Searing fluxes of the living fire thrashed across his skin as he struggled to pull the blades free, until a single arc cut through both swords and allowed him to escape backwards with one in hand.

She struggled to power the aura, but she knew better. Though it was one of her most powerful close combat techniques, it was difficult to sustain with her waning strength. The radiance of the fluxes slowly began to fade as it quelled. The last remaining light glinted across the bloody scraps of metal that remained lodged in her arm.

In her hand she clutched the hilt of the broken sword and watched Shade carefully as he readjusted his grip on his as well, both slick with their own blood. Though Shade fought to retain composure, she knew he had taken serious damage from her last attack. Singed flesh and the dripping of fresh blood tickled her senses and made her smile. Her body felt heavy and a shadow began to cloud her night vision, giving her the final piece of Shade's proclaimed advantage poison. Having exhausted herself to this extent, her adrenaline was no longer hiding it as it coursed beneath her skin. Likely from the arrows she had endured, or the blades, or both. Either way, they were both badly wounded and a resolution would now be met, here in soil soaked with blood, at the ends of broken blades.

Their eyes met in hot blooded stillness. Tragic flame kissed blossoms gently floated between them. The tension that wound finally reached its breaking point, and as the emotional coil snapped, their bodies collided with such force that the falling blossoms receded. Blowing back in a halo amidst the concussive force of their connection.

Each broken blade sunk through flesh and bone, gushing pools of scarlet upon the fertile soil of the grove. And the stillness settled once more.

The last blossom slowly fell in the silence. Pressed shoulder to shoulder, with only the dripping of blood to accent the holding of breaths, until one fell to their knees.

Whisper could feel the sopping warmth against her skin as she collapsed, Shade's broken blade burrowed perfectly in the center of her stomach. Her fading eyes looked up from her grievous wound to see her sword deep in his arm, and sunk at the tragic irony that he would deflect her in the exact manner as she first deflected him. She wearily watched as he staggered back into the grove, sifting through his quiver for an arrow of passable fletchings while he retrieved his bow.

"You... fought with... incredible spirit," he labored. He withdrew an arrow and held it between his sticky fingers. Blood smeared across the shaft.

Though her consciousness was waning, the darkness began to illuminate with a soft, golden glow as Shade channeled the last of his energy and notched his final shot. "I am humbled by your strength, and shall give you a dragon's death."

FINAL

A COLLECTION OF TRAGEDIES

It was only a few moments since Salem's mind was sealed away in the Aviary, leaving the Lady Rhoswan to collect his belonging of interest while the two wolves laid him on one of the slats. "Give him a few minutes and then kill him swiftly. That should be enough time."

"After all this trouble, you only planned to give a few minutes?" one of the wolves argued as he cut Salem's bindings. "We could have killed him in the streets, it would have been less wasteful."

Rhoswan's sorrow turned to menace. "Listen here," she began coldly. "The brain processes faster than you think. A conscious minute to us is hours in my aviary. To a man like him it could be days. Do not question me again, or I will show you first hand."

The wolf sneered as he rolled his eyes. He owed her very little respect, as he was a follower of Howlpack Shade, and not of her. Though they were ordered by Shade to do as she wished, they met with distaste. The wolves were creatures of hunting and stalking, not killing men as they lay in coma.

She turned from their wretched demeanor and ascended the stairs, disappearing beyond the door.

Salem began sweating profusely. Labored breaths over clammy skin, as though he were undergoing incredible turmoil.

The wolf, filled with disrespect for the White Haired Witch, drew his blade and held it to Salem's throat. "He won't have a second longer." The wolf's words were cut short as Salem grabbed his wrist and twisted it sharply, forcing him to loosen his grip on the knife. Before he could force his wrist free, the room spun as Salem pulled him down and curled his leg over the wolf's head, locking him in an unorthodox, yet inescapable arm bar. The arm crackled as Salem pushed, twisted, and pulled, dislocating the wolf's shoulder, breaking the elbow, and snapping the wrist all at once.

The pain was dull at first, as the shock made the situation surreal, but as reality quickly caught up the wolf tried to bellow, only to have his mouth forced shut as Salem shoved the fallen blade up through the soft underside of his jaw and anchored it deep beyond the palate of his mouth and into his head.

Salem gracelessly pushed the body to the floor as the other wolf came upon him with weapon drawn. The shimmer of the blade glinted across Salem's weary eyes as it clipped his hair, thick with the sweat of his mental tribulations. The searing pain of flame and hot wax forced him to drop the knife as Salem grabbed the nearest candle and shoved it deep into his eye. The wolf crumpled and Salem kicked out the knee to mount a tight choke, twisting his weight so the wolf could not balance and effectively disabled any leverage from his upper body.

The wolf fought with one arm and it wound up locked with the choke in an upwards position. The wolf's other free arm was quickly locked down with Salem's legs. Though Salem was certainly not the strongest of the two, he was lethally educated in kinetics and physiology, knowing full well that so long as he kept the wolf's arms in such positions, the minor muscles left to work with would not be enough to overpower him.

Moments passed with silent struggles as the wolf grew weaker, and shortly after the last of the wolf's fight left his body and the weight fell dead in Salem's arms, he released and they both fell to the floor.

The room was a spinning mess of dim shadows and roughhewn stone that slowly filled with the tinge of blood. Every ounce of remaining strength was put into trying to stand, reeling back and forth as he fought to balance as though his head was too much for his shoulders to carry.

Time was a loose concept now, not knowing whether he had been in the Aviary for minutes, hours, or even days. All that was certain was the importance of finding his strength and saving Whisper, for the sake of the world and for himself. Despite his determination his weakness soon overtook him and he toppled to the chill of the stone, succumbing to the darkness.

***

The monks always told Whisper that in the last moments of one's life, the truest of one's values come to surface. For some it is family, others pride. Everyone experiences something different, an epiphany or revelation of the life they had lived, laced with either completion or regret.

She always knew her last moments would be of a single thought and as she wearily gazed upon the flashing light before her she was awash with surprise that it wasn't what she had imagined. Her father's voice drifted away, the thirst for revenge dissipated into the aether, and she began to forget the aura that took the life of her mother. In these last few precious moments, feeling the slowing beat of her heart as her wounds bled her dry, all she could see was him.

The violet sheen that glinted in the black of his hair when the light was just right, the eyes of faceted emeralds that entranced her the moment they first met, and the softness in his voice every time he called her his 'dear Whisper'.

Her chest tightened with regret. Being blinded by rage and driven by a travesty two decades old. It was a darkness that consumed her day and night, disallowing her to feel the light against her skin when it was trying so hard to warm her.

Her thoughts returned to the night in his hovel a broken man, punishing himself in a broken world. Beyond the glamor, beyond the peace, that was when she saw his heart, and she loved it. To her, love was a strong word, and one she wasn't familiar with. The idea of it always felt awkward or disingenuous, but if she were ever to label a feeling with such power, it would be that which she felt that evening. The turmoil in his eyes, the pouring of his heart. The urge to hold him close and assure him that together they could make it through.

Such a shame, to feel this joy so late. A shame to realize something so meaningful, with only seconds left. The tears that welled behind her eyes came forth and streamed down her face, mixing with the dirt, sweat, and blood of her undoings. In her last moments, as she watched the man before her let loose his power, she prayed to the Fates for the first time in her life. Reaching to them with her heart, professing her foolishness, and pleading for a chance to love for the first time. As the light neared enough to drown her vision with blinding purity, time seemed to slow and a voice whispered into her ear. "No."

The electric flare engulfed her completely, with an explosion of crackling energy so grand the trees fell to dust and the earth turned to glass. Her skin turned black, cracking and burning to a crisp as it forced its way through her wounds and destroyed her from the inside out. The energy burst into a pillar of lightning that stretched into the sky, sending a shock wave that thundered for miles before dissipating into an air that snowed white with ash.

Shade limped across the ground of smoldering glass and stood over the charred remains of Whisper. Her hand reaching to the sky in hope of rescue, eyes wide open. With a prod of his bow he tipped the body over, which fell to the ground as a solid husk. Burnt flesh flaked off from the impact.

At her head he lay the flame kissed dire wolf's pelt and set the broken skull atop it as a makeshift tombstone. As he honored her in the best tribal manner he knew, he stopped at the sight of something peculiar. Though his attack had seared her beyond recognition, her eyes remained undamaged and stared lifelessly into the beyond through her brilliant cobalt blue irises. Cautiously, he held his fingers to her neck to check for a pulse and even hovered over the char of her lips to listen for breaths, but there was nothing. "Even in death, your eyes defy me," he said deeply. He took a few silent moments, bowed his head, and whispered a short hunter's psalm to guide her soul back into the energy of the world. He then rose and disappeared into the night, traversing the wasteland of ash and blood back to Freestone.

★★★

The heavy, humid stench of mold and carrion brought Fever to her senses very quickly, shooting up from her makeshift bed of pelts and rotten straw.

A low, deep growl resounded along the rough stone walls of the cavernous room as a monstrous creature peeled itself from the shadows. "She awakens." At first she thought it was Wrath, due to its size and obsidian armor, but as it approached a glisten of blades twinkled from a mane of fur as black as the night was dark.

Fever shifted her legs to ready a dodge if she needed. "Who are you?" Her eyes scoured the room to plan her escape. A single door was set along the far wall, a kris stuck in the table to her left.

"I am Agathuxusen, the Ravenmane. Only one of my kind," he replied, raising his hand to his helmet. He unclasped the base of the neck and removed it, revealing the reddy-tan fur and lion-esque features of the largest Blademane Baku she had ever seen in her life.

Fever's eyes narrowed as the voices in her head began to stir the memories of the Baku raid that took her parents from her. The sound of their screams. The scent of their blood. The sacrifice they made in hopes of her escape. Her pupils strained as her instinct to kill began to boil over, and shadowed serpents began to roil from her black diamond bangles as she prepared to bear teeth.

The Ravenmane tilted his head and pulled the collar of his armor down as far as he could. Emblazioned on his neck was the sprawling black mark of the fatespinner. "I am an Instrument to Ivory. You and I are divine kin."

She barely heard a word he said as they locked eyes. He was fearless, arrogant, confident. She was furious, sadistic, irrational. She was awash in the memory of her first kill, and he could taste the dark blood of her intent. The air slowly churned as they prepared to clash she, an aura of coiling shadow, he, the ripple of growing heat.

Then, the kiss of radiant flame brushed her face as his hands burst into dazzling white fire. The lingering pain of Ashissa's acid trap throbbed across the left side of her face, snapping her back into reality and bringing her to realize the Baku just claimed he was an ally. Her eye squinted with the swelling and the shadowed serpents immediately dispersed. Gingerly, she touched the burn with her fingertips and let her heart race as she felt her beautiful skin turned hideous scar.

"What has she done!?" Her rage was a bitterness that filled the air.

"What are you talking about?" The Ravenmane was unshaken by her sudden outrage, but suspicious of how quickly it seemed her mind changed tide. With a flex of his fingers the flames dispersed and the room began to cool.

"My face, you fool! What has she done to my face?"

The Ravenmane looked around the room and grabbed the kris from the table. With a flick of his wrist he threw the blade into the straw for her to collect. "There is nothing wrong with your face."

She held the blade before her and stared into her reflection. A gasp fled her chest as her psyche collapsed beneath the weight of her blight. The corrosive mist of the glyph scarred her in ways she couldn't imagine and her hideousness disgusted her. She couldn't imagine why the Baku would say nothing was wrong, she was a monster.

'You are better beautiful than not, and the world will see you as you once were.'

Ivory's voice whispered in her ear as Fever noticed time was standing still. *'Even I cannot repair the damage that has been done, but I have graced you with an illusion to conceal the scarring. An illusion that will be broken to anyone who is made aware of it.'*

It was bittersweet. Graced enough that the world would see her beauty, but cursed that she would always see her blight. Time resumed and she staggered to stand, making her way across the uneven floor to the door.

"Where are you going?" the Ravenmane asked, amused by her reaction.

She stumbled through the exit to find herself high atop a ledge of an open cave system, with a brilliant golden tornado of energy pulling mist down through a tunnel in the ceiling. The same as she had seen over Valakhut. Thousands of Orbweavers shuffled below, with a line of nearly one hundred leviathans that each took turns attempting to break the Second Wish from the fissure in the honeycomb stone. Hundreds more were training for combat, while others sat and practiced drawing glyphs and enchantments with their peers.

"What is..." She was immediately interrupted by a furious thrumming of wings as a massive insect flew by, a man in robes mounted on its back. Soon she saw another, and another, until they amassed in a whole platoon of buzzing aerial units. Far below, coalesced around the base of the tornado, other massive demons exited. Some with vicious scything talons the length of the common man. Others with fearsome horns that could gore the broadest of oxen. The only similarity amongst them was the glowing Orbweaver sigil they adorned on their heads.

The Ravenmane sneered. "The demons of the mist are thrall to the Orbweavers, now. An enchantment they call the Mind-shackle Glyph." Together they gazed upon the army of nightmares the world had yet to see, let alone imagine.

"Where are we?" She was awestruck at the many *impossible* things she was seeing all at once. The funnel of mist being used to recruit an army of demons, the hundreds of leviathans the world thought extinct, and the thousands of Orbweavers everyone believed were only a short chain of small covens.

"This is Sabanexus, the lair of the leviathans," he replied. "Beginning of the end." He pointed into the distance at the base of the tornado. The crowds began to part, eagerly awaiting for something to exit. Slowly breaking through the torrent of winds and energy were four monstrous creatures twice the size of the leviathans, armored in thick bony plates. Some walked, some slithered, but all commanded the full attention and respect of everyone in attendance. "Welcome, the four Chitin Kings of the Overworld."

At a distance, she could not make out the details of their twisted figures, but in an unusual sense of dread that made her feel saner than ever, she could feel their strength emanating over her flesh. "They will destroy humanity."

The Ravenmane neither smiled nor frowned as he stared off into Elanta's oblivion. "They will destroy everything."

EPILOGUE

The roughhewn halls of Sabanexus were a dark and dismal gray against the deep blue of Ivory's eyes as she strode with purpose. The Ravenmane accompanied her to illuminate the cavern with an open palm of roiling flame, while the low rumbling of Wrath's heavy steps followed behind. Since hearing of the arrival of the Chitin Kings she was eager to speak with them. The hall began to widen further until they approached an open cave guarded by fearsome demons from the mist – their faceted eyes scoured over Ivory and her Instruments with prejudice, but they backed away to give them berth nonetheless. As the vastness of the cave opened further, the silhouettes of four massive figures could be seen seated against the furthest wall on thrones made of broken stalagmites.

"Such a pleasure you finally made it," Ivory sung sweetly as she opened her arms to greet them.

Each of the Chitin Kings had six glowing eyes that pierced the darkness and watched her every step. Though one growled, none responded otherwise.

"Well..." she replied, "As promised, I have created the bridges to Elanta and have rallied your Orbweavers to your cause. Now, if you would simply uphold your end of our bargain, my Instruments and I can be on our way."

Though she didn't show it, she was prepared to open a portal and flee at the first sign of betrayal. One could never be too careful when dealing with demons, but she didn't want to offend them with distrust in the event they had an unforeseen honor.

One of the Chitin Kings growled again and leaned towards her, outstretching his hand and revealing a platinum scroll tube emblazoned with ancient sigils. Though the bulk of his body was still shrouded with the help of her color-absorbing aura, she could clearly see his bladed fingers and bony armor as his hand approached the Ravenmane's flame. "What is it?" His deep voice rumbled as he spoke.

"Thank you, Vasugomex." She placed her palms together as a sign of gratitude. Of the four monstrous Chitin Kings she had come to know in her journey beyond the mist, he was the only one with bladed fingers. Though she could only see the one arm graciously outstretched from the shadows, she was well aware he had three more that could strike her down at any moment. Arguably, though all four Chitin Kings were incredibly dangerous and intolerant, Vasugomex was the most... open-minded. Patient was a strong word, and the difference between Kings was marginal at best, but he was willing enough to listen to an idea, a plea, or even strike a bargain. Her eyes gleamed as she saw the artifact in all its glory and smiled as she gingerly accepted it. Her fingertips traced the markings in awe as she marveled in its beauty and craftsmanship. "Inside, there is a secret," she wooed, "Created by the dragons and hidden in your overworld." She carefully handed it to Wrath and bowed.

The six eyes of Vasugomex narrowed with intrigue. "What secret?"

Ivory placed her palms together and envisioned the Second Wish at her fingertips. "The secret to destroying honeycomb stone."

Ivory was certain the Chitin Kings had no idea what she was talking about and expected them to care very little. The large, bony hand sunk back into the darkness of their makeshift thrones. "We notice the sword has the same markings as the diamond on your wrist."

Ivory looked down to the bangle, Shiori's sigil blazed within the stone. "They are... part of a set."

Vasugomex could be heard leaning back into his throne, while the chittering of another rustled beside him. "We can taste the power they give you, and it borders on troublesome."

Their distrust made her uncomfortable. "I understand completely. The artifacts are known as Shiori's Wishes, and I assure you I mean no harm to your cause." The Chitin Kings were already defensive knowing she had two *Wishes*, mentioning a third existed didn't seem like a good idea.

The multitude of eyes focused on her with malice. "We will warn you once, and once only," Vasugomex began, "You have been an honorable ally during our bargain, but now our deal is complete. If you cross us in any way, we will make you suffer. Your *Wishes* will not spare you our judgement." Together they shared a silence, quickly broken before the Chitin Kings could decide to forego the diplomacy and disembowel her where she stood. "Be gone, mortal. We have no more business to discuss."

She had never been called a mortal before and the demeaning undertone quickly wiped the smile from her face. She gently tapped her fingertips together as she imagined establishing her authority, but quickly calmed herself enough to turn her back and ignore the confrontation completely. They clearly didn't know who they were dealing with, and without the Second Wish in her hands she wasn't going to risk trying to show them.

With pause to stare down the Chitin Kings and allow Ivory to pass, Wrath and the Ravenmane turned to follow, leaving the Kings in their wake.

"Mortal," she vented to herself, looking back at the platinum scroll case in Wrath's hand. "Not for long."

***

The stench of ash was a blight in the once extravagant pagoda of the Lady Rhoswan. The taste, the despair. A ghost of misfortune that corrupted every silk thread and paper door. A fortune in decadence, a lifetime of attainment – seared, broken, and stained in grim finality.

Rhoswan held the tattered blue silk of one of her favorite dresses as she sat at the edge of her bed, the dying light faintly illuminated the damage she had desperately tried to forget since the burning of the mist.

"Such a shame," a deep voice crossed the room. "The rich, plucked from their cozy pillows and soft clothes."

Emerging from the shadows was Howlpack Shade, encrusted with blood and barely standing, bow in hand. "What a decadent nest you've built, Rhoswan Gray."

"Beautiful birds build beautiful nests," she replied as she feigned awareness of both his presence and injuries. "And it's *Lady* Rhoswan."

He sneered as he challenged her. Calm, cold eyes affixed as he gently tipped her cherry bedside table with the edge of his bow. The antique fell to the ground, loudly spilling its contents. "The wolf does not make concessions to the bird of paradise."

She choked back his disrespect. Wild animals were beyond teaching etiquette. "You fared worse than I imagined." Though the dress was ruined, she daintily folded it as though it were pristine. "You must be getting dull."

Shade leaned against the wall and crossed his arms around his bow. "I haven't fought like that in twenty years," he proclaimed. "That tiny mistborn girl killed eleven of my wolves and managed to deal me significant damage. Far more trouble than she looked."

Rhoswan chuckled solemnly as she recalled Salem saying the same thing.

Shade caught himself trying to adjust the phantom weight of the dire wolf's skull and pelt he once proudly wore. "I will have to hunt myself a new trophy. The fenwights of Setsuha seem like excellent prey, though I don't know how a pelt would feel to wear."

"She killed eleven wolves... how many are left in your pack?" She tried to look him in the eyes, but instead stared down the cold shafts of two arrows, drawn inches from her gaze. He hadn't made a sound as he crossed the room and notched the arrows, though she was not surprised by his paranoia.

"Avert your eyes, bird. I will not chance your witchcraft."

She rolled her eyes and turned away. "High strung as usual, I see. Are you like this with all the pretty girls? Poor, nervous virgin."

Shade withdrew and leaned in the frame of the window, proceeding to answer her prior, more pertinent, question. "Twenty one, less the two I have lent you for the time being."

"Much less since last we spoke years ago."

"The rest are dead. Prey to their prey. There is no room for the weak in my world and now that Ivory has returned and demons roam rampant, perhaps you will appreciate the severity of my methods. If any of the new Instruments fight with the mistborn girl's spirit, we may have some serious trouble."

The Lady Rhoswan rose from the edge of her bed and joined him at the window.

In the past, they had bickered and fought more than enough times for him to tell when she was being halfhearted. "What's wrong?"

She shook her head. "Salem was a good man and Whisper wanted nothing but to find herself. It doesn't make sense for them to die."

"It doesn't have to make sense to us. The jaws of the wolf do not choose what to kill, the laws of nature command it."

"I know, I just wish I had more clarity."

"What's done is done for the sake of the world. We don't know the consequences of our actions, but we know the purpose, and that should be enough." He readied himself to leap from the window. "I will have my wolves float the mistborn girl's body out to sea. The current should take her into the mist and ferry her into the spirit world."

"I think we both know now, there is no spirit world beyond the mist."

Shade nodded softly. "I prefer tradition." He looked out into the darkness, as though hearing an inaudible call. "I must rendezvous with them beyond the grove."

She nodded. "Perhaps a hot bath will bring me some ease."

She turned away as he leapt out of sight and struggled with the emptiness of the room. An emptiness that seemed to follow her into the bath she had her maids pour.

Surprisingly, some crickets chirped beyond the pond. Life was slowly beginning to return to Freestone, though it was a slow and miserable process.

Curls of steam danced off the hot water and rose petals in which she was immersed. Faint candlelight flickered and brought her deep solace. She reached from her bath to the satchel of items she had alleviated from Salem and withdrew the white crystal to examine it further.

She sunk to her neck within the large wooden tub and watched her maid in the corner of her eye as she stoked the coals that heated it from beneath.

"What does this look like to you?" Rhoswan asked the young woman.

"Crystal, milady," she replied sweetly.

"Well, you're not wrong." She looked at it more closely, turning it to examine all of its cloudy striations and grooves. "It's a soft crystal, known as selenite."

"Selenite? I have never heard of it before." The maiden curtsied and prepared to give Rhoswan some privacy now that the coals were good and hot.

"You wouldn't have. It's not from around here." Her eyes wandered as she pondered his acquisition, let alone the purpose. Salem was a man of many complexities, but material attachment was not a trait she would label him with. If he had this stone with him, it had to be important.

She sighed as she closed her eyes, exhaling the tribulations of her day, when a tingling crossed her skin. An unusual static filled the air and she watched intently as the surface of the water vibrated. A foreign aura of inexplicable origin. The static began to visibly shake the air, sending erratic fluxes through her line of sight, when a grim realization struck her ⊠ she couldn't move.

The piece of selenite slipped from her fingertips and fell to the floor as she struggled, but to no avail. Her chin slowly lowered into the water and stopped.

"I really did not think you would try to kill me," spoke Salem from behind her, slowly emerging from the shadows to sit and watch from the foot of the tub. The length of his hair fell across the left of his face, casting a shadow over his eyes through which only the emerald shimmer of his irises could cut. He leaned forward on his knees, wearily bracing his weight, watching her beneath his brow.

Rhoswan looked down at the water and tried to lift her head to keep it from entering the edges of her mouth. "How are you doing this?"

Salem seemed mournful, but laughed a tired, hopeless laugh nonetheless. "Queen's Gaze."

A dumbfounded silence nearly made her forget she couldn't move. "A dragon's eye technique? How is that even possible?"

"I assure you, it is." He momentarily stood to pluck the selenite from the floor and then sat back down. "Believe it or not, it is a technique very similar to your own. Where your eyes create a rune that locks someone's mind in the euphoria of their pleasures, my technique locks someone's body in the paralysis of their fears."

"I know only sorrow for our circumstance, not fear."

"True," he smiled, "But your body does not know that."

The runes flared across her pupils as she tried to lock him in the aviary once more, but this time his mind remained exactly where it was.

"Now that I have experienced your technique once, I know how to avoid it," he assured.

"I only have to look at you, how can you resist?" This was the first time her technique didn't work. As it had always been the bulk of her confidence, the fact that it wasn't ensnaring him filled her with a helplessness she hadn't experienced before.

"The brain is divided into two hemispheres," he began. "The left side controls our consciousness and known identity, while the right holds our id, subconscious, and truest core emotions. It is the left eye that connects to the right hemisphere of the brain, and can be considered the gateway into a person's true self. When you use your technique, you send energy through the left eye of your subject, directly into the right hemisphere of their brain, which induces the coma to which you so eloquently refer to as the Aviary. I had to experience it once to fully understand how it worked, but now that I do, I know that so long as I do not reveal my left eye to you, you cannot lock me away."

"You determined all that from one experience?"

"Only because I was looking for it. Did you know, that because the right eye is connected to the conscious portions of our brain, we are reflexively conditioned to look into the right eyes of others when interacting? You are no different, in fact. You have focused on my right eye in every conversation we have ever had. I made my connection when I noticed you began focusing on my left in our... most recent conversation. I believe it was right before you left me to have my throat slit."

Her mind was blank with what to do. On the verge of sinking beneath the water, unable to use her eyes. It was a nearing finality she could only hope would be thwarted by the mercy of his graces, though she knew she had just proven to him her capacity to bury her own. The only option that came to mind was to stall him. The Queen's Gaze used significant power and he seemed in no shape to hold such a technique for long.

"Using a dragon's eye technique, having no fatespinner. I am beginning to believe in the unbelievable," she said. "Are you really a dragon?"

Salem shook his head. "No, I am not. Technically."

"Then you are enlightened, using some form of technique that mimics one?"

"No," he said once again.

"Then what are you?" None of this made sense to her and though the forefront of her thoughts were focused on survival, the back of her mind stirred with irritation over the unknown.

"As you are an Instrument of the Fates, I am an Instrument of the dragons."

"There's no such thing!" she argued.

"Over the course of time, all that is history, all that is known, there was never one before me." With an open palm he gestured to himself and then lifted the selenite for her to see. "I was a Setsuhan of Snow Leaf, bound to the mountain, serving Savrae-Lyth."

"You're... a Setsuhan?"

"Indeed. Born from selenite, the mate of a crafted pair. It is the reason I have no fatespinner, as Setsuhans are born of the energy within the mountain and thereby have no 'souls' for the Fates to track. The Fates have always been aware of this, of course, but never sought to kill us as they did the dragons because we are bound to the mountain itself and cannot influence the rest of the world."

"But how can you leave the mountain without turning to stone?"

"When the Fates waged the war and the dragons began to fall, I was to be the successor of the Queen's power. A selenite body to hold the power of a dragon queen undetected until a new queen was ready to wield it, one powerful enough to return Shiori Etrielle to the world. Savrae-Lyth's power was concentrated into her heart, and when she tore it out and placed it in me my body severed its connection to the mountain and now uses the power of the Queen to sustain my form. So long as I carry her power, I will not revert."

Rhoswan was at a loss for words. Though the story was dramatically unreal, if any one creature was capable of devising such a transfer it would be the Queen of Drakes.

Salem held a hand over his heart. "Savrae-Lyth did not kill herself to forfeit the war, but to win it once the Fates thought it was over."

"By bringing back Shiori Etrielle? I only just found out she actually existed, but you're saying she's also still alive?"

"Indeed." Salem placed the selenite back into his lapel. "Long ago, the Fates once served as her advisers, until they committed treason and claimed the world as their own. Even between the four of them they could not guarantee her death and instead opted to catch her by surprise and imprison her. Fortunately, Etrielle became aware of their intentions and hid her Three Wishes before the Fates could claim them."

"I don't believe you. The Fates are concerned with the prosperity of the world."

"And Shiori was concerned with the prosperity of life. What seems a minor difference is, in truth, a big conflict of interests in the grand plan."

"If what you're saying is true, then I had no knowledge of the Fates' transgressions. Perhaps there is a way I can help. If the Fates can't track you, they couldn't know I am helping you either. You can't win a war against them alone." She knew Salem to have many traits, but unwavering conviction was definitely something identifiable. If her usefulness could appeal to his plan, perhaps she could compel him to set her free and work together.

He rested his head in his hands as he pondered. They had been close friends for many years and she knew him on a far more personal level than anyone else. Together they shared many stories and created many more. The greatest of which was the Scarlet Ribbon, making them legends in the hearts of Freestone, if not the realm of Whitewater. "You are my closest friend, Rhoswan," he began. "Nothing would please me more than to write the next chapter of the world with you."

She smiled as best she could given her inability to move. It was true, the two of them were an unrelenting force, now more than ever given her new information.

He stood and slowly began to approach her. "However, so long as you are an Instrument of Origin your presence is dangerous to my cause." He bowed his head softly, closed his eyes, and gently placed a hand atop her silky white hair. "I love you, Rhoswan Gray, but I cannot trust you."

Her eyes pleaded in the still moments before he slowly pushed her beneath the surface of petals and fragrant oils. Her arms and legs convulsed as she fought to free herself from the paralysis, holding back the urge to scream away the last of her vital breath. Within the haze of the water she imagined clawing at the edges of the tub, gouging grievous lines with desperate fingertips so deep the water would tinge with blood and broken nails. One by one, her muscles began to cramp as her body tightened and trembled, growing evermore aware of the claustrophobia as the helplessness weighed her like a stone.

As her lungs grew desperate, her instinct to breath filled her mouth with water, breaking what was left of her composure and sending her mind into a terrified fit of survival. The edges of her vision began to grow darker and in her last moments, held captive beneath the surface of the water, she watched in fading terror the beauty of the rose petals as they slowly drowned with her.

Her body surged one last time as her lungs burnt with fluid, flailing away the last of her air until her mouth screamed for mercy, but no bubbles were left.

The last of the petals sunk beneath the surface and the grave churned no more.

Water dripped across the silent decadence of Rhoswan's pagoda as Salem pulled his hand from the tub and shook away the water, wiping tears from his eyes as he struggled to regain his composure. "I am sorry, my friend. Your death is a tragic necessity, and once the new Queen of Drakes is ready to receive her power, I will join you." He strode to the window and looked across the spindly shadows of barren peach groves, breathing deeply the tale of ruination he had added to his collection. "Now, where are you, dear Whisper?"

***

With the ground turned to lightning kissed glass and the trees but piles of ash in the radius of the strike, the grove held a haunting desolation and silence that balanced on the edge of both beauty and dismay. Whisper's body lay strewn and broken, as a monument of the fallen. While her once spirited eyes, open and empty, stared across the void of the sheen beneath her, several small pools of silver lacuna began to appear within her irises, creating a brilliant silver blossom that contrasted sharply against her natural cobalt blue. Slowly, each lacuna bloomed in supernatural brilliance, stretching the silver petals across the ocean of her eyes. The transformation slowed to full resolution, and with a blink of her draconian eyes she filled her lungs with a breath of new beginnings.

CHARACTER REFERENCE

BY REGION

THE REALM OF WHITEWATER

Whitewater is the central realm of the world. At its northern and southernmost points it is greeted by the shores of the ocean, while other realms border its eastern and western ranges. Temperate forests of pine and bittersweet grove scatter across the ridges of green grass and gray stone, up until the snow dusted forests of the north.

Salem Eventide: A subtle streak of violet sheen through his dark hair, though hardly noticeable in contrast to the vibrant emerald green of his eyes. His origin is unknown, but his impact on the realm has been significant. Where once he was a doctor in the flourishing peach groves of Freestone, now he is the Voice of the King. A prestigious position of authority that speaks and acts on behalf of the King when the presence of his majesty is not possible.

Whisper: Orphaned in her infancy and left to grow in the mountainous seclusion of the Monastery of the Eternity Ring, she has known nothing but strength and vengeance as she searches day and night for the man who murdered her family. She is a mistborn, shaped by the mysterious demonic energies of the mist that surrounds the world and feared for her capacity and willingness for destruction.

Lady Rhoswan Gray: Also known as 'The White Haired Witch' for her glamorous platinum hair and mysterious abilities, she is an object of elegance, grace, and power. Close friend and business partner with Salem Eventide, she resides in the city of Freestone where she owns the famous Scarlet Ribbon Estate.

Breon: Personal assistant to Lady Rhoswan Gray, he contends to all of her business affairs and demands.

Howlpack Shade: A highly skilled hunter, tracker, and assassin, Shade is the Alpha of a group of warriors known as the Howlpack. He is the Instrument of Howlpack Sentinel Avelie and traverses the realm to silently execute those who threaten its future.

Wrath: A monstrously large creature, known as a leviathan, clad head to toe in obsidian armor, he is a nearly unstoppable force at the command of Ivory, the Unwoven.

Elder Waylander: Head of the Waylander family and leader of an elite organization known as the Moths, he is a loyal servant and assassin for the King of Whitewater and currently posted in the north to protect the bastion city of Lyre.

Rowan Bastet: Though a foreigner to Whitewater, his proof of loyalty and skill earned him a place among the Moths, serving as Elder Waylander's closest ally and friend.

Casamir Waylander: Son and eldest child of Elder Waylander, he is to be the heir to their name and legacy. However, Casamir struggles with finding his own identity outside of his family's tradition of becoming a Moth of the Realm. Though educated in basic military tactic, his heart loves to invent.

Katya Waylander: Daughter and youngest child of Elder Waylander, she is a gifted healer and alchemist studying in the city of Lyre. Excelling at her studies and spiritual growth at a rate far more impressive than Casamir.

Derin Eywin: The Duke of Lyre, entrusted with governing the bastion city of the north and protecting the Great Library with the command of the largest military force in the realm.

King Liam Whitewater: Also known as 'the Whitewater Leviathan', he is the last of a race of giants that once ruled the mountains. When his adopted human father, Leomund Whitewater, led an army into the mountains to destroy the leviathans, Liam was taken as an infant and raised to be the next king. He rules his people with fairness and grace, gaining the praises of the common folk and the scorn of the noble blooded.

Alexander Tybalt: Judiciar of the King's Council, he is a seasoned general in charge of the realm's armies and judicial system.

Vaughn Cross: A young, brilliant man made Chancellor of the King's Council, he is a prodigy that governs the economic development of Whitewater. He thinks himself above all others, excluding Salem Eventide, with whom he competes fiercely to prove he is the best.

Victor Fairchild: Treasurer of the King's Council, he is a man of high standard and expensive taste. Every bit of wealth traverses his logs as he accounts for the realm's expenses and income.

SETSUHA, THE REALM OF THE SNOW LEAF

The Realm of the Snow Leaf is a massive mountain that borders Whitewater's north-eastern influence. There is ocean to the north and east, the temperate tundra of Whitewater to the west, and the humid jungles of the serpentine Shén Shé to the south. Their freshwater rainforests and pristine rivers have been guarded from outsiders for thousands of years by illusions, enchantments, and the supernatural evolution of its flora and fauna. Nearly everything has developed some form of carnivorous nature that prevents trespassers from invading their lush realm.

Vaexa est'alara: *(Vay-ksa ess-ta-lah-rah)* The youngest of the Setsuhan elders, her name translates to 'White Diamond Dove'. Unlike other Setsuhans, which are made flesh from hard stone, she was sculpted from soft selenite.

The high resonance of her birth stone has made her much more sensitive both emotionally and physically, and has instilled in her a desperation for freedom and adventure beyond the mountain to which she is bound.

Rhys: *(Reese)* The only Setsuhan elder of male form, he was named for the scent of the rain. His pleasant nature has kept him close friends with Vaexa, as he takes joy in her free spirit.

Nuith: *(New-eeth)* The second oldest of the elders, she is named after the dusk, and is often teased for her constant fussing over tradition and safety. A perfectionist at heart, she mothers the other elders to ensure they remain vigilant in their duties.

Luseca: *(Lew-see-kah)* Named for the dawn, she is the eldest of the elders. Though nearly eight hundred years of age, she has more than enough energy to tease the others and find ways to keep everyone in good spirits.

Selva: *(Sel-vah)* Fenwight friend, companion, and guardian of Vaexa since he was a puppy.

Fenwight: *(Fen-wite)* A magical creature born from the earth and stone of the Setsuha. Resembling a massive wolf of mottled fur and moss, their cloudy eyes are blind to anything that does not touch the ground. These spirit wolves travel by melding in and out of trees anywhere within their territory.

Kin'nyi: *(Kin-yee)* A massive cat-like creature clad in bony plates that can individually refract light to make it invisible. Additionally, it has two hearts, five quill-laden tails, and a flap of skin under its stomach that allows it to glide upside down. They are a social apex predator that hunts in packs of two or more, manipulating and corralling prey into desired ambushes.

THE REALM OF EMBERWILDE

The westernmost realm of the world, it only borders Whitewater to the east and the Baku Sands to the south. Glistening ocean crashes at the base of sheer rock faces to its west and north, cooling their otherwise arid climate.

Basic military training is a rite of passage for both men and women, rich and poor, and begins in their youth. When basic rank is achieved, a single white feather is woven into their hair. This signifies they are a true citizen of the realm and have earned their right to liberty. As rank progresses, new feathers are added or colors are changed to reflect their new status.

The Malikah: She is better known as The Phoenix Queen. From the Palace of Roiling Cinders, with its ancient architecture built into the side of an active volcano in the middle of the city of Obsidian, she rules over all of Emberwilde. Few have gazed upon her, but all fear her cunning, intellect, and wrath, leading and empowering her realm with strong militaristic efficiency.

Phori: A highly decorated Brigadier General from Akashra who proudly adorns her rank with the violet plumes that hang from beads woven into her hair. She is one of the few warriors skilled with the exotic two-bladed staff and is the leader of a large military detachment.

Fever: A sultry and seductive assassin from Emberwilde, she is a broken mind that loves to create chaos. Aptly named for the poison induced fever her victims endure before their deaths, she is a highly hunted criminal of Emberwilde.

THE BAKU SANDS

A large peninsula to the south of Emberwilde, its deserts stretch far out into the ocean. Home to several different tribes of lion-folk creatures known as Baku, their individual territories are often fiercely guarded.

Agathuxusen, The Ravenmane: *(Eh-guh-thuk-su-sen)* His origin unknown, he is a massive lion-folk from the southern deserts known as the Baku Sands. Standing taller and broader than a normal Baku, with a mane of jet black, he readily wields highly volatile liquid fire which he uses to melt all in his way – flesh, bone, and stone alike. An Instrument to Ivory, the Unwoven, he obeys her every command in exchange for his fearsome power.

SHÉN SHÉ, THE REALM OF THE GOD SNAKE

A small Realm to the east of Whitewater and south of Setsuha, that is a consuming maze of jungle and sheer, vine laden mountains. The snake-like humanoids and aberrations that inhabit it have an unquenchable thirst for knowledge and a penchant for enlightenment. They can be incredibly dangerous if necessary, but are otherwise very spiritual. Their cunning and monstrous nature, however, keeps them untrusted in the eyes of their human neighbors.

Ashissa: *(Ah-she-sah)* A pure blooded serpentine Shén Shé representing her neighboring realm in search for power through knowledge. She is arguably one of the best enchanters in the world, revered for her mystical aptitude, and feared for her race's innately venomous virulence.

Malison: *(Mal-e-son)* Snake aberrations from Shén Shé that are raised solely as guardians to the pure blooded shamans. They bear hooded heads, four arms, serpentine bodies, and are highly venomous.

THE WEAVE

A separate plane of existence created by the Fates as a safe haven for their fatespinners, where destiny is woven, watched, and altered to create the most favorable outcome in their eyes.

Origin Progenitus: The first of the Fates, Origin Progenitus hatches a new fatespinner whenever a creature with a soul is born.

Howlpack Sentinel Avelie: The second of the Fates, Howlpack Sentinel Avelie is the guardian of the Weave.

Illy the Flux: The third of the Fates, Illy the Flux observes the fatespinners – predicting the future and calculating the necessary changes to make it better.

Ivory the Unwoven: The forlorn Fate, Ivory the Unwoven was once maestro to the deaths of the fatespinners and their cycle of life energy. She has renounced her role as the fourth Fate and now pursues motives of her own.

CPSIA information can be obtained
at www.ICGtesting.com
Printed in the USA
LVHW04s0329280818
588333LV00001B/5/P